THE KYIV FILE

A JACOB HUNTER THRILLER

DAVID ARCHER

DAMIEN WILD

The characters and events portrayed in this ebook are fictitious. Any similarity to real persons, living or dead, is coincidental and not intended by the author.

ISBN-13: 978-1-63696-467-6

ISBN-10: 1-63696-467-2

Printed in the United States of America

www.righthouse.com

www.instagram.com/righthousebooks

www.facebook.com/righthousebooks

twitter.com/righthousebooks

JACOB HUNTER THRILLER

The Kyiv File (Book 1)
The Bogotá File (Book 2)
The Havana File (Book 3)
The Amsterdam File (Book 4)
The Saint Petersburg File (Book 5)

ONE

A MULTICOLOR FLASH LIT UP THE ROOM. FOR A nanosecond, a kaleidoscope of rainbow tones sparkled on the wall, then, just as suddenly, the colors were gone, and the wall was gray again. Before Mykola could blink, an almighty explosion rattled the windows in their frames. Moments later another starburst, another loud boom. The same thing happened three more times, and then the volley of flares ended. A chorus of voices took up a steady chant.

"Slava Ukraini! Heroyam slava!" *Glory to Ukraine! Glory to the heroes!*

Mykola Ovcharenko, staunch new member of the opposition Svoboda Party, found himself in a room he wasn't supposed to be in, searching for a document he wasn't supposed to possess. But possess it he must. With the city of Kyiv in a state of utter panic, breaking into the functionary's room had been easier than he'd anticipated. Three hefty shoves with his strong right shoulder and the wood around the lock splintered like a dry stick of spaghetti.

The official from the ruling party lay dead on the floor, dragged under the desk after Mykola had cornered her and snapped her pale, thin neck. He hated hurting women, but she was the enemy, and this was war.

Find the document and get out.

There was no time to waste. Other rats could return at any moment, see the busted-down door, and create a world of trouble. It seemed unlikely amidst the reigning chaos that he would be disturbed, but Mykola couldn't take chances.

The lack of people in the corridors as he'd made his way to the campaign headquarters told Mykola most of the apparatchiks must have fled, but some surely remained in the building, tooled up with pistols and ready to take out enemy threats. Many would be too scared to go outside and take their chances amongst the riotous mob. Those cowards would be hunched up crying in a corner somewhere, cowering on a stairwell, or in the basement, praying that whoever came for them showed mercy. Fat chance.

Then there were those of another stripe, those who refused to abandon the building to the mob. Idealogues, loyal to the core and prepared to defend the illegitimate proxy regime to the last drop of their miserable blood. Would they show mercy to Mykola? Fat chance.

The Party of Regions and its corrupt president were barely clinging to power. The whole edifice was about to crumble. It was surely just a matter of time. The mob was as desperate as a cornered mother bear guarding her cubs.

Mykola was desperate, too. *Desperate to find that motherfucking document.*

A cracking sound exploded as a small hole appeared in the window, the glass crazing. A projectile fizzed past his right ear before puffing out drywall plaster next to the light switch by the door.

Come on, hurry up and find it and get out of here. You'll be cut down if you don't get a move on.

Five more bullets followed the first. Dots like a line of Braille appeared above the doorway.

He stuck fingers in his ears, gave them a wiggle. The explosions had caused something to go wrong inside his head. The horde's chanting now sounded fuzzy. It wasn't critical to his task, just an annoyance he could do without. If he needed his eardrums looked at by a doctor, he'd organize it later. His own health was of secondary importance to the cause. There was only one priority.

Find the damned document.

But he was having no luck at all. All the papers looked the same; in the hazy smoke now seeping through the bullet holes in the window, the words swam before his eyes.

Mykola took a deep breath to stop himself from hyperventilating and refocused. He blocked the din out as best he could, squinting to see better. Again, with little success—there was only so far mind power can work against the laws of physics and chemistry and his own body's involuntary reactions to stimuli. To make matters worse, the waves of noise down in the city square, surrounded by buildings that corralled then boosted sound like an amphitheater, began to build until they became a howling roar.

He stole a quick glance out the window. The crowd had grown larger since he'd run past it half an hour ago. Sections heaved and rolled around like a living, breathing organism, ripples of motion here and there; other pockets of protesters remained static, waiting to attack or retreat depending on what the field commanders ordered. Sixty feet down and two hundred feet across, citizens of all ages—mainly men but brave women too—taunted the police and security forces. The mob chanted slogans, waved their fists, sticks, flags, crowbars. They hurled bricks and stones and bottles. Whatever they could lay their hands on. Others just stood and watched, mesmerized by the apocalyptic spectacle. Mykola saw the barricades of sandbags and tires and realized he was witnessing the stirrings of a civil war. He grinned when he saw the catapult some genius had constructed to launch gas bombs. He knew that was its purpose because beside the catapult were stacked crate upon crate of fuel-filled bottles, rags sticking out of their necks.

Aligned against the valiant but outgunned people stood a

phalanx of highly trained Berkut, the riot police in gray-and-black camouflage clothing, ski masks, and visored helmets. They would respond to their commanders' instructions without question or hesitation. They grimaced menacingly as they rattled metal shields, pointed semi-automatic rifles, and bashed back with batons anyone brave enough to get too close.

In all his life in this land he called home, Mykola had never witnessed such anarchy and violence.

And hate.

A hundred people had been killed now during these protests that began in the deep, thick snow and freezing cold of January just past. To anyone paying proper attention, the way it all played out should have come as no surprise. A law that banned protesters from hiding their faces behind masks had escalated into a tsunami of frustration and anger. And then, the kicker: Yanukovych's about-face on signing the European Union–Ukraine Free Association Agreement, which had pushed the patience of the law-abiding people of Ukraine over the edge of a cliff. An alliance with Europe was what they craved, a move away from Russia and its authoritarian ways.

Now the movement of protest was turning into a full-blown revolution. Opposing voices from all points on the philosophical spectrum had demanded a stiff broom be swept through the stinking corruption. But those demands were ignored, and here was the result. Rebellion. The momentum was too strong to stop it now, Mykola knew.

Back to the search. He had to find the letter soon and get back to the safety of his apartment before it was too late. But amongst this mess, it was going to require a miracle. 'Where the fuck is it!' he yelled and thumped his fists against the hard wood of the desktop. Sweat poured in runnels from his dusty brow as his hands turned over files, eyes scanning for headings that would tell him he'd found it. He shook his head in exasperation, the abundant sweat now dropping from his ear lobes, beads forming along his hair line. It was just above freezing outside and not much more inside as the building's antiquated heating system limped along, but his body temperature only increased as his frustration grew. The unceasing racket was beginning to affect his thinking. *Have I already looked in this box? Yes. Wait, no, I haven't. What was the serial number on the lid? 409-X or 409-Y? Shit, shit, shit, I can't remember.*

But Mykola would not give up. He would keep looking until he either found it or he was caught and executed. He bent his back and leaned over the desk. Once again, he sifted through the piles of papers, rifled through stacks of cardboard boxes, and flicked through filing cabinets. As he searched, he whistled a famous tune by the Ukrainian band *Okean Elzy*, more as a distraction from the noise than because he liked the song. It wasn't working. He screwed up two scraps of notepaper into little twists and stuck them in his ears. A tiny improvement.

Come on. Concentrate. Find the paper you need, then get the hell out of there.

Through the pieces of paper, he heard the whistling sound of Molotov cocktails sailing through the air. Then the tinkling of glass as the bottles smashed against hard objects. He dared another quick peek outside from his position—for now safe—inside the office on the fourth floor. His heart thundered as he watched the madness unfold on the ancient cobblestones below. The square was a patchwork of bonfires: piles of God-knows-what burned here and there, flames danced from the broken windows of cars lining Hrushevskoho Street adjoining Maidan Square. His eyes watered from the acrid stench of smoking tires and rags, burning paint and other chemicals. Whisps of the putrid fumes leaked through the cracks and bullet holes in the old windows, making him cough and gag.

He wiped his eyes with a handkerchief, returned his attention to the task at hand, and steeled himself for another round.

However long it takes.

And then, suddenly, there it was. THE LETTER. Inside a transparent plastic folder. It had been hiding in plain sight the whole time, in a small pile of correspondence next to the Rolodex by the phone. How had he missed it? Easily. It had been stuck to another file. A quick sniff and taste test identified honey as the culprit. Co-founder of the Party of Regions, Yukhym Zvyahilsky, the fat prick, was known in some circles as the Brown Bear. Seems he shared his totem animal's love of the sweet stuff.

Mykola held the file in trembling hands. He carefully extracted the letter from inside the plastic folder, addressed to Yukhym Zvyahilsky himself. He caught his breath as his eyes took in the bald eagle, the Latin motto, *E pluribus unum*. As per their best intel, the letter came from the highest offices of the United States government. He tried to scan the text to get some meaning, but his English wasn't strong enough. The diplomatic register of the language used was far removed from the schoolboy level he possessed. The title at the bottom under the florid signature left no doubt as to the letter's import. *Senior Tactical and Strategic Advisor to the Secretary of State of the United States of America.*

There was no time to marvel or ponder any further, he had to leave. Get home, make the call and learn the next phase. He knew the letter would be transferred to HQ, but that was a job for later and for someone else.

He grabbed the plastic folder, tucked it under his arm, and ran. Down the corridor, pushing past a couple of people coming the other way with smudged dark rings under their eyes. They staggered around like zombies from those American movies his little brother was fond of. He hoped to be a long way distant before the body of the unfortunate woman was discovered. Once outside, he donned a blue and yellow armband to identify him as a patriot. It should offer some protection—if only peace of mind—as he sprinted through the obstacle course of destruction.

The action had intensified since the first fusillade of flares had lit up the walls of Zvyahilsky's office. Mykola sucked in a huge breath as he saw the raging battles on the square. His patriot's heart told him to end the mission and join the ranks of the protesters. His brain was still functioning well enough to overrule it.

He squared his shoulders, quickly picked out a route that skirted the most obvious hotspots, and took to his heels. He'd only run twenty or so steps when a gas bomb landed a couple of feet away, a pool of fire spreading in all directions. He looked to his legs, wondering if he was alight.

No. I'm not on fire. All good. Keep running.

Five minutes later, sweating profusely from every pore, he rounded the last corner. He had to pull up suddenly. An ambulance crew was dealing with an old woman, blood streaming from a deep wound to her head. His instinct was to stop and render what assistance he could. That instinct had to be suppressed. The mission took precedence over one old woman. Another five hundred meters of gut-busting sprinting and he was home. He wrenched open the main door and bounded up a set of winding stairs until he reached the third floor and relative safety.

His own apartment, where he'd lived alone since separating from his ethnic Russian wife last year. She'd supported Yanukovych, and worse, Putin. She had to go.

Mykola took a cold shower, scrubbed the grime and the stink of fear from his body, and dried off with a rough towel. The wall clock behind his humming refrigerator said it was 9:15 p.m. His boss would be expecting a call before 10:00p.m., as agreed. A pot of moka coffee on a high gas flame whooshed like a steam train, then went quiet. He readjusted his scruffy bathrobe, poured a cup, lit a cigarette, and placed the landline telephone on the table. He dialed, waiting fifteen seconds before a gruff voice answered.

"Dobriy vechir." *Good evening*. "I have it." Mykola could sense the relief in his own voice. "I thought I was never going to find it, to be perfectly honest."

"Well done." The words were technically praise, but they didn't sound like it. No emotion at all. "Take it to the address I gave you, the old apartment building on Antonovycha Street. The passcode to get into inside is K482."

"Not very original." The letter K denoted Kyiv, the number—the year the ancient city was founded.

A barking laugh. "Agreed. But impossible for a patriot to forget."

"Indeed." Mykola took a long sip of coffee.

There was the sound of a match striking on the other end of the line and the inhalation of cigarette smoke. "Listen carefully. Once you get to Antonovycha Street, take the elevator—if it's working—to the sixth floor. You want apartment 34. But first, knock on the door of apartment 33. A man with a black beard will give you the key to No. 34 and another key to a safe inside the flat."

Mykola laughed. "You're joking!"

"The only other option was under the mat. Would you have preferred that?"

"Of course not." The man's sarcasm wasn't disguised, but these were desperate times, and Mykola was of a forgiving nature. Besides that, after a childhood of bullying on account of his red hair and extra-long nose, he had skin thicker than an elephant's hide. "Put the letter in the safe, then go straight home. No stopping to gawk at the mischief on Maidan Square. Understood?"

"Yes."

Just after midnight, Mykola Ovcharenko had carried out the last part of his mission without a hitch and was striding back to his apartment, chest swollen with pride. Echoes of the skirmishes on Maidan Square and surroundings drew him back to the protest. He'd made it to within one block of his destination when he felt an insistent tap on the shoulder.

He turned instinctively. It was the middle-aged man from apartment 33. Mykola smiled at the man, whose own face remained impassive. "Have you come to join the people?" said Mykola.

"No," said the man. "You were told to go straight home."

"Come on, man! This is history in the making."

"I'm sorry, but if you cannot follow simple instructions exactly, then we have no room for you."

Mykola stood rooted to the spot and could only stare as the man whipped out a fat-muzzled pistol from behind his back and took aim. Before he could blink, the man pulled the trigger. Mykola felt a flash of intense pain in the middle of his forehead which, thankfully, ended in a nanosecond before the life spirit exited his body and he crashed to the ground.

TWO

THE SCENES ON THE LARGE MONITOR WERE HARD TO watch. Even for a seasoned operative like Jacob Hunter, the images caused him to wince and curse softly under his breath. Drone strikes on civilian infrastructure were bad enough. When it was a school or a hospital full of children, it was an act of despicable wickedness. But he wouldn't look away. Even when the moist-eyed first responder emerged from smoking rubble carrying a blood-spattered child who was clearly dead. Or when the wailing mother repeatedly beat a fist against her chest as the child was gently placed by her feet.

"Pretty bad, huh?" Grant Fletcher, head of top-secret US intelligence department Skia and Hunter's direct supervisor, clicked a remote to pause the footage they'd been watching for twenty minutes. He fixed a couple of whiskey and sodas, adding ice cubes from a bar refrigerator tucked under a gleaming cherrywood cabinet.

"That's an understatement. It's appalling. Plenty of fodder for war crimes prosecutions at the Hague when it's all over." Hunter nodded his thanks as he accepted the proffered drink. "But there's nothing *we* can do about it. This war is going in so many different directions with so many sides involved, I can't keep up."

"True." Fletcher sipped his whiskey. "Not only do the belligerent armies have mercenaries from all around the world fighting for them, in Russia's case, they've got an entire private army on their side."

"I take it you're talking about Prigozhin's Wagner company?"

"Exactly. Twenty-five thousand plus badasses prepared to do anything to earn a paycheck. Can you imagine the atrocities they're perpetrating even as we speak?" He didn't wait for an answer. "Then there are the alliances: The European Union, the Euro-Atlantic Partnership Council that connects Ukraine with NATO, the People's Militias of the Donetsk and Luhansk Republics, Russia's tiny group of international allies."

"Group? I can only see one obvious ally. Belarus."

"Officially, yes. Lukashenko's regime stands shoulder to shoulder with Putin. Others back Russia without yelling it from the roof tops. Syria and Iran. However, these are minnows, and their support is useless." Fletcher drained his glass. "Then there's the lack of cohesion from *our* side. So many agendas, arguments over the billions we're spending on Ukraine, what weapons and personnel should be supplied. To date, there have been thirty-seven shipments of arms, can you believe it?" Again he didn't wait for a response before adding, "Stinger air defense systems, Javelin anti-tank systems, howitzers, rockets, ammo. You name it. Some say it's too much, others that it's not enough. A coordinated, unified approach to this mess seems a pipe dream, which means we face a protracted engagement with no end in sight."

"Unless someone in the Kremlin or the White House pushes one of those nasty red buttons," Hunter said, side-eyeing his superior.

"Don't even suggest it." The whites of Fletcher's eyes showed bright. "That's a scenario I don't want to even entertain."

"Listen, boss," Hunter sighed. "Why are we even having this

philosophical discussion?" There was an edge to his voice. "Like I said, we're powerless to affect the policy makers even if we wanted to. My opinion, your opinion, that clown fish's opinion"—he pointed at a fifty-five gallon aquarium that took center stage in the converted warehouse Fletcher called home—"they count for nothing."

"Quite right, Jacob. But we have our orders to carry out. We've been flicked an assignment that the Secret Service and the CIA can't handle or don't want a part of. And when I say we, I mean *you*."

"I'm getting a bad feeling about this one already. Who dialed in the order?"

"State Department. You know I can't name names, though. I'll make us one more drink because you'll need it to get your head around what I'm about to tell you."

"Sure, but you know two's my limit."

Drinks in hand, Fletcher continued, "Before I get to the nitty gritty, I'd like to show you the rest of the video. Don't worry, the money shot's only moments away."

Hunter glanced at his Breitling Endurance Pro watch. Nine forty-five p.m. The timepiece was a gift from the vice president presented to the operative anonymously—the VP had no idea he even existed—for saving her step-daughter's ass. The young woman had flirted too closely with a Mossad intelligence officer who spiked a drink and took a bunch of compromising photos. His aim had been to inveigle information out of her about her mother, but it all took a bizarre twist when it turned out that his perversions and greed were stronger than his dedication to the cause. Hunter had organized for the spy to accidentally break his neck and fall off the Brooklyn Bridge, his phone disappearing into the depths of the East River together with the body. Hunter hoped the briefing didn't drag on too much longer. He wanted to get home to catch a classic war movie on cable. Instead, he was watching fragments of a real war.

Fletcher cleared his throat. "What we've seen so far is a collage of footage from various sources preceding the main event. For us at least. Oh, and I apologize for the dead kids."

"What are you apologizing for? You didn't kill them."

"You know what I mean, Jacob." Fletcher fast-forwarded, skipping footage that appeared to be a dashcam covering a drive through city streets before the vehicle stalled in traffic at a set of lights. He pressed another button to go back to normal speed. Then, two seconds later, a blinding flash of light as a missile struck the side of a long gray building a hundred and fifty yards away. A ball of luminescence bloomed in the twilight sky, then came the billowing smoke, ashen and black and laden with fine debris. A burst of loud swearing in Russian came from inside the car that was filming the action.

"What did he say?" said Fletcher.

"Literally *whore*, followed by *bitch*, then *fuck your mother*. With poetic license, I'd equate the entire outburst to 'Holy Mother of God!'"

"Hmmm. I guessed it was something like that." Fletcher slugged on his drink, an ice cube banging softly against his front teeth. He dabbed at his light-brown mustache with a napkin. "You can tell by the tone."

"Russian swearing is so much richer than English, which is tame by comparison. I could give you a whole series of lectures on the nuances of Russian profanity."

"No thanks," said Fletcher. "I've got no head for languages. My high school Spanish wouldn't get me a margarita in Mexico."

Hunter laughed and nodded. "I wish I didn't have the aptitude sometimes."

"You're blessed with a special talent, my man. And that's why you've been chosen to get the letter back."

"What letter?"

The chief inhaled deeply. "Somewhere deep inside that building was secreted a letter written by an advisor to the Secretary of State in 2014. It was addressed to a guy called, and forgive my pronunciation, Yukhym Zvyahilsky."

"Close enough," said Hunter, swirling the last of his drink before tipping it down his throat.

"Thanks. I know I mangled it."

"I've never heard of him."

"Not surprising. It's nearly ten years ago, and you were barely a boy."

"Grant, I was twenty-five years old ten years ago."

"No way. Get outta here!"

"You know perfectly well how old I am. And just about everything else about me."

Fletcher steepled his fingers. "That I do. And I also know you are more than capable of completing this mission. Which I hadn't finished explaining. Our intel reports the Russians didn't hit that building by accident. And it wasn't a false flag operation by Kyiv. The Ukrainians wouldn't dare launch an attack on themselves so close to the heart of their government. If you notice, the historical center of Kyiv has so far been largely spared from serious bombardment. Putin knows hitting the city center too hard will galvanize the West like never before."

"Of course. Putin's officially running a 'Special Military Operation,' not a war. A fully declared war is something he knows he's going to lose. So why hit this building? It *is* close to the center of town. Am I right in thinking it was to get the building cleared out and then access the safe or wherever the letter was kept and... ah...steal it?"

"Bang on the money." Fletcher smiled a lip-smile that didn't show teeth. "Your job is to travel to Moscow, where we understand the letter is now located, and get it back."

Hunter shook his head. "Grant. I'm not sure that's such a good idea. Staying in character for so long is going to drive me insane. That's assuming my cover doesn't get blown."

Fletcher pressed his lips together. "Not doing what I ask you will have unthinkable consequences for our government and the entire course of this war. People are implicated who would rather not be." He paused and walked to one of the many floor-to-ceiling windows, hands behind his back. "People prepared to pay a lot of money to have things go away."

"Hush money, in other words. And I'm the chump who gets them out of a pickle, right?"

Fletcher pointed a finger at his charge. "I'll have no moralizing from you. You get paid an absolute fortune to do what you do. Besides, your contract says you cannot say no to a mission."

The last part was true. He'd signed a contract with no get-out clause. Locked in for another ten years. As for remuneration, that was fine. He sat on a juicy retainer of $500,000 per annum plus bonuses that dwarfed the retainer for each successful mission. His sprawling apartment a block away in Duane Street was twice as expensive as his boss's. "I'm not refusing. I'm just voicing my opinion about my chances of success here."

"You easily passed for a Russian on your last mission."

"It wasn't without its hiccups, Grant. The general smelled a rat right at the end. I barely got out of Kabul alive." He cracked the scarred knuckles of his big hands. "Besides, there's more to this than just *passing as a Russian*, as you call it. I haven't set foot in the country since 2015, when Boris Nemtsov was assassinated. Christ, the whole landscape of the place has shifted seismically. There is literally NO freedom there anymore."

"You don't need freedom, Jacob."

"What do I need? You tell me how the fuck I'm going to pull this one off? This mission has no hope of succeeding."

Fletcher gave a sigh of exasperation. "You've got the chops, don't be disingenuous. What do you need? Simple. In addition to your regular physical and firearms training, I'd say you're going to need one week of solid reading."

"Reading what? Tolstoy's *War and Peace*? That'd take about a week to get through. Maybe the Ugolovny kodeks?"

"What the hell's that?"

"The Russian Criminal Code. I might need to familiarize myself with it in case the FSB throw me into the Lubyanka and I need to hire myself a lawyer.'

Fletcher shook his head slowly. "You crack me up, Jacob, you really do." There was nothing in his tone that indicated amusement. "You'll need to read the latest intel on who's who in the zoo of Kremlin politics. The history of this ongoing spat between Russia and Ukraine. Perhaps a bit of study on the latest in pop culture so you don't look like a dweeb around the watercooler." Fletcher went to his rosewood desk, slid open a drawer, and extracted a slim folder. He handed it to Hunter. "Before you do anything, read this. It's a copy of the original letter you must retrieve and bring back to the United States."

"I don't understand. If there are copies like this, what's the point of getting the original?"

"A copy can be proven to be a fake. In this case, the provenance of the letter is just as important as its sensitive content."

Hunter nodded. "Makes sense."

"The original was signed using a fountain pen containing a specific type of ink. Additionally, there's the chemical composition of the paper, possible latent prints of the author. In short, technically, it can be proved that the original came from the State Department. Read it yourself and tell me your own conclusions."

Hunter skimmed over the formal diplomatic introduction, then chewed his bottom lip as he got stuck into the meat and potatoes of the letter. *We urge the Ukrainian government to rethink its intention to sign the European Union–Ukraine Free Association Agreement. Doing so will undermine your country's relationship with the United States in a highly negative way. Most favored nation status stands at risk of being revoked. In any future diplomatic disagreements, including those that may escalate into armed conflict, you may not be able to count on the support of the United States. Cordially yours, Rufus Constable II, Senior Tactical and Strategic Advisor to the Secretary of State.*

"So the president of the day, Yanukovych, was pressured into not signing the agreement with the Europeans?" said Hunter, looking up from the page.

"Yep." Fletcher portrayed a serious look. "And the State

Department does not want the fact made public." He took a seat at his desk, flipping up the screen of his laptop.

"Who is this Rufus Constable II fella?"

Fletcher waved the question away like it was an annoying mosquito. "A functionary who died mysteriously in 2016 while scuba-diving in the Dominican Republic."

"Knew too much, did he?"

"No speculation, please, Jacob. He's not important in the grand scheme of things. Now, which flight do you want to take next Saturday? Morning or evening?"

"So soon?"

"You're lucky. State wanted you to leave today. I convinced them to push it back, but it wasn't easy, believe me. The panic over this missing letter is impossible to exaggerate. Which means your bonus for this job is gonna be...well...big-name rock stars make less in a year. So my advice—get stuck into that reading."

"Will do."

Fletcher pulled a sheet of paper from the printer tray and handed it to Jacob together with a pen. Skia's waivers contained two unchanging conditions: there would be no rescue mission in the case of his arrest, and a number of crucial human assets would only be made known to Jacob at certain stages of the operation one at a time. Again, a safeguard against blowing the identity of long-term deep cover agents in the event of Jacob's capture and, heaven forbid, torture he was unable to endure. Jacob scribbled his signature and handed it back.

"Oh, and one more thing before you go home," said Fletcher, placing the waiver into a hanging file under his desk.

"What? Haven't I got enough to think about?"

"Remember the name Ardalion. Burn it into your brain. It is your codename. Only a handful of people will know it."

Fletcher's dramatic delivery often ground Jacob's gears. This was another of those occasions. "Who?"

"You trying to get me to break the rules? You'll learn who they are when they approach *you*. Knowledge of these details will put our Ukrainian and Russian assets at greater risk than in any other mission you've completed."

Jacob nodded. He'd been tortured once before, in Nicaragua. He'd somehow managed to keep his mouth shut, but he was saved by a cartel turncoat who put a bullet into the brain of Jacob's sadistic tormentor. Had the torture not ended, he might have spilled his guts.

Fletcher scratched his palm before adding, "The codeword Ardalion will first be given to you moments before you cross the border into Russia. It will prove the people conducting your insertion are the real deal."

"What if I don't hear that name?"

"Abort. And save yourself the best you can."

Jacob sighed. "Understood."

"Once you're installed as an employee of the Ministry of Finance, where intel says the letter is most likely secreted, you'll only have a tick over a month to get the letter, max. Intel says the anniversary of the invasion of Ukraine is the most probable release date of the letter."

"Jesus Christ..."

"I needn't remind you of the embarrassment that will befall this country if you fail to–"

"I get it, Grant!" He stood, snatching his wallet, keys, and cell phone. "Good night."

As he strolled the block to his own apartment, the enormity of what lay ahead hit Jacob in the guts like a sledge hammer.

THREE

FROM HIS WINDOW SEAT, HE WATCHED THE SPINNING blades as the fan sucked air into the engine where the inner workings did their magic. He was heading for Warsaw, Poland. It was a new city for Jacob. He wouldn't have time to enjoy it, though. A contact would be waiting in the arrivals hall of Frederic Chopin Airport to whisk him to a location near the Ukraine border.

The obese man next to him snored, blobs of spittle forming at the corner of his mouth. Probably dreaming of the delicious pirogis he was going to gorge on when he reached his destination. Jacob shuddered. He wasn't what they call a 'people person.' The man grunted and wriggled in his sleep, the hairs on his pudgy forearm brushing against Jacob's arm. Jacob jerked it away instinctively, swearing under his breath. A glance at his wristwatch told him there were more hours left on this flight than he cared to endure. Less than halfway there.

He silently cursed Fletcher for his choice in administrative staff. His secretary displayed appalling organizational skills, especially when it came to travel arrangements. She must be sleeping with Fletcher to be keeping her job; there was no other explanation. As usual, everything had gone wrong. She'd waited much too long to make the reservation, and all the business and first-class seats had been snapped up. Instead of sitting at the pointy end of the aircraft where he belonged, where he could, in comfort, bone up on the boring reading Fletcher suggested, he was stuck in the middle with the stinking, unwashed masses. Even flashing the no-limit platinum AmEx card at the check-in desk had failed to score an upgrade. There was a huge classical music festival happening in Warsaw, and every kooky classical music fan in America was heading there, including his gross travelmate in his stained Beethoven T-shirt.

He donned the flimsy headset and found a passably good movie channel on the inflight entertainment system. He only half paid attention to the action on the tiny screen. Instead, his gaze was drawn to the engine's turbofan. Observing the mesmerizing, swirling spiral, Jacob's thoughts drifted back to the day his entire future had been mapped out for him by fate.

A crisp, cool December day, 2005. The sky was bluer than the rarified air outside the fuselage of this American Airlines plane.

He relived this pivotal moment often. Gave thanks for the disaster that had befallen him. On sober reflection, the dreams he'd held that day on the college gridiron, to become a professional football player in the NFL, were probably never going to eventuate. He was a better-than-average player but no superstar.

The memories always had the quality of a vivid dream.

This time was like all the others.

Neck twisted to track the incoming object, the spiraling ball landed gently in his outstretched arms. A gift from the heavens. The perfect pass, executed by a strongarm quarterback who was rumored to be in the crosshairs of several NFL heavyweight franchises. With accuracy of passes like this, delivered on a dime over fifty yards and under intense pressure from behind the line of scrimmage, it was no wonder.

The crowd in the bleachers erupted gleefully. They knew the holy grail was theirs for the taking. And the vessel couldn't be in safer hands than those of speedy wide receiver Jacob Hunter. He had a mere twenty-seven yards left to run to make the touchdown. Fifteen seconds left on the clock, five points down. The prize—eternal glory as the player who brought home Glenn Bridge High's very first championship. Maybe the talent scouts would come knocking on Jacob's door, too. And why not? He'd smashed some long-standing school records today. Seven catches and three touchdowns. Not sure about the yardage, but he was on track for at least 150. And a fourth TD.

Those stats meant nothing at this moment. Just inert numbers. There was only one priority: escort the pigskin over the goal line and win the game.

But there was one big problem: he was squarely in the sights of three massive and mobile linebackers who had other ideas.

Ball tucked firmly under his arm, momentum carried Jacob forward after he'd reached top speed in the act of receiving from his QB. He was a locomotive. At six-two and 210 pounds and with a head of steam up, nothing would stop him. The linebackers were shepherding him along a path between the middle of the field and the left-hand touch line. Jacob's instinct was to veer infield, try to split them by putting on some sidestepping moves. It was in his bag of tricks; he'd already used it to score a touchdown in the first half.

But the players standing in his way were not only huge, they were fast. Plus they were likely anticipating Jacob might try the same tactics again.

No. There was only one option.

Run straight, run for your life!

And so he set sail for that left corner, rehearsing in his mind the spectacular swan dive that would see him evade the desperate clutching fingers of the last of the linemen. He could already hear the sound of the crowd losing their collective shit as the touchdown was awarded.

The defenders were gaining.

Such a short distance, but oh, so far to go.

Lactic acid was reaching maximum saturation in his legs, the muscles turning to jelly. Each stride a monumental effort. Feet sinking in quicksand. *Fight it!*

A quick look over the right shoulder. Two defenders seemed to have given up the chase. But one hadn't, and he was three strides from Jacob, arms pumping. The ball-carrier was four strides from the goal line.

Push, push, push!

Then, with the white line so tantalizingly close, his world was rocked by a loud *pop*. The sound brought gasps from fans in the lower seats of the bleachers. The hamstring in Jacob's left leg had torn. Blitzing pain like he'd never known fizzed through the back of his upper leg, along his spine, into his brain. The run became a hobble. One yard from the goal line, he could go no further, yet he kept a firm grip on the ball. All three linemen were upon him now. Like a high jumper, he tensed the muscles in his good right leg, prepped to launch his injured body into the air and over the line.

And that was his last thought before he was crunched side-on by an 18-wheeler wearing a football helmet.

Two days later, he woke up in the local hospital with two broken ribs, one arm in plaster, his neck in a hard plastic brace, and the knowledge that the championship had eluded Glenn Bridge High yet again.

In his subconscious, Jacob could hear the hum of the aircraft's engines and the air-conditioning system, feel the bumps through light turbulence, smell the lousy coffee. His memory of the day of the lost championship morphed into a dream of the day of his *realization*.

Snuggled up to Sally-Anne Vincent, his new girlfriend of three weeks, a complexly plotted spy flick played out inside Cinema 2 of the Glenn Bridge movie theater. She'd almost vetoed the outing: the film starred an actor she hated, but Jacob won the argument. He was still hurting from the football catastrophe—losing the game itself and the crippling injuries he'd endured. He'd suffered a serious concussion, and his head ached constantly, assuaged by regular doses of pain killers. Ironically, the longest injury to heal was the torn hamstring. Never mind broken bones, internal bleeding and bruising, or a severe concussion that was an inch away from permanent brain damage. No, it was the stupid leg injury that cost the team the match that still caused pain. Another month of rehab before he could even jog again.

Instead of outpourings of sympathy from his coach and players, he was hit with condemnation. *For not stretching properly!* Which was a load of horseshit, because his position in the team as a wide receiver who ran more than many of his teammates dictated that Jacob was one of the most assiduous warmer-uppers in the team.

It wasn't just the players and personnel who gave Jacob the cold shoulder. At times, it seemed like the entire town had turned against him. Spiteful things were being said about him everywhere, even on the pages of the local newspaper. The editor had a field day belittling him for the loss, but he did it in such a clever, satirical way that there was no comeback. Jacob's father, a retired army colonel, wanted to sue for libel, but Jacob insisted they keep their heads down until it blew over. He expected more support from his mother, who shrank into herself. Her friends came to visit less often, and she herself was reluctant to venture out of the house.

Why do small towns take high school sports so seriously? It was a question Jacob asked himself over and over. He tried to stay above all of the small-town small-mindedness, but it still hurt. The shunning, the ridicule. He was mature for his age, but still a teenager after all.

Thank God he'd found Sally-Anne. Or, in truth, she had found him. He was loitering outside the movie theater not long after being discharged from hospital. She recognized him and struck up an awkward conversation, full of stuttering and blushing and perspiration on foreheads. The attraction was instant and molecular. Jacob quickly realized he could speak his mind with her and there would be no judgment. He admitted to

Sally-Anne that with few loyal friends to count on—none, in fact—he found solace in the make-believe and escapism of Hollywood. He thought he was weird, going to the movies alone, but it turned out he wasn't the only hard-core fan of the silver screen.

"It's not weird at all," she said. "It's the best way to concentrate on the story. When you're with others, there are constant comments and interruptions. I'd rather come by myself."

"Or maybe with another movie buff who won't interrupt?" he'd ventured.

"Exactly." She smiled and nodded.

Before he knew it, they were on their third movie date. The first film they saw together was a steamy rom com, which Jacob found less awful than he was expecting. Mainly because Sally-Anne squeezed his hand during all the gooey moments, snuggling her head into his shoulder and lightly caressing his thigh to the point of excruciating, hormone-raging frustration. He wouldn't push her to do anything she didn't want to do, though. There was something so sweet and innocent about her—the way she dressed conservatively in plaid skirts and woolly cardigans and never cussed—not like the other girls he'd made out with in the past. Not that there were many: despite his jock persona, Jacob's shyness was a huge impediment when it came to developing relationships with girls. Which in turn took second place to football. Everything took second place to football. Until *the incident*. He doubted he could ever pull on a pair of cleats again.

The second movie was a superhero blockbuster, which Sally-Anne admitted she quite liked. Jacob knew that to be true simply by observing her involuntary reactions to what was happening on the screen: cheering, laughing, gasping, and tensing up at all the appropriate moments. There's no faking that. Perhaps it was more a testament to the ability of moviemakers to elicit emotions rather than genuine responses to the medium. Or not, who the hell knew?

Now they were shoveling popcorn into their mouths as a spy thriller unfolded on the giant screen. Jacob had chosen a matinee session, knowing there would be fewer people inside the theater. He was right. They were the only ones there. He risked an arm around her shoulder, which she acceded to with smiling enthusiasm. The heat from her body, rising above the intentionally low temperature inside the venue, was doing things to Jacob he wished it wouldn't. He positioned the bucket of popcorn in the middle of his lap to hide his arousal. For some reason, he feared she would positively freak out if she knew what was stirring in his loins.

Before he knew it, he was swept up in the plot of the thriller. Halfway through, it happened. A pair of Russian baddies were having a heated exchange about how to blow up a vehicle. One suggested using a gas bottle. Jacob burst out laughing.

"What's up?" said Sally-Anne in a habitual whisper, totally unnecessary since there was no one else to disturb.

"The dude said gas balloon instead of bottle."

"No he didn't," she argued. "The subtitle clearly said bottle. I think you need to wear glasses."

"Yeah, the subtitle was right, but whoever wrote the script made a mistake, because he definitely said balloon."

She tugged his sleeve hard. "You never told me you could speak Russian. What gives?"

For a couple of seconds, Jacob was lost for words.

How the hell *could* he understand it? Then he slugged down some Coke before admitting, "I don't have the slightest clue."

FOUR

Clearing customs was a breeze. A smiling official welcomed him to Poland and wished him a pleasant stay. The man barely looked at the incoming passenger's passport before handing it back with care, like it was a birthday card. A refreshing change from the granite-faced scowls you often get at most US international airports. It's like they're trained in hostile expressions and body language.

The arrival hall was crowded, an abundance of musical instruments in cases as the classical music buffs converged in the spacious vestibule. A number of flights had landed within a short space of each other, which only served to exacerbate the dense crowding and lines for everything. It was worse than a Black Friday sale at Macy's.

Jacob readjusted the sports bag that was the extent of his luggage and searched for a sign bearing his civilian code name, Edward Brown. His height helped him better than most, but after two minutes, nothing. A flick of the wrist: 2:45 p.m. There had been a forty-minute delay in landing, which had a knock-on effect with clearing security, customs, and passport control. Perhaps the contact had grown tired of waiting and was answering the call of nature. He'd wait another thirty minutes, rooted to the spot and scanning for the sign, and then implement the alternative plan of calling the number he'd memorized.

A tap on the shoulder. "Mr. Brown?"

He turned to see a squat female in an orange rollneck sweater, a ginger bob haircut, and black square-framed glasses. He couldn't help thinking of Velma from the Scooby Doo cartoon. "That's me."

"Follow me please." No smile, no greeting, no welcome. Without saying another word, she took off toward the sliding-door exit. She made a call, barking something in Polish that Jacob understood to mean *We are on our way*.

The woman set a cracking pace, weaving in and out of humans like they were traffic cones, using elbows when necessary. She even nudged a violin case out of the way with her foot, drawing a snarl from its owner. Out in the cold air, she marched toward the curbside. A black late-model Mercedes with tinted windows pulled up in front of a row of taxis. Passengers lining up in the cold glowered their displeasure as the woman beckoned Jacob to cut the line and jump in the back seat. She climbed in the front next to the driver, two doors clunked, and they were on their way to the Ukrainian border and beyond.

THE POLISH WOMAN'S name was Vera. Not too dissimilar to cartoon Velma, which made Jacob grin. Likewise, she was all business, no pleasure. "The drive will be long and boring. Lots of snow drifts and open fields. Not much else." She shrugged, almost apologizing for not ensuring a more edifying trip. "I hope you have something to keep yourself amused."

Jacob retrieved his first burner cell phone, one he would ditch well before crossing into Russia, from the pocket of his leather jacket, folded up beside him on the back seat. "A couple of language apps to brush up on my Ukrainian."

"Dobrze," said Vera. *Good*. "But you won't need it. I understand you speak Russian fluently? That will be more than sufficient."

"Using Russian won't win me too many friends in Ukraine, will it?"

"Speak with an exaggerated American accent and you will be fine. Try English first, by all means; you may be lucky. Especially with younger people."

Made sense. Then again, what did it matter? He'd be in and out of Ukraine in a little over 24 hours, and interactions with strangers other than sanctioned contacts would be minimal, preferably non-existent. He composed a quick coded message that went to another number before being rerouted to Fletcher. *Arrived safely in Poland, on road to Lviv.* He pulled up the language app in any case, despite Vera's assertion. A hundred or so memorized stock phrases and replies might come in handy. Before focusing on the task, he said: "Any stops along the way?"

"Toilet breaks only. We have food and water in the trunk. Oh, and a couple of Uzis in case we run into bother." The bald goon behind the wheel burst out laughing but said nothing. In fact, he'd not uttered a word the whole time.

Vera turned in her seat and handed Jacob a Samsung S6 tablet. "Please, you can see the route we are taking. The drive to the border will be over in a little more than five hours. Even though I have a special authorization, it could take a while to get through customs at the Korczowa-Krakovets border crossing. One never knows what kind of idiots are on duty in the booths. When we are through, we will hand you over to a Ukrainian man called–"

"The Octopus."

Vera nodded, her glasses slipping slightly down her short nose before she shoved them back into place. "I understand he is known by that name in certain circles, yes. An entrepreneur with tentacles everywhere. He will take you from the border to the city of Lviv. After that, I have no idea what is in store for you. And that's the way I prefer things, so please don't entertain me with details of whatever you're planning to do."

"A lot of what lies ahead for me is a mystery, too. But don't worry. I'm not here for the scintillating conversation."

Vera grunted. "Good."

Jacob knew plenty about the Octopus already. His real name was Matviy Ostapenko, an old-school hard man who ran a popular strip club in Lviv called The Sable. Even a war was powerless to stop the adult industry. Ukraine was known as a hub, if not a source, of human trafficking. Intel said Ostapenko was not involved in the slave trade. Jacob reserved judgment. The Octopus had too much money and influence to be a total clean skin. However, he was a staunch patriot prepared to siphon money from his lucrative businesses to purchase equipment for the war effort. Indeed, he was so dedicated to the cause that he'd willingly changed his lifestyle of overt extravagance to a much more modest one. He reputedly hated the Russians with a passion and could be relied upon to support any actions to turn the invaders back. "Do you have an opinion on this guy, Vera?"

She laughed with her head tilted back. "It's not my job to have opinions. My job is to deliver you to Mr. Ostapenko and return to Warsaw with my driver in one piece." She fished around in the console and pulled out a tattered book that looked to be a collection of crossword puzzles. "Now, if you don't mind?" Her tone left no room for interpretation. *Don't disturb me unless it's urgent.*

She hadn't been lying about the tedium of the road trip. Mile after mile of snow-covered fields, isolated villages, small farms. On the other side of the highway was an endless procession of goods trucks, as well as buses transporting people away from Ukraine. The buses seemed to be filled with women and children. After about the sixth mile of trucks, stopped in the middle of the road or crawling end to end like one enormous caterpillar, Jacob ventured to ask the question. "Where are all the men?"

Vera put her crossword book down, peering at Jacob over the top of her glasses. "Fighting the fucking Russians, what do you think?"

"Surely not all of them?"

"Like I told you before, it's not my job to have an opinion."

That was something they shared. Jacob wasn't barred from exercising natural curiosity, but questioning the essence of his missions and the reasons behind them was not met with approval. Taking a break from reading mind-numbing minutiae about the ever-shifting political situation in Ukraine since 2014, he laid his head back on the soft-as-down headrest. Jet-lag was kicking in big time. The second part of the dream he'd relived on the airplane started up again, like a movie after intermission.

After the shock of discovering he could understand a foreign language—Russian, no less—the medical tests began. A battery of them. Blood analyzed for every health metric known to man. Reflexes tested, heart and lung capacity, urine, stools, the works. But most importantly, brain tests. Wires attached to his skull, other equipment beeping and bleeping all around him. It took five weeks of solid investigation before a full report was written.

The verdict. Acquired Savant Syndrome.

"Rain Man. Is that who you're saying I am?" Jacob couldn't believe what he was hearing.

The doctor with the white beard who looked like a famous country singer assured Jacob that, no, he was *not* that. He was a normal, healthy young man, not an oddity. His new condition, acquired as a result of the collision on the football field, was hyper-focused on one aspect of his mental function. Language.

His mother and father sat in visitors' chairs by his bed in the research lab. An old-fashioned tape recorder appeared from nowhere. Mom pressed play, and Jacob's face lit up like a firework. A young female voice recited a nursery rhyme. He couldn't recall ever hearing this recording in his life, but he recognized the sounds, the words, the intonation. It played for about five minutes. Jacob's parents looked on in astonishment as he recited the strange-sounding phrases alongside the disembodied voice. Not a pause to think, no hesitation, the words tumbled out.

"Do you know the meaning of what you were saying just now?" his mother asked, perhaps thinking her son was a genius.

Pity she didn't think he was so terrific when he snapped his hamstring and lost the football match and she practically shunned him.

"Not all of them, but I totally get the gist of it." He chewed a fingernail as the magnitude of his new ability hit home.

One of the research team, standing a couple of feet away, asked Jacob if he could recite the words without the tape-recorder playing. He did as requested; again, a faultless rendition.

"Do you know who that is speaking?" said mom.

"Yes! It's Natasha." He felt his brows knotting in confusion. "I know her name, but I can't picture her."

She produced a glossy photograph of a young woman with wide, green eyes and hair tied back in a ponytail. His face broke into a smile of childlike innocence as his mother continued, "You can't recall her face because you were only three years old. Do you recognize her now?"

"Yes! Why have I never heard the recording before or seen this photo?" Jacob felt robbed, like something good had been kept back from him, a formative part of his childhood.

"To be honest, son, we'd completely forgotten about them." His father now sat on the edge of the bed like he was riding a horse side-saddle. "It was only after this...thing...happened to you that I remembered the items stashed away in the attic. When your nanny Natasha left to go back to Saint Petersburg, she gave this tape to us. She asked us to play it to you every now and then so you would remember the words. So you would remember her. And we did, but after a couple of weeks, you grew tired of it. Like so many things, it wound up gathering dust under the roof."

"How old did you say I was?"

"Three," said his mother.

A silence fell over the gathering. Then the doctor said, "How did you understand what was going in in the movie? They weren't talking in nursery rhymes, it was...grown-up language."

Jacob squinted as he tried to remember. "I have this vague recollection of Natasha just talking to me. Like, all the time. As if

I was an adult." He shrugged. "Maybe a lot of it sank in and stayed in my brain."

The medicos suggested Jacob might like to undertake a formal course of Russian language study. See how far he could take it. Introductory level, then slowly build up. *Why not?* Jacob thought. *It might be fun.* After figuring out and committing to memory the weird Cyrillic alphabet in under thirty minutes, he read the first text book he was handed, cover to cover, and memorized the content. Then a second, then a third, each more difficult than the next. The complexities of Russian grammar that stumped most new students of the language were tiny hurdles Jacob leapt over with ease. The declension of nouns, conjugation of verbs in all their strange and archaic forms, and exceptions to rules were conquered and stored away in the memory banks for use at any moment he chose. He devoured book after book, on all manner of subjects, and within six months was already reading and comprehending classical Russian literature. He motored through novels by Dostoevsky and Nabokov as though they were reading primers for children.

The best part was that Jacob loved his new talent. In addition to reading, he listened to Russian music, pop songs from the 1980s onwards and watched Russian spy movies that were even cornier than the Hollywood variety. Academics marveled not only at the young man's breadth of knowledge, but also his flawless accent. A clear, native speaker's accent, they said, shaking their heads and smiling. *Must have been transferred on a subconscious level from Natasha*, Jacob reasoned.

Like his father and grandfather before him, upon finishing high school, Jacob applied to West Point Military Academy. The entire process was a mere formality, and he was granted golden passage into the hallowed halls of this prestigious institution. As a place to spend four years, it beat high school's ass. With its motivated students and top-quality teachers, he almost never wanted it to end. Forty-seven months later, he graduated with distinction, having added Spanish to his arsenal. He'd picked it up quickly, *no hay problema*, attaining a high level of fluency. The US Army had approached him with an offer to fast-track his career through the ranks. Things were looking good for Jacob Hunter.

Sally-Anne Vincent, who loved Jacob more than she loved the movies, made the trip from Ohio to New York to be with him and his parents at the graduation ceremony. She sat in the front row, beaming like an idiot, tears streaming down her face. There was no doubt in Jacob's mind she would soon become his wife.

Two months later, Sally-Anne was dead, and Jacob was on a mission to find who had killed her. A mission he had failed at but vowed never to give up on.

"Hey!" A firm hand shook his shoulder. "We are nearly at the border with Ukraine. Be ready with your passport."

"Have I slept the whole time?" Jacob realized he had tears in the corners of his eyes. He blinked them away, then squinted through the open car window, lights glinting off the driver's bald pate as he sucked on a cigarette. The acrid smoke wafted inside the vehicle. He'd have to get used to that; Eastern Europeans were among the heaviest smokers in the world.

"Yes," said Vera. "Just a few minutes to go."

Jacob rubbed his eyes, then blinked a couple of times in response. It was dark now.

"We thought it best not to disturb you." The lowly driver's English was as good as Vera's. "But now, you will need your wits about you."

He climbed back in and slammed the door, eased back onto the road, and proceeded to the check point.

FIVE

A SLIM BLONDE IN A FLUORESCENT LIME-GREEN BIKINI gyrated on a pole twenty feet from their table. Ten feet to her right, there was another pole and another girl. A brunette. Fleshier and rounder than her colleague. Their eyes were highlighted with glitter-laden shadow and thick mascara. Lipstick a crimson red.

Both executed movements that were at once supple and lurid. They performed their act to the rhythm of a thudding rich bass line that rippled its way through a funky electro-pop melody. Occasionally, they would let go of the poles, wander to the front of the stage and bend over, slapping their own buttocks, to the delight of the audience. Men hooted their approval when the women removed their tops in unison and went back to making love to the metal poles.

To an outsider like Jacob, the women looked happy enough. Big smiles plastered all over their faces, flawless skin and dazzling white teeth. Perhaps they were smiling under threat. If they were, what could he do about it? Nothing. It wasn't Jacob's job to rescue them.

A thick blue-gray haze floated ethereally inside the dim cavern that was The Sable nightclub, downtown Lviv. The combined emissions output of what Jacob estimated to be forty to fifty men, a large portion of them puffing away at any one time, equated to a volume of smoke any self-respecting doctor would recommend avoiding at all costs. The fumes irritated Jacob's eyes and choked his lungs. There was so much of the second-hand variety floating about, like a carcinogenic indoor fog, he thought it pointless to refuse when Matviy Ostapenko extended an open packet.

"Thanks." Jacob leaned forward to touch his cigarette against the flame dancing on the end of Ostapenko's silver Zippo lighter. He sucked tentatively on the tip of the cigarette like an amateur as it began to glow red. A cough threatened to explode from his mouth, but he managed to suppress it. He should have trapped the smoke in his mouth and let it escape, not inhaled it into his lungs. Lesson learned.

Ostapenko quirked an eyebrow then chuckled. "I expected you to decline. They tell me all Americans under fifty are into a healthy lifestyle that doesn't include smoking cigarettes."

Jacob tilted his head at a slight angle. "Oh, well. When in Rome."

"Sorry?"

Jacob gave the best Russian equivalent he could think of. "Don't go into another monastery with your own set of rules."

"Ah ha!" The conversation switched from English to Russian, a look of relief creeping across Ostapenko's oily brow. "Your knowledge of the invaders' language is spectacular, Mr. Brown!" Ostapenko fiddled with a set of worry beads lying on the table in front of him. "By the way, will that Roman philosophy extend to you sleeping with one of my beautiful dancers?"

"No," said Jacob, eyes watering in the toxic air. Calling the writhing and hip-swiveling women *dancers* was a stretch. "As much as I appreciate the kind offer, it will not extend to that."

"Maybe you like to take both of them to bed? I will arrange it. You will have an experience you will never forget!"

"Again, I have to say no."

"Why not? They are beautiful girls, very eager to please. Especially when it comes to looking after honored guests from abroad." The man's leer gave Jacob a sick feeling in his stomach. The Ukrainian might be a loyal patriot, but he was still a dirty pimp.

Jacob quelled his disgust by sipping vodka. Pissing off Ostapenko before he'd extracted maximum usefulness out of him was a bad idea. Each contact had to be curated with care; get on their wrong side and an entire mission could be compromised. It had happened to other operatives, and their careers ended either by being fired, if they were lucky, or by getting themselves killed. Jacob puckered his lips as if giving the matter some serious thought, then shook his head while he made a face of reluctant regret.

"You are married and too much in love to be tempted. Am I right?" Ostapenko rubbed his hands together. Jacob saw tan lines on the man's fingers where rings used to be. Hocked, perhaps, to boost the nation's war chest. How noble.

Jacob shook his head. He tipped back the remains of the shot glass of ice-cold vodka to wash down the bitterness building in his throat. "Single my whole life."

"Not a homosexual, are you?" Ostapenko asked with a twisted mouth, as if an answer in the affirmative would be the worst sin a man could commit.

"No." He searched for an excuse that wouldn't offend. "The thing is, I need to get to know a woman for a while before I sleep with her. Call me old fashioned, but it's the way I was brought up. And since I'm only in town for one night, that leaves little time..."

"At least you can look and appreciate the view, yes?" Ostapenko poured himself and Jacob another shot. "Marta and Magda are a pair of dolls. Watch them and enjoy."

"I can do that." His own laugh that followed sounded fake to Jacob's ears, precisely because it was. He hated playing the glad-handing game, but there was no avoiding it. The Octopus would later deliver what had been promised: a basic set of fake Ukrainian identification in case the police or other arms of authority pulled them over tomorrow near the border and got curious. American tourist Edward Brown would arouse suspicion should he be questioned anywhere near the frontier. The elements of his new Russian identity—and there were plenty—would be provided once he'd made contact with the asset in charge of smuggling him across the border.

Most important of all, Ostapenko was offering a comfortable bed where Jacob could get his head down and bank enough sleep for tomorrow's adventure. And that's how he'd chosen to perceive each assignment. Not as a possible date with death, but an exciting game to be enjoyed, milked for its adrenaline and cortisol rushes. To do otherwise would risk fear getting the better of him.

So far, each of his fourteen *adventures* had been carried out successfully. Not without hiccups and snafus. They had to be factored into every job. He'd killed three men and one woman in the line of duty, each one burned into his memory. He hated having to kill, but when it was his life or someone else's, the choice was obvious.

But this job was different. By an order of magnitude.

Inside hostile Russian territory, he would have no known and trustworthy allies to turn to in a scrape. Not one. Every person he met would be a new face. His ability to pass himself off as a native Russian would *not* guarantee safety. He took a deep breath and, not for the first time, wondered why the hell he'd ever signed on with the clandestine organization. Those on the inside called it Skia, after the Greek word for shadow. The word had another meaning—ghost of the underworld. Pretty apt, Jacob thought. Officially, there was no name, because officially, Skia did not exist.

"I am glad you are a normal male who can look at beautiful women, not some kind of degenerate," said Ostapenko, snapping Jacob out of his musing. "The number of these human oddities in the West seems to be growing by the day."

"I thought Ukraine wanted to be part of the West."

A massive roar went up in the crowd. Jacob looked up to see the women had discarded their thongs and were now showing the gentleman their skills at manually pleasing themselves without assistance.

Ostapenko had to raise his voice to continue as the whistling and foot stomping intensified. "I cannot speak for all of my countrymen, but I want Ukraine to be strong and independent. Not a pawn in the games of egotistical generals. And to do that, we have to leverage support from the West. You would be surprised, though. There are many in this country who want nothing of the kind. They are fools. Only an alignment with the West will save us from the monster and his deranged followers in Moscow. A seat at the table, our very existence, requires full membership of NATO, nothing less!" He banged his fist on the table, rattling the ashtray, bottles, and glasses. His eyes glowered in the darkness. He remained silent for a moment, then sighed. The noise abated somewhat, and he was able to speak more or less at a normal volume. "But I digress unnecessarily. Ten more minutes and the girls will stop working and go home for the night. Or maybe your room upstairs?"

"You don't give up easily, do you? As tempting as it sounds, I must decline." Jacob stubbed out the cigarette he had only drawn on twice. He wouldn't accept further offers. His head ached abysmally, and his throat felt like it had been sandpapered. "Rather early to be closing on a Saturday night, isn't it?"

"Curfew. I think it's unnecessary, especially in Lviv. We are a long way from hostilities. But what I think doesn't matter. People caught outside after curfew without a permit can find themselves in a lot of trouble." He refilled his glass, but Jacob put a hand over his. "Fair enough. You have a big day ahead of you tomorrow. We leave at 5:00 a.m., just after curfew. Sleep well."

Alone in his well-appointed room on the top floor of the five-story building, Jacob pulled out a thirty-page file describing the identity he was about to assume. His legend. He'd read it many times, knew every detail, but it never hurt to have one more look. In case there was something subtle contained in it, a subtext, some nuance. But no, it was a straightforward biography of an invented person. In as many ways as possible, it mirrored his own background, but in others, poetic license was used. Soccer substituted for American football was an example. Another, the man spoke fluent English as a second language. Jacob had long ago perfected the art of speaking his mother tongue in a light Russian accent. No documentation to go with the legend, though. Carrying it would be too risky and it would only be provided to him *in situ*.

He punched the pillow. Barely able to keep his eyes open, he laid his head down. The silence ended as the door to the adjoining room slammed abruptly. A burst of masculine laughter and feminine giggling followed.

Ostapenko had taken the pair of strippers to his own lair. Within minutes, he was doing to them what he'd proposed Jacob do.

The Ukrainian proved to be a man of stamina. The sounds of moaning and yelping and laughing went on unabated, and a headboard slammed into the wall. Jacob gritted his teeth, barely able to control the urge to pound his fist against the wall, scream at them to shut the fuck up, even to go into the room next door and beat the daylights out of Ostapenko and toss the women out on their ears.

He did none of those things. Instead, he got dressed, popped open the window, and shimmied down a drainpipe. A stroll around the beautiful, deserted streets of Lviv for an hour or two should give the creep enough time to get his jollies.

Curfew be damned.

SIX

"Go inside that building," said Ostapenko, pointing to a ramshackle barn three hundred yards away. Boards were missing here and there, and others hung at angles where nails had come loose. Its door flapped in the light breeze, which was annoyingly picking up speed to match the falling temperature. A slanting wet sleet fell in the gloom of the late afternoon. "The asset is waiting for you there, Mr. Brown. That person will provide you with further instructions. Slava Ukraini. Udachi tebye. Good luck in slaying the monster!"

The patriot pimp crushed a cigarette out under the heel of his boot and strode back to the Toyota Prado waiting to spirit him back to Lviv. Watching the man retreat, a twinge of guilt nagged at Jacob's conscience. The Octopus believed the story he'd been told, that his fleeting American acquaintance was heading to Moscow to assassinate the Russian president. Never mind. One day, the tyrant's days *would* come to an end. Besides, Ostapenko had ruined Jacob's sleep, which greatly lessened that feeling of guilt. Two close calls with mobile military patrols meant Jacob had had to abandon his midnight stroll and head back to his room at the strip club. Thankfully, the dirty bastard Ostapenko had finished the job, and Jacob was able to grab a couple hours' shuteye.

Jacob watched impassively as the 4x4 revved hard, smoke pouring from the exhaust. The vehicle spat a shower of dirt, snow, and gravel behind it as Ostapenko and his bodyguard departed. Another car, a mud-spattered dark green Kia Mohave SUV, stood twenty yards from the barn. A patina of tire tracks was etched into the mud. It looked like at least one other vehicle had been here recently. Crows cawed in distant fir trees, the only sign of life from horizon to horizon. Jacob's new surname of Voronin, the one he would be answering to until *the letter* was safely in his hands and he was out of Russian territory, originated from the Russian word for crow. An omen perhaps?

Jacob took a moment to regulate his breathing in the freezing night air. Inhaling pinched his nostrils together, exhaling sent out dual jets of steam. He checked his pulse. Eighty bpm, well above his normal resting rate. But not dangerous. *Steel yourself for anything.*

He stood in a paddock you could almost call a swamp in the northernmost corner of Ukraine. He doubted he could have dreamed up a more surreal backdrop. Ostapenko had dropped Jacob off on the bleak outskirts of the recently liberated village of Hremyach, just a stone's throw from the frontier with Russia. From Hremyach, Jacob guessed he would be transported across the border by car. *But how?* He imagined a bumpy trip along potholed roads, hidden under blankets like some refugee in a WWII movie. A requisitioned military vehicle bearing Russian insignia. Big fat Zs emblazoned either side and on the roof.

Or maybe something completely different.

He didn't enjoy jobs like this. Too many unknowns. Yes, he had prepared well for the role he was going to play in Moscow, the intense pressure he'd be under. But the secrecy surrounding his journey there was way over the top. It was like they didn't fully trust him. This cloak-and-dagger strategy *was* a necessary evil in some cases, to ensure plausible deniability for the sacred higher-ups, but it played havoc with his nervous system. Ulcers down the track were not out of the question.

One careful step at a time through the icy mud, clutching a small canvas bag containing US passports, real and counterfeit, plus the Ukrainian documents supplied by Ostapenko. Not needed, as it turned out. They had been stopped twice by cops on their journey from Lviv, but a quick word from the pimp and they were on their way again. He'd need to ditch the fake documents as soon as he received the Russian replacements.

His heartrate climbed again, 120 bpm. His sense of aloneness kicked in. Solo until the next contact materialized. Just a matter of about thirty yards now to the barn, but with the Octopus's car disappearing behind a stand of birch trees and the sound of its engine fading fast, the sense of foreboding couldn't be shaken.

He slipped on a patch of slick ice two feet from the door before regaining his balance, cursing loudly in English before realizing how stupid that was. All thoughts and words, even uttered reflexively, had to be in Russian from now until the mission was completed. He pushed open the door, which screeched eerily on its rusty hinges.

He poked his head inside cautiously. "Zdes' est' kto-nibud?" *Is there anyone here?*

Silence, save for the wind whistling through the gaps in the rotting planks. Jacob took a couple of tentative strides forward, pulling out his burner smart phone and activating the flashlight. Before he could use it, an overhead light flickered and buzzed, went out, then sparked back to life. A low-wattage bulb hanging from the ceiling barely illuminated the 40x40 foot space. Hay bales stacked two high lined the sides and back, and the interior reeked of dung, dust and despair.

And bang in the middle of the barn, sitting on a wooden chair, was a man who could have been Jacob's twin. His face bore no expression, like a department-store dummy. The skin had a pallid, wax-like quality, but that could be a function of the feeble lighting. He appeared to be slightly thinner in the face than Jacob, ten to twenty pounds lighter, and sported a thin honey-colored mustache. Apart from those minor details, Jacob could have been staring into a mirror. The stranger was dressed in an army combat uniform, but from thirty feet away it was impossible to tell whose side he was on.

Jacob stood still, staring, not knowing whether to speak or wait to be addressed. Before he could make a decision, it was made for him.

"Ubey yego!" *Kill him!* A deep female voice came from behind Jacob's shoulder. A quick glance around. No one there. Perhaps it came from outside? He looked back to the man on the chair.

Except he was no longer sitting on the chair, but on his feet and striding toward Jacob. Snarling and breathing hard, his eyeballs bulged, the white sclera huge. Worst of all, he brandished a massive knife that gleamed dully under the hanging lightbulb. He was obeying the unseen woman's unambiguous instruction, Jacob realized.

What kind of weird fucked-up trap is this? Drive a man eleven hours across an entire country only to have him stabbed to death by a crazed soldier in an abandoned barn? Nothing made sense except the will to survive.

Jacob dropped his bag and adopted a low, defensive stance, bouncing on the balls of his feet. Adrenaline coursed through his body. *Fight or flight?* Over the years, instructors had taught him to engage in conflict as a last resort. The smartest move was always to get the hell away from danger.

He spun around quickly to assess his options.

The door was closed. He edged backward until his hand located the handle. He gave it a turn. No good. The woman—or someone else—had locked the two men inside. Escape cut off, Jacob had no option but to fight.

One scenario dominated Jacob's thought process. *If this man is an expert knife thrower, I've got no chance.*

Luckily, his adversary gave no indication he would throw the knife but held the weapon tightly with his right hand in an overhand grip. Jacob's muscle memory from countless hours of field training exercises kicked in. He moved side to side, arms extended and ready for anything. *Stay on the move. Standing still means certain death.* The man kept his center of gravity low as he shifted his position, looking for an easy thrust, soft flesh to embed the blade in. Internal organs. Perhaps he guessed Jacob wouldn't be an easy kill—he was all patience, making no sudden moves that a skilled opponent could counter with blocks, perhaps turn the knife against him.

Then, the man suddenly switched gears from patient and analytical to a blur of motion. Jacob sidestepped furiously to avoid each stabbing thrust. Some came too close, and he was able to block them. One after the other they came.

Stab, stab, stab. Stab, stab, stab.

One slash got through his defenses, catching him just above the navel.

He felt no pain and made no move to see if blood had been drawn. Dodge, dance, then dodge some more. Tire him out, look for a chance to disarm him.

The assailant was showing no signs of weakening. He had abandoned all ideas of finesse. He was swinging big, round haymakers, aiming them all at the left side of Jacob's body. Using a 360-degree defense, Jacob leveraged his powerful thighs to take leaping strides away from trouble. Watching like a hawk and doubly on guard since being nicked, he somehow blocked each attempted stab with the outside of his forearms. If he could only trap the man's elbow and bring him to the ground. That wasn't going to happen; the attacker was wise to it. Confronted with a professional warrior, Jacob knew that skills acquired from training might be great to have; however, a real battle was another matter. It was where primal instinct and intuition took over.

This was one of those battles.

Heart pounding out of his chest, Jacob remembered the chair. He turned his back—breaking the golden rule of knife-fighting defense—and made a dash to the left corner at the rear of the barn. As he'd hoped, the man followed. When Jacob sensed the man was just over an arm's length behind, one yard from the corner, he banked toward the side wall of the barn, pulling the assailant in that direction with a twist of the body and a none-too-subtle head feint.

The man lost his footing like a basketball player taking the candy and stumbled into the haybales, cursing loudly. Before he could regain his feet, Jacob had his hands upon the back of the wooden chair. He strode toward the soldier, hoisted the stool high in the air, and brought it crashing down on the man's head with all his might. The soldier cried out in pain, but that only spurred Jacob on. He smashed the bleeding and fractured skull two more times. The doppelganger's legs juddered and spasmed before they and the rest of his body stilled completely.

Jacob dropped to his knees, two fingers to the man's carotid artery. Nothing. His own heart rate was slowly coming down, the cortisol rush kicking in. Bloodied hands cradling his face, he whispered a quick prayer for the fallen man.

Before he could even begin to formulate his next move, the squeak of the door made him jump to his feet, ready to defend himself against another attack. He had to shield his eyes from the bright lantern that overpowered the lightbulb and flooded the interior with light.

A tall woman dressed head to toe in black—boots, jeans, long puffer jacket and woolen hat—strode inside and placed the lantern on the ground. She gave an appreciative nod. "Otlichno." *Excellent.* "You did as I asked."

Jacob blinked twice, not understanding. "What?"

"I told you to kill him, and you did. Good work."

"What the hell! I thought you told him to kill *me*."

The woman's lips compressed as she nodded. "Ah hah. Yes. I can see the confusion. But I see you've made a thorough job of it."

"I had to. He came at me with that fucking knife." Jacob

pointed at the weapon lying next to his victim's lifeless clenched fist.

"Was he not bound by ropes?"

"I didn't see any."

She took a couple of strides into the middle of the barn, holding up strands of cut rope. "Seems he freed himself. I'm glad he had a sporting chance before you took him out."

"Look. I don't know who you are or what you think you're doing, but I'm guessing you're the asset who's going to take me across the border. Anyway, I don't care. What I do care about is being set up and nearly killed. You must have known he had the knife before he was tied up."

She said nothing.

"Did you know he had the knife?" he roared.

She waved away his concern. "What are you talking about? You handled him perfectly. Anatoly here is—or should I say *was* —a tough soldier from Vladivostok. Raised in an orphanage, no wife or kids. No one's going to miss him."

"Was he a sacrifice?"

"Do not mourn this asshole. He was caught by our soldiers in a small village near here. He committed horrible war crimes. Raped and killed young girls. You have not only done the world a favor, you did it superbly. Not many would have gotten the better of him, let alone escaped with their life." She cast her eyes toward Jacob's midsection, and his gaze followed. A slash in his sweater was surrounded by a small red stain. Nothing to be concerned about.

Jacob paced back and forth for a few moments, gathering his thoughts. "Wait. Did you say Anatoly?"

"Uh huh. That is correct."

"Anatoly Voronin?"

"The very same."

This was Jacob's new identity. He'd assumed it was a mere invention, not that he was *replacing* someone. He put that very point to the woman.

"You cannot simply materialize from nowhere in Russia," she said dramatically. "If you take on this man's identity, a lot of the hard work is already done. Records of this man exist, so you will become him, but with some important differences."

"What are they?"

"I am only guessing, because I don't know what your ultimate mission is, but he was a simple peasant. I assume they will invent a more impressive CV for you. But what the hell do I know? I'm just the hired help."

Another thing needed to be explained. "What the fuck just went down here?" An idea was formulating in his brain, but he needed confirmation for it to make sense. "Why was I put in this dangerous situation?"

The woman squatted, snapping a round of photos of the dead man lying on the ground. "I need photos of the front. Help me turn him over."

Jacob grabbed the dead man by the shoulders and rolled him over onto his back. He saw the Russian flag sewn into the uniform. A massive dark wet patch covering the thighs down to the knees told him the man hadn't urinated for some time. The gaping eyes were a lighter shade of blue than Jacob's. He stood and turned to the woman. "You haven't answered me."

The woman took more photos before squirreling the cell phone in her jacket. "You had to prove yourself."

"Prove myself? No I didn't! I've proven myself plenty of times. This is someone's idea of a sick joke."

The woman crossed her arms. "I have no knowledge of you or your history. I was paid to do a job, and I have only half fulfilled it. You will now come with me. We will hide in the forest until 01:00 hours, then you will be taken across the border. Once you are in the Russian village of Belaya Berozka and in the hands of the installation team, my job will be done."

"How am I getting across? Surely the border is heavily fortified?"

She shrugged her broad shoulders. "Yes it is. The moskali are well entrenched along their side."

Jacob nodded. Her use of the derogatory term for Russians, derived from the Ukrainian word for Muscovite, told him she must hate the neighbors as much as Ostapenko did.

She continued, "There is an official border crossing check point a couple of kilometers from here, but obviously we will not be going that way. It's been out of commission since early in the war. A diversion will be created, we drag their resources away from their main encampments, and we sneak you over at an identified weak point."

"What kind of a diversion?"

She smiled, accentuating a vicious pink scar between the corner of her mouth to halfway up the side of her nose. The woman was still more beautiful than the flawless Marta and Magda combined. "A big one that you won't miss." She picked up the lantern. "Time to get out of here." She beckoned for him to follow her outside and instructed him to sit in the passenger side. Jacob watched as she popped the liftgate and extracted a plastic red canister with a black funnel before marching back inside the barn. Less than a minute later, she was sitting beside Jacob and starting the engine. As they drove back along the dirt track, the flash from a massive fireball lit up the ground and trees in front of them in an ethereal glow. Jacob glanced in the side mirror. The barn was gone, replaced by an orange and yellow ball of fire, clouds of black smoke spreading out in all directions.

"Are you sure that was a good idea?" he asked. "A fire like that will attract attention."

In a flat voice, she said, "There's a war on. Explosions happen all the time." She looked at him intently. "Besides, poor Anatoly deserved a proper cremation."

SEVEN

A few minutes later, she yanked the steering wheel to the right. They exited what passed for a minor highway and headed along another dirt road. Walls of trees either side of the rough track blocked out most of the stars, creating a shadowy tunnel with twinkling specks above. As the woman wrestled with the wheel over the deep ruts gouged into the ground, Jacob craned his neck up and forward, picking out the constellation of Ophiuchus, the serpent-bearer. A tiny dot passed across the void above, a satellite perhaps.

A quarter mile in, the woman found a small clearing and parked the car with practiced ease, like she'd been there more than once before.

"We've got a long wait until this diversion happens," said Jacob, glancing at his watch. Only 19:45 hours. "Now what?"

"You hand over to me your bag, and I will dispose of everything in it."

"Say what!" he objected. "My papers are in there."

"They are redundant now."

"Maybe the Ukrainian ID that I never needed to use. But I need my US passports."

"Plural?" She arched an eyebrow. "You got multiple personality disorder?"

"Sometimes I think I actually do. But no. I used a fake one to get across the Polish border and my real one to leave the United States. And I'll need it to get back in."

"You are really making things complicated for yourself." She shook her head.

"Complicated but necessary. Getting caught leaving and entering my own country with a bogus document would put an end to my career. Probably land me in jail for twenty years or more."

"Makes sense, I guess," she said, holding out her hand. "I'm still waiting for your bag."

He reached between the front seats and grabbed his bag from the back. He unzipped it and handed over everything except his real US passport, which he tucked in his pants pocket after fumbling the other documents to distract her. She gathered the spilled jumble, then flicked through the documents. "You are a sly one. There is an item missing. Where is the genuine passport?"

He shook his head. "You're not getting that one. Sorry."

The woman inhaled sharply. "Don't be stupid. If you get caught with that, the *moskali* will arrest you on the spot. And you have no visa to be in Russia. Prisons over there"—she jerked a finger to the right—"are a lot worse than in America."

"I'll be careful with it, don't worry."

She held out her hand again. "You need to trust me."

Jacob burst out laughing. "Trust you? You nearly had me killed!"

"Then maybe you need to trust yourself more. You won the fight in the barn against the odds. I believe you will–"

"Stop! It's not happening, end of conversation."

She recoiled into her seat, then sprang back forward again. "Listen. I have an idea. I will arrange for your passport to be couriered by diplomatic pouch to the US Embassy in Moscow."

"Oh yeah? So I guess the walking dead, Anatoly Voronin, just rolls up to the American embassy and politely asks for admission?"

She shrugged. "I imagine someone would bring it to you at an agreed place. But we are talking about hypothetical nonsense. Your country has enough assets in place in Moscow to help you out. Getting out of Russia will be a lot easier for you than getting in. I implore you to give me the passport. I have clear instructions: you have to give me everything in your possession, no exceptions, otherwise I must refuse to take you across the border."

He could easily overpower her in the confines of the vehicle, force her to do what he wanted. Make her drive him...where? No. Out here in the boondocks, with war being waged in the near distance, he needed her like oxygen. On reflection, she was right about a number of things. Least of all, trusting her and himself. Fletcher's technical team—people Jacob would never meet—had constructed the chain of events that would lead to his infiltration. *You can rely upon your contacts,* Fletcher said. *But always use your own judgment and discretion.* He reached into the bag and held the passport in his outstretched hand.

"Thank you," she said, taking hold of the document with firm fingers. "Wise decision."

"What do I get from you in return?"

She arched an eyebrow, gleaning an unintended double meaning from his question. "From me you get a dirty Russian soldier's uniform and a smart cell phone with an untraceable SIM..."

"A hundred percent untraceable? In the greatest surveillance state in Europe?"

"Yes. Ukraine has the best computer programmers in the world."

"If you say so. And the Russians are the best at hacking, so when you say untraceable, I'm doubtful."

"Believe me. This one cannot be traced or hacked. It has a so-called GPS spoofing functionality. A fake signal makes it look you are somewhere you are not."

She was all over the detail. "Okay. What about weapons, other things I'm gonna need in case I get into trouble like I did in the barn? I would have preferred to shoot the guy than risk my own life."

She nodded understandingly, a dark ringlet escaping from her woolen hat. "Those things will probably be provided on the other side. I can't promise it, though. All I know is what I have to do."

They sat in silence for a while before she said, "We need to rest. Be prepared for some serious action later." From the back of the car, she retrieved a couple of thick blankets, handing one to Jacob. Then she set an alarm on her cell phone, reclined her seat, lay back, and closed her eyes. Jacob found the lever on the right-hand side and dropped his own seat back. Preserving energy, physical and nervous, seemed like his best tactic at this point.

Sleep came quickly. A dreamless slumber was interrupted by the insistent buzzing of his companion's phone alarm. He jolted awake, suddenly remembering he was in the middle of a wasteland on the fringes of a warzone.

"One hour and fifteen minutes before the diversion begins," she said, stretching her arms before yawning. She pulled a thermos from under her seat, poured a cup, and handed it to him. Hot black coffee with a shitload of sugar, like nectar. She treated him to a shelled hard-boiled egg, a banana, a slice of aromatic black Borodinsky bread, and half an avocado. She had the same. They ate quietly, Jacob having to tell himself not to bolt his food.

He felt the temperature dropping inside the vehicle. "I'm starting to feel cold in here. Any chance you could turn on the engine to get the heater going?"

She obliged, at the same time taking off her sweater. No bra underneath. "I have another idea for keeping warm. Come here, American man. I told you to prepare for some serious action, didn't I?"

When Jacob told Matviy Ostapenko he needed to get to know a woman properly before having sex with her, he hadn't been entirely straight up. He didn't even know this one's name, but refusing her offer seemed like bad manners in the circumstances.

EIGHT

HER NAME WAS MARINA. SHE WAS ENDOWED WITH THE body of an Olympic sprinter: perfectly muscled, medium-sized breasts, powerful upper legs, and a modest layer of fat on her broad hips. When they made love on the folded-down seats, she climbed on top and pinned him with vise-like thighs. He had no doubt she was a trained killer and, if he was off his guard, she could finish him off with her bare hands.

Windows fogged up completely, Jacob started to get dressed in the cramped confines of the front seat. He opened the door, deciding the freezing cold was a better option than hurting himself by dislocating a joint.

"Stop. There is still gasoline in the jerrycan. I will burn what you are wearing now after you and I have said our good-byes."

While he stood shivering, she fetched a new set of clothes from the SUV's cargo compartment. As promised—a dirty Russian army uniform. She was understating things. It was caked in mud and reeked of month-old body odor with hints of blood and gun oil. On the positive side, the underpants and socks seemed to be brand new. He changed into the new gear faster than a stage actor in a one-man show.

Once he was back inside, she said, "The plan was to have you wear Anatoly's clothes, but since he pissed himself disgracefully, you can put on this back-up combat uniform."

He side-eyed her. "Also off a dead guy?"

She made a lip-zip action. "I know nothing."

"What about boots? They seem to be missing."

"Damn it!" She scratched her head before putting the woolen hat back on and pulling it down tight over her ears. "I knew I should have taken them from Anatoly." She paused. "What shoes do you have on? I wasn't paying attention."

"Black oxfords. They don't exactly go with military–"

"What size are you? Quick!"

"American 12, which is...shit, what is it?"

"Let me check." She pulled out her phone, scrolled frantically. "Looks like a 44."

"Listen. Can't you just send me over with bare feet? Say someone souvenired my boots, or wanted me to..."

She looked up from her phone. "Are you out of your mind? It's below freezing outside. Not to mention the mud and slush everywhere. You cannot go over the border without boots. No, no, no." She breathed hard for a moment. Jacob could almost see the cogs spinning in her mind. "There is no chance anything will have survived the fire, so I'm not going back on the off chance."

"Could we ask at nearby properties? Maybe there's a farmer with the same size feet as me. There's still time."

She let out a sarcastic laugh, showing slightly uneven teeth, a gold one near the back. "Pointless. There is no one living anywhere nearby in the farmhouses. Everyone has been evacuated and won't be back until we crush the moskali. Which could be a while unless our foreign allies step up some more."

"What if I say I took the ones I'm wearing from a dead Ukrainian civilian?"

"You would never abandon proper army boots for those..."—she pointed in the direction of the footwell—"tapochki."

Jacob smiled. She had called his expensive Gucci shoes slippers. And she was right about what a soldier would do to protect his feet.

Marina's cell screen glowed as she made a call. "Seryozha? Can one of your men sacrifice a pair of boots and withdraw from the operation?" She listened intently, heaved a sigh of relief before hanging up. "I thought 44 was big. The closest match is a 46."

"Better too big than too small."

She winked lasciviously at him. "I think so too."

Jacob felt himself blushing. If that facial gesture was a compliment or a ribbing, he wasn't sure. He stared through the windshield, nothing but the faintest glow of the stars and the ominous black canopy of the trees.

"Are you a religious man?" Marina said.

That piqued his interest. "I believe in God, if that's what you mean." He didn't mention the mental prayer he'd said for the late Anatoly Voronin.

"Excellent."

He gave her a curious sideways look. "Why do you ask?"

"Because there's a good chance you won't make it to Moscow, let alone back to the United States."

"You have that little faith in me?" He hoped he'd been able to keep the alarm out of his voice.

"No. I have a lot of faith in you and your capabilities. And someone has put enormous efforts into coordinating your infiltration. But I've got a horrible feeling the *moskali* are going to have a lot more firepower across that line. What I'm trying to say is, be prepared for the worst."

"You said there would be a serious diversion?"

She nodded slowly. "Yes, I did. And there will be." Looking at her profile, Jacob detected a small hump halfway down her nose. She turned to face him, all business. For the first time, he noticed that her nose had another defect—it bent ever so slightly to the left, the imperfect feature reminding him of a tough-as-nails cadet he'd boxed against at West Point. He wondered what sort of scrapes she'd been in to sustain such an injury. "That's what I've been told. Apart from the name of the commander over there, Seryozha, that is all I know." She shrugged apologetically. "Perhaps it's time to make your peace with the Lord." She crossed herself solemnly.

Now she tells me.

NINE

AT 00:45, DUAL BEAMS OF LIGHT SWUNG AROUND FROM the left and bore down upon the Kia Mohave. At first, small dots a quarter mile down the road, the lights grew larger with each second. The growling engine told Jake this was a massive vehicle. Not a tank, though—tanks use night vision systems.

"Friend or foe?" said Jacob, his heart thundering like a stampede of buffalo.

She glanced at the dash clock. "Right on time. Friend." She glanced at him with a slight squint. "I hope."

Jacob shifted about in his seat. The codeword Fletcher had given him—*Ardalion*—was still unspoken. If she didn't say it in the next ten seconds, he would make a run for it. His hand grabbed the door handle. His fingers flexed as he looked outside the passenger window. Uneven ground, mud and slush and ice, and worst of all—dark. In this terrain and with nothing to guide him, going on foot—in his oxfords—would be suicidal. If she didn't say the codeword, he'd have to knock her out—kill her if she resisted—and drive hell for leather away from the oncoming vehicle. Then try to find a decent weapon, other items that could help him get back to civilization. He'd somehow make his way back to New York. The State Department and Fletcher would need to find another schmuck.

He realized he'd stopped breathing.

Her eyes widened as the lumbering juggernaut was almost upon them.

Come on, Marina. Say the codeword, for fuck's sake!

"Wait." She narrowed her eyes. "Is that a signal?" The beams, growing steadily brighter as the bouncing vehicle advanced, blinked on and off in some kind of pattern. Jacob didn't need to hear Marina's answer. The message, sent in Cyrillic Morse, was one word. *Ardalion*.

"You okay?" said Marina, reacting to the whoosh of breath Jacob exhaled. He wondered if she could smell his adrenal glands working overtime.

"Yeah, I'm fine," he whispered. "I was starting to get worried."

"Why?"

"The codeword."

"What codeword?"

Jacob smiled inwardly, confidence in Fletcher's organizing skills restored—for now. The message was meant just for him. "Sorry. I can't divulge that." He leaned across the console and gave Marina a peck on the cheek. "I guess this is where I get out."

She gripped him by the wrist. "Good luck, Yakov Hunter." She then switched to perfect English. "Do not become the hunted."

As he walked toward the man in full Russian Army combat gear, Marina drove slowly past, giving a finger-tip wave. The use of the Slavic version of his first name was at once endearing and terrifying. He didn't recall ever telling her his name, but then he remembered his reluctant surrender of the precious passport. She must have had a good look at it. Another wash of relief.

A young soldier appeared from the back of the monstrous all-purpose Ural-4320 truck; this one had been converted into a troop carrier. Over a quiet spell between jobs, Jacob had spent six months learning as much as he could about what the Russian Armed Forces had deployed on the ground in Ukraine. His focus for this exercise had been on vehicles and small arms, which in Russian fell under the umbrella term of *tekhnika*.

The man picked his path with a flashlight, avoiding the thick mud as best he could. Now standing next to Jacob, it was obvious the smooth-cheeked man was barely out of his teens. In full kit and with an AK-12 assault rifle slung over his shoulder, Jacob was reminded of African boy soldiers. In the joyless voice of a seasoned warrior who'd seen too much, the kid said, "What was the message we flashed with the headlights?"

"Ardalion."

The kid grunted then jerked a thumb toward where he came from. "Idite za mnoi." *Follow me*. He trudged to the back of the truck, Jacob's eyes glued to his heels in the gloom, and dropped the tailgate. Someone inside raised the side flap of the tarpaulin cover and extended a hand. Jacob grasped the wrist and clambered up and in.

Inside the back of the transport vehicle sat five other men dressed in uniforms similar to his hand-me-downs. The men greeted him with a hearty hello, their eyes sparkling under an interior light. He took a seat on a collapsible bench next to two other men, with three opposite. Beside him were a pair of well-worn boots one size too big and a pair of sturdy socks. He kicked off his oxfords and wrangled on the footwear. One of the men flung Jacob's shoes out the back of the truck like they were junk. Another pulled up the tailgate, and the one nearest the driver tapped twice on the metal bulkhead separating the troops from the cabin. The engine started with a mighty roar before the driver made a bumpy three-point turn and the truck rumbled off at low speed.

The soldier immediately next to Jacob handed him an AK-12. The man began to speak quickly in Ukrainian. When Jacob asked him to slow down, the soldier politely switched to Russian and slowed the pace of his speech. "In a couple of minutes, missiles and smoke bombs will strike at numerous points along the border, creating massive confusion among the enemy. We will cross the border by traversing the frozen Sudist River, driving through thickets of trees as well as open fields. We will avoid roads before pitching up at a safe house a few kilometers outside the Russian village of Belaya Berozka. There, you will be provided with the materials you need for the next stage."

"I trust there's a great big Z painted on the top of this truck?"

The youth grinned. "You can see it from outer space." His expression then turned serious. "If we get caught and questioned, our story is we're returning to our military base in Bryansk. We had conducted a raid on a Ukrainian village full of Nazis before we heard the commotion and decided to come join the fight."

"Understood."

"But do not worry. We will not be caught. *Tfu tfu tfu.*" The last expression was a shared Russian and Ukrainian superstition; uttering the sounds was meant to ward off bad luck. Jacob caught another meaning: no guarantees.

The truck lurched left and right as it negotiated the ripped-up, muddy track. Jacob gripped the underside of the bench to stop himself from sliding off, bumping shoulders with the men on either side of him. He'd seen videos of the 6x6 Ural-4320 negotiating ridiculous gradients, crossing rivers with the water up to the driver's neck. The truck was a behemoth.

"We captured this vehicle during the siege of Mariupol last year," said Jacob's neighbor to the left, his tone laden with pride. "The dogs still occupy the city, where 20,000 people sadly died, but"—he slapped Jacob on the upper arm—"we have their fucking truck. Ha ha ha!"

There was no verbal response to give, so Jacob merely nodded. Whether the number of casualties was true or not, he had no way of verifying. Even if he could, it was peripheral to the mission.

Soon, the ride became appreciably smoother. Must be out of the mud at last. There was no way to see outside, so it was a matter of guesswork as to what type of terrain they were on. Maybe a field.

The truck picked up speed, perhaps attaining 25 mph. Then faster again, the rattling and jolting replaced by easy cruising. The men hummed to themselves, fiddling with the multiple straps on their combat kit. Then the Ural braked suddenly, sending the human cargo on a sideways lurch.

"What the..." said Jacob.

The screaming whistle of something flying in the air was followed by a thundering BOOM.

Then another.

One after the other, rockets flew toward their targets and struck them.

Jacob cast his eyes at his short-term companions, wide-eyed with excitement and nervous energy, blissfully ignorant of the mission they were assisting with. No doubt they'd been fed the same bullshit that was told to Ostapenko. Marina, too, he imagined. All praying to their God that Jacob would stop the warmongering Russian tyrant in his tracks.

As a particularly loud explosion rocked the truck, Jacob was glad there were foot soldiers alongside him. Strength in numbers was as much a psychological boon as a reality. In truth, the foe on the other side of the border outnumbered and outgunned the occupied country by orders of magnitude, American and European arms shipments notwithstanding. This dinky squad of daredevils would have its work cut out should they encounter trouble.

Please, no trouble.

The shelling stopped for a while as the Ural once again hit rough ground. Jacob shut his eyes, reflecting on the international clusterfuck this conflict had turned into. The war was entering the red zone in terms of brinkmanship. Each side pushed the envelope a little bit further every now and then; territory captured, then surrendered, cluster bomb strikes, retaliatory actions. More audacious attacks on Ukrainian civilian targets. Counterattacks targeting Russian civilians. It didn't take an expert to see who always got shafted—civilians.

How far *would* the West go to ensure Ukraine won the war? Did their collective will even *want* them to win? Jacob often doubted the endgame was the defeat of Russia. What the hell it really was? Anybody's guess.

The wailing of rockets resumed for two minutes, then subsided. In his head, Jacob had counted twenty-eight missiles, but he could have missed a few. The amount of money the State Department was willing to spend to retrieve this letter was mind-boggling. Three minutes of silence was replaced by whirring helicopter blades, the distant humming of motors sparking to life. The Russians were on investigation duty now, hightailing it to the epicenters of the strikes, looking for people to rescue—and perhaps to punish.

The truck started up with a throaty roar and resumed its journey. There was a forward dip before the vehicle straightened up again, and this time, the ride was the smoothest so far.

"The frozen river?" he asked his neighbor.

"Yes." The man tightened a strap under his helmet. The guy was getting more nervous the closer they got to the border. Jacob thought he could sense heat coming off him even in the frigid confines of the truck. "This is the second time we are crossing it."

"Really?"

"Yes." The man nodded as the vehicle growled in a lower gear before once again ascending a sharp gradient, the opposite river bank. "The first stretch was much narrower, so you may have thought it was just a good road." He barked a laugh. "Except there are no good roads out here."

Once they flattened out again, the driver gave two quick, cheeky toots on the horn. The neighbor turned to Jacob, a weak smile on his face. "Welcome to Russia."

"Wonderful. And all without the bother of having to fill in a damned customs declaration!" He said it loudly enough for the rest of the men to hear, and it got the laugh he was hoping for. If anything went wrong between here and the next hand-off, he wanted them not just on his side, but sympathetic to him.

"Anyone know how much farther to go?" He looked at all their faces.

"Six kilometers from the second river crossing," said a bespectacled man in his mid-forties who sat diagonally across from him. *Less than four miles.* Jacob automatically converted metric to US customary units in his mind. He could feel sweat gathering in his armpits, the sticky damp sensation in the cold night worse than a punch to the face. But it was still not worse than the vile stink of the second-hand uniform. The sooner he could take a shower and get clean clothes on, the better.

The farther the truck went, the quieter it got. All the Russian resources must have been haring up and down the points of the border where the missiles hit, looking for dead and wounded, putting out fires, digging up rubble. Jacob wondered if there had been any civilian casualties on either side of the border. He prayed there hadn't. With any luck, poor Anatoly Voronin would be his only victim on this trip.

Another click closer, he figured. He concentrated on his breathing as his eyelids grew heavy. What he wouldn't give for a hit of caffeine right now. He'd been awake for many hours, and energy was flagging. Tough luck, though. No doubt he'd have to stay awake for a few more hours to come.

Reflexively, he cocked his wrist to check the time. Nothing but bare skin and a small scar. His prized Breitling watch was gone, sacrificed to the greater good. He hoped Marina could either sell it for a nice profit or her cuckolded husband got to enjoy it. The wedding band had been a dead giveaway she was playing away from home with Jacob.

The driver shifted down a gear, turned a corner, and stopped. Outside—deathly quiet. A door opened and closed, the kid reappeared. He pulled back the tarpaulin flap and dropped the tailgate. To Jacob's surprise, the kid even saluted him. "We are slightly ahead of schedule. I'm just checking to make sure everything is okay while we wait, sir. Have you–'

The kid never got to finish the last sentence as his torso was sliced open by a fusillade of bullets. Blood spurted over the lip of the tailgate, visible even in the semi-dark of the cabin. The young soldier made a gurgling sound and keeled over, his rifle clanging on metal.

Inside was pandemonium. Eruptions of material as more bullets pierced the tarp. Two men opposite Jacob took bullets to the neck and dropped, their blood spraying to join that of their dead friend.

Jacob hit the floor alongside his three surviving neighbors.

"We're in serious shit," whispered the middle-aged man.

No kidding, Jacob thought but said nothing.

The shooting paused, and everyone held their breath. Then came the sound of the driver-side door opening and clunking shut. The driver screamed, "Pokazhis, ublyudok!" *Come out and show yourself, you bastard!* A second later came a rapid burst of gunfire, deafening inside the truck. All Jacob and his pals could do was grit their teeth, cover their heads, and stay low. His fingers curled around the grip of his AK-12, ready to use it if necessary.

Jacob started counting in his head and reached fifty-five before the shooting finally stopped. It was immediately replaced by a man's primal scream, like a football player celebrating after scoring the winning touchdown. "The enemy is eliminated!" shouted a raspy voice before the back flap of the tarp was ripped aside. The grinning, unshaven man with wild eyes brandished his assault rifle and shook it like he was trying to free the magazine from its housing. The man lying next to Jacob sighed the longest sigh Jacob had ever heard in his life. The driver grunted, "We drive on." He poked his head inside to inspect the damage, saw the dead soldiers, whistled through his teeth, and made the sign of the cross. "Toss them out."

Jacob and the other men stripped the bodies of their weapons and protective gear, grabbed the cadavers by their hands and feet, swung them—one, two, three—and dropped them behind the truck. Then they leapt out and dragged them a couple of yards into the trees, covering them in snow. The dead Russian was left where he lay. No questions were aired about where the mystery shooter had appeared from, no protests about abandoning the bodies. The men just did as they were told.

And the truck rolled on.

TEN

A FINGER STRETCHED OVER THE TOP OF THE STEERING wheel, pointed at a gap in the trees illuminated by the powerful headlights. “We’re almost at the final destination on this leg of the trip, my friend.” Another hundred yards, then a dogleg turn to the right, and the truck pulled up outside a quaint wooden cottage painted cornflower blue, a single light glowing within. Jacob counted four other houses in the little street, each with large front and side yards. No lights were on in any of them.

“Are those other houses also stocked with friendlies?”

“No fucking idea.” The driver shrugged. “All I know is we’ve arrived.” He blew a narrow stream of rank cigarette smoke out the window, followed closely by a ball of spit. “Udachi, amerikanets.” *Good luck, American*.

He jumped out of the passenger seat, his ephemeral comrades waiting for him on the blind side of the truck. A round of hearty handshakes and quietly spoken expressions of encouragement with the brave survivors of the gun attack before they jumped back in and the trusty Ural-4320 turned and headed back to Ukraine. Would the men get home in one piece? Did they have families waiting for them? Jacob bowed his head and prayed for their safe passage and for the souls of the dead men.

The safehouse was nothing like the barebones city apartments you see in the spy movies. Nor a sprawling mansion in the unspoiled countryside. In truth, it was only marginally bigger than the barn in which Jacob had killed Voronin. The modest shack was fronted by a rickety wooden fence with palings missing like punched-out teeth and a steel gate.

He stamped the snow off his boots as he tapped on the door.

"Name?" said the man who opened the door no more than an inch. Even in the gloom, it was obvious he was terrified.

"Ardalion."

A sigh of relief and the waving of hands. "Quickly, we have very little time." The man looked like Jacob's high school geography teacher. He acted a bit like him, too, with bird-like, rapid body movements almost too fast for the eye to see. He was obviously also fastidious with his appearance—collared shirt and sharp-edged trousers despite it being the middle of the night. "I've prepared some hot water for you. Wash quickly, change into your new clothes, and leave. No more than ten minutes, please. This way."

"I was hoping for a couple of hours' sleep," Jacob protested. "I can barely function."

"Too dangerous. Time is not your friend. The Internet is already buzzing with news of the Ukrainian border strikes." He coughed like he smoked two packs a day. The stench of tobacco and the yellowing walls in the little house further attested to his habit. "Do what you have to do and get going, I beg you."

Jacob followed the man into a small bathroom. The showerhead was missing and the toilet bowl was stained with tan streaks. He stripped and evacuated his bowels with much relief. In the corner of the tiny room sat a ceramic basin steaming with hot water. He rubbed his body with a cake of lemon-scented soap then sponged down with a facecloth. A new toothbrush and mint toothpaste on the washstand was a thoughtful touch. Basic amenities, but right now it felt like he was a VIP at a five-star spa in downtown Manhattan.

Inside a plywood closet in the adjoining bedroom, he found an expensive dark blue suit with the drycleaner's plastic still on it. A glance at the label. Henry Poole of Savile Rowe. Overkill, perhaps. A white button-down business shirt, three changes of underwear and socks for a couple days, heavy winter coat, leather jacket, and ushanka fur hat. A shoulder holster for a pistol, but he couldn't find a weapon anywhere in the room. At the foot of the closet lay a clutch bag containing a Russian internal passport in the name of Anatoly Ivanovich Voronin and an international passport in the same name, Jacob's photograph on each. Same date of birth as Jacob. Place of birth, Vladivostok, as far away from Moscow as you can get. A swipe card bearing an address Jacob knew was in the heart of Moscow's elite Khamovniki precinct. A note inside, written in Russian and in a scrawly hand. *The rest of your ID—birth certificate, driver's license, military ID showing your two years' obligatory service, educational documents including university degree and some others—are at your new address in Ulitsa Efremova. Park your vehicle in your building's underground carpark using the same swipe card. Spot No. A-15. Your first Moscow contact, Lilliana Danilova, will be waiting for you at your apartment. She will give you further instructions upon you citing the codeword. Destroy this note now.*

He memorized the details, tore the note up into tiny pieces, and flushed it down the toilet. He dressed in the new clothes and rejoined his host at the kitchen table. The man's eyes wandered, fingers tapping on the table, a cigarette smoldering in a tin ashtray. His nervousness was infectious; Jacob's own vital signs shifted in the wrong direction. Pulse up and sweats starting. *Is this guy a turncoat?*

"Can I trust you?" Jacob poured himself a thick black coffee from a steel moka pot.

"Of course!" His eyebrows furrowed like the question was an insult.

"It's just that..."—Jacob's hand darted across the table and yanked the man toward him—"you're very edgy. If I sniff the slightest danger, I won't hesitate to..."

The man pulled his hand back with surprising strength. "Of course I'm nervous. I've got an American spook in my house, haven't I!"

The man had a point. He was probably recruited for this one-off mission, paid handsomely out of the US State Department's seemingly bottomless coffers. If the neighbors found out, he'd be toast.

"What about my transport?"

"The vehicle out back is fully fueled. There's a cooler with a week's worth of food and drink in case things go wrong and you have to hide out somewhere. A loaded Makarov in the glove box that fits neatly into the holster you would have found."

Jacob nodded. "I was wondering about that."

"Now, please finish your coffee and go."

"Am I supposed to drive to Moscow on my own?"

The man shrugged. "No driver has been provided, and I'm certainly not coming with you."

Jacob wiped the last of the surprisingly good coffee from his lips. He checked the time on the phone supplied by Marina: 02:00. "How long does it take to get there, any idea?"

The eyes stopped darting at last, fixed intently on Jacob. "Seven and a half to eight hours."

"Perfect." The word dripped with sarcasm. His body craved sleep. "Please tell me the car has GPS." Having never driven in Moscow but familiar with its ultra-chaotic nature as a passenger, this was a part of the mission he was not looking forward to at all.

The man smiled for the first time. "Of course there's GPS. This isn't the Third World, you know."

As Jacob eased the late-model black Mercedes 4x4 out of the last paved road in Belaya Berozka, GPS programmed to guide him to his new address via the M3 highway, he wondered, not for the first time: *What the hell am I doing?* He told himself it was for the good of his country and the world at large. And the big bucks.

He pushed the gas pedal until the Merc hit 110 kph on the expressway. He turned the radio on and attuned his ear to the dulcet tones of Russian deejays stuck on the graveyard shift. And, just like that, he was Anatoly Voronin, brand new junior policy advisor to the Minister of Finance of the Russian Federation. If he got out of this one alive, it would be a miracle.

ELEVEN

Lilliana Danilova greeted Jacob at the threshold with the traditional Russian triple cheek-kiss. She gripped him by the shoulders of his suit jacket, slightly crumpled after the marathon drive. He'd left it on because he wanted quick access to the gun under his shoulder holster. Thank God, no cops had pulled him over on the drive from Belaya Berozka. Must have been the fancy car and the ministerial plates that saved his bacon, because plenty of other motorists were stopped, questioned, and detained.

Danilova's fingers were strong, evidence of years of intensive physical training as an undercover operative. Immaculately polished and manicured claws dug in like talons as she looked him up and down with an appreciative eye. He blushed at the ogling attention. Although attractive in a superficial way—the makeup and cosmetic surgery had done wonders—she was closer to fifty-five than forty-five. In her favor, she sported the body of a woman who worked out regularly. Jacob's gut told him she'd probably be handy in a fight.

"Nakonyets." *Finally.* Her dark-brown eyes lit up as she spoke. "Thank God you are unharmed after your arduous ordeal."

He whispered softly in her ear. "Is this apartment safe?"

She made no effort to speak quietly. "Sovershenno chisto." *Clean as a whistle.* "I've personally seen to it."

"You're not going to ask for the codeword before we get to know one another?" said Jacob, pulling back from the woman's clutches. His body screamed for sleep; he'd driven for nine hours with only one stop to visit a gas station bathroom at around the half-way mark. A couple of accidents caused snaking traffic jams that added another ninety minutes to the ETA. This first debrief had better be over quickly or he'd drop dead with exhaustion.

"I'm confident you are who I think you are. However, if you want to dot the i's and cross the t's, very well. What is the codeword?"

"Andromeda." His tone was deadpan. "Now, may we proceed?"

Her tattooed-on eyebrows elevated. She stammered for a moment. "Uh-huh, sure. But...ah...please excuse me while I make a quick phone call to my daughter. May I step out onto your balcony?"

He grabbed her by the forearm and gave a hard squeeze. "Are you going to rat me out because I gave the wrong codeword? Will there be a knock on the door by some goons with machine guns?"

"Wh-wh-what? No, I...ah. Oh dear." The color drained from her face.

Jacob let go of her arm, drifted across to a cream sofa and dropped into it, feeling the embrace of the luxurious cushions. "Relax. It's Ardalion. Why on Earth they picked that one, I'll never know."

The relief brought the color back to her taut cheeks. "You had me worried for a second there, Edik."

He frowned but inwardly was relieved. She'd been given the name Edward Brown, not his real one. "You must not call me Edik or Edward. From now until I leave Russia, we must only use Anatoly or the short form, Tolya, at all times."

"Of course, Tolya. Quite right. As people in the acting world say, you must inhabit the role." Danilova, without prompting, explained her theory on the choice of the codeword. It was a rare male given name of Greek origin. Matviy Ostapenko had a son with that name. No doubt he'd suggested it to Fletcher. Jacob could care less about its origin.

As the woman spoke, she moved about the apartment like she owned it. She opened the freezer compartment of the massive stainless steel refrigerator and retrieved a bottle of Stolichnaya vodka. In seconds, she'd poured them each a shot and brought the drinks to a coffee table next to the sofa. She sat close to him, although there was an empty matching chair directly opposite, raised her glass, and said, "To our mutual success!" Without waiting for him to join in the toast, she downed the contents.

Time to set the dragon straight. "If you don't mind, Lilliana."

She twisted her head toward him. The gap of six inches between their faces wasn't enough to disperse the fumes of alcohol on her breath. "Mind?"

He gave a sharp nod at the vacant chair. "I like my space."

"Fine," she huffed.

He reached for his vodka and slammed it down. Ice-cold, the strong alcohol warmed his throat and stomach. It was just after 09:00 a.m., not the usual time for imbibing. But as he'd said to Ostapenko, *when in Rome*. "Can we please get this over with quickly?" he said. "I've been attacked by a knife-wielding maniac and shot at, then had a crazy long drive from the border. I don't think I've ever needed to sleep as much as I do now."

"Very well." She couldn't hide the tetchiness in her voice. "Wait here," she said unnecessarily. It wasn't as if he was in a hurry to go somewhere else.

He closed his eyes, so near to drifting away, when a thump brought him back to the present. From a leather zip-up portfolio, she pulled out a series of ID documents and flipped them on the table, naming them as she went. Jacob barely paid attention. He'd peruse them at his leisure.

"Seriously, Lilliana. Can't this wait?"

She leaned back into her chair. “Not at all. Everything needs to be ironed out now. You start work tomorrow. Or have you forgotten?”

He blinked hard. This wasn’t right. Surely there was a honeymoon period. He’d need at least a day to get over the adrenaline and cortisol overdoses of the last seventy-two hours. “Come on.” He said it in a protracted way that sounded whiny and unprofessional to his own ears, and he instantly regretted the petulance. Fatigue induced, but still, not good enough. He struggled to sit in an upright position. “I apologize. Since you seem to know your way around the place so well, how about you make me a coffee, extra strong. Then we can get started.” He offered a wan smile.

She grinned, faint lines that had escaped the attention of the plastic surgeon appearing beside her lips. “That’s more like it.”

The caffeine took a couple minutes to kick in, but when it did, the result was transformative. His pulse quickened, his awareness heightened. “You didn’t drop a little something extra in my drink, did you?”

She looked at him askance, sipping at the white wine she’d poured herself while he’d had his eyes shut. The fact she was so anxious to drink booze in the morning was setting off alarm bells, but he’d wait and see. She was his first primary contact in Moscow; hammering her about bad personal habits at this early stage could backfire badly. “Are you joking?” she said, lips twisted as she seemed to take genuine offence.

“Why not? This country is notorious for poisonings and the like.”

She shook her head. “Tolya, I understand your cynicism. Yes, the regime is brutal and murderous. Its critics are not only poisoned, but they sometimes decide they can fly and jump out of windows. But those are not our methods. We prefer–”

“How high up is this apartment?” he interrupted.

Danilova tilted her head back and laughed. “Bravo!” She took a small sip of her drink. “By the way, this is clear apple juice, in case you were thinking I’m some kind of lush.”

Encouraging. Although the strong smell of vodka on her breath told him she'd had more than just the celebratory tipple with him on his arrival. Either that or his faculties were impaired from being over-tired. *Or* she really was a lush and was lying. He'd been in the spying game long enough to know one thing for sure. People lied. A lot.

"What do I need to know for tomorrow?"

"What is your father's job?"

Checking his legend straight up. Maybe that's why she'd wanted to ply him with booze. To see if he remembered the tiny details that go into making up a person's life. Indeed, could the ridiculously circuitous route taken to infiltrate him into Russia have been designed to stress him to the maximum and then check his ability to assume another identity? "Starting with the easy ones, I see," he said, chewing his bottom lip. "Electrical engineer."

"Correct." She paused for a moment. "What's your paternal grandmother's name?"

"Elena. And before you ask, her maiden name is Kozlova. Or should I say was. She died in Khabarovsk in 2005 of pancreatic cancer."

"Good. Her patronymic?"

"Antonovna."

"Correct. What is your sister's favorite song?"

"I don't have a sister. I have one brother three years older than me, Gennady, who's obsessed with the 1980s band Kino. His favorite song is 'The Last Hero.'"

"Well done." She curled a leg under her buttocks, sipping the apple juice so gently it had to be wine. The coquette look didn't become her, but Jacob kept his trap shut. "I think that's about the most obscure detail we gave you."

"No. That honor goes to the birthmark on the back of Gennady's left leg that looks like a forest mushroom."

"You *are* good." A small nod, a small sip.

She continued for another fifteen minutes, grilling him about his childhood illnesses, friendships, his education from kindergarten to university. Famous landmarks in his home town of Vladivostok. Then his work history. Every question answered perfectly.

Then a surprise. "What is my ex-husband's name?"

"Yours? No idea. Stuff about you wasn't included in my material."

She shook her head. "An oversight. Never mind, you will have until tomorrow to learn the main points."

"What the hell for?"

"Because I'm the person who 'recruited' you. I met you at a trade conference in Khabarovsk during the summer, realized you'd be the perfect fit as a policy expert, and convinced the minister's PA to give you a three-month trial."

"The legend says I applied for the job directly myself."

"Change of plan."

"What about evidence of our association?"

"Simple." She handed him an iPad, the screen showing her profile on VKontakte, Russia's version of Facebook. He nearly dropped the device when he saw the photos of himself at a restaurant with Danilova, sharing a platter of seafood, a nest of green beer bottles crowding the table. He'd never set foot in Russia's Far East in his life. "Pretty good CGI, yes?"

"Very impressive." Anyone would believe that was really Jacob in the photo; he almost believed it himself.

"But there's more. Let me show you."

He handed her the tablet, and she scrolled around for a few moments and passed it back. "What the...?"

"Yes, your own profile on VKontakte. You've been on it almost since it started. I suggest you browse through your posts and get a feel for how you express yourself in written Russian. It's important, because you will need to write letters, reports, that kind of thing. Not on a daily basis, but often enough that you need to be good at it. You've also got profiles on Telegram, and some 'dead' ones on Twitter and Instagram, both now outlawed in Russia, but it's good to have a past when it comes to using them."

He scratched his head. Speaking the language perfectly was one thing; writing creatively in it was another. In fact, it was a skill he had never practiced. He blew out his cheeks. "How often will I be required to produce these reports?"

"Not very often. But there will also be simple correspondence. Emails, for example."

"Emails I can handle." He thanked the Lord he'd taken the time out last year to learn how to touch type in Russian. The keyboard layout had taken two months of solid repetitive typing to get the muscle memory fixed in his brain. "But anything beyond that, I may need help. Either from you or someone else."

She cracked a smile. "Again, don't worry. There's a solution. Whatever you do, don't write in English and then use an automatic translation app. It won't work. Even the best software can contain hilarious errors. Not so hilarious if you're 'made,' though."

"Indeed." He actually appreciated the black humor. "So what's the solution?"

"We've been working solidly on AI on our end. There's a heavily encrypted, cloaked program I managed to have installed on the laptop in your new office down the hall. Type in headings, bullet points, all your rough notes—complete with grammatical and spelling errors —and the program will spit out a nicely worded report in perfect bureaucratic Russian." She jerked her head to the left. "You'll also find some other items that you may find useful."

"Such as?"

"A new Udav pistol."

That got his interest. The gun had only been around since 2019. "Not the standard Makarov?"

"Nothing but the latest for you, Tolya." She winked.

"I've never fired an Udav. Do I get to practice?" The 9x21 caliber pistol with 18 rounds in the magazine was a weapon he'd been anxious to try out. It was superior to the Makarov in his jacket pocket in a myriad of ways.

She laughed. "Please use it only in an extreme emergency. Secrete the Makarov you were given somewhere in the apartment, together with the Udav. Do not attempt to bring them to work. The metal detectors will pick them up. You won't see the detectors, by the way. They are fitted into the door frames, front and back entrances. In any case, I have faith you are so good at your job that you will never need to fire either of them."

"Don't worry. I prefer to do my shooting on the range."

"Good to know. Tomorrow I will drive you to work; after that, you drive yourself or take the Metro, your choice. There's a spot for your car where another staff member's is vacant on account of him being fired for insulting the president in the lunch room."

"Got it." Taking the subway, known in Russia as the Metro, seemed the smartest option in a city renowned for its epic traffic jams. "And thanks for the heads-up."

"Never speak badly of the regime at work, even as a joke. And less enthusiasm about the Udav would be nice, too. We don't want you turning into Rambo on us."

He kicked his shoes off, swung his legs around, and lay on his back. "The way I'm feeling now, I can't even imagine that happening."

"Please don't go to sleep on me," she pleaded. "There's a couple more things we need to cover before you can rest properly." She ticked off more items he'd been provided with. A cell phone with a covert communications—or covcom—app installed. He was to ditch the one provided by Marina in the Moskva River. This new one was for secure communications between himself and Fletcher, should the need arise, and with the US embassy's chief spy handler. He also had a printer and other tech you'd find in a serious home office. The larder was fully stocked, he had more clothes than he could ever hope to wear, and, the pièce de résistance, a fancy home gym at the end of the corridor. "I heard you like running, but if the winter weather turns nasty, as it can in Moscow, you've got a treadmill with specifications that Roscosmos would be proud of."

"Excellent." Again, he wondered how much money had been spent on this mission. Millions of dollars, if you factored in the missile strikes. And all for one lousy letter.

When Danilova finished talking, Jacob had a question of his own. "What about backstops?"

"Everything is covered. If you arouse suspicion and inquiries are made, the companies you worked for have real phone numbers and addresses, as well as people to answer calls and vouch for your bona fides. The databases of the educational institutions you"—she made air quotes—"*attended* have been hacked into and updated to show you graduated from them."

"Anything else?"

"Of course." She made him another coffee, this one twice as big and twice as strong as the first. For the next hour, she told him about the research and policy role prepared for him. A selected employee would give him a brief introduction to the workplace tomorrow, introduce him to the staff. Thankfully, this office was relatively small with only twelve employees—including him—answering to the Minister for Finance. She stopped mid-explanation, hit him up with a snap test on the main Russian financial laws and regulations. For the most part, he answered correctly, but he got a couple wrong. Luckily, they were related to recent minor changes to tax law that he may have missed in his intense course of self-study. "Luckily, your role is more a big-picture one. Knowledge of technical minutia is desirable, as they say, but not essential. Everything can be searched and found on databases these days. Your grades and references speak of you as a high-achieving student and employee in the private sector, but not a genius."

He yawned. "I am a certified genius, actually."

"I see." She cocked an eyebrow as she gathered her things. "You've certainly got the language part down pat. As for the rest?

We'll see how you perform tomorrow. I'll be waiting on the street outside your front door at 07:30. Don't be late."

He yawned again. "We've said nothing about the actual mission."

She narrowed her eyes. "Let's not get ahead of ourselves. Settle in first, then we'll talk about the assassination you're going to carry out."

Jacob thought his already overstressed heart was going to burst out of his mouth and land on the plush carpet. *What the fuck?*

"I'd like something from you, Lilliana." Jacob held out his right hand.

"What?"

"Your set of keys to this apartment."

"I'm sorry, I..."

"Non-negotiable, I'm afraid." He tilted his head and gave a sarcastic half smile.

She grumbled and handed over a bulging set of keys. Instead of waiting for the elevator to come, she took the stairwell to the right, two steps at a time.

TWELVE

WITH LILLIANA DANILOVA FINALLY OUT OF HIS HAIR, sleep should have been Jacob's first priority. After what she'd said about an assassination, his internal alarm bells were ringing louder than the famous clock on the Kremlin's Spasskaya tower. Sleep would have to wait a little bit longer.

There were two contacts stored in the encrypted satellite phone. Single letters: F and E. Fletcher and Embassy. Hopefully the boss would answer; the thought of leaving a message and then him calling back after he'd finally fallen asleep was too horrible to contemplate. Eyelids drooping almost to the half-way-closed point, he selected F, pressing the green dial button so hard with his thumb the screen threatened to break.

"Ardalion!" The tone was joyous; exaggerated or real, it was hard to tell with Fletcher. The man was a consummate actor. "I've been anxiously waiting for this call from you. The first thing I want to know is, are you okay?"

"I'm alive."

"Excellent."

"What the hell's going on, Grant?" His hand shook as he stirred a third spoonful of sugar into another extra-strong coffee. "From what I can tell, you've sent me on a fool's errand. If I get out of this country alive with that letter, it's going to be a miracle."

"I'm sorry? Slow down and breathe, I can barely make out what you're saying."

"Bullshit. You can hear me just fine. That dragon's been fed the same lies you told Ostapenko and God knows who else. Is she CIA?"

There was the sound of feet pacing a tiled room. "What dragon?" A pause. "And what's this *you* business?"

The urge to throw the phone against the wall was almost too hard to resist. Instead, he hissed, "Danilova. She thinks I've been sent here to take out Putin with a bullet. I cannot even get my head around that. Who do they think I am? A fucking ninja? The man's protected better than Kim Jong Un. The Ukrainian pimp thinks the same thing. She didn't say it, but I reckon Marina was also lied to. A bit of a coincidence, wouldn't you say?"

"Relax. Danilova's not CIA. She's an Alexei Navalny acolyte. A long-term employee of MinFin and recruited for us by a dedicated handler in the Moscow embassy. She might appear confident, cocky even, but she's walking on egg shells. Be nice to her, you got me?"

"Why? She's flakier than old clapboard."

"Think logically. I know that's your strong suit. Do you believe you would get this level of cooperation if they thought you'd been sent there merely to retrieve a letter?"

"Why not?" Jacob paced the vast floor of the living room. He kept his voice as low as he could. The building was sleek and modern and insulated well enough to keep in—or out—noise louder than an AC/DC concert, but this was Moscow, so it paid to be extra vigilant. Danilova assured him the place had been swept thoroughly for bugs an hour before his arrival and come up clean. He wasn't taking the chance she might have installed her own devices. There was something supremely untrustworthy about her that he couldn't put his finger on. He resolved to give the place a sweep of his own, even if it was only a manual one.

Then a proper sweep—it shouldn't be too hard to find an off-the-shelf detection device in this city. "You didn't have to tell them it was a letter that implicated America in wrongdoing. You could have said...I don't know...it connected Putin with something compromising."

Fletcher burst out laughing, and Jacob had to hold the phone at arm's length until the laughter subsided. "The man is implicated in nothing less than war crimes. And you know what? He doesn't fucking care! It makes no difference to his vise-like grip on power what people dump on him. Can you imagine our Russian helpers on the ground doing somersaults because a letter is going to make Vlad look bad?"

"No," Jacob growled under his breath. The boss had a valid point. No amount of real or invented kompromat would dent the confidence of Russia's president or lead to his political demise. His enemies craved his literal demise, nothing less. "So what am I supposed to do?"

"Like I said before. Relax. Not everyone you're going to meet is in on the fake assassination story."

"No?"

"No. Your key guy is a CIA deep cover agent in the Ministry of Finance. He's sworn to do whatever it takes to help you. His name is Aleksandr Gerasimchuk, and he's been patiently waiting for an important case to work on for ten years. Been through three handlers from the embassy in that time."

"A guy with a Ukrainian surname is on the inside of MinFin?" He paused for a moment. "Actually, now I think about it, it's not such a big deal. Valentina Matviyenko is a key member in Putin's tight inner circle. They say she had a big hand in the decision to invade."

"You have done your homework, Jacob." There was genuine praise in his tone. "Gives me confidence you *will* get the job done."

He ignored the remark. "Tell me more about Gerasimchuk."

"He's the one whose trust you need to gain above all others.

It was Gerasimchuk who undertook all the vetting work and went over your bona fides, so you can rest easy in terms of your ID not checking out. By the same token, you can't risk pissing him off in any way. And if you do, patch it up as fast as you can."

"Why is he so important?"

"He's been assigned as your direct supervisor at the Ministry, not Danilova."

"That *is* good news."

"He's also the man who's going to lead you to the letter. He thinks handing it over to the United States will help secure peace in Ukraine."

"You're joking! It will have the exact opposite effect if it goes public. Why on Earth would he think it would lead to peace?"

The pause went on a little too long.

"Did you hear me, Grant?"

"I heard you. Gerasimchuk is convinced the letter is an official invitation to Ukraine to join NATO."

"What?" Jacob nearly dropped his phone. "Are you fucking kidding me?"

Fletcher gave a double cough. "He's under the impression it's a letter from Anders Rasmussen, who was director general of NATO at the time. We've told him the letter was signed by Rasmussen and representatives of all the other NATO countries. It was ready to be delivered when the Dane had a change of heart."

"I can't believe anyone would fall for that baloney."

Fletcher sighed. "When people are desperate, they'll cling to whatever gives them hope. Gerasimchuk has told us the letter will show the world that NATO really did want to usher Ukraine into the fold, but something derailed the process. Now is the time to right that wrong.

"And it is believable, to a degree," Fletcher pressed on. "In September 2014, after Russia had annexed Ukraine and the east of the country had turned into one big clusterfuck that continues to this day, Rasmussen stood on a podium with then-president of Ukraine, Petro Poroshenko. They–"

"Poroshenko was Zelensky's predecessor. His nickname was the Chocolate King because of his business holdings in the confectionary world."

"Correct. But please don't interrupt me, Jacob. I know you're tired, but it's important you understand Gerasimchuk's motivation so you know how to play him."

"Go on."

"At the press conference a decade ago, Rasmussen bleated platitudes about standing united with Ukraine, said that NATO strongly condemned Russia's violations of international law. Blah, blah, blah. But here's the bit that got Gerasimchuk believing the letter we invented is plausible. The DG said Ukraine was a distinctive and important 'partner' and..."

"Surely that wasn't the first time such a vague term had been used?"

"True. But on this occasion, the NATO chief was standing on stage with the Chocolate King and, well, it was all about the feels. If you watch the footage online, you'll see what I mean. Reporters were brazenly firing questions about Ukraine joining NATO, and neither of the men outright precluded it as a possibility. We've told Gerasimchuk the letter was drafted after Rasmussen's little speech and the radical next step was about to be taken. It just required Poroshenko's signature the next day and NATO membership was in the bag."

"So," Jacob reasoned out loud, "he helps me recover the letter, but I make sure he never lays eyes on the content."

"Correct. And if somehow, he does...well...I'm not sure we'll be able to depend on his loyalty for one second longer. In which case, you will have to–"

"Holy shit, Grant. I've already sent one man to meet his maker on this trip. I'm not anxious to do it again."

"Then you'd better make damn sure he never sees the letter up close and personal." The hiss of a can being opened came down the line. "Otherwise you will have to liquidate him."

THIRTEEN

Danilova parked her state-provided BMW in an underground lot two blocks from Jacob's new place of employment. The Ministry of Finance of the Russian Federation, located a stone's throw from Red Square and the Kremlin in the historic Kitaigorod district, was housed in a five-story gunmetal-gray granite building on 9 Ilinka Street. Its neighbors included the massive Gostiny Dvor Exhibition Center and the GUM department store. Not the place to go if you want peace and quiet; the streets around MinFin were constantly abuzz with locals at work or leisure and open-mouthed tourists. But that was fine with Jacob—hiding in plain sight was often the least stressful way to run a covert operation.

Out on the street, a biting wind howled down the narrow space between buildings on either side of Ilinka Street. Late January and the mercury on a wall thermometer said -13°C, around 9° Fahrenheit. Jacob hunched his shoulders and narrowed his eyes as snowflakes cascaded around him. Danilova strode the snowy sidewalk like she was ruler of the city, not a *chinovnik*, a bureaucratic cog in the giant machinery of Russian government. Sticking close beside her as they elbowed their way toward the entrance, Jacob's heart started to pound, butterflies on steroids bashing around in his stomach. The contents of his conversation with Fletcher echoed in his brain. *Don't piss this one off, don't piss that one off.* That was the last thing he was planning to do.

Danilova crushed her cigarette butt under a solid leather boot and punched a number into a keypad. He looked over her shoulder and memorized her code in case he wanted to get inside without his own being recorded in the system. There was a clicking sound as the lock disengaged, and she pushed the door open.

Jacob drew a deep breath.

This was it.

Crossing the Rubicon. Or was it the Styx, the gateway to hell? He wondered how many Americans had set foot inside MinFin's headquarters, even as invited guests. Not many, he guessed. He was probably the first, and quite possibly the last.

He tapped his escort on the shoulder as she pressed the button to call the elevator to the first floor.

She turned her head. "Nervous?"

"Like a bride on her wedding night."

"I wasn't nervous." She grinned broadly. "Unless you meant a virgin bride, of course."

"Yes," he replied out of the corner of his mouth. "That's exactly what I meant."

"Cheeky boy." She smiled as she held out an arm to stop him entering the elevator car. "On second thoughts, let's familiarize you with the fire escape route."

The pair headed for the stairwell. Inside, a fresh paint smell flooded Jacob's nostrils. MinFin had plenty of money to spend on keeping up appearances, even in a rarely used part of the building. Their footsteps echoed in the empty space. At the exit to the fourth floor, Danilova turned and said, "There's another set of stairs at the back. Gerasimchuk or one of his underlings will show you those later."

Jacob nodded. In a new environment, especially one from which he might have to beat a hasty retreat, it was essential to know every way in and out. No surprise, his searches for a blueprint of the MinFin headquarters had come up empty. His acquired savant syndrome gave him a linguistic gift, but years of practice had helped him hone and develop abilities in other fields. Visuo-spatial skills was one that he excelled in. He would try to visit every floor of the building and, in his mind, create a mind map of every office, corridor, bathroom, and window. It could prove a complete waste of time, or it could save his life.

One more floor, and they were at the top. Inside, there was a bathroom to the right and a long, wide corridor that seemed to bisect the floorspace. They encountered no other people as they strolled the hallway; through glass walls he could see other staff busy chatting on telephones, staring at computer screens, up to two and three monitors crowding their desks, or pecking away at keyboards. Two-thirds of the way along, they stopped outside a private office with a seriously solid wooden door.

She turned a handle and ushered him inside. "This is yours, Tolya."

He shook his head in wonder as he took in the opulence of the room. *The strings she must have pulled to arrange this.* He took another look at her in the cold light of day, with four hours' worth of sleep under his belt. She was more attractive today than he'd given her credit for yesterday. He leapt to a conclusion that could explain his good fortune—she was sleeping with someone who made big decisions. The minister himself?

"What do you think?" she said, hands on hips.

He pursed his lips and nodded as he surveyed the room. "Not bad." A view down onto bustling Ilinka Street and the mint-green façade of the building opposite was a bonus.

"You are playing with the big boys now, Tolya," she said, yanking Jacob from his mental mapping. "Are you ready to play?"

Jacob winked and busted out the famous catch cry of the Young Pioneers, the now defunct Russian equivalent of the Boy Scouts. "Vsegda gotov." *I'm always ready*. Despite the words, nerves were creating an acid bath in his stomach.

"Molodets." *Good man*, she said with a wry smile. "Put your briefcase down, and we'll go and meet your new supervisor."

"GERASIMCHUK, ALEKSANDR NIKOLAEVICH." The man gave the standard full Russian introduction: surname, first name, patronymic. He held out his smooth hand, steady as a rock. Around 50 years old, bookish with penetrating brown eyes behind black-framed glasses, a high forehead crowned with a sparse crop of closely shaved silver hair. A suit that looked a little old-fashioned compared to the stylish outfits he'd seen adorning the younger tigers in the department. His new supervisor was around five-ten, above-average weight that perhaps testified to many years of working in an office environment with little time for exercise. Or no inclination. Gerasimchuk had been working deep cover for so long he must have nerves of steel, though, Jacob thought. Which in this game was often more important than physical attributes.

"Delighted to make your acquaintance. I'm Tolya." Jacob met the man's handshake with a gentle double squeeze and his other hand laid over the top, which made Gerasimchuk raise his eyebrows. It wasn't some kind of secret code, just a gesture Jacob hoped would engender trust. As long as he didn't see it as some kind of physical come-on. The action was met with an equal and opposite reaction. With an added extra. Gerasimchuk leaned into Jacob's ear and whispered in a deep rumble, "Ardalion." An excellent start, Jacob thought to himself as the man freed his hands from the newbie's grasp.

Danilova coughed into her fist after Jacob and his new supervisor had introduced themselves to each other. "I'll let you two get acquainted properly. Catch you both at this afternoon's strategy meeting."

"We won't be gathering in the boardroom today." Gerasimchuk announced it like it was a piece of unusually good news.

"No?" Danilova sounded pleasantly surprised. Clearly the boardroom get-togethers weren't something to look forward to.

He shook his head. "No, Lilliana. The strategy meeting today will be held at your favorite café, The Cigar Club."

"Excellent. The Ministry's picking up the tab, I presume?"

"Naturally. And it gets even better. A cozy meeting today. The three of us will be making up the quorum, no one to disturb us." He smiled broadly and spread out his hands. "That suit you, Tolya?"

"Perfect," he said. With a dash of irreverence he hoped would go down the right way, he added, "I'm sure the café will be at least equal to what I'm used to in Vladivostok."

"We Muscovites pride ourselves on having the biggest and the best of everything in Russia." Gerasimchuk grinned. "If not the world."

"I've heard," said Jacob. The man was laying it on thick, which was reassuring. Playing the role with intent and purpose and not prepared to open up until they were out of the building, where not only the walls had ears, but the ceilings and furniture too.

Danilova bowed almost imperceptibly. "At what time?"

"I'll DM you on the internal system. Expect mid-afternoon."

"Khorosho." *Excellent*.

She gave her hair a flick and exited Gerasimchuk's office. The supervisor gestured for Jacob to take a seat in a chair across from a large, highly polished desk.

"I read that the minister arrived back from a trip to Turkey last night. Will he be debriefing the staff today?" said Jacob, stretching his long legs out under the desk. The last thing he'd done before crashing into the deepest sleep he'd had in years was to scan the most popular online Moscow newspapers so he could be up to speed on latest events. Samsonov's visit to Ankara was headline news.

Gerasimchuk frowned. "You heard right. But he's not in the office today. He's reporting directly to Vladimir Vladimirovich on his discussions with the Turkish minister of Treasury and Finance. Western sanctions are starting to bite hard, Tolya, and Samsonov was over there drumming up support from the Turks. He'll be with Putin all day, I believe. If you're lucky, you'll get to meet the minister later in the week."

Jacob pursed his lips. A postponement of his inevitable meeting with Maxim Antonovich Samsonov would give him welcome breathing space. Confronting the minister was the most horrifying prospect of this assignment so far—being attacked by a knife-wielding soldier and shot at in the dark were better options. The only thing worse would be a face-to-face with Vladimir Vladimirovich Putin, known far and wide by the initials VVP. His gut told him such a meeting *would* take place; with most of his assets believing Jacob's task was to take Putin out, no doubt moves were afoot to set something up.

Gerasimchuk beckoned for the new employee to join him at the window, which offered a glimpse of a colorful old church. "Know what that is?" he said, nodding at a pair of sky-blue and salmon-colored domes. Jacob had to plead ignorance. "It's the Church of Cosmas and Damian. I don't know much about it except that Ivan the Terrible got married there."

Jacob sucked in a breath. "In that tiny little church?"

"Yes. It's incredible a small building like that can have such a huge significance, no? A bit like our headquarters here, I think. Most people walking past wouldn't have a clue about the important decisions made within these walls."

"I guess they wouldn't," Jacob agreed.

"You realize what a big deal it is working at MinFin, don't you?" Gerasimchuk switched the topic unexpectedly before returning to his swivel chair and gestured for Jacob to resume his seat, too. "Many ambitious people would readily swap places with you."

"I do realize it." Jacob nodded seriously despite his real feelings. If he could go back in time to the moment he'd agreed to this suicidal mission, he would also swap places—with anyone. "I am honored beyond words that Lilliana saw promise in me and organized the opportunity for my trial employment."

"She talked you up, that's for sure." Gerasimchuk cocked an eyebrow. "I'm hoping you can live up to the hype." He fixed Jacob with a challenging glare. "Give me your take on Turkey as a trading partner for the Russian Federation. I'll give you five minutes."

Jacob looked at the ceiling for a couple of seconds, then decided the only way to proceed was to ad-lib his lines. "There aren't many countries left that are even slightly predisposed toward Russia these days, but Turkey is one of them." Jacob could feel sweat pooling in his armpits, his heart jumping rope to a zydeco beat. Why was he being hit with this spot test, one straight out of left field? He only knew some broad-brush information about the partnership between the two countries. He *did* know gauche Russian tourists liked to spend their money in the bars and clubs of Antalya, but beyond that, not much else.

He sucked in a deep breath and determined to bluff as best he could for as long as he could—at least for the allotted five minutes. "At the end of the day, relations with other countries, economic or otherwise, also come under the remit of MID—the Ministry of Foreign Affairs—as well as Minpromtorg—the Ministry of Industry and Trade," he said through compressed lips. "My advice to our minister, were he to seek it from me, would be to work together with other kindred ministries, to strive to keep Turkey on our side for as long as possible by whatever means possible. Same goes for any other nations treating us favorably, especially in terms of supplying us with affordable consumer goods."

"The main one being?"

"China, of course."

"Any others?"

An article he'd read a month ago in the British *Financial Times* leapt into his mind. "Then there's Serbia, Mexico, and

Brazil, who have elected to be sensible amid the ill-conceived moves against our country."

"Excellent. Do you think the sanctions will stay active for much longer?"

Jacob chewed a fingernail, pondering the correct way to reply. "Impossible to predict. Once our country ultimately emerges victorious from the Special Military Operation in Ukraine, I'm confident the world will go back to some semblance of normality. Our citizens will be able to travel freely again, and Westerners who love our wonderful culture will come back. Of course, it will never be *exactly* the same as it was before February 24, 2022, but I'm an eternal optimist. Once the West realizes that Russia isn't the one losing out by being isolated, but, on the contrary, is learning how to be more self-sufficient and becoming even stronger..."

"Well done, Tolya." Gerasimchuk tapped something on his keyboard. "That will do for now. I'm sure you're going to be a wildly successful strategist and policy advisor here. I like your broad vision and perspicacity. Exactly what's needed!"

Jacob could feel himself blushing. Maybe this gig wouldn't be so scary after all. "Thank you."

"Don't worry about having a handle on everything. That's impossible. We have plenty of functionaries working for small wages, both here and off-site, who handle all of the minutiae in terms of how many billions of rubles are being spent on this, that, and the other." He clicked a mouse and kept talking while staring at his computer screen. "However, it wouldn't go amiss for you to stay abreast of trends, memorize some key figures once a week." He clicked a button, and a piece of paper emerged from a nearby printer. "Go and fetch that, will you?"

Jacob retrieved the piece of A4 and went to hand it, unread, to Gerasimchuk.

"No, Tolya. That's for you."

It was a list of twenty-five metrics, including GDP, inflation, trade balance, military expenditure, with numbers for the month gone and year-to-date. The money spent on the armed forces compared to the rest nearly took Jacob's breath away. Six and a half trillion rubles—or nearly 70 billion dollars—per annum. Around 4.4% of Russia's GDP.

"I think I can digest those numbers." That was an understatement. He could memorize a hundred more.

"You'll get the email first thing every Monday morning." Gerasimchuk tapped a pen on his desk. "Useful to be able to spout the figures if Samsonov gives you a grilling."

"Speaking of which, do you think the minister's brought good news or bad news back from Turkey?" said Jacob. "The press reports were scant on details."

"For his sake, I hope it's good. Samsonov has been in the job over a decade and has generally kept the big boss happy. But now is the time he really needs to show VVP what he's made of. There are plenty of aspirants willing to take Samsonov's spot if he can't guide the country through this rough patch."

"His job's not a poisoned chalice?" said Jacob.

Gerasimchuk chuckled as he adjusted the knot of his tie. "Every job where you are directly answerable to the president is a potential poisoned chalice. But many are happy to take it in their hands and even take a sip."

"You think he's safe?"

"Our minister is as loyal as they come. As the Americans say, Tolya, he's as safe as Fort Knox."

"Is that what they say?" Jacob spoke through pressed lips. "I've never heard that one."

"I don't suppose you're exposed to much Western culture in Vladivostok." His gaze was steely. Staying in character perfectly.

"Not much, no," said Jacob, blinking like a rube from the sticks. "There is a big Asian influence, though. So many cars directly imported from Japan driving around town with the steering wheel on the right-hand side. It makes for lots of accidents on the roads."

"Okay." Gerasimchuk was dismissive of this piece of trivia,

which he was certainly already aware of. He rubbed his hands together like he was trying to light a fire. “Enough small talk. Let me give you a rundown on what we expect you to produce for us in your trial period.”

“I’m very eager to start.”

Gerasimchuk put a finger to his lips, narrowing his eyes. “An unimaginative if expected answer. We’ll start with...” A ding sound came from Gerasimchuk’s computer. “Oh, dear. This is rather unexpected.”

“What?”

“The minister is here. And he wants to meet you, Tolya.”

“When?”

“Now!”

FOURTEEN

THE MINISTER'S OFFICE DWARFED GERASIMCHUK'S. Twice the size, it was perhaps 1,200 square feet, give or take, with thick carpet, gleaming wooden furniture, a couple leather sofas, and a sprinkling of armchairs. A slightly dusty odor. Clearly, the minister spent less time in the office than the rest of the staff, dropping by only when absolutely necessary. There was little in the way of technology in the room, apart from a huge TV monitor, an old-fashioned handset phone, and a modest laptop taking up a fraction of the space on his expansive desk. Most impressive was the array of bookcases lining three walls, jam-packed with all manner of weighty tomes. Behind the desk, looking on like Big Brother, the obligatory and very flattering portrait of the president. Jacob and Gerasimchuk sat three feet apart on a long sofa, Samsonov opposite in a regal armchair, one leg crossed over the other.

"So glad to have you on board, Anatoly." The minister's eyes drooped slightly.

Jacob smiled as genuinely as he could. "Glad to be here, sir."

"Has Aleksandr Nikolaevich been treating you well?" Samsonov inclined his head, shaved close in a losing battle with baldness, toward Gerasimchuk, who sat calmly, steepling his fingers.

"Very well, sir. He's made me feel at home."

"Aleksandr's a terrific deputy when I'm away." He smiled amiably at Gerasimchuk, then shifted his gaze back to Jacob. "Have you met any of the other staff yet?"

"So far only our mutual friend, Lilliana Danilova."

"A tour is planned for later, Minister." Gerasimchuk sounded almost defensive. "I'll be introducing Tolya to everyone."

"All in good time." Samsonov nodded slowly. "We are an ancient department with a rich history. Time moves at a different pace in MinFin."

Jacob smiled but said nothing. He knew the history of the organization thoroughly. It traced its roots back to 1780, when Catherine the Great issued a decree establishing the ministry, and had changed identity several times between then and the present day.

"If you can inject a bit of youthful enthusiasm and, most importantly, vision, into this outfit, the country can only stand to gain enormously." Samsonov paused, almost wistfully. "You know, when Lilliana approached me with her story about you, well, I was impressed. I simply couldn't say no to giving you a trial run. I'm not normally involved in the hiring and firing decisions here, but sometimes I get my way."

Something in the man's tone told Jacob he was right about Danilova and the boss sleeping together. And that he *got his way* with her quite a lot.

A double knock came on the closed door, creating an echo inside. The minister nodded wordlessly at Gerasimchuk, who obediently stood and admitted a young woman. Dressed in a crisp white blouse and pencil skirt, hair tied back severely in a bun, it was impossible to tell if she was a tea lady or a legit MinFin worker lending a hand. She delivered a silver tray with a large pot of coffee, cream and sugar, and three small cups, as well as an assortment of cookies. "Ah, thank you, Irina."

She nodded, filling the cups to the brim, but made no reply before exiting with a deferential bow.

"Now, what can you tell me about this program you're helping to create?" The minister took a sip of coffee from a fine china cup, peering over the rim expectantly. "It all sounds very promising."

For a second, Jacob's stomach threatened to expel the contents of his meager breakfast of a slice of buttered toast washed down with black tea. Being put on the spot like this was next-level intimidation. Samsonov's entire bearing came across as a combination of amiable and a simmering, underlying menace.

"Oh yes!" chimed in Gerasimchuk. "Anatoly will be working with a team of our best policy experts to–"

"Please, Aleksandr." Samsonov raised his right hand slightly. "I know you have a protective streak, but let the man speak for himself."

"Of course, Maxim Antonovich." Gerasimchuk lowered his eyes a fraction. It wasn't a reprimand, but it was clear the power imbalance was immense.

"I'm all ears." Samsonov folded his arms and nestled into the back of his armchair.

Jacob wondered if the figurative expression *to shit oneself* was about to manifest into reality. Thankfully, Gerasimchuk had had five minutes before the surprise meeting with the minister to clue him in on what *the program* was. Thankfully, not a computer program—he had little knowledge of code apart from a basic course in C++ he'd taken in high school. This program was one of relationships. Indeed, it had been given the name *Nurture.* Jacob held Samsonov's inscrutable gaze, concentrating on trying to keep his own vital signs in the normal range. "The *Nurture* program is about cementing the relationships that Russia already has with favorably inclined nations and developing them to their maximum potential. Encouraging more investment and cooperation from, of course, China, but also expanding our focus toward Serbia, Brazil, Mexico, India, and any other reasonable nation that doesn't blindly kow-tow to NATO and the United States." Jacob drew on his phenomenal memory once again, pointing out the fact that Russia had accumulated a huge stockpile of Indian rupees that it could re-invest in India, basically to keep the trade-flow pumping along nicely with that country. Other currencies were also being squirreled away, largely thanks to Russia's insistence on not trading in greenbacks where possible. He concluded his five-minute spiel by noting there was still plenty of scope for Russia to not only survive, but to thrive, even with its back firmly against the wall in terms of the West's immoral trade blockade.

"I'm sure VVP will be keen to talk to you about this program, Anatoly." Samsonov stood to his full height, brushing a microscopic piece of lint from his jacket sleeve.

Jacob sensed his Adam's apple go up and down. *Stay calm.* "That would be the greatest honor of my life." He caught Gerasimchuk's approving glance out of the corner of his eye. Say only good things about the tyrant.

"I hate to disappoint you, but it won't be for a couple of weeks." The minister closed the lid of his laptop and placed it in a leather carry case. "He's rather preoccupied with military matters at the moment. There have been some serious counteroffensives along the border." He dropped his voice. "I'm sure I'm not revealing anything confidential here, but two nights ago, the fascists struck hard. Thank God no civilians were killed, but a rocket bombardment wiped out some crucial munitions bases and other infrastructure near Belaya Berozka."

"Never heard of it," said Jacob, a little too quickly. It was almost a reflexive, defensive denial, and he chided himself for letting it slip.

"Not surprising." Samsonov chuckled softly. "Neither had I until yesterday. It's one of those remote towns we like to collectively call Mukhosransk. Do you have that word in Vladivostok?"

Jacob nodded. The word more or less meant fly-shit town. English equivalent, bumfuck nowhere. "We sure do. But if the

Ukrainian terrorists strike even the tiniest village, no doubt backed by Washington, that is an evil that cannot go unignored."

"I cannot agree more." Escorting his guests out the door, Samsonov clapped Jacob lightly on the shoulder. "On second thoughts, young man, perhaps I can expedite that meeting with VVP. Let me see what I can do."

FIFTEEN

THE MINISTER'S SNAP GET-TO-KNOW-YOU SESSION LEFT Jacob totally drained of energy. He almost collapsed in his seat as Gerasimchuk closed the door to Jacob's office.

"Holy shit. That was intense." He reached for a bottle of water from a nest of them on his table and glugged half the contents.

Gerasimchuk stood behind Jacob, gently massaging his shoulders. A totally weird situation, but the man's technique was oddly soothing, and Jacob made no move to stop him. Then Gerasimchuk leaned in and whispered softly, "We're still playing the role, don't forget. Whenever we are in this building, we support the regime in every way. Do not slip up."

Jacob nodded as Gerasimchuk's fingers lost contact with the collar bone ligament. "Tell me, Aleksandr Nikolaevich, how on earth does one prepare for a meeting with the president of Russia?"

"You don't have to."

"What?" Not the answer he was expecting.

"Your ability to think on your feet when the pressure is on is like nothing I have ever seen in my life. That is why you will enjoy great success in MinFin." He helped himself to one of the water bottles and unscrewed the cap. "Whatever that success looks like and however long you stay here."

Jacob pushed back in the chair, which rolled a couple of inches on its casters. "No. I don't think I can do it." He cradled his head in his hands. "The pressure will be too much. I'll pass out in front of him and disgrace myself." He was laying it on thick, but he suspected fearing Putin was as much a positive personality trait as admiring him.

Gerasimchuk's eyes bulged out of their sockets. "You must! No one can refuse an audience with Putin."

It had to be done. Jacob slowly removed his hands from his face. "Okay." He looked up at his supervisor and gave half a wink. "Whatever it takes."

A look of supreme relief brought color back to Gerasimchuk's cheeks. "Molodets." *Good man.*

THE HANDSHAKES SEEMED NEVER-ENDING. The ages of the other nine staff working the Policy and Strategy Division on the top floor ranged from early twenties to late fifties, with a slight predominance of younger workers. He mentally matched names to faces, filing them away for future reference. His long-time study of the Russian language and culture made it easy for Jacob to memorize the permutations of names—including the myriad variations of diminutives—that Russians were so fond of.

The last to be introduced to Jacob in the fifth-floor lunchroom was Irina Frolova, the shy woman who had brought in the coffee to the minister's office. "Irina's a tech whizz," said Gerasimchuk as Jacob shook her hand lightly. Heat radiated from her moist palm. She blushed like a peach, and Jacob sensed instantly that she either found him attractive or intimidating. He certainly towered over her small frame. She reminded him so much of Sally-Anne Vincent: similar eyes, nose, and mouth, but even more was her posture and apparent introversion. The similarity caused him to shudder inwardly. Years on and he still hadn't found Sally-Anne's killer. At times he thought he was close, but leads evaporated just as he thought they would bear fruit.

"Aleksandr Nikolaevich is exaggerating." The blush deepened as Irina turned up her internal disingenuous button. If she wasn't at the top of her game, she wouldn't be working at MinFin HQ. "I'm a recent graduate from MGU. I've only been here six months."

"In which time she has made a massive contribution in the IT department." Gerasimchuk spoke the words like a proud uncle.

"Isn't this the Policy and Strategy Division?" said Jacob. "Do we have our own dedicated IT section? I'm a little confused."

"Nothing to be confused about. IT is on the floor below us, and Irina pops up when one of our people has an issue with their computer. She's got a roving commission for the entire building, actually. If someone up here has a problem with their computers, Irina's the first to volunteer her assistance."

Jacob stared at her intently, but she was unable to meet his gaze. "So coffee making is also part of your duties?"

"Ah, not exactly. You see, the minister is related to one of my university lecturers who put in a good word for me, which helped me land the position." She looked embarrassed to admit it. Nepotism and cronyism ran rife in most bureaucracies, and Russia was no different. In fact, it led the pack. "As a way of thanking him, I volunteered to help out with some of the menial tasks. Not that I mind, of course. It's an honor to work here, no matter the job." A slight shake in her voice told Jacob she wasn't being entirely truthful about this arrangement. He suspected Samsonov was forcing her to do some of the unglamorous jobs as payback for his generosity. A shell of an idea formulated in his mind about how Irina could be useful in getting hold of the letter.

"It's irrelevant how she got here," said Gerasimchuk defensively. "Irina graduated from MGU in the top five percentile. She has proven her worth. She helped upgrade the building's security system to a level of unbreachability."

"Impressive," said Jacob. "So no one can get in that we don't want to get in?"

"That's the idea." Irina smiled with a little more confidence this time. "I mean, no one got in before, but with the current global situation, it was decided to ratchet things up a few notches."

A final handshake and Jacob decided that tomorrow his computer was going to suffer a malfunction, and Irina would be called to the rescue.

LILLIANA DANILOVA, eyes aglow to match the bright-red tip, had her right hand wrapped around the cigar like she was about to please a lover. She sucked hard and expelled a chain of perfectly formed rings. Gerasimchuk was happy with a much smaller cigarillo, which he puffed on with an enthusiasm the equal of Danilova's. "These Montecristo cigars are amazing," said Danilova before readdressing the smoldering cylinder with eager lips.

The atmosphere in the exclusive smoking lounge was cleaner than Jacob expected. With only his two colleagues and himself in the small VIP lounge, the modest amount of carcinogens emitted into the air was quickly whisked away by efficient air-conditioning. When Jacob glanced at the menu, it was clear the prices would get some customers' eyes watering more than the cigar smoke.

Gerasimchuk uncorked a bottle of premium whisky and poured two fingers' worth into fine-cut crystal glasses for each of them. Jacob sipped slowly, the alcohol pleasantly warming his insides.

"How do you think your first morning went, Tolya?" said the supervisor.

"Very well." Any day his cover remained intact was a good day.

"Indeed it did. Is it your intention to make friends with the

IT girl?" said Danilova, a tinge of jealousy discernable in her voice. Or, Jacob thought, she'd been on the sauce since early morning, and he was imagining something that wasn't there. "She seemed rather smitten with you."

"I didn't pick up anything," Jacob lied, his fingers drumming on the table top. "Besides, she's at least ten years my junior. I'm not predisposed to romancing women fresh out of college." He fixed her with an ambiguous look. "If anything, I prefer my girlfriends to be around the same age as me."

The arrow hit home, and Danilova visibly squirmed in her seat. She averted her gaze and sent another volley of circles skyward. Jacob toyed with the idea of joining them in the smoking ritual, deciding he would, after all, take part. He summoned an attendant, who took him to a special room where the cigars were kept under glass at optimal temperature and humidity. With no knowledge of the subject, he let the man choose for him and returned to his companions.

"The meeting is now officially underway," said Gerasimchuk. "I will only speak for a short time, and the two of you can contribute when I've finished. Agreed?"

"Yes," said Jacob and Danilova in unison.

Jacob took a tentative puff, the rich and fruity flavor of the tobacco sending his head into a light spin. After washing it down with a sip of the outrageously expensive whisky, he began to think a long-term entrenchment in MinFin might not be a bad thing after all. If only he didn't have to retrieve the letter and save the State Department's ass...

"Were you listening, Tolya?" said Gerasimchuk, tapping a collar of ash into a chunky glass ashtray. "We need to get a couple of things ironed out."

"These things are strong! Sorry, yes I was listening."

"Then you'll be able to tell us what you think your chances of retrieving the prize are."

"First of all, I don't even know where it's located. I was assuming that was at least part of the reason we're here, out of earshot of certain parties." Jacob kept the language neutral, following the golden rule of not naming names wherever possible.

"We thought it best to reveal it to you once you were *in situ*. I believe the prize is...here." Gerasimchuk wrote two words on a napkin. *Minister's safe.*

Jacob stopped swirling the liquid in his glass, the fumes amplified once again as he slugged down the liquor that was never designed to be consumed so fast. "And how do you know for sure that's where it is?"

"I've been in this job for a long time, Tolya. You get a feel for things. Plus I know a lot about who's trusted in the government, and who is watched with a greater degree of suspicion."

Danilova's cell phone rang. She dug around in her voluminous handbag before holding up the iPhone like she'd just found a lost item that had eluded her for a long time. "Sorry, I have to take this. It's a personal matter." She made a hasty exit from the small room.

"Okay," said Gerasimchuk, clapping his hands together. "With a bit of luck, she'll be a while. No more writing on napkins. This place is clean."

"You sure?"

"Absolutely. I know the owner."

"And you'd rather speak while Lilliana isn't here?"

He nodded. "I don't trust her."

"At all?"

"She's sleeping with Samsonov. Compromised to a great extent. History teaches us that sex and secrets are hard to keep separate."

Jacob stubbed out the cigar after his third puff. Any more tobacco and he was sure he'd pass out. Despite Gerasimchuk's words of assurance about the venue being bug-free, Jacob whispered, "She thinks I've been sent here to kill VVP."

Gerasimchuk laughed gently through a curtain of smoke. "I know. She thinks I think the same thing and that the letter is the secondary element of your mission."

If only you knew the letter isn't what you believe it to be. That's what Jacob wanted to say because he was full of admiration for the man. Lying in wait for so long to get a taste of payback against a regime he despised. The man deserved a medal for patience and guts. Instead, he would get betrayal. "Shall I play along with her?"

"Absolutely. I'd like to think she's fucking Samsonov purely for our advantage—getting you inside MinFin being the coup de grâce—but sometimes these things can go off the rails. She may have developed genuine feelings for the bastard. On the other hand, she hates Putin sure enough. I've been hearing her bleating about it since 2010 or thereabouts."

"How on earth does she expect me to pull off something like that?"

"She told me she gave you an Udav pistol. I guess you're meant to take him out with it."

"You can't be serious! The man is closely guarded, his every move planned."

"And that's why you'll never get to kill him. The only person who could pull it off would be a lover. Does Putin even have one? I wouldn't be surprised if he's got no interests in that direction. Totally focused on power, which–'

"Which he gets off on?"

Gerasimchuk gave a humorless grin. "Unfortunately, I think so." His phone chirped. "A message from Lilliana. She can't rejoin us and is taking the rest of the day off. What a shame." He picked up the lunch menu and ran a finger down the side. "Now, Tolya. Fancy some divine foie gras?"

Half an hour and one more whiskey later, lunch was served, and Gerasimchuk began to explain his theory about the letter.

"Two days after the missile strike on the Kyiv building housing the letter, a couple of large men arrived at MinFin. One had a briefcase handcuffed to his wrist. I haven't seen the likes of this behavior since the days of the Soviet Union when *politruks* carried US dollars and other treasures around in such a fashion. These two couldn't have looked more like special agents if they'd tried. Samsonov was at HQ that day and took delivery of the parcel. I know, because I was with him in his office at the time, discussing a possible change to income tax rates."

"How do you know what was in the parcel?"

"He told me."

"You're joking!"

"No. He said it was a piece of evidence that would help Russia win the war."

"Did he go into detail?"

"He hinted it was related to NATO and its duplicitous behavior. There would be an announcement around the anniversary of the launch of the Special Military Operation."

The prize was less than thirty yards from his own office. Jacob could feel his heartrate lift. "And he was happy to reveal that information to you?"

"Why not? We were alone in his office. You couldn't hope to meet a more loyal public servant than me. And Samsonov knows it. I have done everything he's asked of me since he took over as the minister. Besides, he couldn't help but feel so superior, knowing that he was the one entrusted with the document's safekeeping."

"But how are we going to get it out?"

"Like Lilliana, I couldn't help noticing that young Irina was immediately attracted to you. Leverage that."

"The thought had crossed my mind, I must admit." Jacob chewed his bottom lip. The morality of leading the woman on worried him, but not as much as failing to retrieve the letter.

"If you do, be careful. From the scuttlebutt about the building, I've heard nothing to suggest she's opposed to the regime. But that doesn't necessarily mean she isn't. A man like you will be able to figure out which way she leans politically, I'm sure."

"That's not a fait accompli. However, I'll give it my best shot."

"She may know a way of getting past the security features to access Samsonov's office when he's away. Doing it without triggering an alarm and all hell breaking loose, that could be another matter altogether."

"Thanks for the positive words of encouragement," said Jacob with a small dose of sarcasm.

"I have a nagging feeling she may be a little out of her depth when it comes to the minister's arrangements." Gerasimchuk pursed his lips slightly before taking another draw on a post-lunch stogie. "You'll have to sound her out on it. Maybe I'm wrong." He smiled, revealing a set of uneven and lightly stained teeth. "It has been known to happen."

The two men finished a dessert of layered honey cake and coffee, putting the bill on MinFin's tab. Gerasimchuk ushered Jacob out onto the street. The two walked in silence back to HQ, leaning heavily into a biting wind that howled off Red Square.

Logging onto his computer for the first time, two emails awaited Jacob's attention. The first took the gloss off the bacchanalian lunch he'd just enjoyed. A request from Samsonov. Scratch that. An order. Deliver by Friday afternoon a comprehensive report—for VVP's review no less—on Russia's prospects of opening up more trade corridors through Mexico and ways to accelerate the process. Thank God it wasn't Turkey or China or Brazil. At least with Mexico, he'd be able to read primary source material in Spanish, translate it into Russian in his mind, then use the program Danilova had told him about to pop out a, hopefully, high-quality report. He'd have to read the damned thing multiple times to make sure it was good enough to pass muster. A glaring mistake from the new wunderkind would send him to a corrective labor colony—if he was lucky.

The second email brought a curling smile to Jacob's lips. It was from Irina Frolova. Innocent, but he could read between the lines of her short missive. *Hi Tolya. So nice to meet you today. If you need any help with tech problems, I'm only an email away.* A smiley face to round it off. And not just any smiley face, a winking one.

Irina's email had lobbed into his inbox only five minutes ago.

He didn't want to appear too eager by responding quickly. The onerous task set by the minister strangely took some pressure off him. He would read up on all things Mexican for the next...a glance at the clock in the bottom corner of his laptop...four hours, continue at home, and get a start on making notes for the report.

After three hours of bookmarking dozens of websites and searching internal databases with information on the Mexican economy, Jacob flexed his fingers. He took a short stroll to his window, looking down at the white fairytale landscape. It was as if he were looking back in time, or perhaps to a place where time stood still. The secure phone provided by Danilova buzzed in his jacket, hanging over the spine of the swivel chair, snapping him out of his daydreaming.

A short note from Fletcher. The number 825, which meant something was up and he needed to check in. He sent back 303, which meant he'd call as soon as he could. No more messages, which signified it wasn't an emergency. If it was, the next number would have been an immediate reply of 112 from Fletcher. Returning the cell to his jacket, Gerasimchuk's words suddenly rang out inside his head. *I don't trust her.*

SIXTEEN

Jacob put his laptop into sleep mode, made for Gerasimchuk's office, and rapped twice on the door. "Come in," came the supervisor's voice after a brief pause. Inside, his desk was smothered under piles of thick computer printouts bound in black plastic folders.

"Can I ask you for some advice?" Jacob plopped his cell phone on a small piece of spare real estate on Gerasimchuk's desk before pulling up a chair.

"Anytime, Tolya."

"I'm thinking of getting a new phone. This one's getting terrible reception. Calls keep dropping out."

"Mind if I have a look?"

Jacob made a please-do gesture with open palms. Gerasimchuk slid open a drawer and retrieved a SIM-eject tool. He opened the casing of the cell and teased out the SIM card. He placed it inside another phone and switched it on before pressing a couple of buttons, ejecting the SIM, and putting it back in Jacob's cell. He slid open another drawer and passed a device that resembled a TV remote control over the phone like an airport security worker. A light flashed intermittently, but no sound was emitted. Jacob heaved a sigh of relief as the technical surveillance counter measures—TSCM—sweep came up negative. Gerasimchuk then tapped the edge of the phone twice on the desk and handed it back. "A good thumping like that usually fixes most problems. I'm sure you won't have to go and buy yourself another one now."

"Thanks," said Jacob. "I should have thought of that myself."

"Glad you dropped by, actually. I was CC'd on your email from Samsonov about the Mexican matter. Looks like a big project early in your new job." Gerasimchuk walked across to a walnut cabinet and pulled out a bottle of tequila. "Fancy a margarita?"

"You have lemons and salt-encrusted glasses in here somewhere?"

"Let me rephrase that. Would you like a shot of straight tequila?"

Jacob laughed as he gripped the doorknob. "Not this time. Maybe to celebrate after I get this report written."

"Don't hesitate to ask for help from me if you need any." He tilted the neck of the bottle toward Jacob. "But be quick about it."

"Why? I've got a whole week. More than generous, I'd say." A month would have been better, but you have to play the hand you're dealt.

"Lilliana and I have been summoned to a meeting in Saint Petersburg. Many of VVP's closest and most-trusted associates live and work there, as you probably know. I'm guessing the minister wants us to have some discussions with the movers and shakers up there."

"When's the meeting?"

"Thursday. We're taking the high-speed Sapsan bullet train. Departs 16:09. We won't be returning until Monday morning."

"I'll bear that in mind."

"You'll get an official email about it later, but Samsonov himself will be accompanying us on the trip."

The hint was unambiguous. Samsonov's guaranteed absence

opened a small window for Jacob to get his hands on the letter. A finger-tip wave to Gerasimchuk and he headed back to his office to carry on with the mind-numbing economic research for another couple of hours.

With the working day over and enough material saved to get a start on the report, Jacob gathered his things and headed for the elevator. Lilliana was a no-go for a ride home, so he exited onto Ilinka and headed right. He'd studied the public transport options for getting back to his apartment and knew it would be a quick ride, just four stops on the subway's red line.

Red Square and the Kremlin's imposing walls loomed ahead through diagonally falling snow. He tugged his ushanka tight over his ears as the breeze stiffened into a strong wind. His nose and the tips of his ears pinched in the cold. He took a right onto Birzhevaya Ploschad—Stock Exchange Square. Street lights created a sheen on the snow-covered pavement, crisscrossed by a myriad of footprints.

City workers, anxious to get home after a hard day at the office, streamed in the same direction Jacob was going, making for the Metro station Ploschad' Revolyutsii—Revolution Square. From there, he would negotiate an underground rabbit warren to get to Okhotny Ryad station, and from there, a direct and fast train ride back to Frunzenskaya station, a short distance from his apartment. A trickle of people was heading back the other way, but not enough to hamper those eager to escape the city center.

Something wasn't right, though.

As the frigid breeze swirled, a nagging feeling in the gut made Jacob want to pull up and check behind him. He stopped close to the wall of a building to allow the bustle of commuters to flow around him. He glanced sideways as casually as he could. Another man, tall and broad-shouldered, dressed in dark clothes, a black woolen scarf wound around his face, leaned up against the same wall maybe twenty yards away, one leg bent with his foot pressed against the brickwork. He was staring intently at the screen of a cell phone—a classic ploy for modern-day tails trying to look innocent. Day one on the job and already being followed. *Not good, Hunter. Not good at all.* He would walk another ten yards, stop, and check again. If the guy was still visible, he'd double back and try to shake him.

He counted off ten paces, then stopped and spun round. The man was nowhere to be seen. Jacob stood on his tiptoes, adding another couple of inches to his already tall frame. He scanned intently, but among all the scurrying people dressed in heavy winter clothes and hats, picking out the tail was impossible.

He let out a sigh—not exactly of relief—steam pouring out of his mouth and nostrils. Was it his imagination? The strain of the last few days would make a stronger man than Jacob Hunter hallucinate like a crack addict.

He squared his shoulders and took off again.

Underground now, passing kiosks, toothless beggars and guitar-playing buskers, he followed the signs to take him to Okhotny Ryad station. This hub used to be named after Karl Marx and still sported a mosaic portrait of the leader of the proletariat. Back in the 1950s it had carried the name of Soviet Deputy Premier Lazar Kaganovich, who somehow managed to escape Joseph Stalin's purges and live to the ripe old age of 97. These days, the name of the station was the same as that of a nearby street and translated into English as "hunter's row"—innocuous enough, but for Jacob Hunter, it sounded slightly ominous.

As he stood on the platform—not too close to the edge, where he'd present a vulnerable target that could be shoved onto the tracks—he decided to execute a "dry clean" maneuver, just to be on the safe side. A southbound train pulled up with a hiss of brakes. The doors clunked open, and he squeezed through the gap, shoulder to shoulder with the crowd. Inside, he surged through the carriage like an ice-breaker, located the second door, and popped back out onto the platform again seconds before the doors closed behind his back. If someone had followed him, they'd be on their way to the next station now, cursing their mistake.

Jacob, slightly more relaxed, jutted out his chin as he studied a poster on the tunnel wall opposite the platform. Government propaganda posters urging men to join the effort in Ukraine. *Sign up today and defend the Rodina*. Maybe it was working, he pondered, as there seemed to be a disproportionately high number of females compared to males out on the streets. Maybe the men were being rounded up from their beds at night and shunted off to the front. Nothing about Putin's Russia would surprise him.

A tap on the shoulder snapped him out of his mental stroll down theory lane. He jerked his head around, right fist clenched and cocked.

"You don't look very pleased to see me." Irina smiled awkwardly.

Jacob loosened his fingers and sucked in a quart of subterranean air. "What?" He marshalled his thoughts as she kept smiling. Was that potential tail something to do with her turning up here and now? Rather a coincidence. He decided to be direct. "Have you been following me?"

She blushed crimson, gloved fingers rolling over each other. "No! Why would I do that?" She laughed awkwardly. "I live in the south-west of Moscow. This is my line."

"Oh." He found the perfect Russian expression. "Mir tesen." *It's a small world.*

"You can say that again."

"What's your station?"

"Frunzenskaya."

"Don't tell me. You've got an apartment in Khamovniki? I think that's what it's called," he said with a slightly disingenuous squint. "I've barely had time to look around much since I rolled into town."

She tilted her head up to look at him. "Well, I can assure you, you *are* in a nice area. Not bad for a newbie."

He thought about telling her his accommodation had been provided for him and that he wasn't paying for it out of his astronomical salary but held his tongue. Talking to colleagues about their paychecks and perks was a road fraught with danger. He decided to switch the focus to her. In his experience, lots of women liked to be made the center of attention. "So where's your place?"

"Prospekt Vernadskogo." She grinned coquettishly; Jacob didn't think she was even conscious of what she was doing with her expressions. "A modest apartment in a soulless skyscraper three blocks from the Metro station."

Jacob had no idea of what the accommodation costs were in that area—or any part of the city, for that matter. Maybe she still lived with family. As if reading his mind, she began to volunteer information like a criminal looking for a plea deal. She did live with her parents, neither of whom were in the best of health. "I've also got a young son who..."

She didn't get to finish the sentence when a train pulled up. Moscow Metro platforms weren't the ideal place to carry on long conversations; a train usually rolled into the station every couple of minutes. Inside the carriage, neither managed to find a seat, so they stood jammed against one another by the door. He wanted to hear more of her story, but he'd have to wait for a better opportunity. With the elevated noise level in the train and the serious height difference between them, he would have to bend down to speak to her. They'd also have to take turns talking into each other's ears to make themselves understood. Way too early for that kind of intimate communication. So instead of chatting, they stared at the window, watching as the blackness of the tunnel raced by.

As he exited the Frunzenskaya station and headed to his apartment building, Jacob resolved to take the next step and be damned with it. He would create an IT problem tomorrow for Irina to fix and ask her on a date.

SEVENTEEN

"I THINK I MIGHT'VE HAD A TAIL ON ME TONIGHT."

"Jesus. Whaddaya mean, you think?" Fletcher's voice sounded scratchy and angry, emphasis on the high-gliding vowels of his strong Brooklyn accent. "You either did or you didn't. Which is it?"

Jacob kicked off his shoes as he stretched back on the sofa. "It was too hard to tell in the conditions. People everywhere, not great lighting, snow bucketing down. Just a typical Moscow night." He explained the other man's behavior and his magician-style disappearance.

"Yeah, that was a tail, all right." The sound of a rasping cough.

"You sound like shit, Grant. Partying too hard in my absence?"

"I'm being leaned on by State. They want a result out of this. Failure could mean Skia getting closed down—it's that big of a fucking deal, my friend. Post discussions, I polished off a bottle of Jack. But I wouldn't call that a party."

Jacob detected real angst coming from across the Atlantic. Not much got Fletcher flustered; he was as cool as they come. Usually. But a threat to shut his operation down had never been made before. Skia was established after the Bay of Pigs incident, its very existence the best kept secret in the world after the recipe for Coca Cola. Despite Fletcher's words, no one was going to shut it down.

"I've only been on the job for one day. Don't panic." Jacob laid on his back to ease the tension creeping along his spine.

"Easy for you to say. If the operation's closed down, I'm screwed financially."

"Spare me the details. Whatever personal choices you made in your life, they're yours to deal with." Those choices included an ex-wife who'd bled him dry in a divorce settlement and a current girlfriend, who, Jacob believed, wouldn't hesitate to flay his bank account, too.

"You spare *me* the moral lecture, okay?" The sound of a mouthful of drink being swallowed came down the line before Fletcher continued. "Any idea about who might've put the tail onto you?"

"Danilova's the only candidate in my mind. But if it was, I'd say it'd be more to make sure I'm not doing anything wrong than to entrap me and get me into trouble. She's anxious for me to put a bullet between VVP's eyes, remember. She even gave me a gun to do the job with."

"Which VIP's eyes?"

"Vladimir Vladimirovich Putin's."

"Right." A slight pause. "Yeah, now I remember they sometimes call him that. Keep her thinking that's your goal. It's the best way to keep her under control."

"I think she's an alcoholic, Grant. Which concerns me from a control point of view."

"Holy shit," Fletcher moaned. "That's all we need." Another sip of Jack followed by a muffled burp, the ultimate ironical response. "Cheer me up with some good news."

The words poured out: heavy emphasis on the utility of Gerasimchuk, the warm welcome from Samsonov, the general acceptance by the rest of the staff on floor five, and a last comment that, despite Danilova's apparent instability, Jacob viewed her more as an asset than a liability, even *if* she was responsible for setting the tail.

"Just don't do anything to piss anyone off." Fletcher repeated his usual mantra.

"I'll do my best." Jacob tugged off his socks one-handed. "In her favor, this cell phone she gave me is a hundred percent kosher. No tracking. Gerasimchuk proved it."

"What about the apartment you're in, dammit! She was there when you arrived. Have you done a sweep of the place?"

"Beyond a thorough visual check, no. I don't have the equipment. If I get some time to myself tomorrow, I'll check out the local electronic stores."

"They won't have gear sensitive enough to pick up what the pros plant, Jacob, you know that."

Jacob felt his calf begin to cramp. Once he was off the phone to Fletcher, he'd give the home gym a serious trial run. "I guess it would be a waste of time. And you know what? If the phone's clean, as I discovered today it is, then the apartment's gotta be clean. It would make no sense otherwise. Bugging the condo would have limited value, the phone—unlimited."

Jacob could picture Fletcher marching around his Tribeca converted warehouse, wiping sweat from his brow. Time to give him the lifeline, a sense of hope. Without naming her, he told his boss about the IT girl from the fourth floor who was going to help break into the safe when Samsonov and his little entourage were out of town.

"When the cat's away," said Fletcher.

"Let's just hope he hasn't left a mousetrap."

"Don't go in there all gung-ho, okay? You get caught and it's all over."

"You don't need to remind me, Grant. I want to live as much as the next guy."

"Wrong. You need to live more than the next guy. Especially if they are between you and the letter." Another sip, this time a long one. "You got me?"

"Loud and clear."

Jacob ended the call, glad to have the conversation over and done with. He changed into T-shirt and shorts and sat for a while meditating. Fletcher's anxiety distracted him, feeding the demons of doubt in his own mind. The hard prep work was done, he told himself. He'd passed himself off as Anatoly Voronin and, as far as he was aware, at this moment, he was above suspicion. An opportunity was opening up in three days. An opportunity this good might not present itself again.

Meditation over, he switched gears and spent the next two hours working himself harder on the treadmill, weights bench, and dumbbells than he had in months. The equipment Danilova had installed in the apartment was at least equal to the standard of the expensive Chelsea Piers gym he frequented.

At 11:15 p.m., he switched off his computer, pleased with himself that he had just finished reading in the original Spanish a 178-page document produced by an influential Mexican think-tank. It concluded that the future of economic partnerships with Russia was rosy, wars and conflicts notwithstanding. A careful reworking of this very document, combined with a little original content, and his own report for Samsonov would be done.

The last thing he did before falling asleep was to formulate a plan for stealing Irina's heart so she would help him steal the letter.

He woke in a lather at 4:46 a.m.

There was something he'd just remembered about Irina. Something he must have only registered in his subconscious.

A small tattoo on the inside of her left wrist.

A non-Cyrillic letter. The one favored by the die-hard Putinists.

Z.

EIGHTEEN

Jacob logged on to his computer to be confronted by a flurry of emails. Mostly updates on projects going on in other sections of the ministry, news items on financial and economic topics shared by staff members, a birthday announcement for a woman on the second floor. The usual run-of-the-mill stuff you find in white-collar workplaces everywhere. One thing made him smile—staff members had no compunction about forwarding memes and jokes that would be deemed too politically incorrect in America. Including one from Irina. He glanced at the field that showed who the email had been sent to. The naughty joke about a lusty farmer's daughter and a lost traveler had been sent to him only.

Had he been ten years younger, his heart would have been racing. An attractive woman coming on to him, especially in this way, was a dream for lots of men. The wrist tattoo, that was the passion killer. It did make his heart race, but in all the wrong ways.

He wrote back: *Good morning, Irina. I was wondering, if you have a spare moment, could you come to my office? I need help solving a computer issue that's giving me hell.*

Within fifteen minutes, a timid triple tap came on the door.

"Enter!" Jacob called out.

Irina's head poked around the corner, the rest of her following in an awkward stumbling gait. Her eyes stayed glued to the floor as she shuffled to his desk. Then she looked up. "Tolya, I apologize for sending you that joke this morning. It was meant for Galya Voronina, a friend of mine who happens to have the same last name as you. The address field autocompleted, and I assumed the email was going to her." Irina's eyebrows shot up a fraction. "She doesn't even work here!"

Adding the last detail seemed irrelevant, but Jacob nodded approvingly like it made all the difference. "Do you think I'd take exception to a rude joke?"

"Ah...I don't really know you that well. You might."

He let his face muscles relax into a genial smile. "Let me assure you, no joke will ever offend me. Not matter what..."—he paused for effect—"or *who* it is about."

The relief on her face was almost palpable. "Spasibo." *Thank you*.

"I want to be the one thanking you. Please come around here and take a look at something." He had purposely changed the settings to disable a couple of functions. "I can't seem to copy and paste with the shortcut commands."

She side-eyed him. "That's an easy one."

"When you know, everything is easy." He stood, allowing her to take his seat while she tended to the *problem*.

Her slender right hand was a blur as she maneuvered the mouse around his mousepad. Six clicks, her tongue held at the corner of her lips as she concentrated. "Done." She inclined her head to look at him as he towered above her. "Your settings were wrong. I think you changed them accidentally." She offered the hint of a grin. "Although I can't imagine how. Those are default settings."

"I swear, I changed nothing." The lie sounded genuine even to his own ears.

"If you say so," she said doubtfully. "I guess it could have been an accident."

What wasn't an accident was the way he brushed against her body as she stood to let him resume his seat. She didn't flinch or move away; if anything, the pressure from her body increased. Jacob knew if he wrapped his arms around her now and kissed her, she would reciprocate with fervor.

But he didn't. His actions at work would be professional and above reproach at all times. They'd have to be. There was no guarantee his office was free of bugs and cameras, or even that sweet Irina wasn't wearing a mic. He'd watched her closely as she'd changed the settings on his PC, and his original suspicion was confirmed. The Z on her wrist was clearly defined, maybe two inches square.

When she was three feet from the door, he cleared his throat and asked her directly. "Would you like to meet up later?"

She spun around, eyes wide. "For?"

"I'd like to get your take on how the ministry operates. You've been here longer than me. I'd appreciate your insights."

Disappointment shadowed her eyes. "Oh, sure. Breakout room?"

"I was thinking in a more informal environment. There's a restaurant not far from my new apartment. Let me treat you to dinner tonight after work. If you're not too busy, that is. I think you mentioned a young son."

She waved the concern away. "Not a problem. My parents live with us, so Vova will be fine!"

After she'd gone, another penny dropped. Vova. It was a popular diminutive form of the boy's name Vladimir. Had she named the kid after VVP?

If she was as loyal a Putinist as the outward signs suggested, she'd only help him break into the safe if she thought it would help the regime in some way.

Luckily, he had an idea for that scenario, too.

A DEFERENTIAL SOMMELIER IN a ponytail tilted the bottle, took a step back, and waited for the guest to approve of the wine. Jacob took a sip, nodded, and their glasses were filled with a minimum of fuss before the man disappeared like mist.

"Now," said Jacob, swirling the dark maroon merlot, watching as a thin viscous film adhered to the side. "Tell me how much I'm going to love working at MinFin."

"What can I say? You might love it, you might hate it. I've only been there for six months."

"Long enough to form an opinion, no?" Jacob took a bread roll from a wicker basket, broke it in two with his hands, and smeared butter over one half.

Irina shuffled a napkin in her lap. "I don't think it is. Besides, our roles couldn't be further removed from each other. What I do is mundane compared to the policy stuff you're involved with."

"At least you get to meet a range of people."

"Yes, but they only want to talk to me when something's wrong."

"Ah ha. Was that a dig at me for doing exactly that?"

"Not at all!" she protested. "As for my impressions of the workforce at MinFin? Most people seem...nice."

"Nice? That's very diplomatic."

"You get the odd one who's always angry when technology goes wrong."

Jacob nodded slowly. "I knew a few people like that back in Vladivostok. Financial advisors are the worst. They pick bad investments for clients, then blame the software."

Irina laughed along with Tolya.

"It's funny. I barely know you." Her voice was low despite there being no other customers within earshot. "But"—she took a sip of her wine, smacking her lips appreciatively—"I've got a really good feeling about you already. About your character, I mean."

"I didn't take it any other way." He nibbled on his roll and dabbed a crumb from his lips. "You've been dodging the issue, though."

"I have?"

"Yes. There must be people in the building who aren't *nice*, as you put it. Tell me who they are."

"Promise you won't tell on me for gossiping?"

"Cross my heart."

She took a long breath and drank a little more wine. She seemed hesitant to speak out of school. As Jacob expected, it turned out to be petty stuff. And mainly about other women in the office and how they groveled in front of the boss. Of course, the men did, too, but not to the same degree.

"And you don't fawn all over Samsonov?"

"I don't have to. My university lecturer is the minister's cousin, remember?"

Jacob shook his head. "I would've thought that would put more pressure on you, having to live up to the recommendation."

"Believe me, we are all under pressure. Fail to perform, and he has no hesitation in firing people."

Now was the time to play his hand. *Be subtle, Hunter.* "And I guess it's important to be dedicated to the president and the Special Military Operation, too. Dissenters wouldn't be welcome in such an important branch of the government."

The waiter annoyingly interrupted. He strode up to the table carrying an oversized plate in each hand: beef stroganoff for him, baked salmon for her. As he departed, Jacob repeated his observation, since Irina seemed to have forgotten his words or chose not to respond to them.

"Hmm." She inspected the giant fish, whose tail and head jutted slightly over the edge of her plate. "I guess so."

"You don't sound too sure." Jacob turned his head slightly.

She glanced up, a hint of alarm in her eyes. "Oh, no. I am sure. No dissenters, perfectly right."

"I thought so," he said, stabbing a chunk of meat with a fork.

"That quirky tattoo on the inside of your wrist kind of advertises where your loyalties lie."

She involuntarily tugged at the sleeve of her blouse, but it failed miserably to cover up the inkwork. Realizing it was pointless, she pushed the sleeve back to reveal the tattoo in all its patriotic glory. "Oh, this?"

"Who's the artist? I might get one myself."

She looked left and right, then sighed. "It was a mistake, to be honest. Galya and I were out on the town celebrating after I was told I'd landed the job at MinFin. Too many shots, I guess. I can't even remember getting the damned thing. Woke up with a hangover, and there it was!"

"But you're glad you got it, aren't you?"

"Sure." There was no conviction in her voice as she scooped up a piece of pink salmon flesh. "At least it's not on my forehead." She gave a sarcastic laugh.

"Be straight with me," he challenged. "You don't like it, do you? I saw you trying to pull your sleeve down to hide it just now."

"It's no big deal." She rested her fork on the plate. "You know, I'm not really interested in politics."

"But how can you not be, considering who you work for?"

"To be honest, I sometimes wonder whether it's worth staying on. The pay's lousy, for one thing."

"It is?"

"Why do you think I'm living in a shitty apartment with my mama and papa and 15-year-old son."

Jacob gulped. "How old did you say he was?" This meant she must be closer to his age than he first thought. He blinked, reassessing. An internal head shake. She barely looked twenty.

"He's fifteen. Actually, nearly sixteen. Two more years and he could be swallowed up by the military-industrial complex." Her voice started to shake. "He's delicate." She dropped her voice to the softest of whispers. "I think he might be gay. If he's conscripted into the army, they'll...kill him."

Jacob reached across the table and caressed the top of her hand. "Surely Samsonov will get him an exemption from the draft."

"He didn't do much to get my brother out of prison," she said sharply. "Not until I...oh, it's horrible to think about it."

Jacob's knife slipped out of his grasp and clattered on the plate. "What?"

"He made me..." She stared at the tablecloth, then slowly raised her head. "I don't want to talk about it."

"Come on, Irochka. Maybe I can..."

"What can you do? Nothing." She dropped her voice again. "All right, I'll tell you. Have your heard of that American woman, Monica Lewinsky? Yes, of course you have. We've all heard of her. The big difference between me and her is that I wasn't exactly a willing participant." She extended her hands to the side of her body. "But hey, it got Igor out of prison."

"Oh my God," Jacob seethed. Samsonov using his power advantage as leverage for self-gratification was the lowest of the low. "What a bastard."

"Yes," she hissed. "Welcome to MinFin. I've said plenty already, so why not keep going?" The whispering had stopped, but now Jacob thought it more appropriate than ever.

"Shhh." He increased the pressure on her hand. "You said you trusted me. Tell me more about your brother."

The door to the restaurant opened and activated a bell sound, making Irina jump slightly in her seat. Diners leaving. "He attended a protest."

"Lots of people attend protests. Not all of them end up in jail."

"The ones holding up signs and those too slow to get away from the OMON do."

Jacob poured more wine for both of them, finishing the bottle. He asked Irina if a second bottle was a good idea. She said it was the best idea all day. "And you know what else would be a good idea?" She didn't wait for him to respond. Through clenched teeth, she hissed, “Fucking laser treatment to get rid of this motherfucking tattoo. I hate it!”

NINETEEN

"Is this really your apartment?" Irina's eyes glowed as she removed her hat, gloves, and coat. Jacob took them from her outstretched hand and draped them on a peg by the door before hanging up his own winter street clothes. "I can't believe it!"

"It was provided by the ministry."

"You don't even pay for it?"

He shrugged. "I've got a feeling there'll be a large deduction made from my first paycheck at the end of the month."

She stood awkwardly in the hallway. Jacob suddenly understood: Although a new recruit at the office, he was so far above her in the pecking order she feared doing anything without being asked first. He gestured toward the sofa. "Please, take a seat. Coffee?"

She nodded. "Thank you, yes. I've had way too much wine."

"You wouldn't want to wake up with another surprise tattoo, would you?"

She burst out laughing. "Never!"

He fussed about in the kitchen, then brought them both cups of extra-strong percolated coffee. "I'll drive you home after the effects of the alcohol have worn off." Which wouldn't be long; Irina had consumed the bulk of the wine.

She nodded. "Thank you. I don't stay out too late these days. Except for that night on the town with Galya. It's my parents, they worry so much. And I worry about them."

Jacob sat opposite her in an armchair. He eyed the digital clock on the wall. Only 10:15 p.m. Still relatively early. This morning before heading off to the office, he'd combed every inch of the apartment, peering into everything that opened and shut, but found no evidence of bugs. He'd already been careless speaking openly on the phone with Fletcher while he was in the apartment; however, there had been no repercussions. If the bad guys were listening in, Jacob would've been apprehended and thrown into a cage by now. Still, he pushed a CD into the stereo slot and turned up the volume as loud as he could without making conversation unpleasant. Classical. Tchaikovsky.

"Tell me about your son."

For the next five minutes, she waxed enthusiastic about her kid. How he loved to help around the house, doted on his grandparents, tried his best at school. "But the bullying is really getting to him. I've told him to act less effeminately, but he can't. There's something inside him that makes him the way he is, and no matter how much I want it to be different, it never will be. He is what he is."

"Do you get any help from his father?"

She rolled her eyes. "Vova's father was a student from Kenya. Our relationship was short and strained. He lived in a hostel on the outskirts of town for three years, then he was gone. Vova was born after he left."

Jacob sucked in his breath. The kid was possibly gay and half Kenyan. In today's intolerant Russia, this was not a combination for a successful and happy life. "Is there any contact between Vova and the father?"

She tilted back her head and laughed. "You're joking! He had his fun with me, finished his studies, and went back to Kenya with his fancy engineering degree. I wouldn't even know where to start looking for him, even if I wanted to." She sipped her coffee, and with shaking hands put the cup back on the table with a rattle. "At least I got my son as a gift out of the relationship. I love him so much it hurts, but I worry for his future."

The pair sat quietly for a while, listening to the muffled hum of the traffic rolling along the Moskva River embankment.

"How would you like to secure a better future for him?" said Jacob, hearing his own words coming out of his mouth like a salesman's pitch. "One without fear of being drafted into the army or being bullied by his peers?"

"Dream on!" Tears poured out of Irina's eyes. She rocked back and forth on the sofa for a few minutes before pulling herself together again. "We are stuck in this country like back in the days of the Soviet Union. My father keeps saying how much better things were then. Now I'm starting to think he might be right. No, all I can do is keep my head down, try and earn as much money as possible, just battle on day to day. And teach him to be tough and resilient."

Jacob could scarcely credit the transformation from cheerful colleague earlier in the day to agonized mother. He got up from his chair and wrapped an arm around her shaking shoulders. "I think I can do something to help, but it's going to take a lot of courage on your part."

"Do you have any tissues?" It was as if she hadn't heard his offer of a lifeline. Or perhaps she thought it was a bad joke. Or perhaps she didn't have the courage.

He found a box of Kleenex in a hallway cupboard, along with enough domestic cleaning and bathroom products to last through the apocalypse. Danilova and the fixers who set up this apartment must have thought he'd be working at MinFin for years. His gut was telling him that he'd either be out of Russia within days or languishing in Lefortovo prison.

Irina dabbed her eyes and blew her nose, finished her coffee, and demurely asked Jacob to take her home.

"Of course. But you haven't responded to my offer to help your son."

She twisted her lips into a knot. "I don't like being indebted to people."

"You would owe me nothing. But before I set the wheels in motion, I do need your help to get something done. If you agree, your life will be transformed in a way you could never imagine."

"How will my life change?"

"I'll take you and Vova back to the United States."

Her jaw nearly dislocated itself. "*Back to?* Who the hell are you?"

EIGHTEEN MINUTES LATER, Jacob pulled into the slushy driveway of a monolithic light-gray building on Ulitsa Koshtoyantsa, three blocks from Prospekt Vernadskogo metro station.

"This doesn't look like the safest of neighborhoods. Do you want me to escort you to your front door?"

She shook her head before reaching around to collect her bag from the rear seat. Back facing him, she set her jaw and said, "I'll be fine. I know all the local thugs." She forced a smile. "Besides, I'd rather you didn't see where I live. It's embarrassing after your place."

He kept both hands on the steering wheel, quelling an urge to wrap his arms around her and pull her in tight. "As you wish."

With the door half open, she turned to look at him. "I've decided."

Jacob's heart stopped. "And?"

"I'm coming with you."

"Good. And I'm coming with you now. We need to talk some things through."

TWENTY

"No, Jacob. Absolutely not. Out of the question. What you're asking is impossible."

"Then I'm coming back to America without the letter."

With the phone on loud speaker, the huffing and puffing sounds from Tribeca sounded like they were in Jacob's lounge room with him. "Find another way, dammit."

Jacob opened the right-side door of the huge fridge and scanned the two racks of soda cans. "I don't know if I'll get another window like this. The minister and his key people are going to be away in Saint Petersburg from tomorrow, I've got the IT specialist on our side. She's got a grudge against the regime like you wouldn't believe. There will not be a better opportunity." He popped the top of a can of lime-flavored Borjomi mineral water. If he could source this tasty stuff in NYC, he'd be ordering it by the pallet.

"You running around with a fugitive from the Russian law is a recipe for disaster," Fletcher growled.

"Two refugees, Grant."

"What the fuck! I don't want that Danilova woman messing everything up. You yourself said she was flaky as a...what was it again?"

"Old clapboard. But it's not her."

"Who is it? Not Gerasimchuk. No way. He's been a sleeper for us longer than Rumpelstiltskin."

"I'll give you a seven out of ten for that one." Jacob grinned as he tossed the empty can in the trash. "No. I'm taking the woman and her son with me. She won't cooperate if we don't offer them a way out. Man, you've got no idea, but you can feel the repression in the air here."

"That's not our concern. You're a professional. You have never made one of these crazy requests before."

"It's not a request, Grant. It's a condition. She disables the safe alarm, I swipe the letter, then I disappear. They're going to put two and two together and get treason. Her life will effectively be over. She's anguished enough as it is leaving her parents and brother behind, but I told her reprisals won't extend to them."

"You know that's not true."

"Yes. And so does she. But I've managed to convince her that her son should be the only priority in this equation. There's no future for a kid like him in Russia today."

"A kid like what?"

"I'm not going into that, Grant. It's not relevant."

"I need to be clued up about who we're rescuing here. Is he a retard or something?"

"Grant! Please. I'm not arguing the point with you. If State wants this letter back, you've gotta play it my way. Safe Route Blue via the Finnish border. End of conversation."

"You do realize they've started to build a fence along the border. Safe Route Blue–"

"I'm up to speed on this. The border isn't going to be fully fenced for another three years. It's 800 miles long, and I know there have been successful illegal crossings in the last year. And that's without the budget we have. Tell me where there's a gap we can cross, send me the coordinates. Get onto whoever gets things done in Finland. Make it happen."

"The Finns won't like Russian nationals crossing into their territory without visas."

"I understand that they have their rules. Get them to make an exception. It's getting late here, and I still need to work on this report."

Fletcher coughed exaggeratedly. "What? You're planning the great escape and you still want to do that?"

"Anything can happen between now and then. If she can't get into the safe between now and when Samsonov returns, I might have to play the long game."

"How confident are you she can do it?"

"She told me there are myriad redundancies in the security system. If she deactivates one pathway, back-ups will kick in. Meaning she has to do a lot of homework."

"Let me rephrase that. How confident is she of cracking it?"

"Fifty-fifty." Jacob paced the floor of his vast bedroom while a silence reigned over the line. He spoke first. "Well? Are you going to talk to the Finnish side?"

"Yes." The single-syllable reply was long, drawn-out and reluctant. "I'll get onto our team in Helsinki. It's very late at night here, so–"

"It's early morning in Helsinki. There's no time difference between Helsinki and Moscow. Call whoever you have to in..."—he glanced at his watch—"ninety minutes."

"I'll text you when I've got the information you need."

"That's the spirit, boss. I'll be waiting." A kettle whistled in the kitchen, and Jacob terminated the call. A cup of black tea and toast, followed by a twenty-minute drive to the office. Today would be a good day. If only because—all going well—it would be the last day he'd be looking at that smug Samsonov's face, a face in different circumstances he would rearrange with the greatest of pleasure. Hell, he wouldn't begrudge putting a bullet between his eyes on Irina's behalf.

THEY MET for lunch at a nearby fast-food joint. He needed to double-check her commitment, expressed last night under the influence of alcohol and the pressure of emotion. Half-invested wasn't good enough; he had to be sure. The venue was a rebranded McDonald's across the street from the historic Hotel Metropol. The food and the uniforms were the same as before the American franchise closed the books, and the place was busy.

"Looks like the sanctions don't always work the way they're intended," said Jacob, reaching into a cardboard packet of fries. "This one seems to have backfired grandly."

Irina nodded. "Lots of these outlets simply changed identity after the head company pulled out. Trading just as well as before, if not better." She opened a burger wrapper, took the top off the bun, and removed a slice of pickle. "Some of our millionaires have become billionaires since the sanctions, and the billionaires multi-billionaires." She chewed thoughtfully. "So much for blacklists."

"I was rather impressed with your son," said Jacob, watching the crowd of customers for any signs they were being surveilled. Nothing raised his suspicions. "He won't let us down." These were no mere empty words. Jacob had sat with the boy in the cramped kitchen of Irina's apartment. Irina had said she was embarrassed by her living arrangements, Jacob recalled, but there was no need to be. She was doing the best she could to look after herself and three other people on a shitty salary. Her elderly parents had gone to bed, leaving Jacob with the opportunity to test Vova's mental fortitude for what lay ahead. Vladimir—only his mother and grandparents called him Vova—sported what conventional Russian society would call a provocative hairstyle, wore tight-fitting black jeans and a black T-shirt with the motif of a band Jacob had never heard of. Fading out of fashion in the West now, the Goth look took Jacob back to a brief phase of his own youth when he'd flirted with this subculture. For someone being systematically bullied, Vladimir not hiding his sense of self spoke of an underlying courage.

I'd do anything to get out of this place, he'd said. *Things are only going to get worse, especially for someone like me.*

The risks are huge, Jacob warned. *Lots could go wrong if we are caught.*

I don't care, he'd replied. *Just get me out of here.*

Irina stirred sugar into a Styrofoam cup. "I'm proud of the way he won't deny who he is. Even if it comes with negative consequences. I've asked him to be less flamboyant, but he simply cannot conform." Her eyes gleamed as she held his gaze. "We'll be all right, won't we?"

"If we commit to whatever we decide to do, then yes." He sipped his coffee, wincing at the bitter aftertaste. "Tell me how we're going to retrieve the prize I told you about. You've had all night to think about it. What's your plan?"

She shook her head slowly. "I've had more than that to think about. I've not slept more than two hours after what you told me. About you, about...work. And the plan is based largely on hope and optimism..." She paused, looked up from her food, and smiled in a childlike way. "...Tolya."

Jacob smiled. Like Gerasimchuk, she would keep playing the role until the game was won. Or lost.

"Let's head outside." Jacob stood and gestured toward the door. "It's a nice day for a change. We can walk and talk."

Bright sunshine bounced off the walls of ancient and new buildings, reflecting off snow piled up on the edges of the sidewalk. The temperature had risen appreciably, too, and many people paraded the streets hatless, gloveless, and scarfless. It was a brief reprieve, with a biting cold front forecast to hit western Russia at the end of the week. *Tough luck for the locals,* Jacob thought. *We'll be well clear by then.*

"I've created a diagram of the wiring and circuitry for the alarm system, sat there studying it half the night. I think I've found a way I can override the security settings to get into Samsonov's office."

"You think?"

"Ninety-nine percent sure. I only have to switch off the part that connects to his office; other zones can stay on. That should make things a lot simpler. And quicker." She stopped. "On the other hand, if I were to disable the entire system—cameras, locks, alarms, the works, then it might look like the electricity supply had tripped and caused a power outage."

"Isn't there a backup power supply somewhere? A generator in the basement?"

She chewed her nail. "Yes, of course there is," she said.

"No big deal. Just focus on his office and any other infrastructure that might get in our way."

"Okay."

"And the safe itself?" Jacob pursed his lips. "That's going to present the biggest problem, isn't it?"

"For me, no." She smirked.

"What do you mean?"

"It's not an electronic safe. It's the old-fashioned kind with three of those little combination wheels."

"How do you know?"

"I saw it one time when he was putting something in it. He'd called me in to sort out an Excel problem."

"And he didn't say anything?"

She shrugged. "No. He carried on with what he was doing like I wasn't even there. Besides, I'm a loyal employee who passed all the checks."

"Fair enough. I didn't see the safe when I was in his office. Where is it?"

"It's cliché, but he has the thing set into a wall behind a portrait of guess who."

Jacob burst out laughing. "VVP!" The humor was short-lived. No chance the combination was written down anywhere. It was likely Samsonov changed it on a regular basis. Which left only one option.

Breaking into it.

"I've got no experience in safecracking," he said. "It's something of a dying art." He turned to her as they rounded the corner onto Bogoyavlensky Pereulok. "I don't suppose you know any bank robbers, do you?"

"None. All my friends are law-abiding citizens, just like me."

Jacob strode on, hands behind his back, a pose that he believed helped him come up with genius ideas. On this occasion, it wasn't working. He pulled up. "I'm going to have to consult with my people on this one. Maybe we've got an asset in Moscow who can help."

The pair walked briskly until they reached the Alexander Garden nestled between the Kremlin and the Moskva River. On a red slatted bench, Irina scrolled her VKontakte page while Jacob put in the call he was hoping he wouldn't have to make. E for Embassy.

On the third ring, a voice answered. "Code?"

"Ardalion."

"What do you need?"

He quickly explained what he required, using the minimum of detail. Either a person who could crack a safe or someone who could show Jacob how to do it.

"Wait where you are. Someone will be with you in under thirty minutes."

Once the call ended, he sent Irina back to the office. They had spent too much time together as it was. If someone from work saw them together, they might conclude the two were caught up in an office romance, something that was frowned upon at MinFin.

As the sun ducked behind a swelling bank of clouds moving in from the north, Jacob began to shiver. Either he was coming down with something or the enormity of this mission was starting to hit home. Shoulders hunched, he pulled out his cell again and read state-approved headline news on the Pravda.ru website. He skimmed through a feature story on MinFin's *Nurture* program. He shivered again. The article noted that a special report on international trade was being prepared for the president's approval next Monday.

His report.

Unfortunately for VVP, the document would be nothing but a regurgitation of boring and meaningless data from the Mexican government mixed with what journalists like to call filler.

There was no time to start reading the next story on his cell phone. A firm hand clapped Jacob on the shoulder, making him jump in his seat. "Ardalion?"

"Da."

The contact, a man of medium build, pale complexion, and a trim beard and moustache, slithered onto the park bench like a snake. He thrust his legs straight out in front of him and crossed his feet. He refused to make eye contact with Jacob and stared directly ahead. He reached into his pocket and wedged a small package snugly against Jacob's thigh. Out of the corner of his mouth, he said, "Na tebye." *There you go.*

"What is it?"

The man turned his head slowly and hissed, "Babakh!" Then he stood and casually strode away, hands shoved in his pockets.

It's explosives, Jacob realized. The English equivalent of the final word the man had uttered was—kaboom.

TWENTY-ONE

He could scarcely believe this small parcel had been put together and delivered before he'd had time to properly read the news. You can't get a pizza delivered in Manhattan that fast. Inside the brown paper bag were a small block of plastic explosive in a Ziplock bag, a wired detonator cap about the size of a pencil, an old Nokia cell phone, and a piece of paper with instructions written in English. He read the instructions and memorized them. Another item brought a smile and a sigh of relief. Marina had made good on her promise and arranged for his real US passport to be sent via diplomatic bag to Moscow.

The parcel found a home in the inside pocket of his long overcoat. He stopped a random stranger who was smoking as she walked past and asked politely if she had a spare cigarette and could she light it for him. The woman's face broke into a delighted smile; she ran the tip of her tongue along her top lip as she offered him a Marlboro. She even lit it for him, her eyes never leaving his. He took a drag, nodded his thanks, and turned to walk away as her face fell in disappointment.

Several yards farther along the path, he turned to make sure the love-struck stranger wasn't following him. No sign of her. Good. He ducked behind a thick-trunked fir tree. He sucked hard on the cigarette and touched the glowing red tip to the instruction paper. In a few seconds, it caught alight, and he placed it on a bare patch of earth under the evergreen needles. He stood watching until it had burned to ash.

The concept of rigging the explosive to the safe was clear in his mind. What wasn't clear was how much noise it would make, and would it destroy the very thing inside that he was trying to retrieve. The latter, although a suboptimal result, was at least better than the original letter being released. Still, he'd do his best not to turn the letter into a smoldering pile of soot or blow up Samsonov's office.

HE GLANCED up at the ceiling. Surely respect for human dignity precluded cameras being installed above the stalls in the men's bathroom. Assuming even MinFin wouldn't sink to that low level, Jacob placed a small square of notepaper on his thigh. He scribbled a couple of questions the CIA sleeper might be able to answer. Fletcher was onto it from his end, but the Russians might have different information. Perhaps more accurate information. And with Gerasimchuk leaving the office shortly to prepare for tomorrow's trip with the minister, if he didn't ask now, it would be too late.

In Gerasimchuk's office, chaos still reigned. Papers, files, and archive boxes fought for space on his desk. "Don't mind the mess. Just sorting through stuff for the Petersburg trip," he said offhandedly. "I wouldn't want to forget anything important."

"Of course not." Jacob felt his tie squeezing his neck, loosened the knot, and slipped a finger underneath to undo the collar button. The relief was instant. Although the shirts he'd been supplied were top-quality, they were half a size too small. He was sure he hadn't gained weight since leaving the USA; if anything, he'd shed a few pounds under the constant stress. Wearing smart business clothes five days a week wasn't something Jacob Hunter wanted to get used to.

"How's that report going, Tolya? Samsonov tells me the president is very eager to see what you've come up with. If Putin puts his stamp of approval on your work, you can consider your trial period already completed and your journey up the career ladder underway."

Jacob stretched his arms and yawned. "I should have it finished by Friday, ready for VVP to run his eyes over. There are a couple of areas I'm not clear on. Import taxes and excise duties, that kind of thing."

"Excellent." Something on Gerasimchuk's computer screen caught his eye. "One moment." He pushed his glasses back up his nose as he clicked and scrolled, eyes darting left to right as he read. "Oh dear. You'll have a copy of this email in your inbox."

"What do you mean by *oh dear*?"

"It looks like you need to get a move on. The minister would like to see a draft tomorrow morning before we leave for the northern capital."

Jacob inhaled deeply. "It's still in the form of rough notes, and that's putting it mildly. I wasn't planning on sketching out the first draft until tomorrow, so I'm not sure how it'll be ready on time."

A chiding finger waggled from the other side of the desk. "That's not the can-do attitude we've been led to believe you live by. Any chance of speeding things up?"

"Every chance."

"Good to hear." Gerasimchuk clicked his mouse again, then turned his full attention back to his visitor. "I never asked why you dropped by. Is there something I can do for you?"

Jacob coughed into a fist. "Actually, there is. You said before I should seek help if I thought I needed it, right?"

"Of course. My door is always open."

"Maybe you could make some inquiries about the economic situation in some of the outlying areas of Russia. Specifically, these questions." With the tip of his index finger he pushed the piece of notepaper across the table, gesturing to it with a downward tilt of the head.

Gerasimchuk again adjusted his perpetually loose reading glasses, picked up the paper, and twisted his lips. He glanced at his watch and said through gritted teeth, "I wish you had come to me sooner with this. On such a tight schedule, I'm not sure I can assist. Maybe the people in Regional Development can help you. Here's the number." He turned over the piece of paper Jacob had written on and scrawled a URL. Under it was *NSFW*, astonishingly in English. Jacob raised an eyebrow as he thanked Gerasimchuk, impressed he knew the acronym *not safe for work*.

"Any more questions?" The top of Gerasimchuk's silver dome was all Jacob could see as the man rifled around in a side drawer. Then, rhetorically, "I'm damned if I can find my blasted phone charger!"

"Is this it?" Jacob picked up a black plug with the cord inserted.

The head popped back up. "Yes. I'm always misplacing those damned things."

"Me too," Jacob lied. His photographic memory ensured he knew where all his items were at all times, unless somebody moved them. "Anyway, thanks for the tip just now."

Back in his office, Jacob sweated bullets as he assembled all the points he needed to produce an elegant, if unoriginal report. With three quarters of his notes more or less in the order he wanted, he pulled up the software program Danilova had installed on his laptop. Copy and paste the notes into the appropriate field, hit ENTER, wait for the program to do its magic, less than a minute later, hit PRINT.

Sixty-three pages quietly glided onto the tray of his HP printer. Skimming through the material, he nodded and smiled to himself. He flicked an email to Irina, asking her if she could help with another problem.

"More keyboard command issues?" she said. She stood by the

side of Jacob's desk holding a clear plastic bag which contained an assortment of computer parts and accessories.

"No. Everything's working fine." He handed her the first two pages. "Read this, please, and tell me what you think of my literary style."

She eased into the visitor's seat and began to read the text. Done, she glanced up with a blank expression. "Are you serious?"

"What do you mean?" *Was it that bad?*

"This is...incredible."

He smiled smugly. "I know."

"You're quite arrogant for a probationer." Her eyes locked on to the rest of the document. "Let me read some more." She plucked pages at random, scanned them with visible appreciation, and leaned back in her chair. "To be honest, it's a lot more interesting than I thought it was going to be, considering the subject matter."

"Excellent. I'd hate to let VVP down."

"I don't think it would be a good idea to submit poor-quality material to the president." She made a throat-slashing gesture with her tongue sticking out the side of her mouth.

Jacob quickly made a downward motion with his hands. The subtlety of her black humor might be lost if some FSB goons were monitoring the room. "Have you got that other issue resolved?"

"I think so." Her words lacked confidence. "I'm going to run over all the possible options tonight at home."

Jacob felt his nostrils flaring. "Best of luck with it."

She turned to leave.

"One more thing," said Jacob.

"Yes?"

He beckoned her with a finger. "See to this for me, please."

He'd written on a piece of paper: Meet you on the platform. 18:15.

Just before the end of business, at 16:55, he had produced a paper that an entire department of bureaucrats would be proud of.

"How's your English?"

"Not great, but not terrible," she replied, gripping the center pole near the double doors of the rollicking train carriage. "Why?"

He was confident there was no tail on them. He leaned down to speak in her ear, the ambient noise at a high level. "Because I don't want you pissing off the Finns when we arrive. Once we're there, you and I will speak Russian only when

safe to do so."

She nodded, looked up at him, and smiled. In heavily accented English, she said, "I will try my best."

Jacob said, again in English, "And your son?"

"Are you kidding? He speaks it better than me."

Via a hyper-secure VPN, he typed in the letters of the URL that Gerasimchuk provided. A link to high-resolution satellite imagery, updated daily, of the entire frontier of the Russian Federation. There were separate pages for each country Russia shared a border with. Jacob had never before seen such clear high-res pictures of the Earth taken from space.

He clicked a link and zoomed in on the Russo-Finnish border and visually traced its length, slowly scanning back and forth along the line a number of times. A heavy blanket of snow running the entire length of the border and extending to cover almost the entire landmass of Finland and most of Russia didn't make it easy to determine any suitable crossing points.

He rubbed his eyes, aching from the effort of concentration. His vision had deteriorated over the last twelve months, which worried him. His optometrist had warned him that corrective lenses or surgery would be needed in the next couple of years if the condition worsened. And it *was* gradually worsening. Fletcher suggested it could be a delayed impact of the football collision all those years ago. He insisted Jacob go under the knife—or laser—because a vision-impaired agent losing a pair of glasses or contact lenses in the field could prove disastrous. The boss had a good point, and so Jacob had made up his mind that's exactly what he would do.

If he survived this mission.

The new urgency attached to getting Samsonov's report finished was, ironically, a blessing in disguise. With that task out of the way, it opened a window of opportunity to plan the heist and subsequent escape. He leaned back in his chair, stretching his neck and arms. He'd been studying the satellite images for so long he was sure he would dream about them. It was now 01:45, and the traffic noises of central Moscow had faded almost into nothingness.

His body demanded sleep, yet it wouldn't come. He found a selection of calmatives in the bathroom cabinet. He sluiced down a valerian tablet, the go-to choice in natural sedatives for Russians. Jacob had identified two potential crossing points an independent refugee might choose if they were desperate. Suokumaanjärvi, a lake near the town of Imatra that overlapped the border, and the municipality of Rautjärvi in the South Karelia district. But were either of them realistic?

The more he thought about this route out of Dodge, the less feasible it seemed.

The logistics of staging an illegal crossing in a mild summer would be difficult enough. Instead, they were confronted with a harsher-than-normal winter in northern Europe and heightened geopolitical tensions unseen since the end of the Cold War. Suddenly, the plan of escaping through Finland lost its appeal.

The secure cell phone buzzed on his home office desk. F.

"Yeah?" said Jacob. "It's late."

"Just past 6:00 p.m. here. Sorry, but it's urgent. Helsinki says you will be rendered no assistance at the border at any location you choose to cross."

"Right."

"You don't sound too distressed by the news."

He stood and walked to the glass door leading onto the balcony. Moscow might be a scary city, but it was achingly beautiful. The view from this apartment was one he'd miss. "I've been rationalizing it all in my mind, Grant. I've found out there's a six-mile wide border zone to contend with—about two miles on the Finnish side and five miles on the Russian side. That's wider than the Korean DMZ! Electronic surveillance is state of the art, too. Then there's drones, random dog patrols." He paused to watch a garbage truck doing its nightly rounds of the neighborhood. "On top of that, the journey just to get there on shitty roads would be much too long and arduous. If it was just me in an army tank, maybe. But with two others in tow, driving a sedan designed for city streets... And now you tell me the Finns aren't accommodating."

"They're the antithesis of accommodating. Downright hostile to our request, ironically funneled through the State Department. Their Ministry of Foreign Affairs said any Russian nationals crossing illegally would be returned, no questions. The Finns are not well predisposed to Russians right now." The sound of TV news came over the line. CNN judging by the theme music. "Have you got an alternative?"

"I do. Once the job's done, we fly to Abu Dhabi—there's no visa requirement for Russian citizens entering the UAE."

"Then what?"

"We grab fake US passports there so they can fly to JFK with me."

"This is a big ask, Jacob."

"Excuse me? And what you're asking me to do is what, exactly?"

"Your fucking job. What you get paid to do. Not run a personal people-smuggling operation."

Jacob ignored the remark, accurate though it was. "Put a request in to the US embassy in the Emirates. Ask the techs to create two fake passports, for Irina and her kid."

"I'm not sure they've got the wherewithal to do that in the UAE."

"Bullshit, Grant."

Jacob heard his boss curse under his breath. "They're going to tear me a new one at State." A pause punctuated by heavy breathing. "You've got me wondering who calls the shots in this outfit, Jacob."

Another curve ball, best not to take a swing at it. "Good night, Grant."

TWENTY-TWO

Sunlight ricocheted off the snow-covered roof of the neighboring building, creating a small round spot on the man's shaved skull. It reminded Jacob of a spotlight in the theater.

Samsonov nodded approvingly as he flipped over the last page of the glossy, bound report. A team in the media section two floors down had turned the bland text and simple tables into a document resembling a company prospectus, complete with colored illustrations, graphs, all the bells and whistles. Jacob studied the minister's body language. All positive: open trunk and arms, legs uncrossed, the hint of a smile dancing around his lips as he read quietly. Finally, Samsonov closed the thick folder. "I'm sure Vladimir Vladimirovich will be very impressed by your work, Tolya."

Even though the material was to a large degree created by an AI program using the barest of his own inputs, Jacob's chest puffed out as he experienced a weird sense of achievement. It made no sense, but since flying out of JFK a mere five days ago, not much had.

"Would you be happy to give a fifteen-minute presentation in the Kremlin on Monday evening?" Samsonov leaned in, the positive body language continuing. "The entire inner cabinet will be there for a special briefing, but the president is scheduling a face-to-face with you."

"Of course," said Jacob, mustering peak enthusiasm for a meeting that would never take place. He imagined the surreal scene: separated by 20 feet as he and VVP sat at either end of the famous white beechwood table that was crafted by an Italian master in the 1990s. He looked to the left and saw a massive smile splitting Gerasimchuk's face in two like Pacman. Then to the right, where Danilova beamed like a proud aunt. *The foolish woman seriously thinks I'm going to kill Putin.* "Anything I can do for the betterment of the Russian Federation." The last bit was laying it on thick, but the minister's satisfied smile told Jacob the man had bought it.

Samsonov stood, grabbed his briefcase, and signaled for the two aides on either side of him to get ready; it was almost time to leave. He had a couple of parting words to Jacob before the entourage set off for Saint Petersburg. "I'll make sure my PA sends you all the details of when and where. Also the protocols for meeting VVP, dress code, expected behavior, that kind of thing." He touched his nose. "Very strict, as you can imagine."

"Undoubtedly," said Jacob.

"I've heard a whisper he's planning a weekend retreat at Konstantinovsky Palace early in the spring," Samsonov added. "And that you are on the exclusive list of invited guests."

Another glance to the left. Danilova had her thumb and forefinger pressed to her chin. Perhaps contemplating a more feasible assassination attempt further down the track. Such an option might objectively seem more attractive; she'd be thinking Jacob would have more time to prepare, and perhaps it would afford a better opportunity. The more relaxed atmosphere at a retreat away from the super-tight security of the Kremlin, people off their guard. Either way, the woman was wasting valuable thinking resources. The words *It ain't happening* echoed in Jacob's head.

He bowed reverentially. "I would be honored to attend, Minister."

He sat on a park bench in Alexander Garden, Irina next to him with barely an inch separating the two. They'd finished up at the office at 16:30, the minister and his team long gone. By now, the high-speed Sapsan train would be well out of the greater Moscow area. They could breathe easier. At least until tomorrow morning.

Yesterday, Jacob had worried about being seen with her in close proximity. Now he knew it didn't matter. No one was watching him—or her—and even if they were, he was now a clear favorite of Samsonov. The email about Tolya Voronin's upcoming meeting with the president had gone out to all staff. No one would dare spread any gossip about the new boy wonder.

"You don't mind me sitting this close?" Even as she spoke, she leaned in a fraction harder. She said his big body sheltered her from the chilly nip of the breeze. It was sunny, like yesterday, but the temperature had taken a dive and was set to plummet even further. A blizzard was forecast for the weekend. It justified the decision to abandon the idea of escape through Finland; however, if the weather turned too nasty, it could impact flights out of Moscow. If that happened...*that could not happen*.

"It's fine. But we should be going now. Enough time has passed."

Five minutes prior, the same man from yesterday did a brush-by. He dropped a scrunched-up piece of paper by Jacob's feet. It told him how much of the newly developed plastic explosive to use in order to get the safe open but not bring the entire building down. Turned out, a blob no bigger than a pea was sufficient. He was glad to have double-checked, since his own guess would have been way off the mark.

As they walked to the Lenin Library Metro station, he instinctively snaked his arm through the crook of hers. "Last chance to back out."

She glanced up at him, eyes glistening. "My parents are..." She began to sob.

"They're what?"

"They're going to hate me for what I'm about to do."

Jacob pulled up and placed his hands on her shoulders. "You haven't told them, have you?"

She shook her head. "I'm too scared. I know they want the best for me and Vova, but they'll freak out when we disappear."

"It's best they know nothing, believe me. Keep it that way. Tomorrow's just another day. I know it's going to be difficult, for you and for your son. When—not if—the FSB come knocking, their ignorance will be their salvation."

"You think so?"

"I know so." His lie carried little conviction. The FSB would be anything but civil with Irina's mom and dad, perhaps even brutal. Maybe Irina feared the worst herself. Her brother had already been on the wrong end of the law. Only the most naïve rose-colored-glasses-wearing Putinist believed humane due process was followed in Russia.

"You must think of your son." Jacob switched the emphasis. "Your parents have lived their life. It's time for you and for the next generation."

She shrugged. "I know that's logical. Both of them are nearly eighty. But just abandoning them seems so wrong. I love them!" She dabbed at a tear with the back of her glove. "One positive: they've got the apartment to live out the rest of their lives in. It's old and small, the plumbing breaks down all the time, but at least they have no worries about rent. Their modest pension will tide them over."

"They own the apartment?" Jacob could hear the relief in his own voice. "That *is* something to take comfort in."

"I bought it for them."

Jacob did a double-take. "You bought it? No way."

"Yes. In their name. And thank God there's nothing owing on it."

"I don't get it. You told me your pay was lousy."

She tapped the side of her nose. "I might work in IT, but I

know a thing or two about investing. They like everyone at MinFin to have at least half a clue about money. I worked as a financial planner for a couple of years, got some insider information about start-up tech stocks that were about to go boom. And they did. I sold them for a huge profit. Still, with the crazy real estate prices in Moscow, a shitty little apartment was all I could afford."

"Forward thinking." Jacob smiled. "I like that."

"That's not the only forward thinking I've been doing."

"Tell me about it."

She shook her head, then gave him a rapid wink. "I'm keeping it as a surprise for later."

SHE FLAT-OUT REFUSED his offer to escort her home. *I need time to think*, she'd said. *Time to get deep into the system, double-check everything.* Jacob surrendered easily. Not everyone had his photographic memory, and it made sense for her to go over everything time and time again. Moreover, she was already wound up like a clockwork toy. His presence in the family home would only raise suspicions with her parents and exacerbate her nervousness. He could almost smell her trepidation as he stepped out of the train before she continued the journey for another four stops. A quick prayer to the Almighty that she would have the nerve to carry the operation through to the end. And no fuck-ups.

Now at his Khamovniki apartment, he placed the component parts side by side on the marble kitchen benchtop, made a dummy bomb, then pulled it apart again. On site, he could assemble it in under a minute, detonate it, and run like the devil with the prize. As he made himself a coffee and sent a last-minute text of encouragement to Fletcher that comprised the words *All on schedule*, it dawned on Jacob that Irina's kid, at first glance a pathetic figure, would figure as an asset on their escape. All three of them flying out together would present as a nice, normal family unit to casual onlookers. Yes, Vova was what Russians would call a *mulat*, but it wasn't totally unheard of for two white parents to adopt mixed-race children.

He went through the final steps in his head. Mold the plastic explosive into two small pea-size blobs, place them near the hinges, and wire up. Disconnect the archaic phone's ringer, attach the wires to the blasting cap. When he dialed the number, the phone wouldn't ring, of course, but it would send an electrical impulse to the blasting cap. Then, as the brush-by man had so eloquently put it, babakh!

He placed the parts in a bag, took a valerian tablet, and went to bed.

SHE SAT SIDEWAYS on Vova's single bed; he occupied a swivel gamer-style chair, his back toward his computer screen, which showed a kaleidoscope of colors in pause mode. His face was as blank as a sheet of paper, as if the two hours of non-stop playing his favorite game, *Syberia*, shut away in his private oasis, had given him no joy whatsoever. He rested his forearms on his legs as he leaned over, shoulders slouched, waiting for Irina to speak. She scanned the posters on his walls: emo and goth groups she knew nothing about. An image of a young and androgynous David Bowie took center stage on the wall behind Vova's pillow. He was the only person she recognized in this personal hall of fame.

"Are you sure you want to go through with this?" she said. "I'll call it off if you've changed your mind." *Don't change your mind!*

He shook his head seriously. "No way. This is going to be the best thing that ever happened to me. When you told me we're leaving, it was like a giant hand had reached out and plucked me from the edge of a cliff. No more dealing with those shitheads at school. No worrying about getting called into the army. Whatever it takes, Mama, I'm with you all the way."

She sighed. "I'm so glad we took that trip to Estonia two years ago."

"Is that our escape route?" His tone grew more excited.

She chewed her bottom lip. How much to tell him? "No, it's not that. If we hadn't gone, I wouldn't have applied for your international passport."

"Holy shit, you're right. Then I would've been stuck here forever, waiting to turn into cannon fodder."

She decided to steer clear of specific matters relating to the trip itself. The less he knew, the better. "Don't worry about the details. Tolya hasn't even told me half of it." She paused, then something occurred to her. "I'd like you to look your best for your grandparents tonight. Who knows when we'll see them again." *If ever.* "Do you still have the blue jeans and the set of plain polo shirts Babushka gave you for Christmas?"

Vova tightened his lips. "Yes, Mama." He had vowed to toss them in the trash chute or give them to a beggar on the street, but Irina threatened to cut off his Internet access. *Keep the clothes. Just humor Babushka, okay?* she'd said. He wore the items for a week, then stashed them in the back of his closet under a pile of computer cables. Babushka had nagged him for a while, but soon gave up. The grandparents couldn't get their heads around their grandson's odd behavior, why he dressed in black and wore mascara, but they loved him all the same. They were old-school communists who believed in the International Ideal and the brotherhood of man, and the fact he was half African was a source of pride for them. When they heard racist comments on the rare occasions they ventured outside with the boy, they leapt to his defense. And he loved them for it.

"Could you put them on for dinner tonight?" said Irina. "The green shirt suits you best with the jeans. Those Levi 501s cost Babushka her monthly pension, you know."

His displeasure was obvious. The boy despised wearing conventional clothes, even in his own home. "Do I have to?" he drawled.

"Yes. And please remove all of your piercings. You can put them back in once we're out of Russia." He sported three gold hoops in each ear and a silver one in his bottom lip. She'd thanked God the day he changed his mind about the awful flesh tunnels he'd wanted in his ears. Rather, *she'd* changed his mind, this time by threatening to switch his cell phone plan to pay-as-you-go, with no payments coming from her. He had no income, so the flesh tunnel idea was abandoned. A cell phone trumped everything in terms of must-have technology.

She gave him a maternal hug, then left him alone to get changed. She busied herself in the kitchen making a simple traditional Russian meal of meatballs and fried potatoes, listening to her mother spouting the latest gossip about who in the apartment block was cheating on whom. Her father sipped tea and read a newspaper, shaking his head and tut-tutting every couple of minutes.

Vova emerged from his room, his heavy footsteps drawing everyone's attention. His grandparents gasped. Dedushka blinked like he was a mole emerging into the light, and Babushka's bottom lip trembled. She said, "Young man, I barely recognize you. I thought you'd tossed the clothes I bought you away. My, you look...wonderful. Such a handsome young man you've turned into. Come and let me have a proper look at you."

"Thanks, Babushka," he mumbled, blushing as he approached her. "I'm not sure it's really me, though."

"It *is* you," said Irina, stirring sizzling pieces of potato in a cast-iron skillet she'd owned for fifteen years, as long as her son had been alive. "The clothes we wear don't define who we are."

He laughed. "Then why can't I wear whatever I like?"

"You can. Just not tonight. Because tonight is a special occasion." She pulled plates from an overhead cupboard, doling them out like she was dealing cards.

"It is?" said Babushka. "I might be an old woman, but I know there's no anniversaries or anything like that today. What are you scheming at, Irochka?"

Ladlefuls of caramelized potato and onion dropped onto the blue-and-white plates, followed by juicy meatballs in a garlicky tomato sauce. Irina took her seat, smiling wanly. "I'm not scheming at anything. It's just..." She paused to take a deep breath. Deceiving her parents tore at her insides, like a claw was ripping at her intestines. "I've had a little promotion at work, and I think it's worth celebrating."

A look of confusion crossed Babushka's wrinkled face. "Meatballs and potatoes doesn't seem very...celebratory. I mean, where's the cake? The champagne?"

Irina reached across the table and grasped her mother's liver-spotted hand. "No time, Mama. I only heard the news this afternoon. We can have a proper celebration later. Tonight, I wanted a quiet, sit-down meal with all of us here." She glanced at Vova, who was tucking a napkin into his barely worn green shirt. "With my son out of his cave for a change. But no fuss, just..." She struggled to hold back the tears, ultimately failing as two pearls rolled down either cheek. More joined them until the tears were streaming down her face.

"Goodness, girl!" said Dedushka. "This promotion must mean a lot to you."

She dabbed a tear away. "It does, Papa. It really does."

TWENTY-THREE

THE JARRING ALARM NEARLY TORE A HOLE IN HIS eardrum, his cell erupting into AC/DC's "Jailbreak." The last thing he needed was for his hearing to fail. All senses needed to be on fire today, with some extra help from the sixth one. Together with deteriorating eyesight, his value as a Skia operative would only lie in desk work if he went deaf. No thanks.

His hand slapped around the bedside table like a just-landed fish. He located and grabbed the phone, then killed the alarm. He tore the silk sheet off, leapt out of bed, and marched to the shower.

It was only 02:30, and his eyes stung as needles of hot water bombarded him from the showerhead.

Washed, coffee drunk, dressed, more coffee.

Two nervous leaks.

He dialed a cab company using the cell he'd gotten from Marina. He'd never tossed the device into the Moskva River as per Danilova's request. Chucking it in the drink made no sense. Not only because the river was frozen solid, but the very fact that Danilova wanted it gone was suspicious. He gave the taxi company's dispatcher a pickup address for a Natasha Ivanova three apartment buildings down from Irina's. He called Irina to let her know a ride was on its way and that he was driving into the city. "See you soon."

It's safecracking time.

At 03:37 a.m., Jacob turned up his collar as he rounded the corner at the edge of the building, making his way to the loading bay at the back. Icy snow crunched underfoot with each stride. He readjusted the large sports bag on his shoulder as his feet slipped slightly on a patch of black ice. *Careful, Hunter!* Not a puff of breeze, but the cold ate through to the bones of his fingers, leather gloves proving less than a hundred percent effective. A small, shadowy figure waited for him by the rear door. Irina.

"You mustn't come inside with me. It's too dangerous." He pointed a finger over her shoulder. "Wait in my car. It's in the underground parking garage." He held out his hand with the swipe card to open the gate and the key to the BMW. "Click it and you'll soon figure out which one's mine."

She kept her hands firmly thrust in the pockets of her quilted jacket. "I have to come inside with you. You won't get us into Samsonov's office without me."

"Haven't you disabled his alarm?" He tried but failed to keep the annoyance out of his voice. A scurrying sound came from under a pile of folded cardboard about ten feet away, a rat perhaps. He dropped his voice. "You told me you had that under control."

"Well, I have and I haven't."

"Don't speak in riddles, dammit."

She set her shoulders back defensively. "I'm getting to it. He's had someone install an iris scanner. I've walked past it numerous times and not even noticed. It's a flat panel that almost blends into the wall it's mounted into. I picked it up on my final run over the blueprint of the security wiring, Bluetooth and Wi-Fi points."

"Now I think I remember, dammit." Jabon whistled under

his breath, picturing the scanner that had appeared totally innocuous. "That means only his eye can open it?"

"Normally, yes. But this is part of the forward thinking I was telling you about. Last night I hacked into the system, uploaded super high-resolution digital images of my irises taken in ordinary light and using an infrared light generator Vova bought some time ago. He's an even bigger geek than me. My images then overrode Samsonov's data. Once we're out of here, I'll swap everything back. With luck, they won't figure it out until we are long gone."

"My dear, they will figure it out when they find the safe's been blown and the contents pilfered."

"Yes." She shuffled her feet awkwardly. "There is that." She glanced at her cell phone screen. "Cameras are off until 04:00. Any longer than that and it would raise concerns. Armed men will be turning up to see what the problem is. I suggest we make a move."

He drew a long breath. "Right, let's go."

The first part presented no problems. Irina, a highly trusted employee, simply tapped in a code, the lock unclicked, and they were in the building. Her accessing the building this way also switched off all motion alarms. They had no need to use flashlights, as the corridors were all lit up.

They found the internal staircase, where it was dark and they did have to engage phone flashlights. They trotted on tiptoes, huffing and puffing in their heavy outdoor clothing, to the fifth floor. Within thirty seconds, they were at the door to Samsonov's office.

Irina leaned in toward the iris scanner.

Nothing.

"What's wrong?" said Jacob, unable to contain the irritation in his tone.

"I don't know." She stood back, analyzing the panel. "This appears to be a power button. Maybe I need to switch it on first?"

"Don't ask me, this is your area."

She looked at him squarely. "If we try to break in physically, this panel is going to wail like crazy and send a signal to the FSB. MinFin getting broken into would warrant nothing less than a full Alpha Group squad descending upon us." She paused. "I'm going to have to take the chance."

Jacob's heart pounded like a triphammer as she gently pressed the button, which lit up green. She simultaneously stared at the scanner with both eyes stretched wide. A soft double beep, then the sweet sound of a door's locking mechanism disengaging. She quickly shouldered the door open, Jacob right behind.

Leather gloves now replaced by rubber ones, he carefully removed the portrait of the great leader, looking at least twenty years younger in the picture than he was at this moment in time. "Stand by the door." He knelt and fished out the Makarov he'd been given at the safe house. "If anyone comes, shoot to kill."

"What the hell?" Her hand trembled as she took hold of the gun.

"I assure you, doing otherwise will see your son become an instant orphan."

She gripped the handle with no confidence. "I haven't fired a weapon since military training when I was eighteen."

"That's better than I expected." He turned his attention to the safe. He located the hinges—there were three rather than the expected two. He aligned the wired plastic blobs in the gaps between them. This wasn't in the instructions; perhaps this was some kind of bespoke safe. Maybe it was impenetrable. Fingers crossed it wasn't.

He knelt again, extracting a small blanket. He'd read about bomb blast suppression blankets made of ballistic material. Lacking such material, he thought a small quilted blanket might do the trick.

"I see what you're thinking," said Irina. "But I don't see how that's going to succeed when you're basically working in two dimensions."

"See if you can find some Scotch tape."

She rustled around in drawers, coming up empty. "Your office?"

"Yes, I think so. There's an unlocked stationery cabinet in there." He handed her the key. She returned with a roll of tape in under a minute. With the explosive rigged up, the two of them taped the quilt to the wall. They moved out of the office into the relative safety of the far end of the corridor.

"Here goes nothing," he said, keying in the number to set off the blasting cap. He pressed the call button and held his breath.

"Did you hear that?" said Irina, giving Jacob a quizzical look.

"No, I heard nothing."

They both set off for Samsonov's office, breathing hard due to a combination of terror and excited curiosity.

Inside, there was a faint smell of something acrid, the quilt lying in a smoking heap on the floor, and the safe door open a fraction of an inch.

"My God, it worked!" said Jacob. He grabbed the leading edge of the door with his left hand, gave the side by the hinges a wiggle, and the piece of metal came away completely. With the portrait back in its rightful place, no one would guess there was anything wrong—until they wanted to access the safe.

He stuck his head inside it. It appeared to contain one item: a blue metal box, the kind a small business might keep banknotes and coins in. He pulled it out and tried to open the lid, but it was locked. He handed it to Irina and felt around inside the safe for a key to the box. Just about to give up, he switched on his cell flashlight, and there it was, nestled in the back corner.

"It's 03:50 already, Tolya," urged Irina in a breathy voice, unable to disguise her distress. "The cameras come back on in ten minutes. We have to go."

"Ten minutes is plenty. We have to tidy up first. Quick, give me a hand."

He rolled up the quilt tightly, muscling it back into the sports bag. He gave her a large plastic freezer bag. Both of them got on their hands and knees, picked up and stashed small pieces of debris from the floor. Annoyingly, here and there, feathers had escaped from small tears in the quilt. It took five minutes, but Jacob was eventually satisfied there were no obvious traces of their presence left.

"Three minutes, Tolya. Two to get out of the building if we go NOW!"

Curiosity burned inside his chest. With fumbling fingers, he inserted the tiny silver key into the cash box. He flipped open the lid. "What the fuck!"

"What do you make of it?" said Jacob, setting the GPS for Sheremetyevo Alexander S. Pushkin International Airport.

"It's a code of some kind," said Irina.

"Maybe, maybe not. Use your analytical programmer's brain."

"I've been trying, but the more I think, the less sense it makes to me."

"Can I see it?" said Vova from the back seat. They had picked up a shivering Vova at 05:30 a block away from the family apartment. He'd cut a forlorn figure standing under a street light with a rucksack by his feet.

"Why not?" said Jacob, veering to avoid an oncoming car that had wandered into his lane. He executed the typical Russian driver's reaction. Double flash of high beam accompanied by the middle finger and a muttered oath that questioned the other driver's parentage.

Irina turned and handed her son the piece of paper retrieved from inside the safe. Aside from that scrap and a gold wedding ring, the box had been empty.

"BHS followed by twenty-four numbers." Vova's lips moved silently for a moment as he scrolled his cell phone. "I'm working on a hunch here. Where do all the filthy politicians and oligarchs hide their stuff?"

"Off-shore," said Irina.

"Many countries operate as off-shore tax havens," said Jacob. "Beliz, the Caymans, Panama, the list is long." He furrowed his brow in thought. "BHS. Could be the Bahamas?"

"Plausible," said Vova.

Irina held up a finger. "But we're not talking about money. We're talking about a letter. Something tangible that needs to be kept in a safe place."

"More plausible," said Vova.

"And which country is famous for its ultra-secure safe deposit boxes?" said Irina.

"Switzerland," said Jacob, optimism lifting the inflection of his voice. "My God, it's making sense."

"To have a safe deposit box in Switzerland, you first have to open an account," said Irina. "I'd bet the number on that piece of paper is an account number for a Swiss bank. Samsonov's account."

Vova cleared his throat. "Google tells me Swiss bank account numbers have twenty-one digits. We've got an extra three here, so maybe that's not it."

Jacob thumped the steering wheel. "Dammit. The combinations are infinite. I've set my own passwords and codes, with certain numbers and letters just in there as fillers. I mean, maybe you have to remove the first three here, or the last three, or the first two and the last one, or..."

"Or three from the middle," said Vova.

"Right. But, like you said, it might have nothing to do with–" said Jacob.

"Bahnhofstrasse," blurted Irina. "I've just remembered from my days at the investment company. That's what the BHS is in front of the numbers, I'd bet anything on it. Bahnhofstrasse is the street in Zurich where many of the main banks are located."

"Excellent," said Jacob. "Our winter clothes will still come in handy."

"Are we flying to Switzerland now?" said Vova, clearly excited by the prospect.

Jacob turned his head. "No. We still have to fly to Abu Dhabi first. There are no direct flights to Switzerland from Moscow at the moment. Once there, my organization will book flights to Zurich for me and the USA for you two. New York to be precise."

"We're not coming with you?"

Jacob shook his head. "You're both already in enough trouble as it is."

Irina gave him a challenging stare. "But–"

"No buts." He thought about how much Irina reminded him of Sally-Anne Vincent. She had been murdered because of her connection to Jacob. He wouldn't risk that happening again. "I've made up my mind. Either do as I say or I turn back now and drop you back at Prospekt Vernadskogo."

Irina folded her arms tightly across her chest and stared through the windscreen into the inky blackness. Jacob caught Vova grinning in the back seat. The kid was already dreaming of his new free life in America.

They drove the almost deserted highway another fifteen minutes before Jacob swung the BMW into a rest stop two miles from the airport. With their Emirates flight still six hours away, it was too early to arrive and hang about without arousing suspicion. Since Russia had hosted the soccer world cup in 2018, regulations had been introduced to combat loitering in the terminals; even sleeping was officially banned. Better to wait it out, even though their collective nerves were stretched tauter than the skin of a pregnant woman's belly at the nine-month mark. They ate a leisurely breakfast Irina had prepared for the road, airing theories about how the hell they were going to, one, figure out which bank the safe deposit box was in and, two, how the hell Jacob was going to access it without knowing the account number and not having a key.

"Apparently a person from the bank will have one key, and the account holder another," said Vova, neck craned over the glowing screen of his cell phone. "Both are required to access the box." He looked up again. "We potentially have the account number in front of us, but no key."

"And even if this scenario is the correct one," said Jacob, "we have no idea of the name of the damn bank!"

Irina stared out at the dark forest surrounding them, concentrated on breathing regularly. "What if...what if part of that number is simply a street address hiding in plain sight?"

Jacob wiped droplets of coffee from his lips and returned the thermos to the console. "Vova, look up as many banks as you can with branches on Bahnhofstrasse, see if any of their addresses match the numbers at the beginning or the end of the code."

"Will do."

"Let's all look for it," suggested Irina.

Like contestants in a Rubik's cube competition, they searched feverishly for the answer.

"Got it!" cried Vova within twenty seconds. "120 Bahnhofstrasse. Zurich Security Funds AG."

"That's the first three digits in the code," said Jacob.

"Meaning the rest of it must be the account number," said Irina triumphantly.

Vova held up a finger. "Not necessarily. It could still be a jumbled code."

"At this point in the game, I'm going to assume the digits are in order. There's no other way around it. Unless our government can make representations to the Swiss and force them to give us access, which I highly doubt, I'm going to have to get that letter some other way."

"What other way?" said Irina.

"The same way we got this fucking piece of paper. I steal it."

TWENTY-FOUR

THE SHORT-STATURED CONCIERGE IN A BROWN waistcoat with gold trim and a shiny name tag beamed a forced, well-rehearsed smile. Which only exacerbated the negative words he was speaking, accompanied by mini shakes of the head.

"I'm afraid you're not showing up in the hotel's booking system, ma'am. And we are fully booked for the weekend. Perhaps you would like to try another hotel? I can recommend–"

"Zis is impossible," said Irina, giving her slightly broken English an early workout. "I book through one of those apps everyone use these days. I can show you email on my phone." She dug around in her handbag and stared at her screen for a while before flashing a sheepish grin. "Oh. Maybe I..."

"May I simply pay now in advance?" said Jacob, placing a platinum AmEx card on the counter with a flourish. "Perhaps the penthouse suite is available? I hear it's the best in all of Abu Dhabi."

The man's attitude changed in a nanosecond. "One moment while I check for you, sir."

Dancing hands on the keyboard, a bit of mouth twisting, and the man was able to advise that, yes, the penthouse suite was available due to an unexpected cancellation. "Would you like to know the tariff, sir?"

Jacob waved the question away. "My employer is picking up the tab."

"Of course, sir." The man slapped his palm on a silver bell, summoning a duo of obsequious porters. Jacob peeled them off a king's ransom in the local currency he'd withdrawn at the airport ATM, and their suitcases were whisked away on a trolley.

Inside the sprawling suite on the top floor that enjoyed expansive views across the esplanade known as the Corniche, bags were unpacked and laptops connected before anyone had the obvious thought of freshening up with a shower. Jacob sent an email to Fletcher, letting him know they had escaped from the Russian Federation and were safe and sound in the UAE. They had sailed through security and customs, no suspicious looks, no questions asked. That done, Jacob promised Vova a large sum of money if he could come up with a fool-proof plan to secure the letter without having to resort to robbing the bank at gunpoint.

"I've never seen him so focused on a task," said Irina after Vova had set himself up in the second of four bedrooms. "And I don't even think it's the money you offered him. It's a chance for...revenge."

"I'm putting more faith in you and your experience. He's on a plane bound for New York Monday morning." He held his hand up as a call came through on his laptop. Fletcher. "Yes, Grant?"

"Just to let you know, the passports will be ready for you to pick up on Monday morning."

"You're on loudspeaker, Grant. I've got no headphones, and Irina Frolova is here."

"Apologies to you, Irina. But I'd like to speak to Jacob in private if you don't mind."

"I'll call you back in a few." Jacob gave Irina a massive wad of cash, told her to take Vova and buy swimsuits for both of them, towels, hats, sunscreen, whatever they needed at the boutique downstairs. They should buy a couple of English-language novels or magazines and relax by the pool until Jacob came and joined them. Stay alert for suspicious looking characters and not leave the confines of the hotel complex. Abu Dhabi was a safe city, but best not to take chances on the streets. It was one of the few destinations left in the world where Russians could travel more or less freely, which meant agents and operatives of all kinds would be roaming about. The latest estimates of the number of Russian expats who had been able to settle in the UAE since the war started ranged up to half a million. In other words, vigilance must be exercised at all times. And worst of all, once Samsonov discovered the safe had been blown, it wouldn't take long before the Russian authorities found out they'd flown to Abu Dhabi. SVR—Foreign Intelligence Service—agents would be combing the UAE, perhaps with the cooperation of the Emiratis. Unfortunately, they were stuck here until Monday morning when the new passports would be ready. Warnings taken on board and understood, mother and son headed for the elevator. Vova was particularly excited by the prospect of enjoying some sunshine after the bitter winter they'd left behind. Jacob's last words to them: *Keep hats and sunglasses on whenever you're not in the pool, and keep conversation to a minimum.*

Alone now, he scanned the major stories from a number of countries' leading news agencies. The usual doom and gloom but nothing specific to set off alarm bells yet. The app's ring tone snapped Jacob out of his concentration. "You can speak freely now, boss."

"Please tell me you've got the damn letter."

"No."

"Then why the fuck aren't you still in Moscow!"

Jacob breathed deeply, sipped at an ice-cold orange juice. "Because the letter isn't in Moscow at all."

"Christ, where is it? Not still in Ukraine, surely?"

"Switzerland. We think."

"You think?"

The explanation that followed seemed to calm Fletcher.

"Look, I'm glad you're safe. Not so delighted you're carrying the burden of two extra people, but it is what it is. Let me see if we can twist the arm of the bank that's holding the letter, see if they'll cooperate."

"They won't, Grant. Our new NATO ally Finland told us to take a hike. The Swiss will be even more obdurate. They have super strict laws about privacy."

"Obdurate? Will you speak fucking normal English for a change?"

"It means stubborn, Grant." Another slug of juice, the best he'd ever tasted out of a bottle. "There's an even worse scenario that could unfold if you start making representations, even at the highest level."

"Jesus, what's that?" The calm attitude didn't last long. Jacob could imagine Fletcher reaching for the bottle of JD, scratching his stubble, pacing the floor.

"They'll alert Samsonov that someone's trying to access his account. That's assuming he's the account holder. For all we know, it could be Putin himself."

"Shit..."

"And then I imagine I'll be arrested by the Swiss police the minute I try to access the box. Or the SVR will set up a sniper across the street to pick me off as I enter the bank. Any number of scenarios, none of them good."

"You're a smart cookie, Jacob. Or so I've been led to believe. Tell me how we're going to get the letter out."

Jacob moved to the window by the balcony. It was a long way down, but among the handful of guests poolside, he could discern Irina and Vova placing towels on banana lounges and jumping into the crystal clear water. He could feel the exuberance in their body language all the way from the top floor of the hotel. They were gutted about not saying goodbye to Babushka and Dedushka, but little moments of joy like this helped take the pain away.

"I'm working on it."

"So you have no ideas at all? Brilliant."

"I didn't say that. As far as I can see, the options are as follows. One. I impersonate Samsonov, hoping like hell he's the account holder, and somehow convince the bank I lost the key and they open it for me. Unlikely. Two. We hack into their system to turn off the security like we did at MinFin, sneak in and steal the letter. This one's totally unrealistic, since we don't have an insider like Irina to tap into their computers, and I assume the vaults in there are going to be a lot harder to crack than Samsonov's wall safe."

"You know, something's occurred to me," said Fletcher. "How do we know the break-in at MinFin hasn't already been discovered?"

"We don't. But from what I can see in the Russian online press, Samsonov and his team are still in Saint Petersburg meeting with the other big boys and girls in cabinet. I mean, you can't trust a word of the Russian media, but still, if what we've done had been detected, I'm sure there'd be reverberations somewhere."

"You've given me two scenarios. You got any more?"

"Yes. Shock and awe. We hit the bank hard with maximum firepower. A team of special ops guys storms the building and forces the manager to turn over the letter. Maybe take a hostage or two if they want to play games."

"Have you lost your mind?"

"Not at all. If State wants this document as desperately as you tell me, then they'll have to be prepared to employ desperate measures. The one big problem with this approach is that it draws a shit ton of attention. Zurich's a busy city, people everywhere doing their business at all times of the day. People will probably die."

"What about bribing someone in the bank? An inside job? Everyone's got a price."

Jacob rubbed his hand across his face. "Generally, yes. But this is Swiss banking we're talking about. Not the US Congress."

"Very funny."

"Most heists require long-term planning, observation. Cultivating an employee of the bank cannot work because we don't have time. Samsonov returns to work Monday. Moscow is an hour ahead of Zurich, which makes it even more urgent we move swiftly."

"Didn't you tell me he rarely comes to the office?"

Jacob nodded to himself. "That's right. But this Monday he's coming to take me to the Kremlin to debrief Putin. When he sees I'm not there and Irina's not there...the shit's gonna hit the fan."

"Let me get some strategic brains onto this. The more people trying to come up with a solution, the better the chance we'll actually find one."

"Great idea, Grant. At this point, quality information is the most valuable commodity. Get a team of researchers digging into this damn bank, Zurich Security Funds AG. Learn everything about it: its security systems, everything about the people who work there, weak points in the building itself."

"And what are you going to be doing while other people are working their asses off?"

"Me? I'm going for a dip in the pool."

TWENTY-FIVE

THE FLIGHT ATTENDANT SMILED AS SHE POURED champagne. "Your first time in Zurich?" she asked Irina, who had just placed a Lonely Planet guide to Switzerland on her tray.

"Oh, yes." She watched the bubbles turn into a layer of foam which almost immediately retreated like the tide. "I never been to Switzerland before." She held up the book and grinned sheepishly.

"And you, sir? Your first visit?"

"I've been a few times. Berne's my favorite city."

"Mine too!" she enthused. "Some Moët?"

Jacob placed his hand over the glass. Today he needed a clear head. "No thank you."

The woman smiled demurely and went off to find another first-class passenger to spoil. Fletcher's assistant had gotten it right this time. Made the correct bookings as soon as new identities had been created for Irina and Vova Frolova. A slight tweak: now they were Irene and Valentine Frobisher, residents of the proud state of Delaware. The techs working for the UAE embassy had also recreated Jacob's old fake identity of Edward Brown, providing him with a passport identical to the one Marina had forced him to give up. But the bonus was a couple of Canadian passports in the names of Todd and Kendra Ellsworth.

He closed his eyes for a moment, thinking back to the decision they'd made about how to access the safe deposit box. And Irina's courage. She could have backed out, taken the easy road and flown to New York with Vova. Their subterfuge would have a better chance of success with her by his side, and she'd insisted he take her. It made sense this way, but if anything happened to her, he wasn't sure he'd be able to live with himself. His thoughts were interrupted by the sensation of something touching his shoulder. He half opened his left eye to see Irina's cheek nestled into him, the trace of a smile on her face.

Her ability to smile would be tested in about three hours' time when they entered the offices of Zurich Security Funds AG at 120 Bahnhofstrasse.

The plan could go one of two ways. The second way didn't bear thinking about.

"THAT TRIP WENT WELL, don't you think?" Samsonov said to Lilliana Danilova as he dialed Irina's extension to order coffee. He dropped his briefcase on the floor and sat on his swivel chair.

"Very well, in my opinion," said Danilova with unconcealed enthusiasm. "You were brilliant, as usual."

"Thank you. But you are a biased judge." He paused for a moment. "Now we're back, I can't wait to see the final report from your young man." The phone rang out, but he left no message. "No answer from Irina. She must be busy putting out IT fires."

"Probably," Danilova said quietly. "And yes. I'm looking forward to seeing Tolya's report. I have high hopes for him in this department."

"Is that all there is to it?" he challenged. "You aren't infatuated with him by any chance? He's tall, young, and a very handsome specimen. No one would blame you."

"Bah!" She crossed her legs and looked away. "I'm way too old for him."

"Others would argue the point." He winked. "Including me."

"Flattery will get you everywhere," she said, turning her admiring gaze back to him again.

Samsonov decided they'd actually had enough coffee and snacks on the bullet train back to Moscow. He smiled as he reflected on the power and influence his position commanded. Not only did he and his team have the entire first-class car to themselves, they had the entire train to themselves. He stood and walked to the walnut liquor cabinet and pulled out a bottle of French cognac. Something white flashed in the corner of his eye. A bit of fluff on the sideboard. The cleaners needed a severe reprimand.

"Not too early for one of these, my dear?" He held up the bottle, adorned with little gold stars and made his way over to the sofa where she joined him.

"Of course not. You know me." She took the bottle from him and placed it on the coffee table. He made no protest as she slowly ran a finger down the side of his face, then placed it in his mouth. He started to suck softly when she yanked the finger away, pulled his face toward hers, and kissed him for about five seconds before leaning back in her seat as if nothing had happened.

"You are a cheeky one." He poured them each a modest serve of the smooth, oaky liquor. "Didn't you get enough of me in Saint Petersburg?"

"I can never get enough of you, big boy." She held out her hand and accepted the drink. She took a swallow while he stroked her leg. "Why don't you come over to my place tonight? We didn't get an opportunity to make the proper amount of noise in that hotel room. I hate being quiet during sex."

He leered at her. The woman was a wildcat in bed, and it was true, the hotel on the shore of the Gulf of Finland had extremely thin walls for a so-called five-star establishment. Their lovemaking had been restrained, and they'd only managed to do it on one of the four nights. The temptation to say yes was great, but domestic responsibilities came first. "I'd love to, my little pigeon. But my wife is expecting me to come home tonight."

"Damn your insufferable wife." Danilova stood and stamped her foot. "You promised me you'd leave her."

He stretched out his hand toward her, but she recoiled, hugging herself.

"I will," he said. "It's just...the time's not right. With the special military operation and everything, VVP wants his key ministers to appear like solid family men."

"And family women."

"What?"

"Matviyenko. I mean, she looks like a man, but I'm sure she's a woman." She sucked air through her teeth. "God, I need a cigarette. All this talk about your wife gets me annoyed."

"I'm as upset by this as you are. But you must understand, stability and absence of scandal are everything if the president is to maintain the public's confidence."

She began pacing the room. "That's bullshit, and you know it." She turned on her heel and glared at him. "This isn't the West. Politicians like you aren't under constant media scrutiny. No one out there"—she pointed vaguely out the window—"has a clue about your private life. And if they did, they wouldn't care."

"Lilliana...please."

"I need that cigarette." She drained the rest of her cognac. "And I've got some important work to do in my office." She held up her briefcase with one hand, rubbing her thumb and forefinger of the other hand together. "Analyzing monetary policy papers. What do you think, Max? Is there enough cash in circulation at the moment or do we need to print some more to finance the...?" She left it unsaid, but he caught her meaning all right.

The war.

She closed the door gently behind her. Samsonov shook his

head. It wasn't the first time she'd brought up the ticklish question of his wife, and it wouldn't be the last.

Returning the bottle to the liquor cabinet, the white object on the polished wooden surface was more visible now. He bent to inspect it. A small white feather. Where could that have come from? Probably a hole in someone's quilted jacket. He'd had a tear in one before and remembered how the little feathers could escape, even through the tiniest of holes. But for the life of him, he couldn't recall anyone coming into the office wearing such a jacket. He dropped the feather and watched it float gently into the trash can.

Again, his thoughts turned to the cleaning staff. Perhaps one of them, an immigrant Kazakh or a Tadjik, not civilized enough to take off their jacket indoors, was to blame. Neglecting to vacuum with due attention. He made a mental note to have the current company warned that their contract would be terminated unless they got their act together.

He'd drop into Anatoly Voronin's office shortly. It was now 1:45 p.m. The man would be at his desk, almost beside himself with anticipation for what lay ahead. Scrubbed, shaved, and preened for his meeting with Putin, scheduled for 4:00 p.m. First job, though, put the wedding ring back on. If he forgot and arrived home without it tonight, Olga's wrath would make an angry Putin seem like a pussycat. Olga had no clue about his affair with Lilliana, and that's the way he wanted it to stay.

Putin's portrait hung slightly askew over the safe. What were these cleaners doing? Dusting with brooms?

He grabbed either side and lifted the painting up and back, then turned and placed it on his desk. He turned back again to spin the wheel and get the damned ring out. The door barely hung on by its hinges. His eyes bugged, and he was sure his heart rate rocketed to 200 bpm as he slowly opened it.

Empty.

What the hell!

It was now 2:15 p.m. All efforts to contact Anatoly Voronin had come up empty. Phone, email, social media DMs. No reply to any of them.

"You!" He pointed a shaking finger at Danilova. "You recruited him." His cheeks shook as he thundered at her. The reality had hit him the moment he saw the blown safe. Putin really was a bigger danger than a cheated-on wife. Olga might try to fleece him of all his assets, but VVP could end his life with one word. "My ass is on the line here, Lilliana. The president entrusted me with the safekeeping of the...never mind what it was. But now it's fucking gone!"

Danilova's eyes remained firmly fixed on the floor. She muttered, "I'm sorry."

"Sorry isn't good enough!" The temptation to lay into her with fists could barely be restrained. He had never hit a woman in his life, but right now, he was close to making the first exception.

"It's imperative he be found, and fucking soon! God knows when this happened. They could be miles away by now. Do you have any idea where he might be?"

Her eyelids fluttered. "No. I can only suggest his apartment."

"Wait here, and don't move." He turned to head out of the office but stopped at the door. "Give me your cell phone."

"What?"

He marched over to her and ripped the clutch bag out of her grip. He plucked the phone out, threw the bag to the floor, and brandished the cell before her eyes. "I'm going to get this thing analyzed. The team downstairs is good enough. If you are part of this, Lilliana...I swear, you're going down with me!"

"Stop, stop!" she implored. "There's no need to do that. I'm sure there's another way. Perhaps that floozy Irina Frolova knows where he is. She's been all over him since he arrived."

"Floozy? She's no..." Even as he said it, he remembered with a sick sensation in his stomach how he had asked her to perform a minyet on him in his office in return for getting her brother out of prison. She'd agreed without protesting too much, and at the time he had assumed she was into it. Maybe she hadn't been. God, how stupid could he have been!

"Actually," Lilliana said, venom almost dripping from her lips, "I bet they're lying in bed right now, the dirty bastards. They'll be thinking we'd be late back from Saint Petersburg and they could enjoy a late start to the day. We weren't scheduled to return to the office until after lunch. Yes." Her voice lacked all confidence. "That's it."

"But why was my safe broken into?"

The corner of her lips turned down as she shrugged. "How would I know? I didn't even know you had a safe."

Samsonov furiously tapped a pencil on a blotter. "What do you suggest I do now?"

She shrugged. "Send some hard men to their addresses. Employ old-fashioned KGB tactics. Kick their fucking doors down."

"Don't you worry," he thundered, his face an inch from hers. "There are units from Alpha Group heading there as we speak. And when they're finished, I'm sending them to your apartment. They're going to turn it inside out. If I find the tiniest shred of evidence you brought him here to rob my safe, a stretch in IK-2 Mordovia will seem like a trip to a resort in Sochi."

"I swear, Max." She shuddered. He'd known she'd freak at the thought of winding up in the harsh women's prison—the worst female 'correctional' facility in Russia. Using it as a threat should shake the truth out of her. "The man gave me no indication he was anything but genuine. All his credentials checked out, a hundred percent." Maybe she could throw someone else under the bus to save her own ass. "Gerasimchuk vetted him, like he does any new employee. If anyone is to blame, it's him."

"A likely story," he laughed. "If that weasel snuck under the radar, then I'm not blaming Aleksandr. He's been loyal to this ministry for well over a decade."

Nevertheless, no one was above suspicion in this matter. Then he suddenly remembered. Gerasimchuk had been there when he'd placed the letter inside the safe. And...*no!* Samsonov had told him, if not directly, then obliquely, what was in the parcel.

"Wait here and do not move until I return. You understand me?"

She nodded slowly, rolling her fingers over each other in her lap.

As he strode to Gerasimchuk's office, he realized the romance with Lilliana was dead in the water. Instincts screamed something was not only wrong, but way wrong. He should never have listened to her. Voronin was too good to be true. She was a traitor, and her fate was sealed. And now he had to find out if Aleksandr Gerasimchuk, his loyal deputy for so many years, was a traitor too.

His mobile chirped in his pocket. His hand trembled like an aspen tree in the fall. It was his contact at MID, Boris Kirkorov. "Yes?"

"Immigration control confirms Anatoly Voronin, Irina Frolova, and her son Vladimir flew out of Sheremetyevo Friday at 10:45."

"Where to?"

"Abu Dhabi."

"Dammit!" Sweat pooled in his armpits. There was no way he could hide the catastrophe. "Get on to the Emiratis. Do we have an extradition treaty with them?"

"Yes indeed. They're very cooperative when it comes to sending criminals back."

"Find out where they're staying and pick them up immediately."

"Understood."

"Spasibo." He sighed as he hung up the phone. *There's still hope.*

Alone in Samsonov's office, she felt the blood rushing to her face. His threat to send her to IK-2 Mordovia was no idle one. He had ruined the lives of other employees before. Not sent them to prison but had their careers ended with no hope of re-employment in a decent job ever again. However, that had been in response to poor performance, so perhaps fair enough. By comparison with those who were fired from their jobs, her immediate fate was terrifying.

Curiosity got the better of her; she inspected the open safe. *What was it the American wanted so badly?* No sooner had she poked her head inside when two pairs of strong arms gripped her painfully by the elbows and yanked her backwards.

"You're coming with us," one of them growled.

She offered no resistance as the two goons in military-style combat fatigues, shaved heads gleaming under the lights, muscled her toward the door. At the threshold stood Samsonov, arms folded tight across his chest. The thugs stopped obediently as the minister moved to block their path. "Well, you were wrong about Voronin and Frolova sleeping in late," he spat. "They're long gone. Unfortunately for me, your protégé has already checked out of the hotel he was staying at in Abu Dhabi. Which means I now have to let the president know I've let him down. And that's bad news for you."

"Max, no!"

He held up his right hand. "I'm still speaking. Fortunately, the good sheikhs in the UAE are assisting us as best as they can. Hopefully, we'll soon hear where the hell our traitors have gone. I have a hunch, but it'll be nice to have my suspicions confirmed. In the meantime, you and Aleksandr are taking a ride to the Lubyanka, where you've got appointments with electrodes designed to fit snugly in bodily cavities." He shuddered. "Ugh. I can't even imagine the amount of pain those things deliver, but I've heard it's pretty bad. Anyway, Aleksandr's already shackled hand and foot, waiting for you in a van outside. Tell the truth and your ordeal will be over quickly."

"No, Max, please! Let me—" She knew this might happen when she'd signed up for the mission. But not until the American had killed Putin. And she would have escaped by then, her route to Turkey already planned. There would have been a chance at survival, albeit a slim one. But things had taken un unexpected turn, and the reality of her failure to anticipate this alternative scenario was hitting hard. There must be a way to save herself.

"Shut the fuck up. You'll have plenty of opportunity to talk when the interrogation begins."

"I'll tell you what I know...I can put things right. Just don't send me away with these men. Please!"

Samsonov instructed the men to leave him alone with Danilova. "If she doesn't tell me the truth, I'll bring her to the Lubyanka myself." He fixed her with a death stare. "You are going to tell me the truth, aren't you, Lilliana?"

TWENTY-SIX

ZURICH HAD TURNED ON A WINTER'S DAY THE TOURISTS love. Crisp, clean air mingled with the hint of chestnut smoke emanating from the vats where the street vendors cooked on open coals. Sidewalks cleared of snow that fell heavily overnight before the clouds magically disappeared, leaving a china-blue sky to frame the grand old buildings lining Bahnhofstrasse. One of those buildings was the head office of Zurich Security Funds AG.

"Are you ready, Irina?" said Jacob, speaking only English with her now. When Vova had called early this morning before they departed Abu Dhabi, he'd asked her to conduct the conversation on speaker and insisted she and her son stick with English even between themselves. To his surprise, they were only too happy to comply.

"I think so."

"Good." He ran his eye up and down her with unconcealed admiration. "You certainly look the part, my dear." Jacob had spent several thousand dollars on expensive outfits at the hotel's boutique. Irina's new clothes cost more than she could earn in a year. Once the fur coat came off inside the bank to reveal the slinky dress underneath—business glam, the saleswoman had called it—the manager would be eating out of their hands. Finished at the boutique, Jacob had asked their taxi driver to take them to a hair salon where Irina was transformed by a set of dark extensions so long she resembled a shorter version of Cher. Finally, they'd visited a costume shop in the Al Barsha district, where a curly blond hairpiece and matching fake beard turned Jacob into a 21st century Viking.

"Let me do the talking," he said, conscious of how corny the cliché sounded. Irina nodded enthusiastically. "Walk in like you own the place, okay?"

She shook her head, making the long black hair wave like a silk scarf. "Like this?"

"Exactly like that."

Holding hands, they passed through a set of automatic glass doors, standing aside to let an elderly gentleman go by. Then past a bank of ATMs and a ninety-degree turn to the left. Up ahead, the entrance to the main part of the bank. To get in there was no simple matter. To Jacob, it felt like they were attempting to enter the tomb of Tutankhamun.

A pair of tall, broad-shouldered guards in dark suits stood on either side of a metal detector frame in front of the door. Bulges under the jackets could only be weapons. Jacob smiled. "Guten morgen. Mr. and Mrs. Todd Ellsworth. We have an appointment with the manager, Herr Gustav Rinke. I believe he is expecting us."

The man on the left refused to return Jacob's smile, his lips a straight line. The expression of the guy on the right was even more granite-like. He pressed a finger to his earpiece and said something in guttural German. Jacob wasn't strong on the language, and the Swiss version had him completely lost. The faint sound of a reply and the man nodded twice. He turned to the visitors.

"Are you carrying any weapons or sharp objects?" he asked, deadpan.

"No," said Jacob, resisting the urge to say something smart.

"Please hand me your wallets, phones, keys, coins, anything else metallic on your person."

Jacob and Irina complied, and the man placed the items in a plastic tray which he then set on a small table. The second guard waved a detector back and forth over the tray. No alarm bells. The first guard said, "Please, sir, remove your belt and shoes and pass through the metal detector."

Jacob waited on the other side as a barefooted Irina strode confidently through the metal arch. No buzzing, no bleeping. So far, so good. The first guard handed Jacob two trays: one with their personal items, the second with the belt and shoes. If it was this tough getting in, getting out with the prize was going to present problems an order of magnitude more difficult.

"Please," said a finely featured woman in her mid to late twenties, dressed as conservatively as Irina was glamorous, "follow me. Herr Rinke is waiting for you."

Inside the manager's office, which was modest and austere compared to the lavishness of MinFin, Herr Rinke shook his guests' hands, then beckoned for them to be seated in a pair of leather chairs. He sat in his own swivel chair and steepled his fingers with elbows resting on the pine desk. Irina hung her fur coat on a hook and, as expected, the manager's eyes were drawn to the figure-hugging dress. He must have realized he'd been caught ogling. He blinked twice and got straight down to business. "Now I understand you want to open an account on behalf of the Canadian government. This is an honor for our bank, I must say."

Jacob hesitated, sizing up the man. As per Fletcher's intel, Rinke was no pushover. Fifty-seven years old, 5'11" and 220 pounds, deep crows' feet and balding at the crown, but in prime physical shape. Muscles rippled under his starched white shirt.

"The honor is ours," said Jacob. "The Canadian Ministry of Finance understands other governments entrust certain, shall I say, delicate items to your safe deposit box system."

Rinke shrugged, then gave a knowing wink. "Perhaps they do. We do not question our clients about what they put in their boxes; however, I assume it's not restaurant receipts." He chuckled at his own joke. Jacob and Irina exchanged a look and joined in with a laugh of their own.

Jacob turned back to Rinke. "We heard a rumor that Vladimir Putin himself has an account with your bank. Is that true?"

"I can neither confirm nor deny. I believe this is called the Glomar response, no?"

"Indeed it is. I assume you like to watch movies about the CIA. They invented the phrase."

"Really? I had no idea." Rinke leaned back in his seat. "Now before I ask my assistant to bring us coffee and some delicious Swiss chocolates, may I see please your bona fides?"

"Of course. One second." Jacob smiled and reached into his jacket pocket. He pulled out his fake Canadian passport and fumbled it. It fell to his feet, where he nudged it with his toe, pushing it farther underneath the desk. "I'm so clumsy. Excuse me, will you?" He dropped to his hands and knees and crawled forward about two feet, keeping a close eye on the manager's shoes. They were big ones—as big as the Russian soldier's who'd sacrificed his boots for Jacob back in Hremyach. He lay flat on his stomach, arching his back and neck slightly so he could see what he was doing. Then he stretched both arms as far as he could, letting out an involuntary grunt.

"Everything okay?" said Rinke in a genuinely concerned tone.

"Yes." Jacob gripped the man by the ankles and tugged as hard as he could.

The element of surprise worked superbly. Rinke had no idea what was happening, his body sliding from his chair before he could think of resisting the attack. With the heel of his palm, Jacob delivered a violent blow just under the man's right patella, then repeated the blow on the left knee. Not hard enough to cripple the man, but sufficient to cause pain, frighten, and temporarily debilitate.

"Scheisse! Du Arschloch!" *Shit! You asshole!* screamed Rinke, his closed fist banging again the underside of his desk. "What the fuck are you doing?"

Jacob reapplied his grip to the man's left ankle and ordered Irina to do the same. He broke his rule and spoke in Russian. Actions now had to be swift, without misunderstandings. There was no misunderstanding on Rinke's part either. "Who the fuck are you?" he groaned. "Russian spies?"

"Shut up. Resist and I'll put a knife through your balls," Jacob bluffed.

The man's entire body went limp, the threat working perfectly.

Together they managed to tug the big manager out from under the desk to open floor space. Jacob pointed at the door and commanded Irina to prop her chair under the door handle. She carried out the order in the blink of an eye.

A timid knock came on the door. "Alles okay?" It was the young woman they had met earlier.

"Tell her you're fine," Jacob hissed. "And don't try anything funny. Ich spreche fliessend Deutsch." *I speak fluent German.* The last sentence was a lie, but his ability to mimic accents was enough to convince the poor manager.

"Alles okay," he said, tears streaming down his face. Then a calmly spoken sentence that Jacob was pretty sure translated as *Please don't disturb us for the next hour.*

"Good man," said Jacob. "Cooperation is your only choice at this stage. Put your arms out in front of you, or I swear I'll kill you here and now."

The hands appeared meekly. Jacob wound his belt around the wrists and pulled tight.

"This will all be over before you know it. I'm not going to hurt you any further. Your knees will come good in about fifteen minutes, and you will be able to walk, albeit with a limp for a while. Now here's the proposition."

"Proposition?"

"Your wife's name is Katrin, your daughter is Steffi. You live in a beautiful home in Schlösslistrasse in the Fluntern district."

"What...?"

"I can go on. I know what bus Steffi takes to go to school. Where Katrin gets her hair done. And so do my colleagues from Moscow, who aren't anywhere near as nice as I am. Are you starting to get the picture?"

"Ja, ja." His face was starting to turn red. "I...need my heart pills."

Jacob's own heart health almost took a sudden turn for the worse. He gestured for Irina, who was observing the spectacle open-mouthed, to assist in hauling Rinke onto a leather couch by the window. As they dragged, Jacob said, "Where are these pills, Gustav? Let me help you." *Use his first name to try and regain his trust. Play good cop.*

"In the top drawer of my desk. Hurry. If I get too anxious, I could have a heart attack."

Jacob placed the tablets on Rinke's extended tongue, so pale it was almost white. He started to wonder whether this had gone too far. If they lost the manager, there would be zero leverage, and they would never get out, except in the back of a police van. He said a quick silent prayer, which included a plea for forgiveness. Rinke deserved none of the treatment Jacob was dishing out. He concentrated to steady his shaking hand, decanted water from the carafe on Rinke's desk into a glass, and held it to his mouth and tipped up slowly. Rinke's eyes blinked as he sputtered. The pills somehow went down the man's throat, and he appeared to calm fractionally.

Jacob waited a minute before he spoke again. "I need you to give me access to a safe deposit box."

Rinke nodded and gave a short, sharp, sarcastic laugh. "So no new account for the Canadian government?"

"Maybe next time, pal. Seriously, this is the account linked to the box." He reached into his pocket and extracted a photocopy of the piece of paper he'd retrieved from Samsonov's safe, dangling it in front of Rinke's eyes. The original had been sent to Fletcher via the embassy staff in Abu Dhabi. "I need to get into that box, and I need to do it in the next ten minutes." It was an arbitrary time frame, but experience told him being specific with details generally garnered a more cooperative response.

Rinke's eyelids widened then narrowed as he tried to focus. "I can't read those numbers without my glasses. Even if I could, they mean nothing to me. You know how many accounts we manage? I can barely remember my own!"

Jacob breathed in hard. "Of course. I apologize."

Irina had become pro-active. She put her hand under Rinke's right armpit, looked at Jacob, and said, "Let's put him back behind his desk. He can access the numbers from there."

"Can you?" said Jacob. "I hope so, for your sake." He paused. "And for Katrin's and Steffi's sake."

"Ja, ja, natürlich." *Yes, of course.*

Jacob undid the crude knot, freeing Rinke's hands from the belt. To ensure his continued compliance, he secured it now around the man's neck.

Back in his seat, Jacob and Irina watched from behind as the man donned a pair of glasses, then clicked around files until he opened one with a long list of numbers. "Don't go alerting anyone via some secret code on this computer, Gustav. Anyone comes a-knocking again and I pull this tight and no amount of heart pills is going to help you."

"Ja, ja! I'm doing what you say."

"Again I apologize, Gustav. I'm a little nervous because if I return to my boss empty-handed, well, he won't be very happy with me." He gave Rinke an encouraging tap on the shoulder. "All you need to do is find the box number that goes with the account. Then you take us there, open the box, we take the contents. And the last step, the easiest and most pleasant for all of us, you escort me and Mrs. Ellsworth out of the building into a taxi that your secretary will thoughtfully order for us in about"—

Jacob glanced at his watch, a new Rolex purchased duty free at Abu Dhabi airport—"twenty minutes. Agreed?"

"Agreed," Rinke sighed. "And here is the...holy shit...it *is* Putin's box!"

Ten minutes later, the three of them plus a local locksmith, an elderly man with a limping gait that mirrored that of Rinke, entered a darkened corridor. Their arrival inside the vault activated a bright overhead light. The corridor was about five feet wide, with gleaming silver walls on either side. There were twenty rows of square and rectangular doors in three sizes. "The box you want is...here." Rinke pointed to the bottom third of the wall on the right. A medium-sized box.

They stood back while the locksmith drilled the box open, steel shavings spilling onto the floor. Without the boxholder's key, presumably held by Samsonov, the contents could not be opened by the bank's key alone.

"I will leave you now to access your–"

"You're staying," Jacob insisted.

Rinke shrugged. "Protocol demands you must have privacy to view your box. I must also ask you to pay for the repairs."

"Send the bill to the president of the Russian Federation. And just remember *my* protocol, the one about your family. Wait outside the vault door for us and do not move until we come out."

Rinke nodded and escorted the locksmith outside.

Jacob peered inside the box, his heart hammering like a metronome.

An envelope in mint condition bore a familiar address. 2201 C St NW, Washington, DC 20451.

He prized open the envelope, unfolded the letter.

And there it was.

The seal of the State Department of the United States of America and the signature of Rufus Constable II, Senior Tactical and Strategic Advisor to the Secretary of State.

He was in two minds about taking some other documents

that were inside the box but decided to leave them. It wasn't part of his brief to secure anything except the letter.

Let sleeping dogs lie, Hunter.

He could hear Rinke and the locksmith mumbling less than twenty feet away. With Irina staring uncomprehendingly, Jacob yelled out loudly enough for the men outside to hear, "Damn it! It's not here. Put everything back in, we've completely wasted our time!" He then slid the envelope inside his jacket pocket.

"What was all that about?" whispered Irina.

"The bank will, hopefully, think nothing's been stolen, and the cops will be less inclined to throw all they've got into finding us."

"You can't be serious. We assaulted the manager, held him against his will, and forced him to open a private box."

"Yeah," said Jacob, blowing out his cheeks. "There is that. Come on, let's get out of here."

TWENTY-SEVEN

"START TALKING." SAMSONOV BROKE HIS MUCH-vaunted no-smoking in the office rule, lit a Marlboro, and sucked hard. "If I don't like what I hear, you'll be heading for the Lubyanka in ten minutes."

"Do you have one of those cigarettes for me?"

"No, I do not." He broke another rule and slapped her hard across the face. There would be a palm imprint there for sure, Danilova thought. She shook her head to clear the ringing in her ears but made no protest.

"Do not ask me any questions," he barked, trails of smoke escaping his nostrils. "You only answer mine."

She nodded, feeling a wet streak on the right-hand side of her face. Blood or tears, she didn't know. She wiped at her cheek and stole a look. Tears. "He's an American."

"Bullshit," he scoffed. "Try harder."

"I swear, Max. He's from some secret organization no one's ever heard of. He's been trained to pass himself off as a native Russian."

Samsonov rubbed his chin. "Whoever trained him is a genius, then, if what you say is true, which I highly doubt. I've heard many Americans who speak our language fluently. Diplomats, businessmen. There's always a giveaway in their accent, or wrong grammar. But this guy...he made no mistakes at all. Even writes like a top graduate from MGU."

She started blubbering, more than she meant to, but the acting was quickly morphing into genuine emotions. Would she even get home tonight? "I...don't know how he reached that level, but I swear, he is an American."

"What is his plan now? He's stolen a sensitive item from that safe." He pointed at it. "If I don't recover it and Voronin manages to–"

"Brown. His name's Edward Brown." She looked up at him through a blur of tears.

"Did you come down in the last shower?" said Samsonov, lighting another cigarette from the butt of the first. "That's like Ivan Ivanov. Made up, just like everything you're telling me."

"I'm not making it up, Max. He was sent here to assassinate..." Oh shit! Had she just signed her own death warrant? "I mean..."

"Assassinate who? Me?"

Typical of Maxim, thinking he was the center of the damn universe. "No. Someone else in the government."

"Putin. He was sent her to kill the president. Is that what you're saying?"

She looked at the floor. No way would she confirm that. "No. I think the target is Dmitry Medvedev."

Samsonov burst out a staccato laugh. "You must be fucking joking. That lame duck wouldn't be missed by anyone. He's only kept on because of his blind loyalty." He strode to the window and poked fingers through the shades. He marched back to Danilova, putting his hands around her throat. "Where is this fucking American now?"

She felt the pressure building in her face as the blood flow became restricted. "I don't...know."

He squeezed harder. "Think, Lilliana. Think like your life depends on it."

"Please, Max...I swear, I have no idea."

He let go, and she gasped for air.

"Maybe he went back to his old job in Vladivostok." Samsonov's voice dripped with sarcasm. "Anyway, it doesn't matter. I'm pretty sure I know where he went. I only hope for your sake I manage to catch him in time."

"You're not sending me to the Lubyanka?"

"Not yet."

TWENTY-EIGHT

"WE'RE OUT." JACOB CLICKED HIS SEATBELT INTO PLACE as the compact taxi zoomed past a blue tram car.

"Do you have it? Tell me you have it."

"Yes."

"Thank God." The relief in Fletcher's voice was almost palpable. His precious Skia would not be shut down, and his life of plenty could continue.

The taxi driver asked something of Irina, who was staring out the window with blank eyes. "Just a minute, Grant," said Jacob. "What do you want?" he asked the driver sharply.

"I want to confirm which terminal you require." The beret-wearing driver smiled through his thick black moustache, not fazed by Jacob's directness.

"Two please." He turned his attention back to Fletcher. "Grant, I need you to do something for me before we talk about anything else. I just wish I'd thought of it before."

"What?"

"Send someone around to pick up Irina's parents and get them the hell out of Moscow."

"And take them where?"

"No idea. It has to be quick, though. No doubt Samsonov's

figured out that Irina and I have flown the coop with the prize. It won't take long before they send some sadistic foot soldiers to interrogate the parents."

"Where can they fly to from Moscow?"

"They have no international passports," interrupted Irina, able to hear what Fletcher was saying over Jacob's cell. "They cannot leave the Russian Federation legally."

"Nowhere, Grant. They'll have to be hidden inside Russia until we can come up with another plan. Airports are going to be impossible for them, even for internal flights. All the train stations, too. Everyone will be looking out for them soon. We have to assume they've already started."

"What do you suggest?"

Jacob thought for a moment. "There was this brush-by guy in the Alexander Garden, the one who helped me out with the explosive gear. I don't know, but something in my gut tells me the man is solid, dependable, and has initiative. Contact the embassy and get them to mobilize the guy, or anyone they think can help out."

"Okay."

Jacob rattled off the address for Fletcher and made him read it back. "It could be too late, but you must try." It was his own actions toward Gustav Rinke that got him thinking: if he could resort to such violence against innocent people with ease, the FSB would leave nothing in the tank when it came to torturing Irina's parents. "One last thing. Her brother Igor might be there. He's already in the authorities' bad books, did a stint in jail for protesting against the war. He needs protection as well."

"Fuck's sake, Hunter. Anybody else? The pet dog need asylum?"

"That's it. Good-bye." Jacob disconnected the call. Fletcher's sarcasm was the last thing he needed.

The driver glanced in the rearview mirror and swore under his breath. He dropped into a lower gear and pulled over to the side of the narrow street.

"Something wrong?" said Jacob.

"The dummkopf behind was flashing his lights. I want to let him pass, but he has also stopped."

Jacob turned in his seat. The barrel of a monstrous automatic rifle poked out the passenger-side window of the black Renault Megane R.S. Sport parked about thirty feet behind them. He grabbed Irina by the collar of her fur coat and dragged her down to a lying position on the back seat. A millisecond later, a fusillade of bullets ripped through the back windshield. He heard a muffled cry as the driver took several hits to the back of the head before he slumped forward in his seat. His forehead made contact with the horn, which let out a continuous blare.

Irina began to howl like a wolf caught in a trap, shaking bits of glass from her head and shoulders.

Jacob pulled out the cell phone provided by Marina, now containing a Swisscom SIM, and dialed 112, the emergency number for most of Europe, including Switzerland. A woman answered in a calm voice after one ring. He hollered, "Hilfe! Help! We've been shot at. I've got no idea where we are, but it's near Bahnhofstrasse in Zurich, maybe three minutes north by car. We have to save ourselves. Send polizei. Schnell!"

He turned to Irina. "We have to run," he said, his breath ragged. "Open the door and go as fast and as far as your legs will take you. Zig-zag and stay low. Ready...Go!"

He shoved open the door on his side and scrambled out. He was on the cobbled road, which was good news for Irina, more protected on the sidewalk. He would be the primary target, which was even better news for her. Head down and stooped, he duck-waddled to the other side of the street, rounding a line of parked cars. Bullets continued to spit, pinging off metal, embedding in stone and brick, shattering glass, thankfully missing flesh. All the while the taxi's horn continued to blare. Crouched behind a silver Mercedes sedan, he heard dozens of pedestrians screaming as they fled the onslaught.

He raised his head a fraction and peered through the shattered window of the parked car; the Megane was still behind the taxi, the seated gunman's eyes searching desperately for his targets.

Where the fuck is Irina?

The shooter, dressed in dark clothing and reflector sunglasses, a black cloth mask covering his face, emerged from the Megane. He brandished the gun like he was the Terminator.

Jacob held his breath as the approaching gunman's footsteps echoed on the cobblestoned street. He crouched even lower. His best chance was to stay still and hope the first responders would arrive and scare off the assassin.

He pressed his body hard into the back tire of the Mercedes, eyes inches from the ground. He could see the boots of the gunman now, only five cars away, marching down the middle of the street.

Then the sweetest sound he had heard since arriving in Zurich.

Sirens. Multiple sirens. No doubt several local witnesses had called it in, giving the specific location.

Above the wail of the approaching police vehicles and the forlorn sound of the taxi's horn, he heard the gunman swear loudly in Russian and then his fast-retreating footsteps. Jacob knelt and peered through the window of the Mercedes to see the thug slam the passenger door shut. The Megane screeched in reverse, tires smoking, spun in an expertly executed 90-degree arc, and accelerated away down a side alley.

He stood, cupped his hands to his mouth and called out, "Irina!"

No reply. He headed in the logical direction: away from the scene. As he walked, he kept calling her name. *Please, don't be shot.*

Then, a tap on the shoulder. "I'm here. I was hiding behind that bicycle stand." She pointed at a row of at least fifty bicycles chained to a metal frame. "What now?"

The sirens were almost upon them. "We can't afford to be dragged into a police investigation. We have to get the hell out of here and on an airplane to anywhere but Russia."

"Aren't you forgetting something?" She held a hand up to her ear like she was listening out for something.

"Shit, yes." Their small carry-on bags were in the trunk of the taxi. "I hope the bad guys didn't think to search the vehicle."

A minute later, Jacob had pulled the poor taxi driver off the horn, popped the trunk, and sighed with relief when he saw their bags intact and untouched, the State Department letter exactly where he'd left it. He took a pair of scissors he'd lifted from Rinke's desk and hacked off Irina's extensions, removed his own wig and fake beard and dropped them in his carry bag, to be disposed of later. They walked away briskly, melding into the growing stream of afternoon commuters heading home.

TWENTY-NINE

"This is bad news, Lilliana," said Samsonov in a whisper. "A calamity, in fact." He pressed the red button on his cell and put the device on his desk.

"I'm sorry, so sorry," she mumbled, her body shaking like she had a temperature.

"Your apologies are useless to me."

"Sorry, sorry..." It was now an almost trance-like repetition.

The rolling feeling in his stomach, the premonition of looming catastrophe, made him want to throw up. It was worse than the nerves that had nearly crippled him fifteen years ago when he was first introduced to Putin. It was a grand ball in the Kremlin after some prestigious sporting event or other. He had been a junior apparatchik back then, with burning ambition, eager to please but terrified of making the wrong move or saying the wrong thing. Since then, he had become one of the few men in VVP's inner cabinet who could tell him things he didn't want to hear. It was like walking a tightrope, though, and he had to exercise extreme caution. He'd done it well. That was why he was entrusted with protecting the details of the secret Swiss bank account. Soon, that trust would be gone.

He looked down at Danilova, who cut a pathetic figure with

her makeup smudged and face wet with tears. "The spy and the traitor have escaped our SVR agents in Zurich. Not good, not good at all."

He paced back and forth, now on the eighth cigarette since he'd opened the pack. He was in two minds about dragging her ass down to the Lubyanka. His own fists were itching to give her a proper thrashing now that the letter had been stolen and the Zurich-based operatives had failed miserably to get it back. "In fact, those very agents have themselves been arrested by the highly efficient Swiss police. A shit day all round, wouldn't you say?"

She kept staring at the floor, mumbling incoherently.

His phone chirped and vibrated on the desk.

When he looked at the screen, he felt the blood draining from his face. He prayed he wouldn't faint on the spot, giving Danilova the chance to escape. Not that she would get very far. He didn't faint. Instead, he bravely squared his shoulders and took the call. "Yes, Vladimir Vladimirovich."

He remained silent for a few moments while the president said his piece. Samsonov hated to interrupt, but in this case, it was a worse option than being polite. "I'm going to have to stop you there, Vladimir Vladimirovich. There's been a bit of a problem on our end. The meeting with Voronin will not be taking place as planned." He felt sweat beading on his forehead. "We actually have a bigger problem than that, I'm afraid."

When he had finished describing the shameful debacle that had occurred in the offices of MinFin under his watch, he sensed a great weight had been lifted from his shoulders.

"Who is responsible?" said Putin.

Samsonov gulped, his legs involuntarily taking him to the liquor cabinet. "I am, of course."

Then, joyous relief as the president uttered the next words. "Nonsense, Maxim Antonovich. Your ranks were infiltrated, yes, but you were not the one who personally hired them."

"True. However, it is now up to me to rectify the situation. The worst is not that the account number to your safe deposit box has been stolen. We can organize a new box, perhaps at another bank now. The real issue is the contents of the box."

"No need to state the obvious to me."

Samsonov winced at his own faux pas. "The box contained a number of documents," Putin continued, "the most important being the US State Department's letter that was nothing but the documented coercion of the legally elected government in Ukraine."

Samsonov gasped. He had heard rumors about this letter and its latent power. Now it had been snatched away.

"It was my plan to release that letter on the anniversary of the launch of our Special Military Operation," Putin continued, his voice calm and restrained. "It would have swung the campaign heavily in our favor. Perhaps led to its conclusion as support for the Americans would have evaporated in the wake of the revelation. We would have been able to occupy Ukraine in its entirety with only the mopping up of local militias and traitors to complete." Putin then explained how the provenance of the original could be proved. Indeed, he had well-paid experts from Sotheby's auctioneers lined up to do exactly that. Enemies of Russia could claim that copies, of which there were several in existence, were fake. But the legitimacy of the real letter could not be argued. Every effort must now be made to retrieve it, using every resource at the disposal of all the siloviki combined, including the mobilization of foreign assets.

Samsonov glared at Danilova. The enormity of her crime now apparent, he would garotte her happily and get a good night's sleep with no pangs of guilt. "There are others to blame, but the person ultimately responsible for this mess is...Lilliana Danilova."

"Bring her to me. I'll send a cortege in five minutes."

Although it was a short stroll to the Kremlin, officials never walked there. Always in black limos with flashing blue migalkas. Too good for Danilova, who should be dragged there behind a donkey.

"We'll be ready, Vladimir Vladimirovich."

He poured himself a large serving of Hennessy XO cognac and lit another Marlboro. "Go to the bathroom and tidy yourself up, for God's sake." He sneered disdainfully at Danilova. "The president wants to see you."

Her face crumpled like crepe paper, which brought a thin smile to his face. Out of habit, he went to dial Irina's extension to ask her to keep an eye on Danilova in the bathroom. He slammed his fist on the desk and swore loudly. "On second thoughts, you can go looking as you do. Let the president see you for what you really are."

THIRTY

"THAT MIGHT NOT BE THE LAST WE SEE OF THOSE goons," said Jacob as they neared an intersection. Large snowflakes tumbled from leaden skies. "If not them, others will come looking for us."

"Can we get another taxi please?" said Irina, flicking tiny pieces of glass from her fur coat. "I can't keep walking in this weather for much longer. Look at the clothes I'm wearing." She pointed at her chest.

"No taxis." Jacob stopped and turned to face her. "We're not going to the airport now. If it was just me, I'd take the chance. If the Russians identified me at the airport and made a fuss, all I'd have to do was alert the airport police, and I'd be escorted onto the plane."

"But I've got an American passport, too."

He shook his head. "And what if they complain to the Swiss cops, claim you're a criminal on the run? Right now, you *are* an illegal in possession of forged travel documents. You'd be handed over and extradited back to Moscow." Jacob paused. "Then there's the dirty tricks the SVR are renowned for. Sneaky lethal injections in a crowded terminal, for example. You've also got"—he used his fingers to enumerate the methods of assassination—

"novichok, radiation poisoning, garroted in an airport bathroom, twisted neck. You following me?"

He saw and heard her gulp.

"Look, it's just too risky for you—us, in fact—to travel via airports. We must lay low until the heat dies down."

"And how long will that be?"

"I don't know for sure, but I'd say when your brother and parents are also safely out of harm's way, we can think about the final step. Until then, I'm taking you south, to a small Greek island. We've got a safe house there that cannot be breached. We'll find a way to get you off that island and into the USA that avoids the travel hubs. Maybe a cargo vessel or a submarine."

"Submarine? That's the stuff of spy movies."

He raised his eyebrows. "I *am* a damn spy, or have you forgotten?"

She sighed. "So how do we get there?"

He pointed back toward the row of bicycles in the distance. "We're each taking one of those. Then we steal a car." He pulled out his cell phone and made a search for the nearest suburban train station with a parking lot attached and also for the quickest route there by bicycle. He located one at Altstetten, about 20 minutes' ride away.

"That's a long time." She made a face like she was about to cry. "I haven't ridden a bike since I was a teenager."

"You'll be fine. You never forget."

Soon, he had liberated two bicycles from the stand. They weren't the best ones, but they were attached with the flimsiest of chains. Token security, the padlocks yielded with a couple of swift kicks and vicious tugs.

He led the way, quickly getting off the cobblestones and onto an actual bike path. Irina, despite her lack of practice, kept up with relative ease. They crossed a bridge over the Sihl river and headed northwest until they reached Badenerstrasse. As they approached the Altstetten train station, Jacob's heart sank. The park-and-ride facility wasn't an open space with free parking for commuters, but a multi-level garage complete with thick metal boom gates. He had hoped to find a big outdoor parking lot jam-packed with vehicles, where stealing one would be comparatively easy. But this was Europe, where you have to pay for just about everything.

"Drop the bicycle here," he commanded when they reached a quiet stretch of road. "Don't know about you, but I'm done pedaling." He swung his leg to dismount the old mountain bike he'd stolen.

"Thank God," she muttered, alighting from her bike. "Can you believe how much sweat there is under this fur coat? It's ridiculous."

"We'll change into more practical clothes once we get the chance."

"I hope that's soon." She puffed out her cheeks as she leaned the bike up against the wall of a patisserie. "What now?"

His lips curled for a second before he spoke his thoughts out loud. "The parking garage is too problematic. If we managed to break into a car in there, I'd still have to bust down the boom gate, which looks pretty solid from back here. I have no idea what kind of damage that would cause to a vehicle. Could be enough to render the car useless, so..." Just then a plump, middle-aged woman in a pink puffer jacket exited the patisserie. She struggled to carry three white cardboard cake boxes stacked one on top of the other. One hand clamped on the top box, she stretched her neck to one side to pick her way along the sidewalk. With such a precarious load, there was no chance the woman was planning on walking very far. She must have a car. She paused, readjusted her top hand, and began to veer right toward a vehicle. A big, late-model Porsche Cayenne SUV.

"Bingo," Jacob whispered under his breath. He turned to Irina, who was scrolling through her phone, also now rigged up with a local SIM. "Go over to that woman and ask her if she needs help getting those cakes into the vehicle."

"Are we stealing that car?"

"Yes. But we have to be extra careful. Taking an unattended vehicle is one thing, snatching it from the owner quite another. The cops will be looking for us as it is, if not as murder suspects, then as key witnesses. Throw carjacking into the mix, and they'll deploy officers from everywhere to track us down."

"Do you think the police will be able to identify us?"

Jacob gave a small nod. "We were the last people to ride in the dead driver's taxi. There will be records of the pickup, and old Gustav might realize I was bluffing him about harming his family and hand over the CCTV footage. We can disguise our appearance as much as we like, but that will only go so far. We have to keep on the move."

"I understand." She walked toward the struggling woman.

From a distance of about twenty feet, Jacob observed keenly as Irina went to work on the bait-and-switch.

She cleared her throat to alert the woman there was someone behind her. Clever. The last thing they wanted was for the mark to scare and drop the boxes. "Excuse me," she said in English. "You need help?"

The woman turned slowly, her feet shuffling in tiny increments. A smile of relief. "Ja, yes please. The shopkeeper offered to assist, but stupid me said no, I can manage. Ha ha! And now I can't even open the door!"

"Where is key? I open for you."

The woman inclined her head downward and to the left. "In my handbag. Can you reach it?"

"I think so." Irina smiled benignly at the woman as she undid the brass clip of the leather handbag and stuck her hand inside. She pulled out a keyring with the chunky Porsche blipper and held it up for Jacob to see. He looked right and left. The street was empty of both people and traffic, snow now falling gently. As far as he could ascertain, there were no obvious security cameras in the area.

Treading softly, he sneaked up to be next to Irina, on the

woman's blind side. Irina placed the keys in Jacob's hand and said, "You want cakes in back?"

"Ja, bitte." *Yes, please*. The woman shuffled in the direction of the liftgate. "Thank you so much."

"One second. I open for you."

Jacob pressed the button to unlock the door and jumped in behind the driver's seat. Irina wasted no time getting in beside him. He started the engine and took off smoothly down the street as the woman screamed her lungs out.

"Find a hardware store for me," Jacob said, driving as fast as he could without being reckless and drawing attention. He'd recently seen a list of the most surveilled cities in Europe; Swiss cities didn't figure on that list. But that didn't mean they weren't out there. Or traffic cameras that read license plates.

"Found one. It's only ten minutes away."

Nineteen minutes later, Jacob pushed a small shopping cart toward the cashier in the store at the Brunaupark shopping mall. In it, a tool kit, water bottles, waterproof matches, rope, a couple of hunting knives, bungee cords, ground sheets, sleeping bags, gray duct tape, notepads and pens, a basic first-aid kit, and a bright orange reflective worker's jacket plus the wire hanger it was displayed on. He would have liked to grab a tent, but time wasn't their friend. With luck, not many of those items would be required as Ed Brown and Irene Frobisher made their way to the Greek island of Aegina. Unsmiling, the gum-chewing cashier robotically scanned his items, Jacob paid and was soon back in the parking lot. Irina stood next to a shopping trolley return bay, their travel bags by her side. "Come with me while I chose our next ride," he said. "If we're lucky, we won't have to change cars again until we get to Greece." His plan was to keep swapping license plates along the way, maybe two or three times.

Fifty feet away, he spied two good options standing side by side.

"Keep guard. Tell me if anyone approaches."

"Okay, but be quick." She shivered. "I don't like this."

"You think I do? I'd much rather be home with my feet up, watching the ball game on TV."

Jacob donned the safety jacket, hoping it would make his actions look normal if anyone observed him. With the screwdriver from the tool kit he'd just purchased, in under a minute, he'd removed the front and rear license plates from a neighboring white Opel Vivaro van with Danish registration. He swapped them over with a nearby silver Ford Explorer bearing Swiss registration. Neither vehicle had distinctive markings or decals. Initially, the roomier van looked the best option, but the newer SUV offered a better ride and mileage. The fewer stops, the better. He stood and slapped his palms together, ready to take the next risky step: breaking into an alarmed vehicle, turning off the alarm, and driving out of there like a Formula 1 driver needing to win the last race to secure the championship.

"Psst. There's someone coming," said Irina. "Shall we go?"

"No. I've only finished the first part of the job. Let's wait over by that Škoda."

They tried to look inconspicuous as a young couple approached, laden with shopping bags. To his disappointment, the couple got into the Ford Explorer and drove off.

The van it would have to be.

Using skills a career car thief would be proud of, he untwisted the coat hanger, shoved the hook between the door frame and the window, and jiggled until the locking mechanism released. He leapt in the driver's side, Irina already sitting on the passenger seat. He quickly located the necessary wires under the dash to connect the battery to the ignition, fired up the engine, released the handbrake, and drove away, nice and easy.

THIRTY-ONE

It took three hours and forty-eight minutes until they saw the sign that said 'Milano.' Along the way, they encountered some toll roads, slow spots at road works sites, but generally it was an uneventful and smooth run. The Swiss cops were unlikely to send a chopper looking for car thieves, but Canadian-slash-Russian bank robbers, that was another matter. Constantly on the alert, the only vehicles they encountered with sirens wailing was a procession of ambulances near Lake Como.

After making his purchases at the hardware store in Zurich, Jacob had withdrawn as much cash as he could from an ATM: several thousand Swiss francs and five hundred euros, the most the machine would allow. The cash was for paying road tolls and making all incidental purchases as anonymously as possible.

With the GPS system switched over to English, they easily found a parking garage not far from a large shopping mall on the outskirts of Milan. In the darkness of the low-ceilinged third-level, Jacob deftly swapped plates for a French-registered VW Polo about a hundred feet away. First job done. Europe's finest police forces would be scratching their heads, unable to track the Opel van as it snaked its way south.

Second job—buy new SIM cards. The Swiss ones worked

poorly in other parts of Europe, but the Italian TIM brand would be perfect for the rest of their journey.

Third job—acquire new clothes. Irina took a wad of cash from Jacob and went searching for fresh outfits for both of them. He jotted down his sizes and suggested she buy things she'd imagine her son could wear to 'not stand out.' He reminded her to stay alert for trouble. She skipped away, delighted with the shopping assignment.

Fourth job—radical haircut. Jacob located a quiet barber shop and asked the old man, who had been dozing in his chair, to give him a number one buzz cut, then follow up with a skull shave. The barber sparked to life now he had something to do and completed the task in quick time. When he held up the hand-mirror for the customer's panoramic judging, Jacob grinned broadly. This was a style he'd always wanted to try but somehow never had. The result impressed him; perhaps he'd stick with it.

With just over an hour left before the mall closed, the fugitives were now working hard at the fourth and final job before hitting the road again. Eating.

"I never imagined my first trip abroad would be so exciting," said Irina, rubbing her finger around the plate to scoop up the last of the pizza crust crumbs. Three shopping bags with famous labels emblazoned on them sat by her feet. "And Milan! I couldn't have dreamed it up. Even if it is the outer suburbs."

"Sorry it's under such stressful circumstances. Next time we'll visit all the tourist sights."

"There'll be a next time?"

"Perhaps. I'm not very good at making predictions. I was sure I was going to be a professional football player when I was a teenager. Now look where I am. Running from a handful of security agencies and police forces."

"Tell me about when you were a teenager." She leaned in. "I'm curious about this man who is saving me from a life of tyranny."

Breaking all the rules, Jacob shared elements of his past with

Irina. He didn't name places or people, but the gist of it was the truth. She didn't interrupt, nodding and smiling appropriately. As he described his infatuation with a girl who resembled her in so many ways, she blushed deeply. When he told her she'd been killed, the murderer never found, she cried like she had lost a relative of her own.

Dabbing her eyes with a napkin, she said, "I've been dying to ask one question. How on Earth do you speak Russian so well? It's truly amazing."

Again, he told the truth. This time he did use his nanny's name. It was common and anonymous enough.

"Natasha the au pair from Saint Petersburg was your nanny, huh? Positively romantic."

"I barely remember her at all." He explained about the recordings she had left behind that had gathered dust in the attic until he heard them again after his football injury. "But the knowledge she ingrained in me"—he tapped the side of his head—"it's in here forever."

"So it seems." She took the opportunity to eye his face up and down. "You know, I was skeptical when you said you were going to do it, but that bald look really suits you. Like, no one would dare mess with you."

"Thanks." Not one to blush easily, Jacob felt little prickles of heat popping under his skin.

"Should I do something with my hair?" she asked, titling her head slightly. "Mine is so boring."

"Not yet. A woman's hairstyle can take hours and..."

"Not necessarily. Take me to the barber who did yours. I'm thinking one of those masculine cuts a certain type of woman goes for."

Jacob narrowed his eyes. "You know, that's not as crazy as it sounds. Let's go."

They snatched up their belongings and made it to the barber shop just as the old man was about to close for the night. In broken English, he explained he hadn't cut a woman's hair in years and wasn't confident he could create a hairdo that the lady would be satisfied with. Jacob waved a hundred euros in front of him, and the man suddenly became supremely confident in his abilities.

"Is okay," said Irina. "Is easy job. Make me look like her."

He studied the image of Ellen DeGeneres on the screen of Irina's cell phone. "Yes! That I can do."

The man snipped and shaved, wielding scissor and clippers like a maestro for fifteen minutes. The result pleased Irina immensely. "Beautiful," she enthused. As the old man brushed the small hairs from her neck she said, "Pity no time to make blond."

"Not true." The barber took an aerosol can from a glass shelf. "Spray on, instant change. Come out after cuppla washes."

Irina's eyes sparkled. "Grazie mille." *Thank you so much.*

Jacob smiled to himself. She was starting to get the hang of this gig.

Twenty minutes later, he steered the van out onto the main highway and set the GPS to Athens. The route required they pay more tolls and pass through official border crossings into Slovenia, Croatia, Serbia, Northern Macedonia and, finally, Greece.

"Will my American passport get me through the checkpoints?"

Jacob smiled as he stopped for a red light. "Absolutely. Unless something's gone horribly wrong, we should sail through."

"Ah...what could go horribly wrong?"

"It's an unlikely scenario, but moles have been known to infiltrate the US embassy."

She put her hand to her forehead. "Don't tell me, please."

"Okay." The light turned green, and he merged onto the A51.

"And what could a mole do?" Her curiosity could not be contained.

He turned to look at her for a moment before refocusing on the night traffic. "The worst thing I can think of is they might inform the Serbs, for example, to be on the lookout for a Russian national traveling under a bogus US passport."

"Wait! Aren't we traveling through Serbia? Jacob!"

"Relax, nothing's happened for five years. And even the mole they did discover didn't turn over anything compromising. Systems and protocols are stricter now than they were then. I'd bet anything there are no moles in the embassy now."

"Your life?"

"Ah...maybe not."

"Jacob! Turn around."

"And go where? Like I said, we'll sail through all the border crossings. It's a simple procedure, have no fear."

"That's easy for you to say."

"Yes, it is. Because it's true. I suggest you close your eyes for a spell. I'll find us a place to have a real sleep once we cross over into Slovenia."

The digital dash clock ticked over to 10:00 p.m. Irina was dozing, head tucked into a rolled-up sweater. His own eyes began to droop. Although not quite as nerve-wracking as the trek from the south of Russia to Moscow, his nerves were on a knife edge. He'd played it cool for Irina, but having verbalized the potential for something to go wrong, especially at the border crossing from Croatia into Serbia, he began to think there actually could be a snafu. The country was one of the few in Europe that behaved favorably toward Russia and its government, so if they'd somehow been rumbled, the consequences would be dire.

The crossing from Italy into Slovenia was uneventful. One Eurozone country to another, so no checks. Jacob didn't even realize he was in another country until an advertising sign for a restaurant appeared in Slovenian.

Now midnight, he pulled over to check online for somewhere to stay. A small camping ground in the town of Trebnje was an hour and a half away, boasting 24/7 self-serve hot showers that cost a euro for fifteen minutes. Perfect. As he reached toward the button to set the GPS for the camp site, which would have few if any other people staying there at this time of year, his cell phone rang.

Jacob wasn't quick enough to answer it to prevent the loud ringtone from waking Irina. Her eyes sprang open, and she began to moan, as if she'd been having a nightmare. "It's okay, just a phone call."

She blinked hard and rubbed her eyes, moist with tears. "I'm sorry. I was dreaming about Vova, and Mama and Papa too."

He offered his best understanding smile. "Let me get this first, okay?"

She nodded slowly.

"Yes?"

"It's Grant."

"I know it's you."

"Where the hell are you, Jacob? You were supposed to be on the flight to JFK."

"Change of plan. We're in Slovenia, heading to the island of Aegina."

"What the...?"

"Fitting for a Skia operative to be going to Greece, don't you think?"

"Just be careful."

"You don't have to remind me. We were shot at."

"I kind of figured it must have been you. The story's all over the news. The Swiss gendarmes are–"

"They're called the Polizei in Zurich. It's the German part of Switzerland. Gendarmes are in the French part."

"Thanks for the culture lesson." The sound of a familiar television news bulletin's theme music came from Fletcher's end. "Your little escapade is just about to be repeated on the news again. I've already seen it. Highly entertaining."

"I'm putting you on speaker. What are they saying?"

"There's CCTV of you two emerging from the bank, but it's blurry and could be anyone. Nice outfits, by the way. Modern-day Bonnie and Clyde."

Irina laughed out loud, bringing a grin to Jacob's face.

"What else?"

"Some kid managed to get shaky footage of the taxi shooting. The aftermath at least. No images of you, just the dude stalking with his AK-47 or whatever it is. Man, that would have scared the shit out of me. I don't know how you held it together."

"It was worse in Belaya Berozka," said Jacob. "But that's a story for another occasion." He paused for a moment to stretch his neck muscles. "So they've got pictures. Do they have theories?"

"The details of what went on inside the bank have not been disclosed. Except for one version. The media are suggesting you are both a pair of Russian spies."

Irina burst out laughing again. "That's what the bank manager thought we were!"

"So," Jacob continued, "nothing about the Canadian Ministry of Finance?"

"Nope. It would just be plain embarrassing to admit they were duped so easily. Hats off to both of you for that performance." The volume of Fletcher's TV increased, then the sound cut out. "I've heard enough. Now I've got some other new for you. Irina's parents are in good hands."

"What?" she cried out. "Is it true?"

"Jacob's instincts were correct about the brush-by guy," said Fletcher with a hint of pride in his charge. "He's a fixer I'd like to have working for me."

"He is working for you, Grant. Just under a different payroll."

"Good point. Anyway, this guy got the extraction organized in a heartbeat. He had someone in the local area collect Irina's parents and whisk them away. And not a moment too soon. Apparently, he posted a couple of lookouts nearby, and not five minutes after we evacuated Mom and Pop, a couple of cars turned up at the apartment building with maybe six heavies on board. They returned to their vehicles with angry faces, so I'm told."

Irina rubbed her hands together. "Great news. And my brother?"

Fletcher was silent for too long.

"What about my brother?" she repeated.

"Not such great news."

"Was he arrested?'

"I...I don't know. We haven't located him yet, but they're looking hard."

Irina's hands shot to her face as she let out a high-pitched wail.

THIRTY-TWO

"You have let me down, Lilliana," said Samsonov, looking out the window as the 20-foot-long black stretch limo hummed over the city street, their path cleared by the screeching sirens, strobing blue lights behind the vehicle's grille, and baton-waving traffic cops. "You have let the president down, the country." He tuned to glare at her, but she refused to meet his gaze. "But worst of all, you have let yourself down."

She sat mute. Volunteering information that wasn't a response to a direct question would only elicit another slap across the cheek. Pride ruled out blubbering and protesting her innocence. *Calm, calm, calm.*

"You know, Lilliana, soon we'll be driving in Russian cars only." He patted the soft leather of the back seat in the luxury Mercedes Maybach. "These German automobiles are great, but symbolically, it sends the wrong signal to the people. Government officials will very soon be switching to the home-grown Aurus limos. A big step forward for our country, don't you agree?"

"Yes," she said. "A plus for our manufacturing industry."

"Your next trip could be in a Russian-made hearse. So consider your every word when Vladimir Vladimirovich speaks to you." He pulled up the collar of his winter coat despite the heater working overtime in the vehicle.

The car made a left before heading up the ramp that led through the arch under the Borovitskaya Tower at the southwest corner of the citadel. The driver stopped and exchanged a few words and a laugh with three men in black uniforms and broad-brimmed hats before guiding the car onto the sacred territory of the Kremlin itself.

In a dark courtyard, another pair of uniformed men presented themselves with an ostentatious salute, then led the way with Samsonov and Danilova trailing two steps behind. She was unfamiliar with the layout of the labyrinthine Kremlin, having been an infrequent visitor over the years. You had to be invited into its most secret parts. But, as she understood well, not all invitations were created equally.

Inside the Grand Kremlin Palace, Putin's official working residence, were five reception halls; however, Danilova was sure she wouldn't be visiting any of them. Eyes down, she allowed herself to be caught up in the flow, like a leaf on a stream, with no free will of her own. The distance covered before she and Samsonov were ushered into a small, modest office would have been less than a hundred meters. One of the guards closed the door.

Inside were three men. Two giants with crew cuts and unsmiling faces stood on either side of a classic wooden desk, seated between them the most dangerous man in the world.

Danilova stared at the wavy patterns of the wood grain. She thought she would lose control of her bowels as the short dictator gestured for his guests to take a seat on the other side of the desk. She dared a sideways glance at a sweating Samsonov, who maintained a firm, straight mouth, expressionless eyes.

"Let's get down to business, shall we?" said Putin, gently tapping his finger on the desktop.

"You will escape severe punishment if you can atone for your egregious sins." His mouth disgusted her. The thin lips that barely parted when he spoke. "Do you think you can do that?"

Her eyelids fluttered. *The man thinks he's the Messiah.* Before the end of the Soviet Union he, like all his communist colleagues, was an avowed atheist. Now that it was politically expedient to appear as a righteous believer, he had adopted the language of the Orthodox Church.

"Yes," she whispered. "I think I can atone."

"That's a good girl," he said with a quiet menace. "If we can retrieve the letter from the American *and* liquidate him, I will not only spare you from life in a Siberian prison, I will also make sure you still have a job." He looked up at the ceiling. "Perhaps a cleaner, or...no, I have a better idea. A whore for Medvedev!"

Don't react.

"Of course, I'm not being serious. Dmitry has his favorites already. You're not exactly his type." He narrowed his rodent eyes. "But I digress." He reached into a top drawer and pulled out a notepad. He tossed it across the desk to her. "First, I want a confession from you. I want to know your role in this act, the names of others involved, and an admission from you that you were seeking to destabilize the legitimate government."

If only you knew I was seeking to have you killed. She nodded slowly. "Now?"

Putin looked off to a corner of the ceiling. "No. Take it with you, have a good hard think about it. I'm keen to compare your words with what we've been able to shake out of Gerasimchuk." He gave his best friendly laugh, but to Danilova, it embodied evil. "It's amazing how a little physical persuasion can make even the most stubborn opponent spill his guts."

A slight head gesture from Putin and Samsonov stood, gripped Lilliana by the elbow, and led her to the door. Instincts told her to try to shake loose from his grasp; she had to fight instinct now and be guided only by logic and common sense. Her very survival depended on it.

"Oh, and Maxim."

Samsonov turned around. "Yes, Vladimir Vladimirovich?"

"Don't let her out of your sight for the next 24 hours. If she disappears, I *will* hold you responsible for this entire mess. Your career will be over."

"My wife, though...she's expecting me home tonight. I've already been absent for four nights in Saint Petersburg. How would I explain it to her?"

Putin gripped the bridge of his nose, fingers trembling slightly. "Do I have to do the thinking for everyone?" He stared at Samsonov with burning eyes. "Tell her I sent you on an unscheduled, urgent trip to Kazan. Here." He quickly scribbled something on a piece of paper and handed it to Samsonov. "A note from me you can give your hen-pecking wife. Like the ones your dear old mother wrote for the teacher when you were a little boy."

"Yes, Mr. President." Danilova noted the humiliation in Samsonov's eyes. *Good.* "But...ah...where should I take Lilliana?"

"The top floor at the Patriarch's Ponds building is available. Spend the night there. I will send for you both again tomorrow evening. Bring me the truth, Lilliana, or else." Danilova couldn't believe she was to be taken to this location. Her head spun, flecks of light dancing in her eyes, the way they do just before you faint. Somehow, she held it together. The exact address was unknown to her, but many knew of the facility. In fact, she thought it was just a legend. A secret apartment hidden in plain sight in Patriarch's Ponds, one of Moscow's most affluent areas the locals nicknamed 'Patriki.' Rumors circulated far and wide about the acts of depravity that went on there. Interrogations, torture, even orgies for the elite. Samsonov had never mentioned to her that he had been there, but it was no guarantee that he hadn't. When Putin named the place, Samsonov didn't flinch.

"Yes, Vladimir Vladimirovich." A slow nod followed that almost turned into a fawning genuflection. The sycophancy turned Danilova's stomach.

As they followed the heels of the guards back to the limo, she smiled to herself. Even the favorite Samsonov had to eat humble pie now and again. A rapid, silent trip across town ensued, Samsonov busy texting back and forth with his wife. What a pathetic man he was. Too scared to speak to her directly.

The limo pulled up outside an imposing building with a pastel green façade directly opposite the massive rectangular pond after which the district was named, frozen solid.

"Priekhali." *We're here*, said the driver. "Everybody out."

As she was led up the concrete stairs, her footsteps and those of the guards and Samsonov echoing eerily in the void, one thing was firm in her mind. If she was going down, she would try her damnedest to take Samsonov with her.

THIRTY-THREE

Steam came off his breath as he waited patiently in the van for his turn to wash, alternately reading and listening to news broadcasts online. He rubbed his hands together and wriggled his toes to keep the blood circulating.

They'd struck it lucky with the mini campsite. Midwinter meant low demand. Tonight that translated to no demand. They were the only ones needing a place to rest in this neck of the woods. A caretaker's porchlight glowed yellow a hundred feet from the parking lot. Apart from the neon sign on the side of the road denoting the campsite and a globe above the shower block, no other lights burned. Six log cabins appeared to be empty, and there were no other cars in the small parking lot. He paid the twenty euro overnight fee by scanning a QR code set on a pole near the entrance and entering the details for the limitless and anonymous AmEx card.

He scrolled through the headlines of a top Russian government run news site. Nothing about the incident in Switzerland, same for the MinFin safecracking. Five other kindred websites also produced no results. The Russian Internet, true to form, remained as silent as Lenin's tomb. Had it been otherwise, Jacob would have been genuinely shocked.

European media were more forthcoming. Searches for the fugitives who had violated the bank manager were concentrating on Switzerland but also extended into France and as far afield as Denmark. Their escape route was anybody's guess. The plate swapping was bearing fruit.

Jacob's next tactic would be to slightly alter the appearance of the letters and numbers of the current license plates with duct tape, maybe stealing one last vehicle. An escape through the Balkans, he hoped, would not figure high in police theories. There were still plenty of risks ahead in this journey. Hard land borders to cross, where officials could potentially rumble them. On the positive side, in Jacob's experience, border guards were among the most bribable officials in the world; the large amount of currency he had withdrawn could help get them out of any potential scrapes. Or it could sink their hopes altogether should they encounter that rare bird—a totally honest employee for whom bribes were anathema.

Irina's slouched figure moved in front of the fogged-up front windshield. She passed the passenger door, rounded the vehicle, and crawled into the back of the van. The seats were folded down, sleeping bags laid out. It was freezing cold both inside and outside, and getting into the insulated bags as soon as possible made sense. Jacob looked in the rearview mirror as she unzipped the bag and wriggled her way inside.

"You okay?" he said. "I was worried about you. You seemed to be taking a while."

"I took two turns in the shower: one to get clean, another to wash away my guilt."

"You've got nothing to feel guilty about."

"I've been praying Igor is unharmed. Just because your man from the embassy couldn't find him, that doesn't mean the worst has happened, right?" She was fishing desperately for reassurance. "I mean, he could be anywhere."

"That's right. I'm optimistic he hasn't been picked up by the FSB." That was a blatant lie. He had no such optimism, but her freaking out over the sixteen-hour drive to Athens wasn't going to help anyone.

"How can we find out?"

"Find out what?"

"Where Igor is. You must have people who can track him down."

"Let me think about it. Back soon." He half-stepped out of the van, then twisted his body to look at her. "I know it's quiet, but keep your eyes peeled and the doors locked. If anyone comes and tries to get inside, lean on the horn as hard as you can." He told her to arm herself with one of the hunting knives—just in case—grabbed a set of clean clothes, and headed for the shower. He took the other knife, as well as the State Department letter in a waterproof plastic bag tucked inside the pocket of his toiletries bag. He'd transfer it back to his pants pocket when he hit the hay.

The hot water almost scalded his skin, but he nevertheless left it on the highest setting. Rubbing in pine-scented soap squirted from a wall-mounted dispenser, he recalled how Irina had cried her eyes out for a full ten minutes after the call with Fletcher. She'd admitted she'd never been especially close to Igor, but that barely mattered. He was flesh and blood all the same. Thinking about the indignities Samsonov had made her endure to have Igor freed, only for him to be rearrested, were too much to bear. And the tears flowed in a river.

Jacob's gut clenched as he pictured Igor in the hands of the FSB. Irina had shown him a photo on her phone. He was a puny fellow but big of heart. The man had pushed the envelope with the authorities already with his anti-war protesting. If caught, he'd be shown little mercy, Samsonov would see to that. He'd be thirsting for revenge now that Irina had thumbed her nose at him, embarrassed him before the president. Jacob shook his head, wondering whether the trade-off—freedom and a new life for Irina, her son and her parents—was worth the life of her brother. He couldn't come up with the correct answer because there wasn't one.

Sleep proved elusive for Jacob. The bitter cold didn't help matters. He tossed and turned for several hours, thoughts racing through his head. Should they not simply risk flying out of Athens? It was a tough call; however, he couldn't rule out the possibility that all airports were on high alert for the fugitives. He might get through using his real passport, but she might not. He was not willing to risk her life for his.

Irina had no problems falling asleep, exhaustion defeating anxiety. She snored quietly from the moment Jacob put his head down, her body juddering occasionally. A few mumbled words escaped from the realm of her subconscious as she dreamed of God only knew what.

The sun rose weakly just after 7:00 a.m., a crisp, clear, cloudless morning. The neatly clipped grass surrounding the parking lot was white, covered in a crust of frost, small patches of green poking through here and there. They departed the deserted campsite with a minimum of fuss.

As Jacob had hoped, crossing the border into Croatia forty minutes later posed zero problems. The smiling young border guard waved them through, stamping their passports without asking any questions.

Traffic on the E70 was light, mainly semitrailers with a sprinkling of smaller vehicles, gradually building as the hours ticked by. Three hours and twenty minutes later, they had traversed Croatia and had reached the next frontier. The lineup of trucks to get into Serbia was insanely long, perhaps two miles. Fortunately, there appeared to be a measly three cars ahead of Jacob on the Croatian side. When their turn came, both passports were stamped and handed back; they experienced exactly the same procedure at the Serbian booth. They were stopped at a secondary booth, however, where a gruff man in a uniform that strained to fit his portly frame demanded to see in the back section of the van. Despite the freezing temperature, Jacob started to sweat. He whispered to

Irina to be quiet, his request met with an eager and compliant nod as she shrank into the collar of her winter jacket.

"Where you come from?" said the guard in a brusque baritone. It barely qualified as a question.

"A holiday in Switzerland with my wife." *Keep it as close to the truth as possible.* "Exploring the Balkans then home to the States."

"You were in Zurich?" the customs man said with a raised eyebrow.

"Unfortunately no. Geneva." Jacob watched as the guard's head bobbed around like a chicken looking for scraps. "Hey," Jacob added, resisting an urge to give the guard a playful nudge. "I heard there was a crazy bank holdup in Zurich. I'm real pissed we missed all the fun."

"Show me bag." The man pointed at one of the two large rucksacks. Irina's bag. The man peered inside, taking a long time pawing through her underwear. He inspected every zipped pocket, turned over each item in his big hands. He then pointed at Jacob's bag. "Give me that one, now."

Jacob reached for the strap handles, his heart pounding like a locomotive. A crackling sound came over the officer's two-way radio. He answered it in an almost military fashion. To Jacob's ear, able to figure out the gist of most Slavic languages, it sounded like the man had been summoned to urgently assist in inspecting a semitrailer with a suspect load. He barked a reply in throaty Serbian, then turned to Jacob and with a dismissive flick of the fingers said, "You can go on your way."

At 10:15 a.m., while they enjoyed strong coffee and a hot breakfast at a café in the town of Dobanovci on the outskirts of Belgrade, Jacob received a text message from Fletcher. Irina's parents were on their way to a safe house in a small town near the Latvian border. Better news: Igor had been located—he was staying at a friend's house in the city of Khimki just outside greater Moscow. Brush-by guy had asked the parents for a list of people they knew who Igor associated with. They could only come up with two names and one phone number, but it was enough, and the agent hastily and efficiently organized the pick-up. Igor was on his way to be with his parents.

Tears of joy replaced last night's tears of anguish. Her hand crept across the console and rested on the top of Jacob's. "You and your government have done so much for me. A week ago, I could never have imagined I'd be doing what I'm doing now."

He stepped on the gas to overtake a couple of slow trucks. Once safely back in their lane, he said, "I'm as surprised as you are. I thought I was going to die on the Ukraine-Russian border." He managed a wry smile.

"Will you tell me about what happened?"

"Maybe later." He concentrated on the road ahead and dropped the speed by 40kph after a sign warning of black ice caught his eye. "I've probably said too much." He turned to look at her briefly. "Not because I don't trust you. Your ignorance could be your salvation. From now on, I'll only share with you information that is relevant to my mission and that will keep us out of harm's way."

She shrugged. "You know what?" She didn't wait for an answer to her rhetorical question. "I'm happy with that."

The border crossing between Serbia and North Macedonia was hassle-free. Two standard questions on entry: *Why are you here and how long are you staying?* Answers: tourism and flying out of Skopje in two days for the USA. Both lies, but they satisfied the border guard, who stamped their passports with a flourish, wished them well, and even gave a small salute.

"No more roughing it," said Jacob as they passed the sign telling them they had reached the city limits of Skopje, the capital of North Macedonia. "We're staying in a five-star hotel."

THIRTY-FOUR

THE SPRAWLING SPACE AT THE TOP OF THE GRAND OLD building resembled an empty dance floor. Polished wooden boards, benches spread around the edges where the belles waited to be picked by a beau. Windows draped with heavy black curtains, powerful halogen lights in the ceiling that lit the place up like a football stadium.

There were four people inside the room. The two burly interrogators, dressed like they were ready for a session in the gym, had gallantly introduced themselves as Boris and Grisha. And their guests for the evening's show, the esteemed Minister for Finance and the humiliated prisoner.

Danilova was strapped into a hard metal chair, hands behind her back, ankles tied tightly together. The tough rope dug into her skin and delivered a burning sensation. A sheet of black plastic, a couple of square meters in area, had been placed under the chair. Boris said it was to catch spills of bodily fluids; the floorboards were much too beautiful to ruin, after all. She was dressed only in black bra and panties, the clothes she had been wearing placed in a wicker basket. If she cooperated, she'd get them back before the sun came up. She cursed her decision to wear a sexy G-string instead of more modest panties, although to be fair to herself, she could never have envisaged today would turn out the way it had.

Three meters away stood Samsonov, his face expressionless granite. His request to absent himself from proceedings had been denied point-blank. *Putin demands you stay and watch*, said the smaller guy, Grisha. *To the end*, added Boris, flashing a gold-toothed grin. Both of the men were ruggedly handsome and athletic, not the ugly brutes of Western propaganda thrillers. Those movies weren't wrong about the torture, though. That part they got exactly right.

She had so far endured fifteen long minutes of shouted threats and fearsome open-handed face-slapping from Boris. He wore leather gloves; whether or not that made the blows more painful for her or less painful for him, she couldn't guess. Without any doubt, though, each slap hurt like hell.

Stoic, she'd so far not revealed any information, but she knew how these sessions escalated to the point where even the strongest would break. The slaps would turn into punches, some teeth would be lost. Next up could be one of hundreds of different techniques to loosen her tongue. Some were old-fashioned tactics inherited from the KGB, before that the NKVD and the Cheka. Indeed, they were barbaric methods that had stood the test of time since the Middle Ages. Others were newer, developed by sadistic minds in FSB scientific laboratories with humans for guinea pigs.

She would crack eventually; she had no doubt of that.

But to hold on for as long as she could—each minute denying them information a tiny, if pointless, victory—that was a goal worth striving for.

"Give her a drink of water." Grisha, waiting his turn to get physical, barked the order to Samsonov. The minister nodded slowly and approached a small side table three meters away on which sat a carafe and an expensive-looking crystal glass. From her position, Danilova could see there were other things on that table:

metal implements lined up on a black cloth. Among them, pliers, pruning shears, knives. Under the table a bucket, perhaps for water boarding.

Samsonov approached with the glass, his hand trembling.

He doesn't have the stomach for this. Perversely, she wanted him to see her suffering, to know how ineffective he was in this surreal situation. He might despise her for the betrayal, but seeing a woman hurt like this would be an affront to an old-fashioned man like Samsonov. Had it been Gerasimchuk sitting in her place, his attitude might be different. Then again, maybe not.

She opened her mouth as he tipped the glass up slowly. Unable to control her swallowing, she spluttered, spraying drops everywhere as Samsonov poured the water. He pulled the glass away, whispering an apology while she continued to cough.

"Do not speak to the prisoner!" snapped Boris, taking his glove off and standing aside for his colleague to take over. "She only answers to us."

"Sorry. I didn't mean to–"

Boris snatched the glass away. "You are useless. Just stand and watch."

Samsonov took a series of backward steps until he was more or less back on the spot he'd previously occupied. His status in the government meant nothing to these cruel men who answered only to the highest power.

In the brief moment of respite, Danilova glanced across at her now ex-lover. Still in his fancy business suit at what she guessed must be after midnight, he cut a pathetic figure. Putin's trust in him would be diminished now, if not entirely lost.

Grisha, the smaller of the two yet still a big man, stepped forward. He smiled as he donned a pair of black leather gloves. "I know my partner has asked you this same question a number of times. I'm only going to ask it once. Where is the American?"

"I cannot give an answer if I don't know what that answer is," she said flatly.

"Okay, Lilliana," he said with what was clearly mock patience. "You don't know where he is. A great pity for you."

Danilova closed her eyelids tight, anticipating the blow. It didn't come. "Let's try another one. Who is your handler in the US embassy?"

The haymaker, a closed fist to the left temple, came before she had time to reply. Her head rocked to the side as she heard Samsonov gasp effeminately. *The weak shit.* She felt a trickle of blood at the side of her mouth.

"Well?" said Grisha. "You must have a handler."

"No." She shook her head. "This is all I know—Voronin's real name is Edward Brown, and he works for the CIA."

The goon must be ambidextrous because the blow to the other side of her head with his left hand stung just as much as the first. A ripping pain arced through her jaw, surely fractured now. Her tongue probed a tooth which had come loose.

"Bullshit!" Grisha took half a step back, crouched low in front of her, rocking on his haunches. "We know who all the CIA agents are. He's not connected with them."

This was a surprise to her. She tried to smile, but the effort stung in several places along her jawline. "Then I don't know..."

Grisha walked to the table of torture tools, making a show of being indecisive about which one to choose, his finger hovering over them. "This one," he said almost victoriously as he held the pruning shears aloft. The blades shone brightly under the halogen lights.

He strode slowly and purposefully back to Danilova, repeatedly squeezing the grips, then letting them go. She looked at Samsonov with pleading eyes. The blood had drained from his face. He caught her eye and looked away, shame burning his cheeks. *The weak shit.*

"One last chance to tell me the truth," said Grisha. "We're done fooling around. Boris will grip your legs firmly while Max over there will hold the plastic bag into which your cute little toes will drop."

She craned her neck around. "Max! You can't let them do this!"

He looked at the floor as Boris handed him the Ziplock bag.

"Let's get this over with," said Grisha. "Oh, before I get chopping, would you like to know what happened to your colleague, Aleksandr Gerasimchuk?"

She blinked away hot tears, stared straight ahead. Her bravado was gone.

"He rolled over after we told him we were coming for you." He barked a laugh. "Quite the gentleman." He stared a laser beam at Samsonov. "Unlike some I could name."

"Aleksandr is a good man," said Danilova.

The remark earned a cobra-strike slap from Boris, followed by a correction.

"*Was* a good man."

"What do you mean?" She wasn't feeling any pain now, just fear for an old colleague.

"His heart gave out under the pressure," said Grisha. "But," he chuckled demonically, "thank God it was after he told us what we wanted to know. It's awful when a person dies in vain, isn't it, Minister?"

"What?" Samsonov's eyes flickered like he was coming out of a trance.

The prick has zoned out; he's stopped paying attention.

"He's not dead! You're lying!" Danilova screeched. She had never visited Gerasimchuk in his home, nor he in hers. They weren't close. Then why did it feel like her best friend had been murdered?

This time, there were no brutal reprisals for her unbidden words.

"I'm sorry to say, but he *is* dead. I don't know why you're so surprised. The man was near retirement age, smoked like a factory, and was generally in poor health." He produced a mobile phone and turned it around for Danilova to see. Grisha pressed play. In another room that looked a lot like the one she was in now,

Gerasimchuk sat in an iron chair, tied exactly the same way she was. They had spared him the indignity of stripping him to his underwear. Shirtless, but with his pants and shoes still on, his face was a black, purple and red mess, individual features impossible to make out. *Where are his nose, his ears, his eyes?* Lolling in the chair, his mouth was a gaping wound, opening and closing like a fish out of water desperate to breathe. Gerasimchuk gagged one final time before his body went completely still.

"We promised him no harm would come to you if he told us who his handler was. And guess what?"

"He told you nothing?"

Boris pulled a shiny new Udav from the back of his pants. "Incorrect. He told us plenty. And so will you." He placed his feet shoulder width apart, flicked the safety, and racked the slide. "It's amazing what we found at the apartment you rented for the American. Not only this one, but a Makarov too. And not a single shot fired from either of them. A clever man, this American, getting the better of you idiots with brain power alone." He waved the weapon in Danilova's general direction. "Time to confess, every last detail. Otherwise I'll empty the entire clip into your pretty head."

Samsonov must have found his balls, Danilova thought, as he took a few steps forward, encroaching onto the black plastic sheet and said, "Come on, guys. Vladimir Vladimirovich said she could atone for her sins. You have to give her a fucking chance!"

"Were you not told to just stand and watch?" Boris aimed the pistol at the middle of Samsonov's forehead.

The minister held up his hands in front of his face, waving them around like a second-rate mime artist. "Please, don't shoot! She's the one who–"

"Relax, Maxim. I'm just kidding. Lower your hands."

Samsonov complied, and a nanosecond later three bullets in quick succession ripped through his chest.

Danilova screamed for twenty seconds before losing consciousness.

She was aroused from the blackness by cold water splashing in her face. Her eyes snapped open to see Samsonov's spreadeagled body, an untidy, bleeding lump on the floor. Another blast of water. *Is it time for the water boarding? Please, not that...*

Grisha, standing behind her, put down the bucket and said in a calm and controlled voice, "It might seem extreme, but we were authorized to liquidate him. And we have also been authorized to liquidate you, if necessary. Now"—he tapped the barrel of the still warm Udav against her skull—"we don't want to do that."

"No," chimed in Boris. "Wasting ladies is distasteful. But you have a chance. Your pal Gerasimchuk, God grant him eternal rest, told us the name of your handler in the embassy. Unless you want to wind up like poor Maxim here, your body never to be seen again, I suggest you cooperate. Get her to tell you where the American is. The president knows he was sent to Moscow to steal a very important document, and he has succeeded."

"No, no," she mumbled, shaking her head. "That's not right. He was sent here to kill Putin," she protested, unable to hide the consternation in her voice. "And I...I was trying to prevent it."

Grisha shook his head. "Sadly no." He showed her a photo of the blown safe in Samsonov's office, then the CCTV footage of Jacob and Irina leaving through the front door of Zurich Security Funds AG. "They are heavily disguised, but you can tell by the way they walk that it's the American and the traitorous IT woman. She was instrumental in helping the American, as was Gerasimchuk. Sadly, the spies have exfiltrated all of Irina Frolova's family, so there is no leverage in that direction. You"—he banged the gun barrel against her mouth, hard enough to bust her lip and draw a stream of hot blood—"are our only hope. Will you atone for your sins and help us track down the American?" He pressed the barrel firmly against her temple. "Say yes, I need you to say yes. I really don't want to blast your brains all over the floor."

It was now crystal clear she'd been duped from the start. They had used her to settle Edward Brown into the job, his apartment, offering up every comfort of home, all the while she'd naively believed he would assassinate the monster. She'd been deceived by her handler at the Embassy. By Gerasimchuk, who knew the real reason for Tolya's infiltration of the ministry. And finally, by Samsonov, the man who had professed his love for her.

"Yes. I will cooperate."

THIRTY-FIVE

THE BRUTAL PART OF THE INTERROGATION ENDED, JUST like that. The FSB agents untied Danilova and escorted her via the stairwell to the floor below. They entered a luxurious apartment with high ceilings decorated in French renaissance style: Gold, cream and olive-green shades dominated the décor. The agents set up in the lounge room while Danilova was instructed to clean herself up in the bathroom. "Take as long as you want," said Grisha. "We'll be waiting here. Coffee or tea?"

"Coffee. And some cognac."

"We only have vodka."

"That will do."

She spent fifteen minutes under jets of hot water, alternately crying in despair and vowing to get revenge. She dried off with a soft towel, put on her clothes, and met Boris and Grisha in the opulent lounge room. Her Winstons and lighter had been placed on a small table next to the armchair Boris directed her to sit in. With fumbling fingers, she lit a menthol cigarette and inhaled greedily.

It was as if the torture and murder upstairs had never happened.

Boris held out her cell phone. "We've analyzed this device and found a number of messages in some weird code we've been unable to decipher. Who are you communicating with?"

"A woman from the US embassy."

"Who is she?"

"She works as a policy analyst. Been there for five years. She's been my case officer for two of them."

"Name?"

"Elizabeth."

"No last name?"

A shrug. "She told me it was Harrington, but that could be fake."

"Was she also Gerasimchuk's handler?"

A look away—how she hated looking these animals in the eye. "You already know that, you told me!"

Grisha said, "Set up a meeting with her."

Danilova nodded. "She may contact me herself in the next couple of days. She'll be aware Edward Brown is on the move. For all I know, he's already safe and sound back in the States."

"For your sake, he'd better not be," said Boris, helping himself to one of Danilova's cigarettes.

Her eyes flickered for a moment as an ache flared under her right ear. "Look, there's a regular meet scheduled for Friday. Perhaps–"

"Not soon enough," said Boris, looking at the screen of his own cell phone. "It's already Tuesday."

"But I'll need time to recover from the...interview." Danilova had seen her reflection in the bathroom mirror. Not pretty. Her face and neck were red raw and covered in welts. Bruising would bloom in a day or two. It would require at least a week to regain her normal appearance. "A rendezvous when I look like this will arouse suspicion."

"Doesn't your husband beat you up?"

She frowned. "You know I don't have a husband."

Grisha's eyebrows lifted, like he'd had a brainwave. "We'll get our best disguise people on to it. They work their magic with the makeup, no one will suspect a thing. But if the woman does notice something's not quite right with you, blame it on Samsonov."

Boris burst out laughing. "Brilliant idea. He'd have been rightly pissed that his lover had betrayed him." He stared hard at Danilova. "News of Samsonov's untimely and mysterious demise will not be made public until you have completed your assignment for us. Which is great news for you. Gives you leeway." He pushed Danilova's phone across the table. "Go on. Text your handler. Do you think you can persuade her to divulge what we need to know?"

"I know I can," Danilova lied.

The green-eyed, ginger-haired woman turned up the fur collar of her gray gabardine winter overcoat. She spoke in English, a flat mid-Western accent. "You've got a sense of humor, my dear. Park Zagadka? It means Mystery Park, doesn't it?"

"Yes, it does," agreed Danilova. "But that fact hadn't crossed my mind when I asked you to meet me at this location."

"You've dragged me a long way from the center." Elizabeth smiled sweetly. "So spit it out. Why here?"

"I had to, Elizabeth," said Danilova. "The farther away from the center, the better." She added a white lie. "Plus I have a relative in this neighborhood who I'd like to visit later." It was a great aunt, and she was buried in a cemetery a few blocks away.

"You haven't been compromised, have you?" An expression of minor alarm cast a shadow across Elizabeth's face. "I couldn't bear the thought of having to abandon you!"

"Oh, no, nothing like that. But I have to tell you, after Voronin or Brown or whoever he is did what he did at MinFin, the shit has hit the fan, as you Americans like to say." She glanced over her shoulder, making a show of looking for danger. This secluded section of the park in the far northeastern corner of greater Moscow, however, was deserted, with the exception of the occasional dog-walker.

Danilova was wearing a wire, and there was a miniature camera installed in the top button of her coat. The FSB had earlier set up a network of surveillance equipment in the vicinity of the bench they sat upon, with agents listening in and watching from a van parked on the edge of the recreation area. There was every chance CIA or other American spies had been placed in the park to look out for Elizabeth's well-being. A quick countersurveillance sweep came up empty, but there were no guarantees they hadn't missed something. As such, the approach today would be softly-softly with no abduction or violence in the park.

Elizabeth screwed up her eyes. "What's that on your face? Are you okay?"

"This?" Danilova pointed to her bottom lip. "Maxim. He likes it rough, but sometimes he can take things a little bit too far."

"What an asshole." Elizabeth touched Danilova's lip with her gloved fingertip; over the last eight hours, the injury had swollen to such an extent the makeup expert could do nothing to disguise the lump. Danilova shivered more than could be explained away by the cold mid-morning temperature. "I often hate myself for getting you involved in all of this." Elizabeth crossed her arms. "And I'm jealous as hell knowing you sleep with that creep."

Sitting together on the park bench, like a couple of close friends, no passer-by would imagine their relationship was as intimate and passionate as it really was. And now, Danilova had to put all their romantic history out of her mind; the torrid first night they'd shared at a resort in the south of France—at a time that seemed like a hundred years ago, when Russians were free to roam the planet like everyone else. The rest of that holiday, when both women had attended an international trade fair, was a simmering mess of wild partying and hot, steamy sex. Being with Elizabeth was nothing like Danilova had ever experienced with a man. Not that she didn't enjoy men, she absolutely did. But with *her*, it was next level in intensity.

And then it all went to hell when Putin, with his Napoleonic ambitions, had to go and ruin it for everyone by invading Ukraine. It especially hurt Danilova: with the rise in intolerance toward same-sex attraction in Russia, going abroad for a holiday now and again with Elizabeth was taken off the menu. Their irregular clandestine hook-ups in Moscow had to be planned very carefully and were moments to be treasured.

Life wasn't perfect, but it was tolerable. Until that one fateful day, when they were sneaking an afternoon quickie at a rented apartment, the American woman suggested the unthinkable. *With your help, we can take him out.*

The opportunity was too good to pass up. Playing a key role in the liquidation of the tyrant. She had said yes, with alacrity.

But, as she had since learned, there wasn't and never had been such a plan. Over the last couple of hours, Danilova scolded herself for ever believing such a fairy tale could come true. Elizabeth had used her, just like the other assholes in her life had used her.

Could Danilova betray *her*, though? She thought for a while that she loved the American spy, but perhaps it was just a long-term infatuation. Even now, she was gripped by indecision. As she stared at an empty playground under the snow-covered branches of a stand of evergreens, the moment of clarity she so desperately sought arrived. She would go along with the FSB's demands, get the information out of Elizabeth, and then play it by ear. They wouldn't kill Elizabeth: there was a weird unwritten law among intelligence agencies that each other's operatives were not to be killed. Kidnapped, tortured, imprisoned, yes, but not killed. That rule was sometimes broken, but for the most part complied with. An exception would definitely be made for Edward Brown.

For her efforts, Danilova would likely end up in IK-2 Mordovia, which sucked. But it was prison, not death. She wasn't prepared to die, especially for traitors. Even ones she loved.

"Why did you do it?" said Danilova suddenly. The questions she would ask had been provided to her by an odious FSB agent, Colonel Gavriil Solovyov, the man leading today's operation. She was allowed to improvise if she thought going off script would elicit more information.

"Do what?"

"Get me involved in a plot that can only ended badly for me." She gritted her teeth; feigning indignation wasn't required because that's exactly the emotion she was experiencing. "You've destroyed my trust in you, Elizabeth." The tears that leaked out of the corners of her eyes were real, too. "After everything we've been through together."

The woman's hand sneaked across and rested on a thigh, sending a bolt of desire through Danilova's entire body. *This isn't going to be easy.*

"Would you have agreed to infiltrate our man if you thought the goal was to steal one measly document?" said Elizabeth.

"Definitely."

"Honestly?"

"Yes! I'd have done anything for you. Now I don't know..."

"So what's the problem? In your own way, you've helped us in our ongoing battle with Putin."

"What was in the letter?"

"To be honest, I have no idea."

"So it could have been anything. A fucking phone bill!"

Elizabeth scoffed. "Don't be ridiculous. If it was locked away in a safe, then you can be sure it was of enormous value."

Time to switch tack. "I've seen the footage from Switzerland. Brown was there together with a woman from work. I think they formed a secret relationship. I know they robbed a bank's safe deposit box. Why would they do that?"

Elizabeth shrugged. "I don't know anything about it."

"Really?"

"Yes." The tone of Elizabeth's voice took on a sharp edge. "That's beyond my pay grade." She stood and adjusted the strap of her handbag over her shoulder. "I'm not sure why we are even having this conversation. You summoned me, so I assumed it was something of vital importance."

I'm losing her.

Danilova threw her arms around Elizabeth's neck and whispered in her ear, "I love you so much." She sensed the American rubbing her cheek against hers, slowly positioning her mouth over the top of hers, kissing with an incandescent heat. The beautiful American loved her too.

What a pity.

"Quickly now, we have to go. I think I've got a tail."

"You can't be serious," said Elizabeth, her eyes darting left and right.

"I can't be sure, but I believe someone's following me."

"Who?"

Danilova gripped the woman by the elbow, steering her through a copse of trees and along a slushy path. "FSB, probably. They must be putting it all together. I recruited Brown, now he's gone with whatever they were trying to protect so badly. They're going to point the finger of blame at me."

"Jesus. Are you sure? The backstops are all still in place for Anatoly Voronin...they can be verified."

"Have you got people in the park with you for protection?"

"What? No, of course not! I came on my own to–"

Elizabeth had no time to finish as they reached the edge of the park. A trolleybus pulled up right in front of them. The doors hissed open, and the women stepped inside.

"I need to get back to the office," Elizabeth huffed. "If you're right and–"

"Nonsense. Now that I think about it, I must have been imagining there was a tail." She linked her arm through Elizabeth's and pulled her in close, mouths inches apart. "Actually, I was just playing a game with you. I wasn't lying when I said I had a relative living close by. My aunt. Only she's at work, and I happen to have a spare key. Let's make the most of the opportunity we have. Okay?"

Elizabeth nodded eagerly. "You are a devil, Lilliana!"

THE FSB MAINTAINED hundreds of empty apartments all over Moscow, thousands around the entire Russian Federation. This one-bedroom apartment in the unfashionable Babushkinsky District sat on the tenth floor and overlooked an unkempt pond. Mostly covered in ice, the top half of a shopping trolley thrust out defiantly from under the surface. A handful of women pushed strollers around a web of pathways, some stopping to chat with their neighbors. On the far side of the pond, a group of tracksuit-wearing youths squatted in a circle, chewing sunflower seeds, drinking beer, and shouting at passersby, who, understandably, scurried past as quickly as they could.

Danilova flicked a cigarette butt out the window and closed it. She looked back to the double bed, at Elizabeth's beautiful naked body half covered in a white sheet, one of her plump, pale breasts exposed. They had enjoyed an hour together, now frantically exploring each other like new lovers, now easing back into whispers and cuddles. The American woman dozed, but it was time to act. A gentle shake of the shoulder and Elizabeth opened her eyes.

"Fancy a cup of tea?"

"Sure." Elizabeth rolled over onto her side, and Danilova playfully slapped her backside, then headed for the cramped kitchen. Tea ready and poured, she twisted a capsule and allowed the fine white powder to cascade into the steaming cup. She didn't know exactly what the drug was that Colonel Solovyov had handed her. She guessed it might be a version of sodium pentothal, the so-called truth serum. Torture was the easiest way to get information, but also the messiest.

"Come and get it," Danilova called, setting the cups on the table.

Elizabeth appeared with messy hair, tucking her blouse into the top of her pants. Without speaking, she slid onto a chair.

"Drink up," said Danilova. "My aunt is due back soon. She's not very tolerant of unorthodox relationships, I'm afraid."

"Have I got time for a shower?" said Elizabeth after she'd finished her tea.

Danilova glanced at her watch and puckered her lips like she was mentally calculating the arrival time. "If you're real quick."

The sound of the water running and the woman's off-key singing were enough to drown out the tapping at the door. Danilova opened it with the heaviest of hearts.

"Where is she?" said Solovyov, a small man with the reddish eyes and twitching mouth of a nervous rabbit. Without waiting for an answer, he pushed his way past, Boris and Grisha right behind. Boris carried a medium-sized black bag that looked like the kind doctors keep their equipment in. He placed it on the table and started pulling out the same tools she had seen back at Patriarch Ponds.

"No, no!" hissed Danilova, waving her arms about. "Not these two assholes. This wasn't part of the deal. Why are they here? You mustn't hurt her."

Solovyov smiled reassuringly. "No one is going to get hurt. We're putting on a show for your...girlfriend." He pronounced the last word with undisguised revulsion. He pointed at one of the chairs. "Strip to your underwear and sit down."

It suddenly dawned on Danilova. She knew exactly what would happen next. Her mock interrogation. Despite Solovyov's assurance, she knew she'd be copping more hits, for the sake of realism. Hopefully the animals would hold back a little. Add to that the effect of the drug, and Elizabeth would cough up whatever secret information she possessed.

The tiny room went quiet as the shower and fan were switched off. Then the squeak of the bathroom door opening.

Danilova gulped. *Maybe Elizabeth doesn't know more than she's said already. Shit, shit, shit!*

"Show time," said Solovyov, for some reason in English. He glared at Danilova as Elizabeth's soft footsteps padded down the short hallway.

Elizabeth's eyes bugged. She dropped the towel she was drying her hair with. "What the fuck!"

I'm sorry, Danilova mouthed, tears streaming down her face. *Please forgive me.*

THIRTY-SIX

The chiefs of the FSB, Alexander Bortnikov, and the SVR, Sergei Naryshkin, leaned forward in their seats, hanging on the president's every word like their lives depended on it. Summoned separately, it was a rare occasion for them both to be seated at the table with the president at the same time.

"I need you both to act fast and decisively," said Putin. "I don't know how you're going to do this from a technical perspective, but here's what has to happen."

Both security bosses had their symbolic notepads in front of them, pens poised. Unnecessary, because when the president gave you an order, no matter how complex, you remembered it. Every. Fucking. Word.

"I'm authorizing a reward of 10 million euros for information leading to the apprehension of the man we knew as Anatoly Voronin, also known as Edward Brown," said Putin. "We know precious little about the man, and only have his physical description. A Colonel Solovyov from the FSB, an old colleague of mine from Saint Petersburg, has been acting under my direct authority. However, despite his sterling efforts, we have been unable to find out what we need to know. Facial recognition programs, as well as DNA and fingerprints the criminal left behind have yielded nothing from our databases of known spies. The man is a phantom, it seems." He paused to drink water from a crystal glass. "He and the traitor Frolova have melted into Europe like snow in spring. It's time to widen the net."

"May I ask–" Bortnikov raised a finger tentatively.

"You may not ask anything until I have finished speaking!" thundered Putin. He loosened his tie before continuing. "The reward announcement should be seeded in online forums where members of intelligence communities lurk. Take out ads in all the major newspapers across the world, pay for them through offshore shelf companies, set up an untraceable email address for receiving any tips. Whatever it takes. Just keep it anonymous. I'm hoping that a turncoat from the US side with the knowledge we require will not be able to resist the bait. Americans are driven by greed, so my hopes are high." Another drink of water. "Now any questions?"

Bortnikov opened his mouth but quickly closed it again. "Not from me."

"Me either." Naryshkin finished jotting something in his pad, then pocketed the pen.

"Good," said Putin. "Make it happen!"

Joe Weale squeezed the neck of a bottle of Corona Extra between forefinger and thumb as he tipped it up to his dry mouth. Through a beer-induced haze, he stared across the silver expanse of water at Cabo San Lucas. He'd lived in this Mexican town for ten years, renting a cheap one-level brick and stucco place on a dirt road only a couple hundred yards from the marina. He eked out a living by leading ex-pat Americans and Brits on scuba diving expeditions, tours of the local points of interest. He spent a big chunk of his paltry income on booze and horses that ran too slowly around the Hipódromo de las Américas in Mexico

City. Last year, his income in pesos equated to less than twenty grand in greenbacks.

"Another one, Joe?" said the barman, noticing there was nothing left in the bottle except for the slice of lemon. "You drinking very slow today, gringo."

"What's the hurry?" He picked up his phone. Still no reply from Imma, his new girlfriend. They'd been living together for a couple months, but he was already sick of the arrangement. What promised to be a beautiful relationship based on a mutual appreciation of alcohol had turned into a car crash of mutual animosity. She had promised to pick him up in forty minutes, but he was enjoying the beers a little more than usual today. He sent her a text. *I'll walk home. See you later.* There was nothing to go home for. A woman who got drunk as often as he did, kept an untidy house, and yelled at him. Last night, she'd come at him screaming and wielding a knife. She was fifteen years younger than him, and hanging off her apron strings was a snot-nosed, underfed brat she'd had with a man who was languishing in prison for armed robbery and paid nada in alimony or child support.

"Here ya go," said the barman, sliding a bowl of salted roast peanuts in front of Joe. "A beer plus a pre-dinner snack on the house."

Joe tilted the bottle toward the barman. "Cheers, Miguel. What would I do without you?"

The man scratched the mat of curly hairs on his chest as he pondered the question. "I'd say without me, you would get into not so many bar fights, no?"

Joe smiled, his sun-cracked lips spreading wide.

He was three gulps into beer number five for the afternoon when his cell phone burst into song. The ringtone, Van Halen's "Jump," meant it could only be one person: a prize jerk-off from the past. His inclination was to let the call ring out, but curiosity got the better of him. The number belonged to Marcus Virtanen, a Skia operative who had left Joe for dead in the hands of a cocaine cartel in 2017. Joe blamed the horrors he'd endured at the hands of the sadistic Colombians for turning him into an alcoholic and a sociopath.

"Hey, asshole." It had been almost three years since their last conversation. A bitter one. "Did you ring to apologize for abandoning me in Medellin all those years ago?"

"I tried to come back for you, man. I swear on my mother's grave."

"Don't lie to me, Marcus. What the hell do you want?"

"Listen to me, Joe. I've got a juicy proposition for you. I can't take the lead on this one since I'm still on Skia's payroll."

"I don't wanna hear about it."

"Is five million euros worth a minute of your time?"

Typical bullshit from Virtanen, but it didn't hurt to listen. "Start talking." He slugged half the bottle of beer in one gulp. "You've got exactly one minute."

When Marcus had finished, Joe said, "Okay, you got me interested, and I got nuthin' to lose. What next?"

"I need you to write down a passcode, an email address you will create and later delete, a set of coordinates, and the number of a bank account in Panama."

"One second." He flicked his fingers at Miguel. "Bring me a pen and piece of paper, amigo. And a pack of Marlboros. Muy rapido."

Miguel finished serving a tanned young woman in a revealing bikini, reluctantly tore himself away, and brought the requested items to Joe.

"Okay," said Joe into his beat-up cell phone. "I'm ready." He lit a cigarette and sucked in the smoke.

Three minutes later, Joe ordered another beer, this time with a celebratory tequila chaser. His heart rate and blood pressure now climbing steadily, he knew he had to get home and get the job done before he passed out from the excitement.

Here it was.

His ticket out of poverty and misery.

And all he had to do was send one lousy email.

He staggered back to his hovel; thankfully, Imma was still out with the brat, shopping or whatever. He flopped onto the tattered office chair and, squinting at the screen, logged on to a generic email provider. Summoning dormant spycraft skills he hadn't used in over six years, he cloaked the email address and sent a carefully worded message.

In thirty-six minutes, a reply landed in the inbox of the brand-new account. He clicked it open and scanned the words, scarcely believing what was happening.

Thank you for your information. We have verified your lead with satellite images. Once the product has been picked up from the location you indicated, the agreed payment of 10 million euros will be transferred immediately into the Panamanian account you nominated.

Joe picked up his cell phone and dialed Virtanen. "Hey, ass-wipe. It's done."

"You won't regret this. Now we wait."

THIRTY-SEVEN

THE SHOWER OF SALTY SPRAY FROM THE PASSING JET ski splashed Irina on the face and neck. She yelped and instinctively wiped her mouth with the sleeve of her sweater, also wet from the spray. She stood, yelled an unintelligible obscenity and shook a fist as the lout arced around behind them and sped off at a great rate of knots. "Suka! *Asshole!* And that water is freezing cold. I thought it was supposed to be warm in Greece."

Jacob laughed and rubbed droplets of water that had landed on his newly shaved head. "It's still winter, what do you expect?"

She didn't reply, just reached into an insulated picnic hamper and pulled out a thermos of strong coffee. "Want a drink?" She was already holding the plastic cup out for him. He took it with a nod of thanks, slurped some down, and handed the cup back.

After changing course slightly, Jacob secured the main sheet to the cleat with a slipped hitch, took hold of the tiller, and sat next to Irina. "No need to exaggerate about the weather, by the way." He shielded his eyes against the glare of the midday sun. "It's at least 20 degrees." A quick mental calculation translated it to 68°F. With the light northwesterly blowing, it felt more like 63°F. Add to that the brightly shining sun and total absence of clouds, and in his opinion it was a perfect day for sailing. "And perhaps don't draw attention to us by yelling at idiots on jet skis. We're supposed to be hiding out, remember?" They were virtually unrecognizable in head-to-toe black waterproof pants and hooded jackets teamed with stylish reflector sunglasses, but yelling at strangers was probably a bad idea.

"Sorry." She pouted. "But he intentionally came too close."

"I know. It's a problem." The presence of a lone jet ski on this strip of the east coast of the island had him a little worried. *Surely the FSB hasn't tracked us down?* He hadn't anticipated they'd have company out on the water at this time of year except for local fishing vessels. He turned to look behind him, but the jet ski was already out of sight. Must have disappeared behind that headland. He reassessed the whole idea of a day on the water. "Actually, I agree with you. Far too cold to be out on the sea. Let's go back."

With the sailboat—rented from an apathetic man in a hut for a fistful of cash—returned to the dock, they jumped on e-bikes and headed to the safe house, nestled high in the hills among thick groves of olive, pistachio and orange trees. The island of Aegina had been chosen as a location for the European safehouse due to its relatively sparse population and lack of tourist activity compared to other Greek islands, but it still offered enough infrastructure to be able to hide out for an extended period.

The simple farmhouse sat at the top of the hill that overlooked the sparkling sea below and offered views back toward the interior of Aegina. Constructed of rugged blush-pink stone quarried on the island, it occupied fifteen acres of prime land. The design of the building focused on one main priority—security. Observation towers extended from the roofline at the four corners of the modest square building, each tower equipped with thermal imaging cameras to ensure panoramic coverage at all times. No intruder could get past without being detected. At least, none had in the eight years the Aegina safe house had been in existence. For communications, two parabolic dishes crowned the terracotta tiled roof.

The house itself reminded Jacob of an iceberg. Not much to

see on the surface, but underneath in a hidden basement lay a treasure trove of communications equipment and enough armaments to fight off a small army. Even Jacob had been unaware of the full capabilities of this mini-fortress until they arrived and the caretakers showed him around. Irina was still unaware of them.

"I'm glad you're back," said Skia agent Anastasia Metaxas, one of the home's two permanent residents. The other was her husband Yanni, who was out in the nearest town getting supplies for the evening meal. "I've received a message on the secure line from Mr. Fletcher. You need to check it out straight away." Jacob and Irina had been ordered to surrender their the cell phones on arrival. Yanni took them away, telling them the phones were being stored in a lead box and would be returned when it was time to leave. For the duration of their stay, all communications would be limited to responding to incoming messages via the central system. For emergencies, they were provided with dumb burner phones with local SIMs. Irina had protested in vain; for Jacob, it was a welcome relief from the stress of following news reports online. The house had a well-stocked library of books in a number of languages, so all was not lost. There was also an inground swimming pool and a passably good gym on the premises.

Using a checkered dish towel, Anastasia wiped her hands, speckled lightly with fresh parsley she'd been chopping. "Please come with me, Irene. Let me show you around the garden. Not looking its best in winter, but still a lovely place for a stroll."

When the women had gone outside, Jacob entered the unoccupied third bedroom, lifted a rug in the middle of the floor, and entered a code in a recessed panel on the hatch. The lid unlocked, and he headed down a metal ladder. Lights came on automatically as he descended. At the bottom, three corridors led in different directions; he took the one to the left. At the end was the 500 square-foot comms room. He logged on to the desktop PC to access Skia's ultra-secure email server. As expected, there was one item in his rarely used inbox. A damned long one.

Hi Jacob. Or should I say Ardalion?

So glad you and Irina made it to the safehouse in one piece. According to chatter among the intelligence services, Swiss police are baffled by what went down in Zurich. Somehow they've decided you fled to France or Denmark, and the cops in those countries are looking high and low for two Canadian or Russian bank robbers. Denmark, Jacob?! You never fail to impress me.

Now, please do not be alarmed by what I have to tell you next, however, as always, remain alert. Elizabeth Harrington was yesterday picked up by Moscow militsiya and handed back to the embassy. Apparently Harrington was wandering the streets in an incoherent state. She was physically unharmed. I can reveal to you now that she was Lilliana Danilova's and Aleksandr Gerasimchuk's case officer. Intel from your brush-by man tells us both Danilova and Gerasimchuk have not been sighted for the last 48 hours. More troubling is the disappearance of Samsonov. As a confidante of Putin, the minister's failure to keep the letter safe will have made the tyrant's blood boil. I wouldn't want to be in Samsonov's shoes, that's for sure.

We can assume the worst—that Danilova and/or Gerasimchuk have revealed information regarding your identity and the purpose of your infiltration. They may have paid the ultimate price. Fortunately, both of them had the wrong idea about your real mission and no knowledge of your exit plan, but it hardly matters now. The Russians know the State Department letter is gone, and with it one of Putin's best opportunities to turn the course of the war in Ukraine quickly and to his advantage. Unfortunately, Harrington has revealed to us she was betrayed by Danilova, who administered her with some kind of drug before FSB agents subjected her to an interrogation. Her recollection of the grilling she underwent is hazy to say the least; she has no idea of the questions she was asked, and, consequently, what her answers might have been. She claims she is ignorant of your location and therefore could not have given the FSB that information. Apparently, rumors are running wild in the Moscow spook community that the Swiss bank robbery is linked to Putin personally and that he is prepared to unleash the entire might of the SVR in tracking down whoever took his property.

As a precautionary measure, Harrington has been relieved of duties and sent home to undergo hypnosis. The CIA think she might have known something on a subconscious level and the FSB coaxed it out of her. My theory—they got nothing out of her and sent her on her merry way. The Aegina safehouse is known only to a handful of carefully vetted people. You, me, the Metaxases, now Irina, and three other operatives. I'm confident none of them have disclosed this information.

What I want you to do now is this.

Nothing, apart from maintaining normal vigilance.

On Saturday coming, a navy submarine will be passing through the area. You and Irina will be picked up by a team of officers in a Zodiac and transferred to the sub, and from there taken to a naval base in Italy. I'll let you know their ETA as soon as it's confirmed. In Italy you will board an aircraft carrier that will bring you back to Portsmouth, VA. No ticker-tape parade, unfortunately. Until then, keep your head down and do not leave the compound until further notice.

One last request. Please confirm the letter *is in your possession.*

Grant.

Jacob rubbed his pate, feeling the tiny hairs that were starting to make a comeback. He'd attack the new growth with a soap and razor tonight. Of course, there was no need to maintain the disguise any more, but he dug the new style. Irina was right. It made him look like a badass. He began to compose the reply.

Hi Grant. All good here. We have to stay until the end of the week? Awesome. This place is like a resort. Yes, the letter is intact and in my possession, locked away in this nuclear fallout bunker together with our cell phones. I'd rather keep my precious private items here than in a Swiss bank. Perhaps we could interest Mr. Putin in renting out a space in the safe here in Aegina?

I'm assuming Irina's family members are OK since you didn't say otherwise.

Looking forward to a ride in a submarine. That will be a first!
Jacob.

He logged off the computer and headed upstairs. Through the vertical blinds in front of a pair of French doors, he made out the two women in the distance, chatting like old friends. Irina's temporary blond hair stood out starkly against the lush greenery of the trees. His mind wandered back to more innocent times. He imagined Sally-Anne Vincent, the tragic loss of a young life, so full of potential. How alike she and Irina were: beautiful, brave and smart. What would become of her in America? Only time would tell, but he was optimistic. For her role in assisting Jacob, she would no doubt be rewarded handsomely. A lump sum of cash, or she might be offered a plum job. Skia could do a lot worse than hire her.

He exited the house onto a covered portico, made his way to meet the women, called out, and waved to them. "Coming!" yelled Anastasia. She smiled with relief; no doubt she would have kept Irina outside indefinitely until Jacob emerged, to ensure the integrity of the house's systems.

He met them on the short flight of steps that led up to a broad wraparound deck. "It's getting cold quickly." He rubbed his hands together for emphasis. "I thought you'd like to come inside now."

Just as Anastasia was ushering her guests inside, a black Toyota RAV4 appeared in the circular driveway, leaving a small trail of dust in its wake. A tall wiry man with a swarthy complexion, short black hair and luxurious moustache clambered out of the vehicle. He pulled a brimming shopping bag from the back seat, as well as a couple of bottles of wine.

Over a simple dinner of grilled sardines, bread, and a green salad with olives and pistachios from the farm, conversation turned to what lay ahead for the guests.

"You know, we both have no idea why you're here," said Yanni, pouring wine across the table. "Just that we have to make sure nothing happens to you until you leave."

"You only have to put up with us for another couple of days. I'll let you know the exact time when my boss tells me."

"I have a question," said Irina, putting her knife and fork down gently on the table. "We were out on the water earlier when a man on a jet ski appeared from nowhere. He came close to the boat then disappeared."

"Yes," said Jacob. "It was rather curious. Not the time of year to be out having fun on a jet ski. I don't know why, but his presence out there seemed wrong, somehow."

The Metaxases exchanged a look of apprehension. "How far out were you?" said Yanni.

"If I had my phone, I could give you the exact coordinates, but from memory, I'd say a quarter of a mile from the dock, course north-north-east. There was a headland not far from where the guy appeared."

Yanni gave a quick nod. "There is a family of...eccentrics... living behind that headland. Sticky beaks, I think the expression is. They give a lot of the locals a hard time."

"What do you know about them?"

"Long-time residents. In fact, many generations of them have lived in the same house. They think they own the entire island."

"Have they ever been up here snooping around?"

Anastasia, now clearing away the table, waved a rolling pin like a caveman with a club. "No one snoops around on my watch!"

Everybody laughed, yet Jacob couldn't shrug off a feeling of unease.

THIRTY-EIGHT

She sat wedged uncomfortably between the two men who had brutalized her at Patriarch Ponds. Colonel Solovyov had decreed they would be the perfect escorts to hand her over to SVR representatives in Turkey. After all, they had already gotten to know each other so well, why introduce an unknown element into the equation?

It was a four-hour flight from Sheremetyevo to Antalya, and every minute ticked by too slowly for Danilova's liking. Economy class, to boot. What a joke. It might have been better had they finished her off, like they had Samsonov. But she pushed negative thoughts out of her mind. People were going to pay for the indignities and pain she had suffered. Boy, were they going to pay.

As the airplane jetted its way through the skies, she kept her arms tucked by her sides, happy to let the bookend thugs have the armrests to themselves. The slightest body contact with either of them and she pulled away reflexively. Half an hour from landing, a patch of bad turbulence jolted her body left and right; no matter how she tried, she couldn't avoid touching the bastards. Such was her revulsion, at one point she thought she might have to use an airline barf bag for the first time in her life.

Almost as bad as their touch were their cheap, clashing aftershaves. Nauseating. She knew the difference between the good stuff and the bad stuff because Samsonov always wore the good stuff. Not that it made any difference now. Neither Danilova nor the newly widowed Ludmila Samsonova would get to enjoy that musky scent anymore. Too bad, so sad.

At 5:32 p.m., the Aeroflot Airbus A350 touched down smoothly in the Turkish resort town of Antalya. No time for the beaches or historical or cultural tours of the city. She was told it would be a quick handover, with the commander of the upcoming raid to meet her personally.

"Come on," said Boris. "Let's offload her and be done with it."

Grisha, who had the aisle seat, stood up the second the fasten seat belt sign was switched off and ripped two small rucksacks down from the overhead locker. Danilova had no luggage, no personal items, nothing. She wasn't sure her return alive to Moscow was even on the agenda. "You're lucky me and Boris didn't end you back in Moscow. You've got one chance to redeem yourself. Don't fuck it up."

She sneered at him, knowing he'd not dare lay a finger on her in the crowded airplane.

In the arrivals hall, the FSB men corralled Danilova toward a man in a charcoal-gray suit. Tall, broad-shouldered and blond, he commanded attention like a traffic accident. There was something so compelling in his bearing, she knew he had to be dangerous. He introduced himself as Ivan Melnik.

"She's all yours," said Grisha. He turned to his colleague. "Let's get out of here. The traitorous bitch makes me sick. I know a great bar by the beach. A couple of beers should wash the bad taste out of my mouth."

"Not so fast," said Melnik. "You are not on a holiday. You are all coming with me. Orders from Moscow. You must do exactly as I say."

The smiles vanished from the FSB men's faces just as one materialized on Danilova's.

IT TOOK five hours to drive from Antalya to the western port town of Kusadasi. Whether it was a scenic route or not was a mystery to Danilova. Not because she couldn't see out of the darkly tinted windows, but because she wore a blindfold for most of the way. Overkill, but the SVR was never famous for its subtlety.

She was able to speak freely, however, with no insults or slaps or reprisals of any kind. Melnik turned out to be the perfect gentleman. If he was playing a role, then he did it superbly. It didn't matter how he acted or what he did, though, he was a government rat. She trusted him about as far as she could throw him.

A hundred or so kilometers into the 400-kilometer journey, he pulled over at a roadside café and ordered the frowning goons to sit inside while he and Danilova enjoyed a pastry and a Turkish coffee. He removed her blindfold. "No need for this anymore. It was an order, but I can't see the reason for it." He smiled, showing a set of too-perfect white teeth.

At a secluded booth table, he said, "I don't know much about why you're part of this, but I heard a rumor you've been given the chance to make up for some kind of big mistake you made." He lit a pungent, unfiltered cigarette and offered one to her. She took it. "Is that true?"

"I'm not keen to talk about it." She inhaled and blew out a trail of smoke, then brushed a stray piece of tobacco from her top lip.

"I understand." He rolled up his sleeves, revealing tattoos that Russian men generally only acquire in the prison system. She eyed them, trying to understand his meaning in the gesture. Was it *I'm also a victim of the system, an ally*? Or was it *Look out or I'll fuck you up badly*? Perhaps there was nothing of the kind intended. It was like a sauna inside the café. Perhaps he was just feeling warm. "However, I have a job to do. Deliver you to a colleague of mine. He's in charge of an assault team that's going to the location where a couple of fugitives are holed up. The ones who robbed a bank in Switzerland. Apparently, they stole something that belongs to the president. He's real pissed, as you can imagine."

"What?"

"Oh yes," he said laconically. "We know where they are."

She held up a finger. "Can I ask a question?"

"By all means." He flicked ash into a stained plastic ashtray.

"How did you find them?"

He patted his wallet. "Money talks."

"What does that even mean?" She narrowed her eyes and tucked her chin into her neck as the cryptic answer baffled her.

"It means someone in the American's organization has rolled over and ratted him out for a large amount of cash." He stubbed out the cigarette as a waitress in a floury apron brought them their food. "Everyone has their price."

"Do you have a price? Could I buy my way out of this shit if I paid you the right amount?"

"You've got no personal belongings apart from the clothes on your back." He drummed his manicured nails on the table. "Do you have a stash secreted somewhere on your person?" He leered. "Perhaps you're carrying it...internally?"

"Ha!" She laughed bitterly. "You men are all the same." If she was going to be totally honest with herself, in other circumstances, if she did have a roll of cash inside her body, he was exactly the type of male specimen she'd like to do the searching.

He nodded, icing from the sweet treat falling onto the Formica table top. "In many ways, yes. That is true. Men are brutes."

"Why am I even here?" She had no appetite for the food she'd been given. She raised her voice. *Let's push the envelope.* "I mean, what's the fucking point?"

"Shh," he said as a handful of other customers began to stare. "I don't know. I'm just the delivery guy." He took the last bite of his pastry, gestured at hers, and she made a please-take-it gesture. He began demolishing the second one.

"I don't believe you." She crossed her arms.

"I'm telling you the truth. Any ideas that I have would just be theories."

"Share some of them with me."

He wiped his face with a napkin, checked his watch, and stood. "No. I don't think I will."

"I need to pee." She made for the bathroom.

He grabbed her arm. "You aren't leaving my sight. You can piss behind a tree on the highway."

Around three bends, Grisha and Boris stood either side of her, cracking lewd jokes as she squatted behind a boulder on the highway in the bitter cold, urinating onto the snow. Of all the indignities and pain she had suffered, this was the pinnacle.

But she wouldn't make a fuss.

Bide your time and take your chance when it presents itself.

THIRTY-NINE

THE BLACK MERCEDES VAN PULLED UP IN A QUIET SIDE street outside a squat coral-colored building. Melnik escorted Danilova and the two FSB men inside, greeting a woman at a reception desk in rapid Turkish. She said something back to Melnik, and they shared a laugh. Boris and Grisha, standing off to one side, wore expressions of tired matter-of-factness. No holiday for them, but their brains had already switched back to duty mode.

The new arrivals stomped up a staircase to the third floor. They walked along a short and narrow corridor to a door, then Melnik knocked three times. A commanding "Enter" came from inside. The space was set up like a classroom, with a dozen or so desks spread about evenly. Men with military haircuts but wearing casual clothes sat behind the desks.

At a blackboard in the front of the room stood a muscular man in his late forties wearing a button-down business shirt and tie and holding a ruler in one hand. He sported a network of pale scars on his stubbly face and wore a patch over one eye. The blackboard was covered in scrawled chalk writing: names, dates, coordinates, other numbers.

Melnik coughed into his fist and said, "Major Tikhonov. This is Lilliana Danilova."

"Glad to see you, Ivan." The man extended his large hand to Melnik. The SVR man acknowledged the greeting with a hearty pump, then quietly told Boris and Grisha to go back to the van and wait until called upon.

"You." The major glared at Danilova, his one eye squinting. "Take a seat at the back next to Private Galaktionova."

The lone woman in the group had to be the one Tikhonov meant. Raven black hair, alert, chestnut eyes, an inquisitive expression.

Danilova's feet moved as if behaving of their own accord. She sat in the unoccupied desk at the rear, an arm's length from Galaktionova. Again, she wondered what the hell was going on. And only now did she realize that the major was speaking in perfect English.

"We now have the last piece of the puzzle," he said. Melnik stook by his side, arms folded. "For the benefit of our new friend, Lilliana Danilova, let me explain why I am speaking in English. Due to the limited time available and resources on the ground here in Turkey, we have had to assemble a team with, how do you say, an international flavor. Yes, I would have preferred a crack unit of Russian special forces, but it's simply not possible given the time and logistical restraints. Now." He looked directly at Danilova with his one good eye, wide open this time. "I've been told you understand English very well. Is this correct, or will I have to repeat everything in Russian for you?"

"No need for that." She kept her pitch as flat as possible. Pissing this guy off seemed like the worst idea she could possibly come up with. "English is fine."

"Very well." He began to explain the audacious plan: to storm a property on the island of Aegina under the cover of darkness, neutralize the American and anyone else on the premises, find and retrieve the document that Putin wanted, and evacuate as fast as they could. None of the people in the house was to be left alive.

"Even children?" said a man in the second row. His shaky tone made it clear the prospect didn't fill him with joy.

"Analysis of the satellite imagery tells us there are no children on the property. We have detected four adults only. But, if there are, the orders are clear. No one left alive."

More details poured from Tikhonov's mouth in a rush. To Danilova's ear, it seemed the man viewed this assignment as the peak of his career.

"A 10-member squad, made up of nine of you assembled here, including Danilova, will land on a quiet strip of shore on the eastern side of the island at approximately 02:00 a.m. on Saturday, February 2nd." He pointed at a set of coordinates with his wooden ruler. "Maya Galaktionova. You will pair up with Danilova. Between now and when we return from the raid, you will not let her out of your sight. Understood?"

Out of the corner of her eye, Danilova caught the woman nodding with great enthusiasm.

"In ten minutes, we will drive in a small convoy to the compound five kilometers from the private dock where we will be launching a long-distance Raptor class patrol boat. Vladimir Vladimirovich has redirected this vessel away from the Ukraine effort, which tells you just how important this mission is." He tapped the ruler on the blackboard. "For the rest of today and most of tomorrow, we will practice drill after drill after drill. Exercises will include time on the rifle range, the use of flash-bangs, night gear, swimming, rope climbing, and abseiling." He glared at Danilova. "If you deliberately injure yourself, you will be put down like a lame horse. Do you understand me?"

Danilova nodded slowly. "Yes."

He chuckled softly. "I'm being facetious. You won't be doing much of that risky stuff. And you certainly won't be going near firearms, in case you get any funny ideas. You are delicate cargo, a negotiator, if you will. Galaktionova will be right beside you to make sure you behave yourself, and also to make sure nothing happens to you. Think of her as your personal bodyguard."

Danilova sensed the woman's chest puffing up with pride, given such a key job with great responsibility.

"This mission, so vital for our country, could theoretically be carried out successfully without your participation. And if it were up to me, I would prefer you were not here. A middle-aged woman, who is, from what I've been told, an unreliable drunkard and, let me not be impolite...no, what the hell, let's call things by their proper names. A slut."

Danilova felt her face redden under the verbal onslaught. He seemed to be thoroughly enjoying his humiliation of her. She glanced at Melnik, the 'gentleman,' for a sign of sympathy, but his face was a knot of disdainful disapproval. *All the same, the whole lot of them.*

"You are only here because the president has ordered it. I don't know the specifics of your treachery; however, you've been handed one...ONE!...chance to redeem yourself."

What the fuck am I supposed to do? was what she desperately wanted to ask. She said nothing.

As if reading her thoughts, Tikhonov continued, "As I said, you will not be shooting or handling any weapons during the one and a half days of intensive training. When I say training, it's more like a dress rehearsal for the most important role you'll ever be given. The one that will save your life."

Her breathing accelerated, yet she strove to remain outwardly calm. She kept her hands folded in her lap and stared over Tikhonov's shoulder at the blackboard.

"Once the letter stolen from our president has been secured," the major said, "you will be taken to the American, and you will put a bullet into his brain. Should you fail to pull the trigger, Galaktionova will liquidate you. Is that understood?"

This was all sounding like an implausible suicide mission. And perhaps it was. She couldn't see the faces of her 'teammates' since she was seated at the back of the room, so it was impossible to judge their level of enthusiasm. The Russians among them wouldn't be wishing her well, that was certain, but the mercenaries probably couldn't care less.

Tikhonov handed a couple of large glossy photographs to Melnik. "Take these to her."

Melnik handed the prints to Danilova: a man and a woman in their late seventies to early eighties, and a younger man, who bore a resemblance to the others. Their son? All three sported cut, bruised, and bleeding faces, along with the blank expressions of the chronically tortured.

"I see you are putting it all together in your mind," said Tikhonov. "They are the parents and brother of the traitor Irina Frolova." He slid his hand along the length of the ruler in a suggestive manner as he stared at Danilova. "Should the American fail to hand over the letter, which you will recognize because it bears the emblem of the US State Department, Frolova's relatives will be executed immediately."

THE HULL of the 17-meter long vessel thwacked the surface of the water intermittently. A relatively flat sea meant the Project 03160 high-speed patrol boat could attain close to its maximum speed of 89 kph. ETA 02:14. Current time—01:58.

"Remember," said Galaktionova in a husky voice that grated like sandpaper. "We follow behind the troops and wait on the perimeter of the property until I receive the signal for us to go forward. Don't even think about trying to run after we land or I will cut you down like a dog."

Danilova took a deep breath of the cold air in the bowels of the boat. The brainwashed bitch sitting next to her epitomized everything that was wrong with Russia. "Don't worry. I'm not stupid."

"Good to hear." Galaktionova patted the front of Danilova's Gortex suit hard with an open palm. "Don't forget. Stress the importance of their cooperation."

"I'm sure after Voronin takes one look at these photographs, you'll have nothing to worry about." She couldn't delete the man's Russian moniker from her mind.

Galaktionova squinted and touched her earpiece as a message came through. She turned to Danilova. "Landing in one minute. We follow the others out, get into the inflatable landing craft that will take us to shore. Then we ascend to the perimeter of the property and wait until we are called."

FORTY

FROM THEIR POSITION BEHIND A SMALL OUTCROP OF boulders just on the other side of the target property's fence line, the only thing visible were the stars. The night was perfectly silent, save for the distance soft sound of small waves crashing on the shore. Galaktionova had made Danilova adopt an awkward position: kneeling on hard, pebbly ground. Her hands and knees were bound with zip ties. The bitch herself was comfortable; having spread out a small piece of ground sheeting, she sat on her butt, legs crossed.

"I reckon we'll be hearing fireworks pretty soon," said Galaktionova, her voice edged with anticipation. "Once the jammer puts paid to their thermal imaging cameras and alarm systems, or the sniper takes them out if he can't, the real action's going to start."

"You're not worried they'll be able to defend themselves? The Americans wouldn't leave their man in a vulnerable position."

"You must be joking," Galaktionova scoffed. "We've got enough gear to knock out a small army base, let alone a farmhouse with four occupants." She counted off the assets on her fingers. "AK-12s, flashbangs, smoke grenades, and an explosive ordnance disposal expert to disarm any nasty booby traps."

"Sounds like you've got everything covered."

"Yes." Danilova could make out the woman's smile in the faint light afforded by the stars. "And even if we fail to stop the alarms, our firepower will be enough to take them all out."

"But won't a lot of noise bring the local police force?"

Galaktionova snickered. "They'll get the job done so well, the loudest noise will be the gurgling of their throats after they've been sliced open." She checked the dim glow of her watch. "The troops have been gone five minutes. The call will come any time now. Get your speech ready for the American and the traitor woman."

Danilova wriggled her hips. Her lower legs were starting to go numb; her kneeling pose was limiting blood circulation and the stones starting to cause unbearable pain. "I need to sit like you." She winced. "I can't stay like this for much longer."

Galaktionova crawled a couple of paces forward and swung the rifle butt, connecting with Danilova's neck. "Shut up, traitor! I'll tell you when you can move."

And then, all hell broke loose.

FORTY-ONE

JACOB SAT IN THE BUNKER OFFICE, RECLINING IN THE swivel chair, headphones pressed to his ears. The other occupants of the house were asleep, but sleep would not come for Jacob. Too many thoughts raced through his mind.

One final call to Grant Fletcher before Jacob and Irina departed the farmhouse. "Any update on Irina's family?"

"Just spoke to the people looking after them a couple hours ago. They're doing fine physically but anxious to get out of Russia, as you can imagine. It's going to take a bit more organizing for that to happen. We've got people working on it as we speak."

"That's a relief." Jacob rubbed his eyes.

"You'll need to be down at the dock in two hours," said Fletcher. "Take a big ol' flashlight, hit 'em with some morse code to let them know you're friend, not foe. Try, oh, I dunno, Ardalion."

"What? Are you sure they're coming so soon? It's the middle of the night!"

"Don't blame me. I don't organize the navy's schedule. To quote the worst cliché of all time, it is what it is."

Yeah, thought Jacob. *Such a bad cliché it's the second time he's used it in a week.* "Okay. I'd better rouse Irina then."

"Grab something to eat, take a hot shower, do all those human things. Who knows how long you'll have to wait again."

"For once in your life, that sounds like pretty good advice."

He was about to say his good-byes when the ear-splitting sound of an alarm penetrated the so-called noise-cancelling headphones. *Whoop, whoop, whoop.* Like an air-raid siren on steroids. He found a blinking switch and slapped it to kill the alarm. The wailing siren would surely have woken the other three inhabitants of the farmhouse. Hopefully, the sound hadn't reached the attackers. If it had, they'd be picking up the pace to get the job done.

He shouted into the headset mic, "Gotta go, Grant. The property's been breached." He could hear his boss cursing loudly as he ripped off the cans. A glance at the bank of monitors to his left told the story. Grainy images of men in full combat gear crawling on their hands and knees about four hundred feet away. A message on one of the screens said: *Backup cameras engaged.*

Jacob breathed a sigh of relief. Intruders had jammed the signals on one set of cameras, but redundancies were in place for this very scenario. He gave a silent vote of thanks to whoever had designed this deceptively secure little fortress. At least now he knew how many grunts he was dealing with.

There was no time to waste.

Jacob's heart pounded like a freight train as he stood in front of the gun cabinet. His phenomenal memory failed him for two seconds. *Fuck!* He wondered whether he'd lost it before the number appeared in his brain like a flashing neon sign. He punched in the code Anastasia had given him and yanked out two M16s and four magazines. He prayed he would get to the surface on time.

Running back to the ladder, he took another look at the screens. The soldiers were up on their feet and moving a lot faster now. *They heard the alarm, dammit!* It wasn't easy clambering up the rungs with two Armalites swinging from his shoulders and clanging into the frame. Squeezing the magazines tight under his armpits slowed his ascent. One clip slipped and landed on the floor with a bang.

He kept climbing hand over hand until he was able to push open the hatch.

Inside the spare bedroom, he adjusted the rifle straps on his shoulders and burst into the hallway. He called out, "Irina!"

"In the kitchen!" came a chorus of three voices. The kitchen was located exactly in the center of the house, maximum distance from doors and windows.

"What's the plan for these situations?" said Jacob, staring into Yanni's eyes. He knew there was a contingency. There had to be.

"We head down into the bunker," said Yanni, brandishing what looked like a Glock 17. His wife held an identical pistol. "Send a distress signal to the Greek police special forces. I used to work for them. They will be here very quick."

"No!" spat Jacob. "Irina will be sent back to Russia."

"But..." said Yanni.

"No buts. *You* head down there if you want. We can't keep them all out of the bunker forever. There's too many of them. I counted eight on the monitor." His sketchy plan was to try and take out as many of the enemy as possible; hopefully, stragglers would retreat.

"I stay with you!" said Yanni.

"And me," echoed Anastasia.

"No bunker, I'm claustrophobic,' said Irina. "Is that second machine gun for me?"

"It is." Jacob forced a grin, even though panic gripped his very soul. "Do you even know how to use it?"

"I've had military training. A long time ago, but I need to try."

"Just don't aim it at any of us."

Deafening gunfire erupted. The glass in the French doors exploded into the living room. "Quickly!" said Jacob. *This is not supposed to be happening.* "Everyone, duck behind the kitchen island. We can use it as a barricade." *Not a very good one, but beggars can't be choosers.*

He pushed himself toward the edge of the island closest to the shattered door, instinctively shielding the others with his big body. *Think, Hunter, think!*

A complete, eerie silence descended.

Then came the creak of wooden planks on the deck outside.

Jacob dared a quick look over the top of the island benchtop. In the dim light, he could see silhouettes of two soldiers, clad head to toe in combat kit. They stood two feet apart at the entrance, wielding guns that looked the size of telegraph poles. He ducked down again, gripping the rifle butt, finger on the trigger, ready to fire. He whispered to the others, "Stay calm."

He leapt to his feet and unleashed a burst of gunfire, catching both of the enemy combatants in the throat and head. Some bullets ricocheted off their protective gear, but enough of them got through. They toppled to the floor like felled trees.

Irina screamed like a banshee by his side, but the Metaxases remained quiet.

Deep, angry voices on the deck. Stomping boots, the sound retreating.

"They're probably heading for the back door," said Yanni. "I go." He was already on his knees and scrambling away.

The three remaining behind the island breathed hard, like horses at the end of a long race. Jacob knew the women would be churning inside, adrenaline flowing.

Two gunshots in rapid succession boomed from the back of the house as a fog of acrid smoke drifted into the kitchen. The shots sounded like they came from a Glock. No machine gun fire was returned. *Four down,* Jacob said to himself.

No time for any more thoughts as a flashbang exploded in the dark, then another. Irina screamed again, but this time, there was no cowering. Jacob sensed it happening but could do nothing. His hand reached out to stop her, but it was too late. She was up on her feet, wielding the assault rifle like she was born to do it. The screaming continued, turned into a hysterical war cry as she fired wildly in an arc.

Two muffled thuds as more bodies hit the floor. Jacob sensed a wet spot on his cheek. Maybe a bottle of olive oil had broken on a shelf and its contents sprayed everywhere. He felt a spasming, kicking motion against his thigh and glanced to his right.

Irina had fallen awkwardly, landing on top of Anastasia, who grunted, trying to crawl out from under her. The legs kicked again.

Irina groaned as blood leeched from a ragged hole in the fleshy part of her shoulder. Not spurting, thank God. Not an artery.

"What do we do now?" said Anastasia. "We have to tend to her wound."

He held up a hand. "No. Not yet. There are two more on the loose somewhere."

More powerful shots, then a guttural screech.

"Okay," Jacob huffed. "I'm pretty sure that was the Glock. We wait a little longer and hold our breath."

No more shooting noises came. No more sounds until a panting Yanni returned. "I think that was the last of them."

"Okay. Let's get Irina down below, claustrophobic or not, and get her patched up. We've got a submarine to catch in..."—a quick look at his watch—"one hour."

"Understood," said Anastasia.

"And you two are coming with us," said Jacob. "Ever been on a sub?"

"LOOKS LIKE THE PARTY'S OVER," said Galaktionova triumphantly. "I can't wait to see what damage the boys have done up there."

"Why...no...signal?" Danilova could barely speak, such was the pain in her knees. "I...think...Voronin..."

Galaktionova gritted her teeth. "Shut up. It's coming."

Three minutes went by and still they waited. Then Galaktionova touched her earpiece as someone began speaking to her, and the color drained from her cheeks. "Understood." She looked to her captive. "New plan. They have taken too long. We have been ordered to go back to the boat."

A satisfied grin crept across Danilova's face, and for a moment, the pain in her legs receded. She said nothing as Galaktionova grabbed her by the left elbow and yanked her to her feet. She hobbled as the barrel of the AK-12 poked into her lower back. "Hurry up, bitch."

Danilova stumbled on the rough ground, then regained her footing and staggered on. Another three paces and she fell when her boot landed in a hole. "Ow! I've twisted my ankle."

"Then you are fucking ballast."

She heard the sound of the weapon being shouldered and prepped for action. Danilova whispered a quiet prayer for her eternal salvation. Dying in a foreign field. At least it had a romantic flavor to it.

"Opusti oruzhie!" *Drop the gun!* said a deep male voice.

"Tolya?" Danilova couldn't believe her ears.

Galaktionova tossed her AK-12 to the side, her hands shooting up in the air. "Please, don't shoot!"

"Who's the bitch now?" said Danilova. She looked pleadingly at Jacob. "Can you cut the zip tie behind my back so I can strangle her?"

"Show him the pictures!" Galaktionova couldn't hide her desperation. She tried to turn around but copped a rifle barrel in the middle of her back. "Once you've seen them you better hand that letter over to me."

"Shut up." He turned to Danilova. "What pictures is she talking about?"

"Cut the ties and I'll show you."

Jacob forced Galaktionova onto her stomach and placed his foot on her neck; Danilova smiled with delight. Hands liberated, she reached into the front pocket of her jacket and extracted the photographs. Jacob studied them for a moment using the flashlight of his cell phone, then put them in his own pocket. "Fakes."

"What?" Galaktionova mumbled. "Not possible."

"These are doctored images. I've had confirmation the people in them are fine. Now"—he released his foot from her neck—"the lovely Lilliana and I are taking you prisoner."

"There's a boat waiting for me. There are more soldiers waiting to land. I demand you let me go and–"

Danilova whacked Galaktionova across the back of the head with the AK-12. "She's lying, Tolya. Only the driver is left on the boat."

Jacob ripped the microphone from Galaktionova's uniform, turned it on, and spoke to the man on the other end. "Listen good. All of your troops are dead, apart from one woman, who we have taken prisoner. Turn around and leave Greek territorial waters. NOW!" He threw the microphone to the ground and crushed it under his boot. He gave Galaktionova his friendliest smile. "Now would you prefer a Greek prison or Guantanamo Bay?"

FORTY-TWO

"You look different somehow," said Fletcher as he popped the cork of a chilled bottle of Dom Perignon. "I can't quite put my finger on it."

"I guess I've lost a few pounds over the last couple of weeks. I'm back on my strict fitness regime."

"I can see that. But it's something else."

"Is it the bald head?"

"No. Although I have to say, it does suit you. More than I could have ever imagined." He ran fingers through his own short crop of hair. "I wonder if my Samantha would like the chrome dome look on me."

"No offense, Grant. Your head's the wrong shape for it. Looks like a blimp from side on."

Fletcher narrowed his eyes. "I guess after the success of the mission, you can get away with that kind of shit. Not every boss would be as accommodating as me. But getting back to you, I'm seeing a kind of contentedness in your face. A relaxed look around the eyes."

Jacob took a sip of the champagne and smiled appreciatively, even though he was convinced expensive champagne tasted more like vinegar than the cheap stuff. "I have been sleeping better, despite having put three men in their graves. I thought I'd be having nightmares about it, but strangely not."

Fletcher waved his fingers around like he was pondering some great conundrum. "Is it because of your...friendship with Ms. Frobisher?"

"Irina has changed my life in so many ways. Her act of bravery probably saved me and the two Greek agents, for one thing."

"Indeed." He paused for a moment to take the label off a banned Cuban cigar. Once he'd gone through the snipping ritual, which reminded Jacob of a circumcision, he leaned back in his lounge chair. "You know, I think your outrageous payment for this mission should be trimmed. Significantly."

"Why's that?" The aroma coming from the cigar smoke took him back to Ilinka Street for a moment. He wondered how the staff at MinFin were coping with so many staff missing, including Samsonov and Gerasimchuk, both dead, according to Danilova.

"Because of the burden you are placing on the economy. You were supposed to bring back one lousy letter. Instead, yes, you got the letter, but also three Russian and two Greek citizens. The taxpayer will have to foot the bill."

Jacob shook his head. "The Greeks will go home after they've had a vacation here. And Irina, her son, and Lilliana will find work easily. All of them are super smart and eager to start new lives."

"What about the safehouse, Jacob? That's a bust. We need to set up another one. Again, at great expense!"

"Not my fault. Someone blabbed, and it wasn't me."

"We know who it was."

"What!"

"Yes. We received an anonymous email with copies of correspondence between Joe Weale and Marcus Virtanen. The Russians' ad was answered by Virtanen, but he got Weale to be the patsy who made the first contact with them."

"No prizes for guessing the 'anonymous' email came from Moscow?"

"That's right. So no prize for you." Fletcher chuckled at his weak joke.

The smoke smelled too good and the temptation was too great. Jacob reached for the cigar box and helped himself to one. *No inhaling this time.* "Speaking of outrageous expenditure, how much did the strikes at the Russian border cost? The infrastructure Lilliana set up for me to infiltrate the ministry?"

"Irrelevant, Jacob."

"I disagree." He stood and walked to a window, admired the spectacular view of the Hudson River, bustling with all manner of craft.

"Then there's the cost of guarding Irina's relatives." Fletcher was on a roll. "Not a cheap exercise. But that will pale into insignificance compared to the cost of getting them to the Land of the Free and setting them up with jobs."

"The parents are too old to work, Grant."

"You know what I mean."

They finished the bottle, and Jacob stood to leave. Before he could say good-bye, the phone on Fletcher's desk rang. The chief's expression transformed from happy and relaxed to shocked in a split second.

"Yes, Mr. President. We have retrieved the letter."

Jacob stood rooted to the spot, unable to credit what he was witnessing. Unfortunately, he could only hear one side of the conversation. He cupped his hand to his ear and said in a half-whisper, "Can I hear what he's saying?"

Fletcher nodded. "May I put you on speaker, sir? Jacob Hunter is with me."

The answer must have been yes, because the voice known to the entire world burst forth from the speaker attached to Fletcher's old-school desk telephone.

"Congratulations on a job well done, Hunter. The country thanks you for your service."

Jacob gulped. "Thank you, sir."

"Now do you have that letter with you, Fletcher?" said the president.

"Yes, sir. I've been waiting for the State Department to contact me about it."

"I'm very glad you refrained from handing it over immediately. This entire unfortunate case has come to my attention, and I've made an executive decision."

Jacob's heart was beating out of his chest.

"And what's that, sir?"

"The damned thing is too dangerous. I want it destroyed."

"I'm not sure I heard you properly, sir. Did you say destroyed?"

"That's exactly what I said."

"How?"

"I don't care how. Shred it and then set it on fire would be my suggestion."

"Of course, sir. But how will you know I've done it?"

"If I find out you haven't, I will shut down your entire operation. It's costing more to run than a small African nation. I will also have you blacklisted from any future employment in the United States, revoke your citizenship, and...well...I'm sure I can think of something else. Now will you do as I say?"

"Yes, sir."

Jacob couldn't go home now. No way. Even though Irina was patiently waiting for him at his apartment. Tonight, he was going to tell her exactly how he felt about her, hoping she felt the same about him. But first he had to witness Fletcher shred and burn the letter. This was history in the flesh.

After that ceremony was completed, Jacob had a feeling more booze would be opened.

As usual, his instincts didn't let him down. By the time the clock ticked over to midnight, he and his boss had polished off a second bottle of champagne. The dregs were poured into the ashtray, turning the burned letter and cigar ash into a dirty black slush.

Waiting for his taxi on the street outside Fletcher's building, Jacob checked his cell. A missed text message from Irina.

He smiled.

She *did* feel the same way about him.

Don't miss THE BOGOTÁ FILE. The riveting sequel in the Jacob Hunter Thriller series.

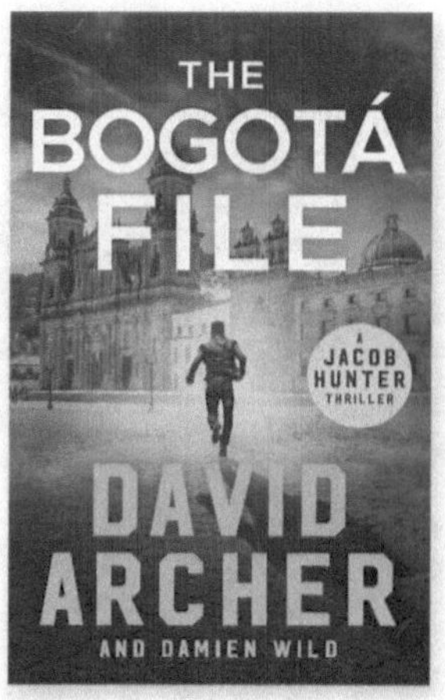

In the heart of Bogotá, Colombia, a wealthy businessman vanishes, abducted by a powerful new drug cartel under the command of the ruthless Adolfo Sanchez. Jacob Hunter, a skilled operative for the top-secret organization Skia, is tasked with finding and rescuing the kidnapped businessman, Paul Brohman.

Assigned the codename "Montoya," Jacob navigates the dangerous criminal underworld, leveraging savant-like linguistic skills and undercover expertise. As he delves deeper, Jacob uncovers a web of corruption involving the CIA, with agents working against the government's interests.

But the stakes skyrocket when Jacob discovers the true motive behind Brohman's abduction – a conspiracy to flood American neighborhoods with drugs, orchestrated by CIA operatives backing a rival presidential candidate. With the incumbent's re-election campaign hanging by a thread, Jacob must confront the shadowy figures orchestrating the plot.

From the bustling streets of Bogotá to the dense jungles of southern Mexico, "The Bogotá File" is a gripping thriller packed with unexpected twists and heart-pounding suspense. Will Jacob uncover the truth before it's too late, or will he become another casualty in this deadly game of international espionage?

Scan the QR code below to purchase THE BOGOTÁ FILE.
Or go to: righthouse.com/the-bogota-file

NOTE: flip to the very end to read an exclusive sneak peek...

DON'T MISS ANYTHING!

If you want to stay up to date on all new releases in this series, with this author, or with any of our new deals, you can do so by joining our newsletters below.

In addition, you will immediately gain access to our entire *Right House VIP Library,* which includes many riveting Mystery and Thriller novels for your enjoyment. Including a prequel novella to this series!

righthouse.com/email

(Easy to unsubscribe. No spam. Ever.)

ALSO BY DAVID ARCHER

Up to date books can be found at:
www.righthouse.com/david-archer

ROGUE THRILLERS

Gates of Hell (Book 1)
Hell's Fury (Book 2)
Ice Burn (Book 3)
Judgement by Fire (Book 4)

JACOB HUNTER THRILLERS

The Kyiv File (Book 1)
The Bogota File (Book 2)
The Havana File (Book 3)
The Amsterdam File (Book 4)
The Saint Petersburg File (Book 5)

PETER BLACK THRILLERS

Burden of the Assassin (Book 1)
The Man Without A Face (Book 2)
Unpunished Deeds (Book 3)
Hunter Killer (Book 4)
Silent Shadows (Book 5)
The Last Run (Book 6)
Dark Corners (Book 7)
Ghost Operative (Book 8)
A Fire Burning (Book 9)
Dawnlight (Book 10)
Dead Ice (Book 11)
No Loose Ends (Book 12)

ALEX MASON THRILLERS

Odin (Book 1)
Ice Cold Spy (Book 2)
Mason's Law (Book 3)
Assets and Liabilities (Book 4)
Russian Roulette (Book 5)
Executive Order (Book 6)
Dead Man Talking (Book 7)
All The King's Men (Book 8)
Flashpoint (Book 9)
Brotherhood of the Goat (Book 10)
Dead Hot (Book 11)
Blood on Megiddo (Book 12)
Son of Hell (Book 13)
Merchant of Death (Book 14)
Extinction C-14 (Book 15)
A Vengeful God (Book 16)

NOAH WOLF THRILLERS

Code Name Camelot (Book 1)
Lone Wolf (Book 2)
In Sheep's Clothing (Book 3)
Hit for Hire (Book 4)
The Wolf's Bite (Book 5)
Black Sheep (Book 6)
Balance of Power (Book 7)
Time to Hunt (Book 8)
Red Square (Book 9)
Highest Order (Book 10)
Edge of Anarchy (Book 11)
Unknown Evil (Book 12)
Black Harvest (Book 13)
World Order (Book 14)
Caged Animal (Book 15)
Deep Allegiance (Book 16)

Pack Leader (Book 17)
High Treason (Book 18)
A Wolf Among Men (Book 19)
Rogue Intelligence (Book 20)
Alpha (Book 21)
Rogue Wolf (Book 22)
Shadows of Allegiance (Book 23)
In the Grip of Darkness (Book 24)
Wolves in the Dark (Book 25)
Olympus Must Fall (Book 26)
Children of the Empire (Book 27)
Wolf at the Gates (Book 28)

SAM PRICHARD MYSTERIES

The Grave Man (Book 1)
Death Sung Softly (Book 2)
Love and War (Book 3)
Framed (Book 4)
The Kill List (Book 5)
Drifter: Part One (Book 6)
Drifter: Part Two (Book 7)
Drifter: Part Three (Book 8)
The Last Song (Book 9)
Ghost (Book 10)
Hidden Agenda (Book 11)

SAM AND INDIE MYSTERIES

Aces and Eights (Book 1)
Fact or Fiction (Book 2)
Close to Home (Book 3)
Brave New World (Book 4)
Innocent Conspiracy (Book 5)
Unfinished Business (Book 6)
Live Bait (Book 7)
Alter Ego (Book 8)

More Than It Seems (Book 9)
Moving On (Book 10)
Worst Nightmare (Book 11)
Chasing Ghosts (Book 12)
Serial Superstition (Book 13)

CHANCE REDDICK THRILLERS

Innocent Injustice (Book 1)
Angel of Justice (Book 2)
High Stakes Hunting (Book 3)
Personal Asset (Book 4)

CASSIE MCGRAW MYSTERIES

What Lies Beneath (Book 1)
Can't Fight Fate (Book 2)
One Last Game (Book 3)
Never Really Gone (Book 4)

ABOUT US

Right House is an independent publisher created by authors for readers. We specialize in Action, Thriller, Mystery, and Crime novels.

If you enjoyed this novel, then there is a good chance you will like what else we have to offer! Please stay up to date by using any of the links below.

Join our mailing lists to stay up to date -->
righthouse.com/email
Visit our website --> righthouse.com
Contact us --> contact@righthouse.com

facebook.com/righthousebooks
x.com/righthousebooks
instagram.com/righthousebooks

EXCLUSIVE SNEAK PEEK OF...

THE BOGOTÁ FILE

CHAPTER 1

ONE DAY BEFORE DEPLOYMENT TO COLOMBIA

JACOB HUNTER HAD BEEN ENJOYING THE BRIEF stopover in his home town of Glen Bridge, Ohio. For the most part, the trip down memory lane gladdened his cynical and scarred warrior's heart. The cool, late October weather, strolling along familiar streets. Jerry's bakery on Main Street, still pumping out that delicious sourdough bread, brownies, and muffins folks drove twenty miles for. The library he'd spent countless hours in, reading history and classic adventure stories by Mark Twain. The old playground where he and his only true friend Magnus Ohlson played one-on-one hoops, with 6'6" Gus usually taking the honors.

It wasn't all pleasantries, though. Jacob was on a private mission of vengeance. However, before he could exact said vengeance, he first wanted to make sure his hunches had some foundation beneath them. He wasn't the type to dish out violence for the sake of it. There had to be a reason—a very good reason. And when he found it, there was no holding back.

First, he had to speak to a number of people, tell them what his hunches were, get their views on the matter. To see if he was on the right track. These folks were old schoolmates and a couple of teachers whom he hadn't spoken to in many years. They'd long since abandoned little-old Glen Bridge, spreading out in all directions. Those with career ambitions, at least, had fled. There wasn't a helluva lot to keep a person in town once they'd graduated high school. Many of the people he most wanted to talk to lived at opposite ends of the country; a couple in Canada, Europe and the UK, one as far away as New Zealand. Jacob was sure these people knew things, important things, that they held the key to a riddle he'd been trying to solve for close on twenty years. And to get the information he wanted, he was convinced only in-person conversations would work. Phone calls, emails, messages— people had and would continue to dodge answering them. Get 'em face to face, though, and the chance of receiving honest answers rose exponentially. Especially with Jacob's powers of persuasion.

So he'd brought them together in the old home town, like Detective Colombo rounding up the witnesses and suspects and grilling them all in one spot. Jacob had created a closed Facebook group, ostensibly dedicated to a fancy Glen Bridge High School reunion—one that was never going to happen. The woman he'd rescued from his last mission in Moscow, IT guru Irene Frobisher, formerly known as Irina Frolova and to him always Irina, had put together a bunch of promo material for the fake reunion that few could resist. A good many old classmates were going to be mighty pissed when they turned up to the non-party tomorrow night.

He'd reached the pointy end of the week-long investigation. As a result of some fruitful and at times animated conversations, he'd narrowed his focus down to one man.

And now, here was that vile man, trussed up tightly and cooking from his insides like a Thanksgiving turkey. To reel the rube in, Jacob had treated him to a free lunch, a couple of beers, some bullshit palsy-walsy chat, and voilà: the dude was putty in his hands. To get him to follow Jacob to the trap was a cinch: the promise to ogle photos of a couple of women who used to attend Glen Bridge High but were now involved in amateur porn on the

Internet. It had the sicko salivating at the prospect. *I've got a computer set up at the place I'm staying*, Jacob had said. *Because it's so hot, almost illegal, I can only show you that stuff using a special encryption.* Those magic words did the trick. Jacob could barely keep up with the guy as he marched down Main Street.

"Hey, isn't this your old place?" the asshole had asked when they reached the address. "I recognize them big trees with the tire swing. Still there after all these years."

Jacob nodded. "Yeah. My parents are friends of the couple who bought it from them." A lie but swallowed eagerly. "Guess they liked the house pretty much the way it was. Tire swing and all."

"We gonna stand here gasbagging all day, or are you gonna show me videos of those dirty women?" The perverted man had been practically hyperventilating.

Fast forward thirty minutes and the man, now getting acquainted with Jacob's interviewing methods, could barely breathe.

Jacob slackened his two-handed grip around the man's throat, thick as a small pumpkin and nearly as hard. The fella managed to inhale a couple of massive gulps of air before Jacob reapplied the pressure. Jacob's fingers ached with the effort; it was like squeezing solid rubber, not flesh and ligaments. He gritted his teeth and pressed harder. Another thirty seconds of choking and it would be lights out for the guy, permanently. Jacob couldn't afford to kill him, though: he needed a confession to make it all worth the effort. The app on Jacob's iPhone was recording everything. Irina would later edit the sound file with AI to make the man's voice sound less strained, like he was voluntarily laying it all on the line, then she'd delete Jacob's voice completely. Jacob would anonymously send the doctored file over to the homicide cops in Columbus. After that, hopefully, justice would be served.

Simpering Steven Finkel, one of the few graduates of 2005 to stay put in Glen Ridge, was the best suspect Jacob had found in many years of searching. Physical evidence was scant to the point of being non-existent, and the leads Jacob had been chasing over the years had gone cold. A confession it would have to be. As a bulwark to his theory, the classmates Jacob spoke to believed that yes, Finkel could very well be the killer.

Jacob let go of the suspect's neck and took a step back, regarding the brute through narrowed eyes. He remained silent, wanting Finkel to be the first to speak.

The man's shaking hands shot to his fat neck as he gasped for air, his mouth opening and closing like a whale's blowhole. He blinked away pearly tears. "I'm...not the guy...you want," he managed to huff. "I never done nuthin' to her." The denial was followed by vigorous shaking of his closely shaved head.

An extended finger poked right in the middle of the man's throat, hard and fast, causing him to gurgle as his spider-veined eyeballs bugged out. "You *are* the guy, Steve. People have ratted you out." Jacob's voice was soft and reassuring now. "You are the psychopath who killed someone I loved very much."

"No!"

"Yes, Steven, yes."

Finkel open his spittle-covered mouth as if to scream for help. Jacob fired him a laser stare that shut down that thought in a flash. "Don't you dare yell out," he added for good measure. Jacob paced back and forth, tapping the blade of a long knife against the palm of one hand, then against his thigh. "Now either you open up and tell me the truth and I call the cops—that way you get to live—or you continue to stonewall me and I slit your throat here and now." He tilted his head slightly to one side and showed one open hand and one upraised knife. "Your choice, Steven."

Jacob put the knife down on the ground in an act of conciliation. "Last chance, fat man."

Finkel swallowed hard a couple of times, no sign of an Adam's apple in his blubberous neck. "I'm very thirsty. Can I have a drink of water, Jake?"

"Do *not* call me Jake, understand?" Jacob thundered. "We're not in the schoolyard."

"Sorry," came the timid reply. "I didn't mean..."

"Can it, asshole." He was already sick of the man's sniveling. At high school, Steven Finkel had had the reputation of a mean bully, but also a coward. Seems he hadn't changed much. Adding to Jacob's irritation, a piece of gristle from the T-bone steak he'd demolished thirty minutes ago was wedged between his teeth and annoying the shit out of him. Not nearly as much as the sweating tub of lard tied to the chair in front of him, though.

Jacob paused a second to scan the surroundings in his parents' dimly lit basement. True, it was someone else's property now. There was so much familiarity about it. His mom and dad had sold the house five years ago and moved to Florida to enjoy the sunshine in their twilight years. The new owners at 198 Hotham Drive, Jeff and Alice Millard, were, as far as Jacob was able to determine, at work in their legal practice in downtown Columbus, hence no cars. Their two teenage kids were at school, five blocks away at Glen Bridge High. No one should be returning home any time soon.

One thing the Millards hadn't attended to, even after five years of ownership, was fixing the defective side door to the garage. There was a knack to jiggling around in the lock with a paperclip or piece of bent wire. Get it in the right spot, and the door opened obediently like Aladdin's cave. The worst burglar in the world could break into this garage. The Millards' lack of care was understandable, though. This was a safe neighborhood in a safe town, Jacob remembered. Break-ins were few, crimes against the person very rare.

But not unknown. Like everywhere, innocent people sometimes got themselves killed.

Jacob placed his boot in the middle of Finkel's crotch, barely able to wriggle his foot into position on account of the captive man's broad, spreading thighs. With a bit of effort, though, he got there. He gave a firm double-pump push with his foot. Finkel yelped, sweat streaming from his face like a leaky faucet. "Ow! Don't kick me in the nuts!"

"You'd be lucky to find any nuts in that pool of lard. Now why did you kill her? Tell me!"

Jacob's high-school sweetheart, Sally-Anne Vincent, had been murdered nineteen years ago. The cops had worked hard to find the perpetrator but came up empty. Now it was a cold case, all but forgotten. Jacob would never give up trying, though. Steve Finkel, unemployed deadbeat and someone Jacob had suspected from the beginning, was firmly in the crosshairs.

"I didn't do it. I swear. You gotta believe me!"

"Don't lie to me." Jacob jammed his foot even harder into the man's balls, drawing a high-pitched squeal. "I've spoken to ten independent people, *ten*, Steven, who swear blind you were totally obsessed with Sally-Anne in high school. I noticed it at the time, too. But I dismissed it as me being overprotective of her and you just being a pathetic loser. But those ten people believe you really were crazy enough to have killed her. And I tend to agree."

"I wouldn't hurt a fly..."

"I would," said Jacob, administering a lightning-fast open-handed slap. It gave off an echoey crack but was delivered with only a fraction of the force Jacob could have unleashed.

"Ow! Why did you do that?"

"Because...you're a fucking murderer, Steven."

Finkel shook his head hard, tears and gunk from his lips fanning left and right. "You don't seriously think I hurt Sally-Anne...do you?"

Jacob sighed heavily. "I think you might have, yeah. But then again, it takes a degree of courage to kill someone, and you've never been a brave fella, have you?"

Finkel's mouth turned upside down into a spittle-covered frown moments before Jacob delivered a slap to the other side of his jowls, this one with plenty of power.

A scream. "Please stop..." Finkel jerked back in his chair, mumbling incoherent words. Tears poured down his marshmallow cheeks like there was no off switch. "I honestly don't know anything."

Jacob pressed his forefinger and thumb to his chin as he coolly regarded Finkel. The slumped shoulders, vacant stare, and wracking sobs were too real. A coward like Finkel would have had 'tells' if he was lying. There were no tells, dammit.

Finkel looked up, ropey snot dangling from both nostrils like a slimy Goth piercing. "I wish I could help you, I really do. I liked Sally-Anne, but not in that way. I know you loved her. She..."

But Jacob wasn't listening anymore. He took a pair of scissors he found on a workbench and cut the snap-ties around Finkel's wrists. "Get up, dickhead. We're done here."

Much as he wanted Finkel to be the killer, Jacob's gut told him he was wasting his time. A jolt of shame coursed through Jacob's mind as he realized he'd derived a small amount of pleasure from roughing the man up. Not his style, but Finkel was so loathsome the enjoyment obtained was almost justified.

"You know what?" Jacob grinned and folded his arms across his chest. "I believe you, pal."

"Then why did you–?"

"To be absolutely sure. Look on the bright side, Steven. Now that you're vindicated in my mind, you get to live. That's a pretty good deal, huh?"

The cops' theory back in the day, that it was some opportunist, probably an out-of-towner, a drifter, who had murdered Sally-Anne and left her lying in a snowy ditch late December 2005, was most likely correct. Finkel was innocent.

Standing on wobbly legs, Finkel smudged the tears away with the back of his pudgy wrists. He gave Jacob a feeble smile, one that said *please don't hurt me anymore*. But his tiny brain couldn't help but spit out the first stupid thing that came into it. "You know, you're going to regret doing this to me."

"No, I'm not." Jacob shook his head. "I wasn't even here. You weren't here, either."

"Yes I was. And I'm not as dumb as you think I am. I'll be able to prove we were here."

Jacob raised his fist as if to strike, and Finkel's hands went up defensively at the same time as his head ducked to the side.

"You mean your cell's GPS will leave a trace of your movements?"

Finkel dared to look back at Jacob through his fingers. "Yes." He reached into his pocket, fumbled around, and then surprise pulled his eyes into big round circles.

"Looking for this?" Jacob dangled the phone in an outstretched hand. Before Finkel could answer, the banged-up Samsung dropped to the concrete floor. Jacob's size 11 right boot stamped on it repeatedly, shards of glass and plastic crunching. He smiled benevolently at Finkel. "Time for a phone upgrade, pal."

CHAPTER 2

Paul Brohman tugged up his zipper and moved away from the raised urinal. Tonight's celebration was a day early, but the icing on the cake would come tomorrow. One step closer to exposing the conspiracy. Some semi-incriminating background files were already in his possession. Stored on his laptop, a USB and, for good measure, uploaded to the Cloud, from where they could be retrieved and submitted to Deputy Director McDonald in Langley.

But those files were full of circumstantial evidence and meant nothing until he got the final piece in the puzzle. The piece that would lead to arrests and jail sentences. For whom? That remained to be seen. Brohman had his firm suspicions, but as of now, that's all they were— suspicions. But dear God, he hoped he was right about this.

Tomorrow, at 7:30 a.m. sharp, Miguel would meet him outside the National Shrine of Our Lady of Carmen, the candy-striped church that towered over the historic La Candelaria District. Inside the church, Miguel would pass on the secret recording. It only cost $500, but to Miguel, it was a king's ransom. And it was money well spent— enough to expose the dirty turncoat and stop an unthinkable crime.

First, though, Brohman badly needed a woman to slate his strong carnal urges. A sex addict who saw no need to be treated or cured for his affliction, he washed and dried his hands meticulously and headed back into the belly of the night club.

He wobbled back from the bathroom, tipping finger waves of apology as he bumped into people on the way to the bar. He couldn't see, or even sense, that he was off balance; only those around him could see it. If he collided with others, it was because *they* were drunk. He forgave them, of course. Paul Brohman was famous among friends and colleagues for being a happy drunk, never violent when he'd had too many beers, tequilas, vodkas, or whatever the locals were imbibing.

Now, at 11:45 p.m. on a Wednesday night, the smooth-talking American from Dallas, Texas, had reached that special state of inebriation, the state where you think everything's under control, you are the smartest guy in the room, the best singer and dancer, and women find you *irre-fucking-sistible.*

And to be fair, Brohman was a very good-looking hombre. Smooth, wrinkle-free skin due to good genes. Brilliant white teeth never affected by nicotine. A rock-hard body, low BMI. Working out for two hours every day without fail for the last ten years meant he not only looked sharp in a suit or Speedos, he had the stamina to party all night if needed. He shunned the popular party drugs, especially now that he was forging a new path in Colombia. The risks of falling into a dangerous trap here were immense. No cocaine or funny little pills for him. Good old alcohol was his poison of choice, and he would stick to it. He trusted it, knew its effects, and could deal with the consequences of even the worst hangover. Of which he had suffered many.

Yet even when tanked to the gills, his tall, well-muscled figure, thick, stylishly cut blond hair and classic chiseled features, teamed with the body of a welter-weight boxer, were the assets that got him laid when he was out on the prowl. The financial mogul generally had plenty of luck with the ladies. On the other hand, his distinctly Nordic look sometimes had negative consequences among the male population of Bogotá. Especially in the night clubs he liked to frequent.

"Oye, mira por donde vas, gringo!" A man dressed like John Travolta in Grease eyeballed Brohman with an accompanying sneer.

The only word Brohman understood was the last one. The intent was clear, too. *You are a guest in our town, so don't be a jerk.* If it came to a fist-fight, thanks to five years in the Marine Raiders as a younger man, he had the skills to defend himself. Even when he'd had too many drinks. Brawling was always a last resort, and he never initiated trouble. True to his happy drunk persona, Brohman gave the man a shrug and a beatific smile of innocence. It worked perfectly, as the young man made a conciliatory hands-down gesture and allowed Brohman to go on his way.

Straight back to the bar. One more beer, then home.

He nodded at a couple of men at the far end of the bar. They waved at him, gave polite smiles, then resumed their conversation. An Englishman and an Australian, like him they were businessmen working for Fortune 500 companies with branches in Colombia. Unlike him, these dudes were married and most likely heading home soon if they wanted to avoid the rolling pin.

Pepe's nightclub, in the pumping Zona Rosa to the north of the Colombian capital, was a popular spot for some R&R with both ex-pats and locals. Brohman's style when he visited was to network early with the foreign crowd until he'd had enough of their boring conversations, then ditch them and switch to predator mode. Quite often, Brohman would pick up a cute señorita and take her back to his apartment.

Tonight, though, he wasn't feeling it. There was no new meat at the market as far as he could tell. Just women he'd bedded already, wise enough to know he wouldn't go back for a second bite. Like a vampire, he craved fresh blood, young and virginal if possible, but after a lean trot, he'd happily bed a new woman aged between 25 and 40. No one would guess Brohman himself was the wrong side of 50.

Ten feet from the bar, he spotted a gap opening that he figured on sidling into and occupying. Out of nowhere, he felt a sharp poke in the right side. He turned to offer his customary apology, but the words froze in his mouth. The woman flicking her hair from side to side was the most breathtakingly beautiful he had ever laid eyes on. A dress not much bigger than a handkerchief revealed medium-to-large breasts, but the legs, his favorite part of a woman, were so perfect he almost drooled. She was slightly out of his preferred age range, but this was an opportunity only a fool would pass up. He detected a touch of African heritage, perhaps, maybe some native Mayan blood infused with that of the Spanish colonizers. Whatever the lineage, she fit squarely into the category of drop-dead gorgeous. She stopped flicking her hair, flashed him a wicked grin, then barked a collage of rapid-fire Spanish he had no hope of understanding.

"No hablo español," he said loud enough to be heard above the funky music. "Hablas inglés?"

"Si, I do," she replied with a coquettish pout. "But not very well. I watch you from the other side of the bar. You are a very handsome man. Americano?"

He nodded as he felt the smile on his face broadening. Her come-on was so strong, he considered for a moment whether she was a hooker. Dammit, she was so beautiful he might even consider compromising his principle and pay her for sex if he had to. Without broaching the question, the only thing he could think of to say to this radiant goddess was the lame cliché, "Would you like to have a drink with me?"

"Si, señor. Con mucho gusto!"

As Latino music, heavy on trumpet and drums, throbbed in the background, he extended a hand to help her mount her seat; she'd be lucky to be five foot tall, although the stilettos added several inches.

His gut told him she wasn't a prostitute. A gold-digger? Quite possibly. The version he wanted to believe was that she was a horny modern woman looking for a one-night stand with an experienced stud. And why not? This was far from the first time a hot female had approached him in a bar with devilry shining in her eyes. In Rio de Janeiro, where he'd spent two years in the early 2000s making a stack of money investing in coffee futures, it was even easier than here. It was almost like he needed a repellent to keep women away. A handsome blond man was considered so exotic, getting laid was almost unavoidable. Less of a certainty here in Colombia, but his strike rate was still impressive.

Five minutes later and $50 lighter, he'd learned the woman's name was Carolina. Without prompting, she even volunteered a last name, Ortega, which, in his eyes, made her even sweeter. Only an innocent from the countryside would do that. Carolina was 23 years old—*bingo*—and, of all things, crazy about baseball. She had been raised in a small village outside of Medellín, where her family had been farming bananas and rice for four generations. They made a basic living selling their produce locally. She found country life utterly boring, so last year she'd moved to the capital.

"To chase your fortune?" said Brohman, ogling her cleavage over the top of his glass. "To become a pop star, maybe? An actress? You've certainly got the looks and sparkling personality to be a roaring success."

She giggled like a schoolgirl before sipping her drink. In the glass was a Colombian specialty, a Pacific mule: a blend of vodka, strawberry liqueur and peach schnapps, ginger ale and lime. It purportedly kicked like the animal it was named after, so Carolina said she would only have a couple.

As the volume of the rhythmic cumbia melodies pouring out of the speakers increased, he leaned in closer. "Do you like this kind of music?"

"Si, mucho." She placed her hands on his thighs, squeezing gently. "Our Colombian music is very romantic, no?"

"It sure is," he agreed. The heady scent of her perfume, a subtle blend of frangipani and jasmine, wafted across to him. Combined with her own natural musky odor, the aroma was activating responses in his basal ganglia, the part of the brain in charge of primal instincts. Those instincts were telling him, *Get this woman out of the bar and into your bed before she changes her mind and disappears.*

"Would you like to take a walk with me?" he said, struggling to place his empty beer glass in the middle of the coaster. "It's a nice evening for it."

"Si," she said with an eager nod. "And then we go back to your place?" She paused for a moment. "To fuck."

Oh, my, Brohman thought. This was going to be one of those nights legends are made of.

Before he could respond to her brazen offer, she hopped down from the barstool, grabbed his hand, and led the way to the exit. He thrilled at her intensity, her sense of purpose. In his professional life, he valued people who knew what they wanted and let nothing stand in their way. With her attitude, Carolina would kill it in commerce. He never mixed business and pleasure, though, so he wouldn't be offering her a job.

His mind raced as they walked; they would soon be as one, bodies entwined on his king-size bed, going at it like rabbits until the early hours. Her small fingers felt oddly cold as they interlaced with his larger ones. No problem, she'd be very warm soon enough.

They slalomed past a group of people near the bar, stomachs gyrating and arms twirling to the cumbia music. Brohman's eyes remained riveted to her perfect legs, which led all the way to the holy grail. His heart thundered with the anticipation of his conquest.

Before exiting the club, Carolina extracted a token from her purse, exchanged a couple of words with the attendant, and fetched a gabardine coat from the cloakroom. Bogotá might be near the equator, but due to its elevation of 8,660 feet above sea level, it enjoyed a temperate climate. Brohman was fine with the cooler evenings; his suit jacket never came off when he was out on the streets. There was a loaded ultra-compact Beretta 950 Jetfire snuggled in a holster under his left armpit. He might like to avoid fights, but he was smart enough to be extra careful in this city. Although Pepe's bouncers used metal-detector wands to stop weapons entering the venue, Brohman got a pass because he paid all the managers to turn a blind eye.

Out onto the bustling Calle 82, aka 82nd Street, the night's bracing air was like a refreshing glass of water. Despite the flashing neon lights of the bars and clubs, the honking of the traffic, the shouting street vendors, and people scurrying about like ants, a feeling of immense calm descended upon him. He and Carolina were in their own little bubble, and nothing else mattered. They ambled their way along the sidewalk, hand in hand like long-time lovers. They'd walked about fifty yards or so when she tugged on his arm. "Hey. I've got an idea. Let's go down this alleyway, guapo, and have some fun." Her voice was husky, almost breathless. "I can't wait to feel you inside me."

"I'm not sure about that, my dear." Calling him 'handsome' certainly appealed to Brohman's ego, but his conservative side rose to the surface; he hated that side because it squashed spontaneity. "It will be much more comfortable back at my apartment. It's a quick trip by cab."

"Look at the traffic, mi amor. It will take over two hours to get to your place." She pulled him with surprising strength toward the dark entrance to a narrow laneway. "Don't be, what do the gringos say? A pussy? Come on, Pablo, show me what you got in your trousers."

She was right. You only live once, and at this surreal moment in time, he was convinced Carolina had more pluck in her than any person he'd ever known. For once in his selfish, misogynistic life, he might even be...in love?

No. Strike that. He was sobering up now, gusts of chilly night air accelerating the process. Two failed marriages to women with smart lawyers, who continued to strip him of a large percentage of his vast fortune, was lesson enough. Never again.

Carolina was a heavenly vision, but he wouldn't allow himself to be hypnotized into complete submission by her beauty. Still, the effects of the Cialis tablet he'd dropped earlier this afternoon were beginning to make themselves known in his loins: her idea of coupling down the laneway now seemed an inspired idea.

The alley ran between a closed souvenir shop, its steel shutters awash with multi-colored graffiti, and what used to be a taco joint but was now boarded up. Before he knew it, Brohman was tiptoeing carefully around a couple of homeless guys sitting on either side of the alley like bookends, their bearded faces barely visible under filthy blankets. In front of them were woolen hats containing a handful of lousy coins. Brohman couldn't help himself. He turned back, peeled off a couple of Ben Franklins, and dropped one in each hat. The men grunted; whether it was in thanks or not was impossible to tell.

Carolina strutted down the lane like a model on a catwalk, her generous hips and butt swaying like a metronome. She suddenly stopped about twenty yards in. Lights from the windows of buildings along its sides cast a gentle light, spotlighting an area free of trash. She leaned against the brick wall, one leg tucked up against it at a 45-degree angle. Her hand disappeared under the front of her dress. She finger-rolled a black G-string down her legs, under her shoes, then flung it away disdainfully. "Come and have a taste of the good stuff, guapo." A fleshy tongue ran around her plump lips, unenhanced by cosmetic intervention.

He was upon her now, unbuckling his leather belt, ready to drop his trousers, hoist her up in the air, and impale her against the wall. Her glistening eyes stared back at him, unblinking, challenging him. He wrapped his arms around her waist, closed his eyes, and leaned in for a kiss.

"Atáquenlo, muchachos!" she screamed around the side of his neck.

What the fuck?!

He heard the approaching pounding footsteps an instant before a savage blow connected with the side of his head. But it was time enough to take a slight evasive action that stopped him being KO'd. Whoever—and whatever—hit him achieved just a glancing blow.

The reprieve was temporary.

He turned to see two big men lined up against him. They were dressed head to toe in dark clothing, one brandishing a baseball bat, the other a huge knife. He cringed as he took in those scruffy beards: they were the 'homeless' assholes he'd just donated $200 to!

This was a fucking set-up. A honey trap. He couldn't believe he had been stupid enough to fall for it.

But they wouldn't get him with the simple weapons they had. He reached into his jacket to grab the...

"Looking for something, guapo?"

He spun toward the sweet voice. Carolina stood, feet set shoulder-width apart, aiming his own pistol squarely at his head.

"You fucking bitch!"

With his back turned to the men, one of them delivered a vicious stab kick to the side of the patella, and Brohman dropped like a stone. "That's no way to talk to a lady, pendejo!"

The pain stung as if someone had poured boiling water down the back of his leg. The men descended on him in a second, like wolves pouncing on a wounded fawn. He struggled gamely for as long as he could—a matter of ten seconds. A powerful hold that threatened to snap his wrist put an end to all resistance. He knew it was time to submit: these gorillas were too strong and too well-trained to be bested by a middle-aged ex-Marine Raider with seven—or was it eight?—large beers under his belt. Snap ties went around his wrists, and the men frog-marched him down the alley away from the busy street.

Incoherent words full of derision and laughter exchanged between Carolina Ortega—definitely not her real name—and the goons added to his humiliation.

As they neared the other end of the alleyway, which exited onto a smaller, less busy street, a rough hessian bag went over his head. He heard car doors open and another two male voices.

There was a shove in the small of the back and arms around his shoulders, guiding him into the passenger seat. There was already someone sitting next to him. Someone with a big and menacing presence.

The car took off like a rocket, the music on the stereo blasting out the same cumbia music that had been playing in Pepe's. "Where are you taking me?"

Instead of an answer, the presence beside him unleashed a massive closed fist under Brohman's rib cage, sucking the air out of his lungs.

Through the clearing fog of alcohol, the clues were now so obvious he couldn't believe he'd missed them. One: the bitch understood every word he had said in English, despite claiming to not speak it very well. And two: how the hell did she know it would take two hours for a cab to get to his apartment? She knew where he lived, dammit. She had known *everything* about him. His captors, too, must know *everything* about him. Including his side role with the CIA. A role he should have taken more seriously, thinking with his head more than with his dick.

If the hombres who snatched him were anything to do with the new cartel, his future looked bleak.

There was only one positive to be drawn from this horrific experience.

He was still alive.

www.ingramcontent.com/pod-product-compliance
Lightning Source LLC
LaVergne TN
LVHW041114080826
845145LV00007B/1811

* 9 7 8 1 6 3 6 9 6 4 6 7 6 *